"So you have no interest in me except for what I've been able to do for you."

Her features hardened. "I came to you with a business proposition. You *know* how grateful I am for what you've done for me—"

"But it's all work and no play, even though you're separated from your beloved by thousands of miles?"

Those blue eyes looked haunted. "What do you want from me?"

"How about honesty?"

"I'm being honest…" Her voice trembled.

"The heck you are—" he whispered fiercely. Having taken all he could, he pulled her close so their mouths were almost touching. "I'm feeling something I've never felt before, and I know you're feeling it too, but your guilt is preventing you from admitting it. The fact that guilt is getting in the way means you couldn't possibly love this man the way you should."

A strangled moan escaped her lips.

"I'm going to kiss you, Jasmine, and then we'll know for a certainty."

Luc found her mouth and coaxed her lips apart. In the next instant he felt her begin to kiss him back with such answering hunger it took his breath.

He'̲̅ ̲̅ong, and now that it l them to a re.

TAMING THE FRENCH TYCOON

BY
REBECCA WINTERS

All rights reserved including the right of reproduction in whole or in part in any form. This edition is published by arrangement with Harlequin Books S.A. The text of this publication or any part thereof may not be reproduced or transmitted in any form or by any means, electronic or mechanical, including photocopying, recording, storage in an information retrieval system, or otherwise, without the written permission of the publisher.

All the characters in this book have no existence outside the imagination of the author, and have no relation whatsoever to anyone bearing the same name or names. They are not even distantly inspired by any individual known or unknown to the author, and all the incidents are pure invention.

First published in Great Britain 2014
By Mills & Boon, an imprint of Harlequin (UK) Limited,
Eton House, 18-24 Paradise Road, Richmond, Surrey, TW9 1SR

© 2014 Rebecca Winters

ISBN: 978-0-263-25101-2

51-0414

Harlequin (UK) policy is to use papers that are natural, renewable and recyclable products and made from wood grown in sustainable forests. The logging and manufacturing processes conform to the legal environmental regulations of the country of origin.

Printed and bound in Spain
by CPI, Barcelona

Published in Great Britain 2015
by Mills & Boon, an imprint of Harlequin (UK) Limited,
Eton House, 18-24 Paradise Road, Richmond, Surrey, TW9 1SR

© 2015 Rebecca Winters

ISBN: 978-0-263-25101-2

23-0115

Harlequin (UK) Limited's policy is to use papers that are natural, renewable and recyclable products and made from wood grown in sustainable forests. The logging and manufacturing processes conform to the legal environmental regulations of the country of origin.

Printed and bound in Spain
by CPI, Barcelona

Rebecca Winters, whose family of four children has now swelled to include five beautiful grandchildren, lives in Salt Lake City, Utah, in the land of the Rocky Mountains. With canyons and high alpine meadows full of wildflowers, she never runs out of places to explore. They, plus her favourite vacation spots in Europe, often end up as backgrounds for her romance novels, because writing is her passion, along with her family and church.

Rebecca loves to hear from readers. If you wish to e-mail her, please visit her website: www.cleanromances.com.

CHAPTER ONE

May

WITH HIS BANKING business done in Cyprus, Luc had taken a rare morning off to visit Yeronisos before flying back to France. He'd always had an interest in archaeology and the tiny island off the coast was thought to be the site of the temple of Apollo. They'd dug up foundations, walls, coins, amulets, wine jugs, and much more. So far the items had been traced to Alexandria, three hundred miles away.

Evidently Cleopatra, queen of Egypt, had possessed the resources to build here on the top of these seventy-foot cliffs that kept visitors away. Yeronisos was so inaccessible they called it a virgin island because it had remained much as it had been when man had first come there over ten thousand years ago.

Luc had walked around the excavations for an hour and found it a totally fascinating place where he could indulge his passion, but then a boatload of male teen-agers had arrived in a dinghy to disturb its tranquility. Instead of studying antiquities, they'd come to cliff dive, a foolhardy pursuit with the waters churning at the base because of a swift current. There was a sign that forbade it, but this group paid no heed.

Deciding it was time to go, he descended the steep steps. The warm May sun forced him to put on his sunglasses to cut the glint reflecting off the deep blue water. When he looked out, another dinghy was approaching. He returned to the speedboat he'd rented and started untying the ropes at the dock.

While he was doing so, the boat pulled in behind him and more young divers jumped out. He recognized their eagerness as they scrambled up the side of the island to get to the top and challenge the elements.

Stepping into his boat, he happened to glance at the last guy to leave the dinghy. But it turned out to be a young woman wearing a backpack. She had a pair of the most fabulous long legs he'd ever seen. A T-shirt over her bikini couldn't hide the voluptuous mold of her body. A dark braid circled her well-shaped head.

As she passed him, he found himself staring into an incredibly lovely face. Classic, with high cheekbones and a provocative mouth. She reminded him a little of Sabine, the girl he'd loved and lost in a plane crash years ago, but sunglasses covered this woman's eyes so he couldn't see their color. With her attention focused on the top of the cliff, he doubted she'd noticed him. She'd come here with all those hormone-filled idiots?

In the background came the excited shouts from the divers already launching themselves into the dangerous, swirling waters. One by one, they jumped into the huge swells and then had to swim for their lives to reach the rocky walls of the cliff. When he heard several bloodcurdling screams among the shouts, his emotions suddenly morphed into gut-wrenching pain as he was transported back to his last year in high school.

During those years he and his friends had felt immortal. In their crazy exuberance, they'd decided to go skydiving. But it had ended in horror when their plane crashed against a hillside. Out of the six, four of them survived. The other two had perished, one of them being Sabine.

His fear for the divers' safety intensified, causing his body to tense. Any one of them could be killed doing something so reckless. Luc knew all about it. He broke out in a cold sweat watching the attractive female make her way to the bottom of the steps that would take her to the top of the cliff. He thought of Sabine and couldn't bear to see this woman hurt or possibly killed doing something so reckless.

She was young like they'd once been, eager for adventure and heedless of the danger. Didn't she know her body could be tossed against the rocks and knocked unconscious or worse? Fearful for the welfare of this beautiful woman, he climbed out onto the dock again and called to her.

She stopped and turned around. "Yes?" she answered in French. "Were you speaking to me?"

The sight of her made his heart beat faster, a reaction he hadn't felt for a woman in years. "Haven't you read the sign? No cliff jumping! You heard those screams. Don't you realize that what your group is doing could end in fatalities?"

Her arched brows frowned. "If it's your job to enforce the rule, you should have stopped the group in the first dinghy."

He moved closer to her. "It's anyone's job to stop

a bunch of headstrong young people from bringing harm to themselves." Without thinking he said, "I'd hate to see a lovely woman like you lose your life for a thrill. Have you no concern for your family or loved ones who would be devastated if anything happened to you?" Luc would never forget the pain.

She stared at him for a full minute. One corner of her mouth lifted in a mocking curve. "*Félicitations, monsieur.* That's the most original pick-up line any Frenchman has ever thrown at me and believe me, I've heard the best of them."

Frenchman? That was an odd thing for her to say since *she* was French. Her response stunned him in more ways than one. "You think that's what I'm doing?"

"It looks that way to me. I'm wondering how often you loiter at the dock, lying in wait for an unsuspecting, accessible female to detain."

"What?" he almost hissed the word.

"If I'm wrong...*je regrette.*" She shrugged her shoulders. "Is it possible you never did anything so daring as cliff jump when you were young? Might I point out that you took your life in your hands just coming out here in your speedboat rental?"

Luc had to tamp down his temper, caught between his concern for her welfare and her provocative insinuations about him. "In what way?" his voice grated.

"Surely you know the Mediterranean has its share of great white sharks. What are you? Approaching forty? I hope you're still a good swimmer in case you should meet with an accident at sea. A rental boat isn't always reliable, but try to enjoy your sedentary day anyway instead of attempting to ruin it for everyone else. *Ciao.*"

In the next breath, she started up the steps with surprising speed to reach her destination.

Between the disturbing flashback and their shocking conversation, Luc had been thrown into a particularly foul mood. He got in the boat without looking back. Once he'd started the engine and edged away from the dock, he headed for the mainland.

When he thought about it, he could imagine that many a man had lain in wait for her, thus her ready defense, which was damn off-putting. The female who'd clashed with him was probably twenty, maybe twenty-one, but he'd found out she could take care of herself without effort. Before the plane crash he might have done exactly what she'd accused him of doing in order to get to know her.

To his chagrin, the vision of the captivating young woman stayed with him long after his flight home, as he picked up his car at the airport and drove to his villa in Cagnes-sur-Mer outside Nice. In that moment when he could imagine their outing ending in tragedy, the memory of the plane crash had swept over him. He'd wanted to spare her from plunging to her death. Instead she'd managed to get under his skin.

Though born with an adventurous spirit, he was no longer willing to take risks when life was so precious. Over the last fifteen years he'd grown particularly cautious when it came to making landmark business decisions that could affect not only his professional life, but his family's welfare and reputation.

The plane crash had changed him into a different person. He'd learned the meaning of mortality. That caution had also kept him out of involved personal relationships that could put his emotions in jeopardy.

It was the reason he hadn't cut the motor and reached for his binoculars to watch her defy danger because she thought she was immortal. He needed to put her and the incident out of his mind.

Jasmine reached the top of the island with only a little time to spare. The dinghy full of guys eager to cliff dive had been rented for two hours. Since this group of teens had room in the boat for her, she'd ridden to the island with them, glad she didn't have to drive a boat herself.

While they jumped, this would be her one and only chance to take pictures of the excavations before she couriered the negatives to the publisher. With this last task done, the book could be printed by the end of the month and ready for the distribution date. She was no photographer, but it didn't matter as long as they turned out.

To her chagrin, the encounter with the man at the dock had shaken her. He wasn't anything like André, the French guy with the seductive way of talking. She'd dated him a little at university before dropping him because he'd turned out to be way too controlling. But just now, when the stranger in sunglasses had come at her about the dangers of cliff jumping, she had been reminded of André, and her adrenaline had taken over in a negative way.

With hindsight, Jasmine realized she'd been ruder to this man than any male she'd ever met. The trouble was, with his unruly black hair and strong masculine features, he was *all* male and breathtaking in those white shorts that hung low on his hips.

Her instant attraction to him had come as a tremendous surprise. That was why his erroneous conclusion about her reason for being there had caused her temper to flare. She wasn't some foolish teenager, yet he'd put her in that category. Little did he know, she thought the cliff jumpers were crazy too, but she'd grown up with older brothers and knew you couldn't stop them if they saw a challenge.

If only the man had just stopped there, but he hadn't. It was the mention of family that had hit a nerve where her guilt lurked. Where did he get off implying that Jasmine didn't care about them? The intensity of his attack had caught her on the raw, creating a negative reaction in her that went volatile.

In retaliation, she'd hurtled little insults back at him like darts thrown at balloons, hoping to damage his ego, but she doubted he'd felt them. He was most likely in his early thirties. Being rock-hard lean and fit, she imagined he could outswim a shark. Deep down, she knew he was the kind of man who could have any woman he wanted and didn't need to hang around some lonely outpost waiting for an opportunity.

For the next hour, she concentrated on her task, trying to shake off the encounter. Once finished, she went back down to the dock and ate her lunch while she waited in the dinghy for the others. The speedboat had long since gone. She wondered what the man had been doing there in the first place, but why she cared was quite beyond her when she was still smarting from their confrontation.

Pretty soon, the first dinghy filled up and took off. A few minutes later, the others divers came running. She learned that one of the guys had cut his lower leg open. Someone had wrapped it in a towel, but he needed medical help. They left for the mainland, where she'd parked her rental car at the boating concession.

Jasmine looked around, but didn't see the man with whom she'd traded insults. She was relieved he hadn't been there to watch them come ashore with the injured teen. She could just imagine his "I told you so" smirk as the guy was lifted into the ambulance.

There was something wrong for her still to be thinking about him. Determined to put the incident behind her, she got in her car and drove the short distance to Nicosia. From the airport there she would catch her afternoon flight back to France.

Later in the day, when the plane began its descent to the Nice airport, it dawned her that the stranger had spoken with a distinct, cultured Niçois accent. A small shiver raced through her body to think he might actually live here, but the chances of bumping into him again were astronomical. How absurd to imagine such a thing happening.

For the second time today, she had to ask herself why it mattered when she had earthshaking events on her mind and little time to accomplish all that had to be done by midsummer.

July

When the phone rang at six-thirty a.m. Friday morning, Jasmine was awake, but she hadn't gotten out of bed yet. To her shock, she'd been dreaming about the stranger on Yeronisos again. Visions of him had been filtering through her mind for the last two months and she was sick of it. Her fantasy of seeing him again was absolutely crazy!

Thank heaven today was her twenty-sixth birthday, the day she and her papa had planned out in detail before his death. She could put aside the memory of this man who'd been haunting her dreams and deal with real problems. Jasmine glanced at the caller ID. Sure enough it was Robert Lambert, her grandfather's attorney, calling right on cue.

Jasmine clicked on. "*Bonjour*, Robert."

"*Bon anniversaire* to you, Jasmine. I know it's early, but we don't have a lot of time before the staff meeting at ten in the conference room."

"I'll be ready." She'd been getting ready for this day for a long, long time.

"Excellent. Per your grandfather's wishes, you will be interviewed in his laboratory for tonight's six o'clock news. The arrangements have already been made. He wanted it announced over the air before the day was out to quiet anyone who wasn't on board."

"I'm all prepared for it."

Not only had her grandfather hated publicity, he'd never let outsiders step foot inside his laboratory. For him to sanction a television interview in the place where he'd worked all his life indicated an intimacy between him and Jasmine the viewers couldn't possibly misinterpret.

"Meet me at nine-thirty to discuss one more matter with you before everyone else arrives at ten. Do you have any questions?"

"No. At this point I want to thank you for all you've done and are doing to help me. I couldn't do this without you. Papa knew that."

"We both miss your papa. Knowing where he is

now, I'm sure he's happy this day has come for many reasons."

"I agree. See you soon."

They both clicked off.

It was really happening.

The second she hung up, her phone rang again. She glanced at the caller ID. This time it was her parents. Recurring guilt stabbed at her because she was spending yet another birthday away from home. Thankfully it would be for the last time.

After picking up, she cried, "Mom? Dad?"

"It's your dad, my darlin' birthday girl. We miss you so much, we gathered the whole family together and decided to fly over to celebrate this weekend with you."

A soft gasp escaped. "You mean you're *here*?"

"Yes. All twelve of us. We just landed. Your mom's helping Melissa with Cory, or she'd get on the phone. Your three-year-old nephew has a hard time sitting still. We'll be at the house in an hour."

Jasmine could hardly take it in. They had no idea about the elaborate plans she and her papa had made. They didn't know that today she would be attending a board meeting that was going to change history.

Instead of phoning them after it was over as she'd intended, she would have to divulge the secret she and her grandfather had been planning the minute they arrived at the house. In truth, she was thrilled they'd come. She'd never needed their support more. "I—I can't wait to see you," she said in a tremulous voice.

"You don't know the half of it, Sparkles. See you in a little while."

"Oh, Dad—" Emotions of love and guilt made her

throat swell before she heard the click. He'd called her that from the time she was a little girl. What made this so hard was the fact that she hadn't always been home for important events.

Since her grandparents had died, she'd been working secretly behind the scenes to develop a perfume to help save the company. Her papa had sworn her to secrecy, even from her parents.

For the last few months, she'd felt estranged from them, which had never happened before. Her dad was particularly upset for her mother, who was missing Jasmine terribly and didn't understand why she hadn't been home for so long. When they'd hung up, Jasmine had felt his crushing disappointment and it had almost destroyed her.

But now that it was her birthday, everything was going to change. Within a month she would set certain things right and then go home to her family and spend the rest of her life proving her love for them. Her silly idea of marrying a cowboy was a fantasy of course, but she *was* going home for good!

After hanging up, she alerted the housekeeper that her family would be descending within the hour. Then she hurried to shower and wash her hair. To her shock, the stranger's comment about her lack of concern for her family's feelings unexpectedly flashed through her mind again, pressing on her awful guilt..

It infuriated her that the memory of his off-base remarks lingered to torment her. She couldn't believe that after two months she was still thinking about him when she had a board meeting to dress for. Jasmine had never attended one, but knew she needed to wear something conservative.

Her new three-piece suit with the knit jacket, pencil skirt and shell in soft peach would project the right image. Not over-or underdressed. She'd wear her hair caught back at the nape and put on her small pearl earrings. This was the kind of outfit her grandmother would have worn to such a meeting with Jasmine's papa.

Luc realized he needed a break from banking business and was ready for a relaxing weekend. But when he called his good friend Nic Valfort to go deep-sea fishing, he learned Nic was on a trip to the States with his new wife and wouldn't be back for another three days.

Somehow Luc needed to throw off this obsession over the woman on Yeronisos. Why in the hell couldn't he get her out of his mind? He'd found himself fantasizing about her, which was ridiculous when he knew he'd never see her again.

Somehow he had to think about something else. Being with Nic would have helped. He and Nic had met at college and had been friends ever since, like their grandfathers, who'd done business together in the past.

Between the plane crash that had marred Luc's life and the tragedy that had befallen Nic's first wife, the men had suffered grief at different periods and could relate. Luc enjoyed being with him whenever they could break away.

But since Nic's second marriage, they hadn't seen much of each other. His friend was ecstatically happy with his new American wife. After he got back from California, Luc would call him so they could get together.

As for tonight, there would be a party with his family to celebrate one of his cousin's birthdays. While he was getting ready to leave his suite, his assistant, Thomas, buzzed him. It had better be important because he was already late.

"Oui?"

"I just got a heads-up from one of our sources in Paris. Turn on your TV. Hurry!"

"More terrorism?"

"This news could be worse for us depending on the outcome."

A frown marred Luc's Gallic features. He reached for the remote in his desk drawer and clicked on to the six o'clock news. He paid Thomas well to keep his ear to the ground.

"Good evening, everyone. On this Friday, we're coming to you from Chaine Huit in Paris, France, with breaking news that is already rocking the international perfuming community. Today, a stunning announcement came from Grasse, France, the perfume capital of the world, causing a negative fluctuation in the stock market."

Tension lines deepened around Luc's mouth.

"Within the last twenty-four hours, the iconic House of Ferrier has undergone a dramatic new change in management."

A cold sweat broke out on his body. *What change?* No one had informed Luc.

The former biggest moneymaker in the perfume industry was one of the bank's top clients and had been for ninety years. But two years ago the head of Ferriers had died and the business had slowly started losing revenue. A few months later, Luc's own grandfather had passed away of a bad heart, making Luc the CEO of the bank.

Though the world didn't know it yet, the quarterly gross sales reports indicated a declining percentage in Ferriers's profits. Not totally alarming yet, but still, Luc was worried. Since his grandfather had been Maxim Ferrier's banker, Luc had been the one to take over their various accounts in order to maximize the assets in an unstable economy. It was one of the reasons he'd gone to Nicosia in May and again in June.

But without the proper leadership he'd worried about the future of a company that had been part of the backbone of the French economy for close to a century. If it failed, the economic structure of Southern France would be jeopardized. Like many other businesses, Ferriers had stayed alive all these years. If it continued to go downhill, the bank would be affected.

"Two years ago, the world lost the greatest perfumer of our time, Maxim Ferrier, at sixty-eight years of age. Balmain, Dior, Givenchy, Caron, Guerlain, Chanel, Balenciaga, Estee Lauder, Rochas, Fragonard, Ricci, Lentheric—all the great major perfume houses considered him an icon the world will never see again.

"Since his death, the company has been run by the family and other staff who made up the board while he was alive. But today, they have finally appointed a new head."

Luc ground his teeth. As he'd already found out, none of them had the Midas touch of the legendary perfumer himself. Who in heaven's name would they have found and brought in to turn things around? Absolutely no one from any other perfume house in the world had Maxim Ferrier's genius. Not in this generation. Probably not for another hundred years.

"Spill it!" Luc muttered furiously to the TV anchorman, who knew this broadcast was making the kind of news the media lived and died for and was milking it for all he was worth.

"Our station is the first to announce the name of Jasmine Martin, a total unknown, who has been put at the helm. She's an unmarried twenty-six-year-old with no formal job experience and has brought no resume to the position of the multibillion-dollar corporation."

"What?" In a state of shock, Luc shot to his feet.

"It's an unprecedented move since only two men have ever held that coveted position in the Ferrier perfume empire…Maxim Ferrier, and before him, his uncle, Paul Ferrier, whose father had run a flower farm in the very beginning. Right now, we're taking you live to the sacrosanct laboratory of the brilliant perfumer in Grasse. Our anchorman, Michel Didier, is standing by there, ready to interview her."

While Luc walked over to the TV screen to get a closer look, the other anchorman introduced himself.

"Good evening from our network in Grasse. I've been invited inside the room where Maxim Ferrier himself developed his famous formula for Night Scent, a perfume that won every award and still tops perfume sales around the globe. This is a privilege for me and all our viewers. The whole world is waiting to meet you, Jasmine. May I call you that?"

"Of course."

As the camera panned in on her, a cry of shock escaped Luc's throat. *No—it couldn't be!*

Hers was the beautiful face he'd seen at the dock

on Yeronisos! He took a deep breath, trying to comprehend it. The woman who'd given Luc battle before he'd watched her charge up those steep steps, possibly to her death, was *Jasmine Martin? The new CEO at Ferriers?*

His dark head reared. He'd never thought to see her again. Yet there she was in the flesh, that fiery beauty he'd been fantasizing about every night.

How was it that she of all people on this planet had been made head of one of the most iconic companies in France? She was a daredevil who'd insinuated that Luc was on his way to middle age before she'd ignored him and gone straight up the cliff to jump off. He rubbed the back of his neck in consternation.

It defied logic that a woman so careless with her own life was now running a billion-dollar corporation. Luc was so incredulous over what had been announced, he couldn't make sense of anything.

This evening she wore her hair caught back at the nape. Instead of wearing a T-shirt and bikini, she was dressed in a peach-colored suit that revealed her gorgeous figure.

Behind her were stacked rows of hundreds of bottles, reminding him of the wizard's shop in the Harry Potter film he'd seen with two of his nephews. Those magic potions that still delighted moviegoers everywhere.

Yet the potions behind this woman had worked their own special magic in the cosmetic world, yielding billions of dollars in revenue.

"I have many questions to ask. But for all those watching our broadcast around the globe, this question is foremost in everyone's mind. How did *you* of all people, of all women, get picked, and at such a young age?"

An impish smile broke out on her alluring face. Luc's breath caught. The memory of their heated exchange had caused him one restless night after another since his return. Twenty-six meant she was older than he'd thought, but it still rankled that she'd dared to accuse him of trying to pick her up.

She folded her arms and lounged against the edge of the lab table.

"You're going to get your scoop now, Michel," she teased with that same audacious maturity, so at odds with her lack of judgment when it came to her safety. There was a twinkle in her dark blue eyes. The first time they'd met she'd been wearing sunglasses. Luc had to admit he'd never seen anyone so natural in front of the camera. "I'm Maxim Ferrier's youngest grandchild."

Grandchild?

The well-known anchorman was taken by total surprise and looked as blown away as Luc felt.

"Since I came along last of his twenty-one grandchildren, he nicknamed me Jasmine. That's because Jasmine is the flower harvested last in October. He said it was his favorite flower because of its beguiling scent. Though my parents named me Blanchette after my mother, his name for me stuck."

Michel shook his head. "Just keep talking. I won't interrupt because I'm speechless and enchanted, and I know everyone else is too."

Her gentle laugh reached down to burrow inside a disbelieving Luc, who couldn't comprehend any of it. "I used to hang around my papa. I thought of him as this amazing sorcerer and pretended to be his apprentice. He never seemed to mind."

"Obviously not," the journalist interjected. "Tell the audience why you think he chose you to run the company."

"He once told me I was the only one in the family who got the nose. Not his own children and not any of his grandchildren got it, he said. Just me. I thought he meant I had a Roman nose like a horse. I was so hurt I ran out of the lab crying. He had no idea how much I loved him, but I was horrified that he thought I was ugly."

The anchorman laughed heartily, but Luc's throat closed up with emotion. Children were so literal, as he'd learned from being around his own nieces and nephews.

"Then he came after me and explained what he meant. He said I was so smart, he thought I knew what a nose was. He said I had a beautiful nose like my grandma. But he was referring to the fact that after sixty years, another perfumer had been born in the family, someone like himself who could identify scents. That person was *moi* and he was overjoyed."

Michel smiled. "No wonder he named you to succeed him."

"I still can't believe he did that and I am still trying to come to grips with it. No one could ever fill his shoes. I'm stunned to think he believed I could."

"I'm not surprised you're in shock," the anchorman commented at last. He stared at the camera. "*Mesdames et messieurs*, you couldn't make up a Cinderella story as unusual as this, not in a hundred years. I wish we had more time for the interview. Before we have to end this segment, the audience wants to hear about your grandmother.

"We know she was a great beauty right up to the time of her passing. Not only was she a devoted wife, she was a great intellect who authored several books."

"She was fabulous."

"While you were growing up, you must have known over the years that the international press touted them the most beautiful couple in the world. The French have called them the Charles Boyer and Marlene Dietrich of the modern era. American media labeled him more handsome and sophisticated than Cary Grant. She has been compared to Grace Kelly and Princess Diana. What do you say to that, Jasmine?"

"What more can I add? They were beautiful people from that era, inside and out. She loved him so much, she died three months later."

Luc hated to admit it, but part of him was spellbound by her and knew the anchorman was too.

"After seeing this broadcast, people will say you inherited her beauty."

"No woman could ever compare to her. If you could have heard my papa on the subject. If ever a man loved a woman…"

Luc heard the tremor in her voice and couldn't help but be moved by her humility. He could never have imagined this side of her after their explosive meeting on Yeronisos. *Unless this was all playacting.* If so, she was the greatest actress he'd ever known.

"Is it true he never gave an interview in his life?"

"That's right. He disliked publicity of any kind. I'm only doing this one interview because our family has been besieged by the media for years. The outpouring of public sentiment over their deaths has been so touching and overwhelming, I hoped to be able to thank them through your program."

"It's a personal honor for me, Ms. Martin. Would it be too forward of me to ask if there's a special man in your life?"

"Since you asked so nicely, I'll answer with a 'yes, it would.'" But she said it with a mocking little curve of her mouth that made Luc's emotions churn in remembrance of her erroneous assumption about him. The anchorman was quick to recover, but he looked embarrassed. Luc knew what it felt like to be slammed by her like that, although she'd been gentler with the other man.

"Message received. Wasn't your grandfather the one who coined the phrase, 'Provence is God's garden'?"

"Oh, no, but he often expressed that sentiment to me."

"While you've been talking, I found another passage in your grandmother's book where she quotes him. He must have been writing about you.

"'Jasmine seems to be a flower made for nostalgia. It grows in doorways and winds over arches, linking it to the intimacy of home. It begins to bloom as the days become hotter, and it releases its scent at the hour when tables are set in the garden or in narrow lanes. It is associated with the melancholy of dusk and the conviviality of summer evenings. Its fragrance permeates the air, making it a background for love.'"

She cleared her throat. "I remember him saying those words. I think Papa had a love affair with flowers all his life."

Watching this interview had tied Luc in knots. The

woman he'd met two months ago was nothing like the flower just described.

The anchorman nodded. "For those of you who still aren't aware, the book Jasmine's grandmother wrote, *Where There's Smoke*, is the definitive source on the life work of Maxim Ferrier. It's being reissued in a second edition with several sections of new information to coincide with the announcement of the new head of Ferriers and will be out on the stands tomorrow. When the first edition of the book came out, it became number one on bestseller lists worldwide. I confess I was enthralled by it."

"Thank you. Grandma worked on it for years. After my papa died, she had it published to honor him."

"No one knew him better than she did, except for you, who came in a close second." Again Luc saw the secret curve in her smile that reminded him of the way she'd smiled at him before letting him have it. The sensation twisted his gut as much now as then.

"Let me read one last thing your grandmother quoted from her husband. 'An exceptional perfume has a top note to entice, followed by the rich character of its middle note. Then comes the end note to bind all three, supplying the depth and solidity needed to make a lasting signature.' He was a poet, wasn't he?"

"Papa was so many things, I hardly know where to begin."

"I wish we didn't have to stop. Thank you for letting us see inside your world. It's been an honor and privilege."

"For me too."

"Congratulations on your new position, chosen by the head man himself. What greater endorsement, *n'est-ce pas*?" He turned to the camera. "That's it for now from Grasse. Back to you in Paris."

Luc shut off the TV, stunned out of his mind by her interview. A bomb had been dropped. He was still trying to recover from the fallout. Pacing the floor, he realized this meant he would be dealing with *her* in the future. His heart thudded at the very thought of it.

Now that the news had gone global, anything could happen and probably had behind closed doors at Ferriers. He couldn't imagine the members of the Ferrier board, twice or triple her age and most of them family, tolerating the granddaughter to become the head of the company. If they knew what Luc knew...

This was nepotism at its best. Either Maxim Ferrier had become senile toward the end, or she'd had him wrapped around her little finger because she'd inherited his gift. But that gift didn't mean she had the grasp for business or the necessary ability to run one of the most famous companies in existence. There'd been no mention of her education. She had no work experience. As far as he was concerned, she had no common sense either.

The Ferrier board had to have the same opinion about her and would soon find a way to vote her out. But until then Luc would have to be extra careful how he proceeded when the day came he had his first business meeting with her. Frankly, he couldn't imagine it after their explosive encounter on the island. Yet, to his dismay, the thought of being with her again charged every cell in his body.

"Luc?"

It had been a long time since Thomas had walked in without knocking, but Luc understood why. His assistant looked dazed. "I never saw or heard anything so amazing in my life."

"You're not alone, Thomas."

"She's more beautiful than her grandmother was, if that's possible."

It *was* possible. The image of her standing at the base of the cliff had never left him. But there were imperfect parts of her the camera hadn't seen, parts that he felt spelled a lot more trouble for Ferriers.

"I still can't believe she's the new face and power at Ferriers. She may be Maxim Ferrier's favorite and worth millions herself, but she looks too young and defenseless to go to battle against dynasty builders with three times her age and experience."

Luc would have thought the same thing if he hadn't been the recipient of her words, which could slice and dice a man to shreds in seconds. His assistant wouldn't see her as a defenseless woman if he'd watched her attack that rocky island on those breathtaking limbs of hers with the strength and agility of a military frogman.

Thomas's eyes gleamed. "This means that from now on you'll be meeting with her instead of Giles LeC—" he started to say, but Luc stopped him right there because he didn't want to hear it. He needed time for the news to sink in first.

"I'm late for a party and have to run. See you on Monday." He left by his private exit. It opened into a hallway leading to the private parking lot with a security guard.

Ever since the incident in Cyprus, he'd fought the temptation to find out who she was. A simple phone call to the boating concession that rented dinghies would have told him what he wanted to know, but somehow he'd managed to stop himself in time.

Dieu merci he hadn't let the desire to meet her in person and set her straight about a few things outweigh his innate caution. Otherwise, she truly would have had the last laugh knowing the director of the Banque Internationale du Midi *was* a voyeur stalking beautiful young women throughout the Mediterranean while on vacation.

The bank couldn't afford to lose one of the biggest accounts since its inception. No matter how acerbic her words, no matter how shallow he found her for being willing to throw her life away for a thrill, no matter how disappointed he was in Maxim Ferrier's decision to put a young loose cannon like her in charge, Luc could do nothing but stand by to watch a catastrophe in the making. And despise himself for being more attracted to her than ever.

CHAPTER TWO

ON WEDNESDAY MORNING, Jasmine saw her family off at Nice airport. She'd promised them that in a month she'd be on her way back home in Idaho for good. Before they boarded the jet, the pain in her parents' eyes revealed their disbelief that she would keep her promise. That look had stabbed her with fresh grief.

They didn't know that the glimpse of her life she'd described in front of the TV camera on Friday belonged to the past. Her grandparents were gone. Once she'd carried out her papa's last wishes—wishes no one else in the whole world knew about except her and his attorney—there was nothing more to keep her in France. But until she'd carried out this plan and moved back to Idaho, they wouldn't believe she really did want to go home for good.

After assuring them that she would arrive in time for their thirtieth wedding anniversary party in August, she headed for the Banque Internationale du Midi with a growing pit in her stomach.

"Papa?" she said to the air growing hotter by the minute under a July sun. "I carried off the first part of our plan on TV. Now I hope to pull off this second part, but I'm nervous. In case I get into trouble, I'll need your help or I won't be able to put the third part into motion. Do you hear me?"

Last Friday's media announcement had turned the entire Ferrier clan inside out as she had known it would, as her papa, though dead now, had known it would once Robert had read the will at the board meeting.

She knew positively that several of them, including non-family members of the board, had hoped to be named successor when the will was finally read. Of late they'd made no secret about it.

Jasmine's French mother and American father, along with her siblings, were known as the American faction of her grandparents' progeny. They didn't want to be involved in company business.

But all the other Ferriers lived in France and existed to promote the company. Some of them were situated in Paris with key positions at the perfumery. The rest had never left the environs of Nice that included Grasse. All of them worked for Ferriers in one capacity or other.

In the beginning, there'd been one small foundry in Grasse. In time, thirty distilleries dotted the Basses-Alpes, and the Alpes-Maritime regions. Her papa had his own small private lab in Grasse and eventually divided his time between the perfumery in Hyeres, and the other one in Paris. Little by little, the company expanded until he'd had the big perfumery built in Grasse.

Naturally everyone in the extended family had a huge vested interest in everything that went on. Jasmine loved them all. They were wonderful people. But when it came to families doing business together in a company with a history and heritage like theirs, emotions ran off the charts. Envy, pride and, in some cases, even greed had crept in.

For them to hear that Jasmine of all people had been named, as Michel Didier had said—a woman, the youngest nobody in the family—it had to be the lowest blow of all time.

Her grandfather had been such a private person, it was in keeping with his character to hide his secret agenda until his one great desire had become a fait accompli. Being that he was without a doubt the kindest, most enlightened, generous man she'd ever known, Jasmine had taken his private confidences to her heart. She knew he was counting on her.

Though her papa realized everyone would be upset and hurt one way or another, he'd had a nobler purpose in mind and was using his willing granddaughter to help right a wrong that had gone on since he'd been a small boy raised at La Tourette, the Ferrier home in Grasse.

The family's adverse reaction over Jasmine having been named was nothing compared to the furor that was coming. Tears filled her eyes. "I won't let you down, Papa."

She drove her Audi into the financial district of Nice. The bank that the House of Ferrier had done business with over the years was housed in a former cream-colored palace of neoclassic design. It lay just ahead surrounded with palm trees and exotic flowers. Everything was riding on this visit. Nothing could be accomplished without the bank's help. It was crucial Jasmine get the CEO on her side.

After pulling around to the public parking area,

she reached for the file folder she'd brought with her and entered through the main doors. A security guard nodded to her. "May I help you?"

"I'm here to see Monsieur Lucien Charriere on urgent business."

"Do you have an appointment?"

"No, but I'm hoping he'll have time to fit me in to his busy schedule." Her papa had always dealt with Raimond Charriere, but she'd learned from Giles Le-Clos, Ferrier's comptroller, that he'd passed away within months of her papa. His grandson Lucien had taken over.

"Without an appointment I'm afraid it would be impossible for him to meet with you. If you'll call the bank and ask to be put through to his office, his secretary will know how to help you."

"I'm sorry, but my reason for seeing him can't wait. If you'll please let him know that Jasmine Martin from Ferriers is here in the foyer, I'll wait as long as I have to."

The name Ferrier had always been the magic word and caused the older man's composure to slip. Without asking for picture ID, he pulled out his phone and spoke in hushed tones to the person who answered. When he hung up, he said, "Someone will be right with you. I didn't realize who you were."

"That's perfectly understandable." In a minute she heard, "Ms. Martin?" Jasmine turned in the direction of the man who'd just spoken her name.

"I'm Thomas, Monsieur Charriere's assistant." His eyes fastened on her with blatant male interest. "If you'll come with me, I'll show you to his office. He's on the phone, but he'll be through with his overseas call shortly."

"Thank you."

They walked on marble floors and down the north hallway to a suite that had been modernized. But nothing could hide the fact that it had once been a royal Italian residence of the House of Savoy before Nice was made an arrondissement of Grasse.

Before they reached the double doors of the inner office, they opened. Silhouetted over the threshold stood a tall, thirtyish male who immediately reminded her of…the bad boy at the dock on Yeronisos!

"You!" The shock of seeing him again, of finding him *here*, of realizing who he was, left her reeling. Her fantasy had come true! How was it possible?

Today he was immaculately turned out in a banker's suit and tie. His black hair, almost unruly, looked like he'd run his hand through it a few times out of frustration or habit.

Already he needed another shave and it was only eleven in the morning. She knew what he looked like underneath his clothes. Rock hard and lean, with a hungry look around his compelling mouth and nose. He had the genes of his Ligurian ancestry, which had given him moody black eyes. She hadn't been able to see their color behind his sunglasses.

A woman wouldn't be a woman if she didn't notice him. Jasmine had noticed him all right, and hadn't been the same since. As she'd discovered on the island, he was a standout in any crowd or alone.

She recalled her grandmother's description of her grandfather the first time they met. *The tall, fit, suntanned man with the penetrating black eyes and hair stood before me. He was so handsome he took my breath away.*

Jasmine could relate, but that pit in her stomach enlarged because this man's glittering gaze traveled over her, making every feminine corpuscle in her body quiver. He was still angry over her insults. She could feel it, but she was angry over his too!

Here she'd been afraid that Raimond Charriere's grandson would be a hard sell, though she'd come prepared to influence him until he couldn't say no to her request. How could she possibly have known that the CEO of the most prominent banking institution in the South of France was the man she'd accused of lying in wait to pick up defenseless young women?

A moan escaped her lips. Jasmine could appeal to other bankers, but because Ferriers had done business with *this* bank since the beginning, she wanted this man's help above all. Otherwise, her plan could be dashed to pieces and all would be lost. She couldn't let that happen! Somehow she had to salvage the situation. But after their caustic exchange on the island, his icy smile told her he'd show no mercy. She knew that much in her bones, and it put her on the defensive. She spoke first.

"I take it from your silence that you didn't expect me to survive my outing on Yeronisos."

His eyes narrowed on her features. "From your long, quiet assessment of me just now, I take it you're equally astonished that despite the sharks, I made it back to the mainland in the rental boat in one piece."

She'd just made things worse. "I should have called for an appointment."

One dark brow lifted. "But as you've already demonstrated, you like to live life on the edge so I'm not surprised you didn't go through normal channels. I hardly recognized you from the television broadcast on Friday evening."

Red-hot heat enveloped her. She'd never blushed in her life, but there was always a first time, as she was finding out. It crept from her toenails to the top of her head, missing nothing in between.

"I can only wonder what to expect next." His deep voice cast the final net to capture her total attention.

This was going from bad to worse. "Do you think we could start over again?"

His hands had gone to his hips in an utterly male stance. "I'm not sure. If I were to say it's a pleasure to meet you, would you assume that one of my secret sedentary activities is to trap hapless females who have the misfortune of entering this old man's lair?"

He wanted an apology. So did she, but since Jasmine had come to him on a desperate mission, it was up to her to cauterize the wound before it bled out of control.

"I'm sorry for the way I reacted on the island. You were right about the danger. One of the guys cut his leg open and he had to be taken to the hospital in an ambulance after we reached the boating concession."

The dangerous glitter in his eyes started to dissipate. "Fortunately for Ferriers, its new CEO survived to live another day."

This man wanted a full apology.

"I didn't honestly believe you were a predator, but your assumptions, especially the one that I gave no thought to the family that loved me, provoked me to say things that shocked even me." Which was the truth.

His black eyes studied her as if he were trying to weigh her sincerity. "I concede that in my concern for your safety, I was a little harsh in my assessment."

A little?

When he extended his hand, she had no choice but to shake it. Of course she was thankful for this overture on his part. *You need him on your side, Jasmine.* But the second she felt skin against skin, warm waves of sensation traveled through her body, throwing her emotions off balance.

"Please, Mademoiselle Martin, come in and be seated."

"Thank you, but before I do, I have a favor to ask."

"I'll leave the door open," he murmured dryly.

She fought another retort. "I thought you accepted my apology."

A faint smile hovered around his lips, without the ice this time. "So I did. What's the favor?"

"I don't want anyone at Ferriers to know I'm here. Could you tell your assistant and the security guard at the main entrance to keep absolutely quiet about this visit?"

After a moment of reflection he nodded. "*Bien sûr.* I'll take care of it now."

While he was gone, she walked across the oriental rug and sat down on one of two blue striped silk love seats facing each other around a coffee table. The couch was upholstered in a blue and white toile she found part of the charm of the elegant room.

Jasmine heard the doors close behind her, sealing them inside.

He rejoined her, cocking his dark head. "Now you

don't have to worry. Would you care for tea or coffee? Perhaps a soft drink?"

"Nothing, thank you."

They were circling each other, metaphorically speaking, trying to size each other up. He took a hand out of his pocket and sat in the chair opposite her. Both hands were ringless.

"Congratulations on your new position as head of the Ferrier Corporation. I dare say you're the most famous CEO in modern French history at the moment." The wryness of his tone wasn't lost on her.

One thing she already knew about him. He was a man who spoke his mind. She didn't know if that boded well or not for the shock he was about to receive.

"Thank you, except that I won't be the head for much longer."

"I can't say I'm surprised," he came back with urbane sophistication. "Please don't misunderstand me, but after the introduction on television about your lack of experience and work record, I gather the board is having difficulty following your grandfather's wishes, no matter that you were his personal choice of successor."

Jasmine hadn't seen that assessment coming so fast. It was *her* jaw that went slack, not his. But she couldn't take offense. He was discussing hard business facts and understood how things worked at the top. A shudder went through her to realize he wasn't the president of the bank for nothing. Her uphill battle had already begun.

"Yes," she admitted. "Giles LeClos has called another board meeting in two weeks for a vote. It doesn't leave me much time to accomplish what has to be done. That's why it was urgent that I see you today if I could. I appreciate your being willing to meet with me without any advance notice."

Her words brought his well-honed body forward. "Surely you must realize that your company's association with our bank over the years means you have instant access, if necessary. I'm glad you came in this morning. This afternoon I'll be out of the city on business, so it's providential that I was still available for this emergency meeting."

"That's what it is, and I'm very grateful." She bit her lip. "First of all, this has to be between the two of us and no one else. I realize you've been meeting with Giles LeClos, who's been in charge since Papa's death. But he mustn't know I've been here or he'll misunderstand and believe I've gone behind his back. In time, he'll be told, but not yet. Will you give me your promise on that?"

He sat back, examining her face with an intensity that made her feel he could see inside her soul. "Go on."

She had to take that as a yes. "Look—there's no point beating around the bush. My grandfather's company has been mismanaged since his death and now it's in huge trouble. No one is more aware of it than you. I intend to save it, but I'm going to need your help."

"You mean in two weeks you plan to pull it out of the red?" Granted his tone was incredulous, not mocking. "Isn't that a little ambitious, even if you have Maxim Ferrier's nose?" She winced. "I realize that sounds cruel, but you've never run a corporation and the bank has continued to extend your loan until it's at the limit."

"I'm very aware of that."

"Then you have to know there's nothing more we can do for you." He shook his head. "Perhaps another bank might be willing to underwrite a second loan for you, but it wouldn't be a wise business decision. Aside from the fact that your revenues are diminishing with little hope of recouping, there's no one at the head who instills enough confidence for the banking board to take a financial risk. Please don't take that as a personal attack against you."

"I won't. I didn't! If I were sitting on the board, I'd have little faith in me too. An empty-headed cliff-jumper who doesn't have a clue about business and is so spoiled by millions of dollars she wouldn't recognize a paycheck if she saw one doesn't exactly fill the bill. Right?"

"Again, those are your words, not mine."

Nothing appeared to faze him. "I believe you. But before you show me the door, I was hoping for the sake of the partnership that has lasted ninety years between your bank and Ferriers, you could find some time to let me make a proposition to you."

His eyes *did* flare at that remark, letting her know she actually had surprised him.

"Not the kind you're thinking, if you were thinking it," she added. "There's a matter of great urgency I need to discuss with you, but it will take some time. We can't do it now when you're already pressed to leave your office on other business. Could you possibly come tomorrow or Friday to my grandfather's laboratory in Grasse? This is vital, or I wouldn't ask."

Jasmine held her breath and prayed while she waited for his answer. She could hear his mind working.

"It would have to be late Friday afternoon. Four-thirty, maybe five. I could give you a half hour, then I have other plans."

Relief flooded her system. "Thank you for being willing to meet me halfway. It's more than I deserve." Jasmine got to her feet. "The lab is the little building on the south side of the perfumery. Just ring me when you're there and I'll let you in." She handed him a piece of paper with her phone number on it. *"À bientôt."*

At four on Friday, Luc left his office and headed for Grasse in his car. Half a dozen times in the last two days he'd reached for his phone to call her and cancel. Each time, he'd get so close, but then he couldn't follow through. The telltale throb in her voice when she'd said it was a matter of great urgency kept nagging at him until he couldn't sleep.

He was a fool to meet with her. It gave her hope when there wasn't any. But as she'd said, for the sake of the business both companies had done together over the years, he'd be churlish not to accommodate this one request. His grandfather had revered Maxim Ferrier and would probably have gone the extra mile before he had to turn his granddaughter down. Luc could at least do the same.

Keep on believing that lie, Charriere. You know damn well why you're breaking the speed limit to get there.

In a few minutes, he took the turnoff for the perfumery and wound around to the south side, where he saw the lab and a red Audi parked in front of it. He'd programmed her number into his phone so he wouldn't lose it. When he called her, she answered on the third ring.

"Bon après-midi, monsieur. I can't tell you what you coming here means to me." Her comment sounded heartfelt. He honestly didn't know what to make of her. "Every time my phone has rung, I've been afraid it was you calling to cancel because you'd thought the better of it." If only she knew. He got out of the car and walked over to the entrance. "I'm opening the door now."

He heard the sound of the electronic lock and there she was clad in a long-sleeved white lab coat that couldn't camouflage her gorgeous figure. The stains on it looked fresh. "Come in."

There were a few windows open at the very top of the room, but it was semi-dark. This was Maxim Ferrier's inner sanctum. It smelled and felt like Luc had just stepped into an old-school chemistry lab with all its paraphernalia from the nineteen-fifties. There was a worktable in the center of the room. Three walls of stacked shelves with fascinating bottles surrounded them, just as they'd appeared on TV.

She indicated an upholstered swivel chair, the only concession to modern-day décor. It was placed in front of an old oak desk pushed against the wall, piled high with notebooks.

Above it were two framed diplomas, both issued from the Department of Chemistry at the Sorbonne in Paris. The older, yellowing one had the name Maxim Tricornot Valmy Ferrier printed on it. The more recent white diploma displayed the name Jasmine Ferrier Martin. There was a ribbon attached beneath the glass that read, *With honors.*

He swallowed hard when he realized what it meant. No one with an empty head received credentials like that.

"I had two reasons for bringing you here. First, I wanted you to see where I work while I disabuse you of a few false notions about me. I *have* been working for years, but always alongside my papa behind the scenes when I wasn't at university. He paid my salary by putting money into a fund on a regular basis so I could draw from it. Please—sit down, Monsieur Charriere."

"Luc," came his quiet response.

"Luc," she amended. "I dislike formality too. Call me Jasmine. I'd prefer it."

He eyed her soberly. "This is where I eat crow, I presume."

"You're wrong. This is *not* payback time. I'm in deadly earnest when I say I need your help. If I can create a setting where you will really listen and not rush to judgment, that's all I ask. When you've heard me out, if you still can't see a way, then I won't ask again."

"Fair enough," he muttered.

"Thank you." She took a deep breath. "When you and I collided on Yeronisos island, I'd caught a ride in one of the dinghies with those teenagers so I wouldn't have to drive out there alone. My reason for being there was to take some pictures of the excavations.

"I've never been cliff jumping or anything dangerous like that in my life and never will. I too thought those guys were foolish and worried that something could happen, which it did."

Luc was eating a lot of crow by now.

"My grandmother's book was coming out again the day after my twenty-sixth birthday. She was an amateur archaeologist and had written a section about their travels. She'd lost the pictures she and Papa took together on Yeronisos island, so naturally they hadn't been included in the first edition.

"That's why I went out there and took some in order for them to be included in the second edition. She and Papa had gone there looking for Cleopatra's tomb. The location of that tomb somewhere near Alexandria still remains unknown."

"I know," he ground out. "I've tried looking for it myself."

"*That's* why you were there that day! I wondered."

It was all making sense. "I have an interest in Egyptian archaeology. After doing business in Nicosia, I went out there for the morning before I had to get back to Nice. I thought maybe she and Mark Antony had been buried on Yeronisos beneath the remains of the temple of Apollo, but I saw no signs of their crypt when I was there."

"I'm afraid it's still a mystery."

Luc darted her a glance. "Little did I know it was the new head of Ferriers who climbed to the top of that cliff like one of those amazing warrior women of the Amazon depicted in the myths of the Greeks. All that was missing were your sandals and the lasso of truth."

"If I'd known that two months later it was you of all people I would need to come begging to, I—"

He eyed her frankly. "You would have reacted the same way."

A smile hovered around her beautiful mouth. "My dad and brothers taught me early how to defend myself."

"Tell them they succeeded admirably. It hurts to admit I was impressed how well you protected yourself. You halfway got me believing I was a lech."

She was more of a mystery to him than ever. He'd seen the expert way she'd handled the anchorman—disarming him completely instead of the other way around. Michel Didier hadn't seen it coming either when she'd shot him down for asking a question about her love life.

Jasmine Martin wasn't Maxim Ferrier's granddaughter for nothing. Luc had a feeling she'd inherited her grandfather's shrewd business sense after all, or he would never have chosen her to be at its head.

He watched her pace the floor for a minute before she looked at him. "It's true I don't have years of experience behind me, but I have something else that didn't come out during the TV segment. My grandfather's full confidence."

Luc was listening. "You made that clear during the interview."

"Except that what you heard has little to do with why he named me to head the company. It wasn't because I inherited his nose. Incidentally, mine is nothing like his. There's only one Mozart born in this world. The truth is, Papa needed me to do something he couldn't do while he was alive."

At this point she had Luc so baffled and intrigued at the same time he grew restless and got to his feet. "Go on."

"Forgive me if I'm taking a long time to get to the point, but it's necessary so you'll understand. My grandparents had two homes. A ranch in Idaho in the U.S., where my grandmother was born. The other was the Ferrier family home in Grasse. They raised four children, two boys, two girls, all of whom are on the board except my mother, who was the youngest.

"She grew up loving the ranch and had little interest in being a part of the family perfuming business. She ended up marrying my dad, an Idaho cowboy who had his own ranch close by. My elder brother lives in the original ranch house. My other brother built a home on the same property. We're all just one happy family."

"Am I to assume that explains your strange comment about the 'Frenchman'?" Luc surmised.

"Let's put it this way. American men are very different than Frenchmen, and I've known two Frenchmen who haven't ingratiated themselves to me, thus the comment I made to you. But getting back to the point, I was my parents' third and last child, born on the ranch. My older brothers and I loved our life there, but every time our family traveled to Grasse to visit our grandparents, I found myself snooping around this laboratory and all Papa's stuff.

"If ever my parents or grandmother couldn't find me, I was with him, smelling all the slips he prepared. I loved doing what he did. No dollhouses and tea sets for me. This lab became my own tree house, so to speak.

"I loved it when he'd take me walking with him in the early evenings. He said it was a perfect time to smell the fragrance in the air. During those times he'd tell me he was creating a new perfume. I'd try to create one too and he gave me ideas. I was entranced.

"We used to play a game. He'd test me to find out if I knew what essential oil or chemical he was using. I'd stay up half the night in my bedroom at his house with all his used slips. I would study everything so I'd be ready for his questions the next day."

Luc was entranced by all this too.

"By the time I was twelve, I begged my parents to

let me stay with my grandparents for the next nine months and go to school here. My mom adored them and understood how much I loved to be with them. To my joy, she and dad allowed it, but they said I could only do it that one time because they'd miss me too much otherwise. At the time I didn't understand the great sacrifice they made to let me live with my grandparents.

"Before I had to go back home the next June, Papa picked me up and put me on this table I'm leaning against." She patted it. By now she'd mesmerized Luc. "That's when he told me I had the nose.

"But he said I had to keep it a secret. When I turned twenty-six, he would put me in charge of the company. But if he died before that birthday, he would leave instructions that the board install me as the official head after I came of age. In the meantime, he encouraged me to stick by him whenever I could.

"I thought he was kidding at making me the head of the company. I didn't believe he really meant those words. I hardly understood them, but he made me feel special and I adored him. I ended up staying with my grandparents in the summers and during holidays. He let me hover at his side and taught me how to cook up a perfume recipe.

"I met the people he worked with, the farmers, the workers at the distilleries, the workers at the warehouses. He took me on trips with him and grandma to Morocco and India and Nicosia. He taught me the difference between the soils in those climates, and the soil in Grasse, where the sweetest flowers are grown. We also spent time looking at ancient artifacts wherever we went. I couldn't get enough.

"After college in Paris, he asked me to come back to Grasse and work with him in here. Just the two of us. No one else was ever allowed inside. It was during that time he started confiding in me about certain issues in his life that had plagued him since childhood. I learned devastating things that broke my heart.

"Before his death, he asked a great favor of me. He'd devised a plan to remedy his pain, but it needed my help to execute and couldn't be carried out until he died." Her eyes filled with tears. She stopped talking for a minute and stared at him. "This is where you come in, Luc."

Was she playing him?

Unbelievably his cell rang just then. He checked the caller ID. His mother was phoning. They'd just returned from the Orient and his sister had planned a big family party. "Excuse me for a moment, Jasmine. I have to take this."

"Of course."

He walked over to a corner and picked up. "Maman?"

"The party started an hour ago. Where are you? Everyone's waiting!"

"I'll be there in a half hour."

"That long?"

"I had business. It couldn't be helped. See you soon." He clicked off and turned to Jasmine, haunted by more questions that needed answers.

"You gave me an hour," she said, reading his mind. "I understand you have to go, but I haven't come to the most important part yet. Could I meet you at your office next week when it's convenient so we can finish this conversation? You need to hear about the great injustice that has been done. I must have help to solve it. Hopefully *your* help."

Must?

Looking into those fabulous blue orbs of hers, he realized it wasn't just her company that was in trouble. Otherwise he wouldn't have caved and said, "I'll tell my assistant to put you down for eleven a.m. on Monday morning." *Get this over as soon as possible, Charriere.*

CHAPTER THREE

ON SATURDAY MORNING the flower market in Grasse brought hundreds of tourists and natives flocking, Jasmine among them. She waited until she saw the truck from the Fleury flower farm make their delivery. As soon as it was unloaded, she hurried over to the stand and bought a tub full of violets she arranged to have loaded in her car.

With time of the essence, she hurried back to the laboratory to prepare a fresh batch of the recipe she'd been perfecting for over a year. The older batch had passed all her tests and she'd had amazing results when she'd worn the perfume out in public.

But this batch would contain the essential oil that came from this new strain of violet that hadn't been available until very recently. It produced the sweetest scent she'd ever smelled. The difference between the old and new strain of violet was so significant, she literally danced for joy through the next two days while she cooked up her recipe.

By Sunday night, she'd prepared two dozen little bottles of samples, hardly able to wait to give them out.

While she wrote notes in her ledger, she paused. "Papa? I wish you were here to smell this. I'm going to try it out on Lucien Charriere. Tomorrow is my chance to win him over to your plan. If he bites, then the second part of it can get under way.

"But I got off to such a bad start with him I don't know what to think. He has every right to consider me a lightweight. In fact it's a miracle he agreed to come to the lab on Friday. Wish me luck."

As she was locking up the lab, she received another call from Giles. But she had nothing to say to him yet, so she'd been putting him off and would continue to do so until after she'd met with Luc tomorrow. If nothing came of their meeting, then she needed to find another banker, even if Luc had explained she probably wouldn't be successful. At some point, she'd get back to Giles, who no doubt wanted to be sure she'd cleared her calendar to be at the next board meeting when they voted her down.

On her way out to the car with one of her new samples, she saw that Fabrice Guillard, one of the chemists who worked at the perfumery, was waiting for her in his Peugeot.

"*Salut*, Fabrice. What are you doing here on a Sunday night?"

"Lying in wait for you," he said in a seductive voice.

She laughed. If she could believe him, then she wished Luc were here to witness the irony of the situation. But she had an idea someone on the board, possibly Giles, wanted to know what she was up to and had encouraged Fabrice to ask her out. If they were trying to find information that could fortify their claim that she wasn't the best choice to be CEO, they were using the wrong person to do it.

Fabrice pretended to be wounded. "You hurt me,

mademoiselle. I saw your car and hoped I could take you out for a bite to eat." The attractive, divorced Frenchman with the light brown hair and eyes had recently been brought into the company and was all the talk among the females at the perfumery.

But like André Malroix, a former boyfriend of Jasmine's, and a lot of French men, Fabrice had that ability to chat her up in a seductive way, causing her to believe she was the most beautiful woman on earth. Jasmine had fallen for it until André showed his true colors. She didn't know Fabrice's true colors and didn't want to know because he seemed like the same type. His intimate way of talking irritated her and she wasn't in the mood.

"Thank you for asking, but I have other plans. My advice for you is to wait for one of the girls after work tomorrow. I can promise you'll have better luck with Suzette. I heard she finds you intelligent and fun to be around."

"*Oh, là là*. I think you're afraid of men, *chérie*."

"If you're talking French men, you're absolutely right."

"Why do you say that?"

If he got her going on her list, they'd be out here all night. If he was innocent of an agenda and only wanted to be with her, it still didn't matter. "I don't think you want to know. Have a lovely evening, Fabrice. *Ciao*."

Even though Luc had braced himself for his eleven o'clock appointment, Jasmine Martin's appearance in the doorway of his office had managed to upend him until he was reeling from sensation after sensation. While he watched her take a seat, the mold of her body did amazing things for her summery print skirt and blouse in blues and greens on white. With legs that went on and on and a mouth that was temptation itself, how in the hell was he going to focus?

The buzz from the intercom drove him across the room to his desk. Thomas wouldn't have bothered him if it weren't important. He picked up his phone. *"Oui?"*

"You've had three calls, all urgent. Now Monsieur LeClos is on the line and says it's vital he get in touch with you today."

With two years of diminishing earnings reports, things were getting hotter at Ferriers. Luc knew Le-Clos wanted another extension of their existing loan and was going behind Jasmine's back.

He darted her a glance, then checked his watch. "Tell everyone I'm in conference and will return calls after three, no sooner. In the meantime, Ms. Martin and I will need lunch brought in. With that exception, I don't want to be disturbed."

"Très bien."

After hanging up, he turned to her and rested against the edge of his desk with his hands braced on either side. "Let's start with my visit to your lab on Friday. You stated at the time that you'd asked me to meet you there for two reasons. After eating crow, I never heard the second reason."

She re-crossed her elegant legs. "If you hadn't had to leave, I would have told you."

"Well, I'm not going anywhere now. The time is yours to explain. You made a comment on Friday when you said that you *must* have my help to solve a great injustice. That sounded cryptic and quite a different matter from the fact that your company is in arrears on your loan payment. Why don't you begin by telling me about this injustice. Against whom?"

Her hands went to the arms of the chair. She stared into his eyes without wavering. "Against the rightful heir to the company."

"Rightful heir?" Maybe he hadn't heard her correctly. "In principle, all of you Ferriers are heirs."

She nodded, drawing his attention to her glistening dark sable hair. "That's true. All the Ferriers born to my grandparents are Papa's heirs. But Papa wasn't the legitimate heir to the Ferrier dynasty. Ferrier wasn't even Papa's legal name. Not in the beginning."

Dumbfounded, Luc walked toward her. "What was it?"

"Tricornot."

First the revelations during the television interview that had knocked him sideways. Now this… "Who *is* the real heir?"

"Papa's cousin, Remy Ferrier."

At this point, Luc was confused. "According to the media from years ago, he was the wealthy no-account alcoholic who crashed one sports car after another. I heard he was a womanizer who failed at several marriages and a race car business, then went off somewhere never to be heard of again. You're telling me *he's* the real heir?"

Whatever he'd said caused her to jump out of the chair and start pacing. He'd obviously offended her. "I'm sorry, Jasmine. I was only repeating the gossip that circulated when I was a younger man."

She finally stopped pacing and turned to him. "Remy was a good-looking man who attracted women in droves with or without his money. He never knew if they loved him for himself or not.

"Yes, he did love fast cars and he did crash quite a few of them because he loved speed and should have raced in the Grand Prix with his friend Marcello. He was that good. When he realized he was getting too old to race, he designed a revolutionary race car, but the business he tried to establish along with it failed because he couldn't find enough backers."

"But he had millions."

"No. He had nothing! His father cut off his funds. His one marriage failed, and yes, he drank too much. But that isn't who Remy really is." A world of sadness had entered those blue eyes.

"Is he still alive?"

"Very much so and living in Grasse."

"You're kidding—I don't understand. Why hasn't anyone heard about him in all these years?"

"Because he's been quietly working on his own flower farm, which is thriving."

"Flower farm?" Lines marred Luc's features. "And yet he's not associated with your family's perfume business?"

Her lovely jaw hardened. "No. But once upon a time Remy *was* the business, the *integral* part," she emphasized to the point that it raised hairs on the back of his neck. "But his birthright was stolen and given to another."

"Stolen?" Luc was confounded by what she was telling him.

She nodded and sat back down again. "On behalf of my papa, I've come to you. He despised being the head of the company and never wanted any part of that aspect or the fame. I'm here to make certain Remy attains his rightful place at last. With a loan from you, I can make that happen."

A loan, he mouthed. "We've already had this discussion, Jasmine. Are you talking about another loan for you personally?"

"For me, for Remy, for Papa, for the very preservation of the company. That's why I've continued to darken your doorstep."

Darken was hardly the word, but the revelations continually pouring out of her had him stymied. "Are you talking a real Jacob and Esau story here?"

"In a way."

"Explain the twist to me."

"The culprit wasn't Remy or my grandfather."

"Then all the accolades heaped on your grandfather are still true?"

"Of course. Just as all the ugliness about Remy's supposedly profligate life was the work of someone as close to a monster as you can get."

Luc rubbed his lower lip with his thumb. "Who would that be?"

"Remy's father."

More confused, he shook his head. "You mean the brother of Paul Ferrier? I don't remember his name."

Her gaze held his. "Gaston was Paul's brother. But Remy's father was Paul Ferrier, the tyrannical head of Ferriers all those years."

"What?"

The things she was saying now were even more astounding than her announcement that she was Maxim Ferrier's granddaughter. While he was attempting to sort out all this new information, there was a tap on the door.

Luc walked to the entrance and took the tray of sandwiches and salad from his assistant. "Remember," he murmured. "No disturbance now, no mention of who's inside my office. One slip and you're fired."

Thomas went stone-cold sober. "I swear I won't say a word," he promised before closing the door.

Luc walked back to the table and lowered the tray. Jasmine looked up. "Thank you for lunch."

"I'm hungry too. Join me."

She reached for a half sandwich and coffee before settling back in the chair. He fixed himself a plate and sat down. "Whenever you're ready, I'd like to hear this amazing tale from the definitive source."

"That's *moi*." Her head flew back, unsettling the hair sweeping her shoulders. Her comment had come out solemn rather than teasing.

"Papa's father was a Tricornot, his mother a Valmy."

Luc made a sound. "I remember seeing those names on your grandfather's diploma."

"Yes. They died, so he was adopted by his mother's sister, Dominique. She was married to Gaston Ferrier. They couldn't have children so they gave Papa their last name. But the situation was doomed at the outset because the three of them lived in the family home in Grasse with Gaston's brother, Paul Ferrier, his wife, Rosaline, and their son, Remy."

Luc poured himself some coffee. "How did they all stand to live together?"

"For Papa and Remy, it was a natural phenomenon because they didn't know anything else. But it was on Paul's insistence they lived together in order to keep the perfume recipes from falling into the wrong hands. He was a tyrant and it was his way of controlling everything to ensure the family business secrets stayed hidden from the rest of the world.

"Paul had a nose, but not a good one by anyone's standards. Gaston tried to take care of the business, but was in fragile health. From the very beginning it was Remy who did the flower farming and virtually ran the whole business from distillation to marketing. Remy had that special gift to know the precise moment when to harvest, when to cut the flowers and prepare them for enfleurage.

"He knew every inch of ground, every flower, the seasons, the farmers he worked with, the demands of the market. Without Remy, Ferriers would never have become a great operation. But Paul destroyed his own son in the process."

Totally intrigued he asked, "In what way?"

"Remy didn't have the nose. The family discovered that Papa did."

"How did that happen?"

"While Papa was fiddling around in the perfumery laboratory, he found some discarded slips of paper with different scents on them. To Gaston's great astonishment, Papa could identify some of the various oils."

"Exactly what happened to you!"

"Yes. Both families were stunned. The normal person can pick out three, maybe four components. A *nose* can detect a mixture of a hundred or more ingredients in their precise amounts, and blindfolded, pick out the various scents from the essential oils that contribute to a recipe. Even as a child, Papa exhibited this ex-

traordinary gift to a much greater degree than anyone
dreamed, including Paul."

"But if Maxim wasn't Paul's son, then how did
he inherit his ability to create perfume? He couldn't
have gotten it from his birth or adoptive parents." Luc
reached for another sandwich, completely engrossed.

She shook her head. "There's no explanation as to
why one person has the gift and another does not. By
some inexplicable reason, Papa was gifted. And he
was the only nose in the Ferrier family dating back
ninety years who didn't have a Ferrier gene in him."

"But he had the genius to create scents." Luc was
finally getting the picture. "Fascinating since he had
the greatest nose this generation has seen. So the true
Ferrier was replaced by the adoptive son."

"More than replaced!" she cried. "Paul idolized
him, gave him everything…his time, his posses-
sions. He ignored his own wife, who by then was in
a wheelchair. Papa became his *raison d'être*. Remy
was virtually invisible to his father. Paul Ferrier was
a terrible, terrible man." Her voice shook. "He kept
Remy tied to him to do the work, not giving him time
off to race cars in the seasonal rallies with his Italian
racing friend, Marcello. Remy was his father's slave."

"That's the worst story of its kind I've ever heard,"
Luc murmured emotionally. He was pained for people
he didn't even know.

"You don't know the half of it. Remy's mother
begged him to leave and make a different life for himself, but he loved Rosaline and wouldn't leave her in
her crippled condition from arthritis. Paul forgot his
wife and son existed."

Tears escaped her eyes. "You can't imagine how

this killed my grandfather. It was all so unfair. To think he was set on the exalted Ferrier throne because he'd been blessed with a very keen olfactory sense, and Remy was not. Papa loved Remy, Luc!" she cried.

"He grieved over the situation and knew Remy was the greatest flower farmer in the South of France, that he ran everything seamlessly and should always have been at the head. When Remy turned twenty-nine, Paul cut off all money that should have gone to his son, money Remy had earned. Six months later Paul died.

"As soon as he passed way, Papa begged him to come back to Grasse and take over the business. But by then Remy was in a bad way and refused to talk to anyone. Papa heard he was in Paris trying to build a race car business. He sent him money through Marcello to help him get started, but Remy never touched it.

"Papa begged him to come back and run the whole company, but Remy's pride wouldn't allow him to go there. Too much damage had been done. All these years Papa has kept in touch with Marcello, begging him to talk to Remy for him and get him to come home. But Remy couldn't do it."

Luc knew there had to be a lot more to the story than she was telling, but he let it go for now.

"Remy had started drinking heavily by then and his business failed. Later on, he married and they had a son, but their marriage fell apart. His wife left him because there was no money, but his son stuck by him. They came back to the house and small property Remy's mother had left him. He began flower farming again, but he's had no contact with the family."

She wiped her eyes. "Papa had to live with that

sorrow for the rest of his life. I became his confidant. Papa put me in charge because he expected me to fix what he couldn't while he was alive.

"He hated the honors Paul bestowed upon him. All he'd wanted was to create perfume. Remy should have run the empire. This ate Papa alive. Behind all the success, both their lives were a giant sore that never healed because Paul forgot Remy even existed."

A shuddering breath came out of her. "Papa developed a plan to restore Remy's birthright and change the map for the future betterment of the company as soon as I was put in charge. With your help, I can give Remy back his dignity and set him up to run Ferriers the way he should have been able to do years ago. He'll make it greater than it has ever been.

"But because of his wounded pride, Remy will never accept the position unless he feels he has something vital to contribute." Her eyes implored him. "So I've come to you for the loan that will accomplish the miracle."

Luc couldn't have foreseen this coming, not in a million years. He was still trying to grasp the enormity of the Ferrier family tragedy.

"You have to understand Remy has a great business mind. Papa wanted him installed so he can run the show as only he knows how to do. Once, when Papa went to South America for six weeks, Remy was put in charge and went to Paris. He ran the company without a hitch and brought in new accounts without effort."

Once.

"I know what you're thinking. But when Papa asked him to do it, he did it flawlessly."

Luc closed his eyes for a minute while he digested what she was asking.

"Remy's brilliant, Luc. So's his scientist son, Jean-Louis, who runs his own firm in the Sophia Antipolis complex here in Nice and is helping Remy. Today he sells the harvest from his crops independently. The kind of crop he's been cultivating could bring millions of dollars to the family business if he had the money to buy up more property to grow more crops. I know where to lay hands on the kind of land he needs.

"I have the figures worked out to show how we can recoup our losses. Papa kept the business on top as best he could, but since his death, one bad decision after another has been made. Everything's here on paper." She got up and handed him the folder she'd brought in.

Jasmine had pled her case and had won him over emotionally without showing him anything. But financially, all the negatives against the idea had been stacking up. "How old is he?"

"Sixty-six."

Ciel! That was old for the bank to go with a supposed recovered alcoholic. Maxim Ferrier couldn't honestly have believed his cousin could take on the whole board at Ferriers and gain their trust. Certainly Luc's bank wouldn't consider it, no matter that his pipe dream was well meant.

"Through my sources I know he stopped drinking a long time ago," Jasmine read his mind. "He lives with his son and his wife and their children."

Luc shook his head. Granting another loan of the size she was talking about meant taking a huge risk, one his bank couldn't afford. Though he could pass this by the banking board of directors, to win a nod would take a miracle. Everything was against it. *He* was still against it for the obvious reasons.

She unexpectedly got up from the chair. "If I have to, I'll put up the family home and the property surrounding it for collateral."

Mon Dieu. For her to risk losing such a personal legacy was unfathomable to him. Clearly she was in this for the fight of her life, and it would be a fight. But he had to admire her because she was willing to risk everything by taking the moral high ground. All for the sake of the true son.

"I can read your mind, Luc. You think it would be a risk to loan more money, but there's a saying: to win without risk is to triumph without glory. You'd be doing a great thing. Please remember something else. I came to you first. If you decide we can't do business, I'll go elsewhere until I find the right banker. This isn't a threat. I'm just being practical and I'm in a hurry."

She got up from the chair, but he grasped her arm before she could leave. She spun around in surprise. "Don't go out that way, Jasmine. Use my private entrance so no one in the bank will see you leave."

Her eyes flashed a midnight blue as she eased her arm from his grasp. "That's all right. I've asked too big a favor already."

A pretty impossible favor. One he couldn't see himself granting. "I'm sorry, but in all honesty I don't believe the banking board will be willing to do business with you under such circumstances."

"In other words, the answer is no."

"I'm afraid so. But please—let me walk you out."

Without taking no for an answer, he headed for his

private entrance. Together they left via the rear exit.
He followed her to the Audi she'd parked around the
side. After she'd climbed behind the wheel, accidentally giving him a brief glimpse of her gorgeous legs
where the material rode up her thigh, she lowered the
window.

He put a hand on top of the car and leaned toward
her. "Just a minute," he said, causing her to pause. "Before you leave, what's that scent you're wearing? It's
sweet and fresh, like the way spring smells."

"It doesn't have a name."

"You mean it's a recipe you just cooked up for the
fun of it," he teased, remembering her comment from
the broadcast.

A faint smile hovered at the corner of her mouth.
He really was in trouble now. "Something like that."

Luc studied the shape of it longer than he should
have. "Promise you won't think I'm playing up to your
good side if I tell you I like it more than anything I've
ever smelled on a woman?"

Her smile deepened. "I believe you. Do you know I
get that same response from almost every man I meet
or work with? I've been wearing it off and on for a
year now. What you're responding to is the pure scent
of the Parma violet."

"Violet? So that's what it is! I couldn't put my finger on it."

"They've all but disappeared, that's why."

He frowned. "What happened?"

"In the nineteenth century around Grasse there
were large plantings being grown for the perfume
industry. Sadly in the eighteen-nineties a synthetic
violet fragrance was discovered and was soon manu-

factured cheaply, putting an end to the production of the natural oil.

"But Remy has brought the Parma violet back to Grasse from Italy. Over the last few years he's spent his time cultivating it and perfecting several unique varieties for their scent. His best one comes from a cultivar with a very strong constitution. When he can plant more, it's going to create a brand new niche that's been missing in the Ferrier perfume market."

"And what is that?" Luc asked. He'd never met such an incredible woman.

"A scent men *like* to smell on a woman. In general, women dress and buy scents to suit themselves."

A scent men like to smell...

Yes…they did. *He* did.

The novel marketing idea blew him away. So did her vast knowledge, which continued to humble him.

"Paul Ferrier had no clue his son was a genius. He considered him baggage." Luc grimaced to think a father could do that to a son. "With the help of Jean-Louis, Remy has developed a secret weapon that will soon put Ferriers in the black again. You were my first choice for a backer, but I'll find another to get him what he needs. Mark my words."

She put on her sunglasses. "I realize I'm lucky you didn't throw me out after I barged in last week. For you to feed me just now tells me why Papa dealt with your bank exclusively over the years."

With that comment, she turned on the engine and started to back out. Before leaving the parking area she waved to him. "You summed me up in a big hurry on Yeronisos island, so I don't know why I expected anything else from you in regard to Remy Ferrier. But

I thank you for your time and for being up-front so no more time is wasted. *Au revoir, monsieur.*"

At the end of Luc's work day, he took the chance that his friend Nic hadn't gone home from work yet, and drove to his office in the technopole research park of Sophia Antipolis. He wound around the pine-covered hills to reach Valfort Technologies.

Not that long ago Luc had participated in a massive four-day search of the park with police dogs, hoping to discover the remains of Nic's first wife, who'd been missing for three years. Miraculously, her body had been found and it had been discovered she'd been shot and buried in the heavily wooded area. What had been meant to be a kidnapping had turned out to be a murder. Only a man with Nic's strength could have gotten through such a horrendous ordeal.

Every time Luc came here, he was reminded of his friend's pain, but the knowledge that Nic had found love again drove away the darkness. Luc needed to talk, and there was no one who listened better than Nic.

Monday evening wasn't the greatest time to drop by, but Luc decided to take a chance anyway. Robert, Nic's assistant, smiled when Luc stepped inside. "I'll let Nic know you're here."

"Is he with a client?"

"No. He's through for the day. This is a good time."

A minute later, his dark-haired friend, sporting a new tan, invited him into his office with a bear hug and shut the door. "It's good to see you! Sit down. Want a soda? Coffee?"

"Nothing right now. I called last week to see if you

could go deep-sea fishing and found out you were on a trip to California. Looks like it agreed with you."

"We had a great time, but I have to admit I'm glad to be back." Nic was a new man since his marriage. Luc hardly recognized him. "Laura and I were just talking about getting you and Yves together for dinner on Saturday night at our house. Are you still seeing Gabrielle?"

"No. That was over weeks ago."

His friend perched on the corner of his desk. "That settles that. Something's wrong. What is it?"

"I've met a woman."

A chuckle escaped Nic. "Since they throw themselves at you, I'm not surprised."

Luc shook his head. "This one is different."

"In what way?"

"In ways even you can't imagine."

"You mean you're interested for the first time since—"

"Yes," Luc cut him off. "But it's much more than that."

Nic started to smile. "Are you saying what I think you're saying?"

He raked a hand through his hair. "I don't know. I'm in trouble, Nic. Real trouble. Do you have time to talk?"

"After the years you put up listening to me talk through my pain, you know I've got time. First of all, who is she?"

Luc couldn't stay seated. He walked around for a minute. "Did you happen to see the news on TV about the new head of the Ferrier Corporation?"

"Who didn't? I think every male watching on six

continents was blown away by the gorgeous grand-daughter of Maxim Ferrier." When Luc didn't comment, Nic eyed him in disbelief. "*She's* the woman?"

He nodded. "Jasmine Martin."

Nic let out a whistle. "How long has this been going on?"

"Since a week ago Friday, but we met two months before that when I went to Nicosia on business. We ran into each other on Yeronisos island."

"Literally?" He grinned.

"Not exactly. But that's a whole story in itself."

"Does she feel the same way about you?"

Luc rubbed the back of his neck. "I don't know what she feels."

"How could you not know something like that?"

"It's complicated. She came to me for a loan."

"*Eh bien, mon ami.* Why don't you start at the beginning? I want to hear about what happened on Yeronisos, and then I want to know why a woman who's worth millions of dollars on her own came to you for money."

"I don't think she *is* worth millions or she wouldn't have said she'd put up the Ferrier personal property for collateral."

A whistle came out of Nic.

For the next half hour, Luc unloaded to the friend he would trust with his life. It felt good to let it all out and try to make sense of it. When he'd finished, he said, "I never saw anyone so invested in another person's happiness. It's been a revelation to me."

"I agree it's a gut-wrenching story," Nic murmured.

"It is, but much as I would have liked to grant her request, I had to turn her down for the loan. Remy

Ferrier has too many problems that wouldn't inspire confidence in the banking board." He rubbed his jaw for a minute. "She mentioned something about Remy's son, who was helping him. Since you work here at the complex, do you happen to know of a Jean-Louis Ferrier? I'm curious. Jasmine said he had an office around here somewhere."

Nic nodded. "I've only met him once. It was after the search for my wife. I stopped by to thank everyone in the complex who'd been a part of it. I learned he's a scientist running a firm in the next section east of me. It seems his team is on the cutting edge of technology for some new miracle processes involving plants and animals. Because of my technological background, I found our conversation fascinating."

Luc sat forward in the chair with his hands clasped between his legs. "I didn't know there was another Ferrier related to Remy here in Nice."

"Small world, isn't it? To my knowledge they're focusing primarily on understanding the cellular mechanisms that underlie the development and physiology of plants and animals, which provides the foundation for biotechnology innovation. From the way he explained it to me, there's this molecular circuit that acts as a bio-timer to control the diverse growth pathways in plants and animals."

Luc took a deep breath. "When Jasmine said Remy was working with his son, I didn't realize what she meant." *Because you didn't give her a chance?*

Nic eyed him thoughtfully. "This discovery allows farmers to save on both man power and shipping, as naturally maturing crops will not all flower at the same time, leading to the less than optimal use of resources.

This technique to synchronize the flowering, to maximize the yield or reduce the cost of harvesting, is revolutionary because you can do it all at the same time
and potentially reduce wastage.

"If Remy is trying it out with his Parma violets
and is having success, then it could revolutionize the
flower industry. More harvests in one season could
mean additional profits for the farmer."

"So *that* was the secret weapon she'd talked about,"
Luc blurted. It seemed he'd jumped to another conclusion too fast without knowing all the facts. Times
had changed since Remy ran the company. Luc felt
the banking board wouldn't think the sixty-six-year-
old farmer was the right person to take over, but Nic's
explanation about his son's work had thrown a new
light on the situation.

His friend smiled. "Besides being a beauty, she's
definitely unique. So tell me what else is wrong."

Luc got to his feet. "I never wanted to feel this way
about a woman again."

"Obviously she's into you too."

"There have been moments along the way when I
thought— Oh, hell, I don't know. I can't read her yet."

"Give it time, Luc. Once you get past the business
part, then you'll be able to explore what could be between you."

"I'm afraid I ruined it when I turned her down for
the loan."

Nic stared at him. "Why don't you bring her over
on Saturday night so we can meet her?"

"After today, I don't know if she'll ever speak to
me again."

"Want to take bets on that?"

Luc's brows lifted. "I'll think about it and let you know," he muttered. "Thanks, Nic. I don't know what I'd do without you."

"That makes two of us."

CHAPTER FOUR

JASMINE'S JAW WENT taut as she headed for the house Tuesday evening. Yesterday she'd given Luc Charriere the grand performance of her life, but it had all been for naught. This was supposed to be the honeymoon phase of her inauguration with the company, but her failure to get Luc on board had come as a crushing blow.

She gripped the steering wheel tighter as she took the exit leading away from the lab, which she'd left early. The thought of walking over to the perfumery and facing Giles's wooden expression, let alone the many phone calls that needed answering, was too daunting.

Good karma hadn't been with her yesterday. Otherwise, the scent she'd been wearing might have made him curious enough to delve into that file she'd left and rethink his position. Though emotions had welled up inside her and she'd laid it all out, he'd turned her down flat.

When he'd come to the laboratory last week, she'd read those negative signs coming from him, the kind you picked up by osmosis. Part of her understood he had legitimate reasons for making his decision. She'd heard them running through his mind. But she hadn't wanted to accept them.

You're a fool, Jasmine. An imbécile. *Idiote.*

She dashed the tears from her eyes. After the experience on the island, she should have known his answer would be an emphatic no. Shaken by the depth of her intense attraction to him in spite of how things had turned out, she decided to go home and put Luc out of her mind once and for all.

To unwind after her session with the man who'd watched her climb Yeronisos—a spine-tingling thought—she took the long way back to La Tourette, passing the sloping fields of acacia, geranium, tuberose and jasmine blooming beneath the afternoon summer sky.

She scanned the horizon. Her favorite view was of the flowers growing up against the white stucco farmhouses. Beyond them, the rocky promontories knifed skyward. Between the crags, the many little villages of pale cream and red lay in repose. Normally this drive helped her relax, but for some reason she was feeling a new restlessness.

If she were being honest, Lucien Charriere was responsible for it.

That's why she couldn't focus on anything. A new hunger had been aroused in her while she'd poured out her soul to him. His compassion for what he'd heard couldn't be denied. It had been there in his eyes, but he still believed that extending a new loan was a bad business decision and there was nothing she could do about it.

He'd given her all the time she'd needed to state her case when she knew his assistant had to put his other clients off in order to accommodate her. She could still feel his hand on her arm. Her body still throbbed from his touch. His mention of the scent she was wearing had established an intimacy between them so strong it had raised her pulse.

Tortured by this new sense of yearning to know what his mouth tasted and felt like, she drove on, winding up the steep hillside on the other side of the gorge. He was nothing like the Andrés and Fabrices with whom she'd worked, those who thought they could sweep you off your feet with their specialized love verbiage.

Luc wasn't like any Frenchman she'd met, who, young or old, single, married or divorced, hit on her all the time whether she wore perfume or not. Luc had maintained an aloofness balanced with just the right amount of professional courtesy and interest. How insane was it that he was the only man of her acquaintance to produce this physical response in her. To think about him all the time like this was madness.

Soon, she reached the fieldstone house on the family estate. Long promenades of cypress trees flanked her progress. The smell of the orange trees told her she was close to La Tourette. The house had emptied of family who'd gathered here the weekend from last, and now were gone. Though she'd wanted them to stay longer, her father's ranching responsibilities meant he needed to get back home.

Jasmine got out of the car and hurried inside. She found Sylvie in the kitchen. "I'm home for the night," she told the housekeeper. "If I want dinner later, I'll fix it myself."

The wiry fifty-year-old Provençale from Aix was

a literal dynamo. "I've already put your meal in the fridge whenever you want it."

"Bless you." Jasmine blew her a kiss and disappeared upstairs to her bedroom. She opened the French doors onto the terrace and walked out. Grasse, the queen of the French Riviera, lay below, a sight implanted in her heart. Beyond it shimmered the blue Mediterranean.

When she'd left this room earlier in the day, she'd been Jasmine Martin with an agenda that had consumed her from the moment she'd turned twenty-six and had been made the head of the company. But standing here now, she realized she wasn't that same person anymore. Suddenly she felt like she was teetering on the edge of that cliff in Cyprus, terrified and in pain all at the same time.

How could meeting one man have done this to her so fast? It was insane!

In her world as a chemist, there was an explanation for this phenomenon called flash point. It was the lowest temperature at which a flammable liquid like essential jasmine oil will give off enough vapor to ignite when exposed to flame. Flash point was also the critical stage in some process, event or situation at which action, change or violence occurred.

That's what had happened to her. She'd been at her lowest point when she'd entered the Banque Internationale du Midi. But when she'd discovered Luc there, she'd ignited as if she'd been torched by flame. In that instant, a change had occurred, altering her state. She now stood at this railing a transformed woman, filled with those age-old longings called desire.

Jasmine couldn't believe it had finally happened

to her. She'd thought herself impervious. When she'd discussed it with her mother, Blanchette had laughed gently and warned her that the day would come when Jasmine would be overcome by her attraction to a man. Just pray he would be the right kind of male, worthy of her.

Why did it have to be the man she'd clashed with on the island? Why was he the man she needed in her corner? One who had the power to put Remy on the throne at Ferriers. But he had chosen not to, and there wasn't a thing she could do about it.

Jasmine had put all her eggs in one basket by appealing to him first. It had made sense to turn to the banking institution Ferriers had relied on for close to a century. But Luc wasn't his grandfather. He was a savvy modern businessman with modern ideas, a man of today. She should have known deep down he would never let sentiment overrule his good sense and practical thinking.

She'd argued her case on sentiment and lost. Jasmine needed to prepare a list of other bankers to contact. It was time to move on to her next target and forget she had ever known Luc Charriere.

After changing into jeans and a top, she went downstairs to the den to begin her search. Before she could get busy, her cell phone rang. It could be anyone. Much as she didn't want to talk to a soul right now, she didn't dare ignore it. Maybe it was her family. She had to be sure everything was all right with them.

When she saw Luc's name on the caller ID, she almost dropped the phone. She'd thought she would never hear from him again. *Be as businesslike as pos-*

sible, Jasmine. Don't let your voice shake. She clicked on. "Hello?"

"Good evening, Jasmine. Am I calling at a bad time?"

"No. I just got home from work. What can I do for you?"

"Since you left my office yesterday, I've taken another look at your file."

Her pulse thudded off the charts. "Why?"

"I've done a little homework and am curious about this land you mentioned."

What?

"There's no price or description on it. You've indicated nothing about it but its existence. If I were to consider your proposition further, I'd need to know what we're talking about here."

She couldn't believe he'd called her back. She couldn't believe he was still thinking about it. Naturally he wanted to know how much money she needed to borrow, but she had been so convinced there was no hope, this phone call shocked her.

"You did mention you're in a hurry," he said quietly.

She cleared her throat. "Yes."

"Under the circumstances, are you free in the morning to show it to me with the Realtor?"

Jasmine was so thrilled he was willing to go this far, she did a little jump. "Absolutely, but I haven't contacted a Realtor yet. Let's just say I've had inside information and know it's been put on the market."

"Why doesn't that surprise me?" The comment made her smile. "Then if it's all right with you I'll drive to Grasse and you can show me. Where shall we meet?"

Not at the house. She never knew when one of her aunts or uncles might drop by. It was the family home to all of them. Though Jasmine lived there, her grandparents had always said everyone was welcome to come and stay as long as they wanted. Their deaths hadn't changed anything in that regard.

"Do you know the old abandoned abbey on the upper road?"

"*Bien sûr.* Shall we meet there at say nine a.m.?"

"I'll be there. Thank you for at least being curious enough to listen to me."

"I owe it to Ferriers. They've been one of our best clients for decades. *A toute à l'heure.*"

Jasmine heard the click before she was ready to hang up. He'd been cordial just now, but still all business. She no longer felt like jumping.

When she thought about it, he was probably humoring her by being willing to look at the land she had her eye on. As he'd said, this was what a banker did who'd been a friend to the company for so many years, even if he still planned to turn her down.

Tomorrow she'd be all business too and kept telling herself that throughout the night.

When Jasmine awakened the next morning, her bedding was all over the place. She'd had a restless night.

After showering, she dressed in her generic uniform, which consisted of a short-sleeved, light blue blouse and matching cotton skirt. At work, her clothes took a beating even with a lab coat. Once she'd shown Luc the property, she would head directly to the lab.

Relieved to hear from her folks that all was well at home, she fastened her hair at the nape with a match-

ing blue elastic and went down the old black staircase
to eat breakfast. On the way, she passed hundreds of
small framed photos lining the walls. Remy's mother
had arranged them years earlier. The history of the
Ferriers was written here, and Remy was prominent
in many of them.

Jasmine paused in front of the one she loved best.
Remy—ever devoted—was standing in the garden of
white Parma violets behind his mom, who was in her
wheelchair. She held a bunch of them he'd grown and
picked just for her. Jasmine knew the story behind
every picture.

Remy and his mother both had dark red hair. In this
picture, he was developing into the handsome man he
would become.

"Whether Luc helps us or not, you're going to be
in charge soon, Remy. Just wait and see."

She removed it from the wall and put it in her large
straw bag. Then she rushed the rest of the way to the
kitchen to drink a half cup of tea and grab a plum. It
earned a frown from Sylvie before she hurried outside
to her car parked on the gravel drive.

The same warm-growing-hot morning greeted her,
but this day was different from all the others. Her body
knew it, otherwise her heart wouldn't be racing. She
wished it were only because she needed her plan to
work, but that would be a lie.

Jasmine couldn't wait to see Luc Charriere again.
All the reasons she shouldn't be interested in a Frenchman she needed to do business with didn't matter.
Chemistry had taken over. As a scientist, she knew
she couldn't fight it.

The solution would be to avoid him. If, by some

miracle, the loan was granted, then Remy would be the one working with him in the future. But if Luc turned her down again, as she suspected he would, then that would put an end to everything and they'd go their separate ways.

To dwell on him was idiotic. She knew nothing about him. Being a Frenchman, he had a lover of course, but he'd be discreet. You couldn't be a French male without one. She knew what the field workers talked about all the time. Women. Jasmine often plopped on a straw hat and helped with the harvest. It was a revelation.

She learned about the ones they'd already been with, the ones they were planning to be with, the ones they were getting tired of. The ones their friends were seeing, the ones they'd stopped seeing, the ones who were stepping out on their husbands, the ones who wanted to step out with them.

Aside from her papa, Jasmine had always preferred American men. They loved women too, but they weren't as open about it. She liked the strong silent cowboy types like Hank Branson, the guy she'd had her first big crush on.

As soon as Remy was installed, she planned to go home and get married. It probably wouldn't be to a cowboy like her father. But that didn't matter. She wanted to get back to the ranch on the other side of the Teton mountain range and prove her love to her family. Jasmine had promised them she'd come back to live. She loved ranching too and longed to start her own family where she could be around her married siblings.

Jasmine was retiring from the world of perfume. Hopefully a grandchild of Remy's would inherit the gift to make up a recipe that would keep Ferriers on top. But that was no longer her concern.

Neither was Luc Charriere, who could never be part of her American dream.

But her body groaned when she drove up to the ruin of the old abbey and found him lounging against a dark green Jaguar convertible with his arms folded. His masculine body filled out his white linen shirt with contrasting buttons to perfection. Her eyes dropped down to his powerful legs covered in beige twill pants. Italian leather sandals completed the picture.

She sighed audibly at the sight of him with that five o'clock shadow. For a minute she was imagining him in a western shirt and a Stetson.

Which was true? The clothes made the man, or the man made the clothes? What a ridiculous question when the evidence stood before her. The *man* made the clothes! At least this man did. With the riddle solved, she got out of her car.

But she bet he'd never ridden a horse. That alone was a huge strike against him.

The new head of Ferriers didn't dress fit to kill. Spoiled women who came from a background of wealth—and Luc had seen and worked with a lot of them—couldn't spend money fast enough to adorn themselves in the latest designer fashions.

That wasn't the case with this woman. With a face and body like hers, Jasmine Martin didn't need to. She had other tantalizing assets, including a mind and thoughts that were so far removed from the superficiality of this world, he marveled. She moved with the kind of femininity a man enjoyed and was compelled to watch.

"*Bonjour*, Luc. I can't thank you enough for being willing to meet me here. I'll admit I was surprised to hear from you at all."

"*Bonjour*, Jasmine." Since losing sleep over her last night had nothing to do with business, her comment had touched on dangerous ground. "I decided to give more thought to what I read in your file, but—"

"I understand the buts," she interrupted him. "This is not a commitment from you. If you'll follow me, we'll be there in approximately one minute."

With her suggestion, there was no risk of them being thrown together in the same car where they would be in touching distance. Danger avoided, for the moment.

He gave her a nod and they were off. She drove fast across the dips and crests of the hillside. After winding around a bend, she slowed to a stop beside a field lying fallow. Luc pulled behind her and got out. She hurried toward him.

"Ten days ago, one of my inside sources informed me this land is available again. This is exactly what I've been looking for, but I'd need to move fast."

"Tell me about it."

"The monks farmed this land for years. When the old abbey burned, the property was put on the market. It sat for a long time. The only company with enough money to do something with it wanted to turn the whole place into a subdivision for middle-income housing. For the last year, the owner and would-be buyer have gone the rounds in negotiations, but they fell apart because of public pressure to keep the land free of buildings."

"I'm violently against these hillsides being exploited," he asserted.

Emotion seemed to turn her eyes a darker blue. "You're one of the good guys in the banking business."

"I'm a native Niçois. This land is my home too."

"You sound like Papa. With our perfect climate and soil, both he and Remy lamented seeing these fields sold off to hungry developers. It's a tragedy that the cost of labor and the growth of synthetic perfume components have made flower farming less rewarding. Nowadays many of the perfume houses go to their source of oils in North Africa and India. Papa fought to keep Ferriers from going the same route."

He flashed her a smile. "Now *you've* taken up the flag."

"I'm going to try with everything in me." A pulse throbbed at the base of her creamy throat. His own pulse picked up her beat.

"How big is this property?"

"We'll have to get the figures from the Realtor, but at one time I understand they had as many as fifty thousand individual plantings of vegetables like carrots, onions, fennel and leeks. If I were to approach him and tell him the company wants to plant violets and nothing else, I know that will satisfy the public. We'll need to erect a couple of sheds and of course a rock wall with a locked gate to make certain the integrity of the plants remains constant."

She reached in her bag and pulled out an eight-by-ten framed picture that she handed to him. "This is Remy and his mother Rosaline when he was seventeen.

Those white violets were his pride and joy in the past. Today he's developed a new strain that no one else in the world has, and no one will. He calls it the Reine Fleury after his mother.

"It grows in sun and light shade. As we say in the perfume world, it's a good doer. The blooms are prolific. In May, you can pick a bunch for the house every week until September. One of these flowers alone will fill a room with its fragrance. When the perfume comes out, it will be Ferrier's new weapon."

She'd already used it on Luc. He swallowed hard. No matter the defenses he was trying to put up, this woman was getting to him, breaking them down so fast he was growing alarmed. Luc would have to stand on his head to get the board to back this loan. Even employing his son's technology, Remy Ferrier himself was a question mark with baggage a mile long.

"Who's the Realtor?"

"Charles Boileau at the Agence Alpes-Maritime. Does his name mean anything to you?"

He handed her back the picture. "My grandfather had several dealings with him. By now he would be getting on in years."

Her eyes searched his. "What aren't you telling me?"

"As I recall, he mentioned the word crusty, but then so was my grandfather."

An unexpected laugh escaped her lips, delighting him. "What do you think would be the best way to approach him?"

Luc could feel the urgency in her. Between her passion for the project and Remy himself, plus the fact that she *had* created a new scent that could put Ferriers at the top of perfume sales, he could feel himself weakening.

"Tell you what. I'll call the agency right now. As soon as he's available, we'll go see him together, today if possible. *You* have a singular effect on everyone you meet so I want you with me. If he and the owner are agreeable to a sale and give you a price I can work with, then I'll consider taking it to my board of directors."

"Wait—" she cautioned as he reached for the cell phone in his pocket. "There are two things you need to know first."

What now? More revelations she'd been holding back? Maxim Ferrier's granddaughter was so full of them, she had him spinning. "Go ahead."

She bit the underside of her lip. He'd love a bite of her himself and despised his weakness. "I'm not the official CEO yet."

A grimace marred his features. "Then what was that announcement about on Friday?"

"Papa left instructions that I was to be given a month before I was installed to take over the reins. He realized I'd need that long to put everything into play. But he wanted the announcement to the public made immediately to make it more difficult for the family to counteract his move."

Ciel! "If you're not the legal head yet, I can't go to the board with this. Why didn't you tell me the truth when you first came to see me?"

She stood fast. "After our precarious beginning, I didn't think I'd be able to get anywhere with you if you knew."

Luc decided he was all kinds of a fool to be taken in by her.

"I have no doubt you'll soon be hearing from some of the family on the Ferrier board, as well as Giles, claiming a show of no faith in me. If I know them, they're already getting ready to vote me down at the next meeting a week from Friday. By preventing my installation, they'll promote the ascendancy of one of them."

No doubt. "What else haven't you told me? Don't hold anything back now," his voice rasped.

Her hesitation spoke volumes about what was coming. "Remy knows nothing about my plan yet."

Luc was incredulous. "What are you saying?"

"Exactly that."

When it registered, he said, "You mean you've had no contact with him?"

"None. I've never met him and I don't even know if he'll let me talk to him. But once I'm armed with that loan, I'll find a way." Out of dark fringed lashes, the blue burned hot with determination.

The shock of those words blocked the air he couldn't take in or out.

"I realize I should have told you all this before you offered to meet me here."

Luc took a fortifying breath. Yes, she should have told him everything, but it was also true he'd offered. With her charismatic powers of persuasion, he'd been her willing victim. She'd had those invisible hooks into him before he'd known what was happening.

"But I was afraid if I did..." Anxiety was written all over her expression, bringing out a protective instinct at odds with his frustration. "I was afraid you'd turn me down flat. This is so important. Not only is the company's life at stake, but Remy's."

The woman standing before him was a mystifying combination of warrior strength and feminine softness meant to disarm a man down to his stronghold. She'd done it to him as no other woman had done since the plane crash.

"After what I've told you about his life, can't you see that when I approach Remy and ask him to take over the company, all the negotiations have to be wrapped up behind the scenes? With the remarkable gifts he'll bring back to the company, he has to believe *I* believe in him and what he's doing."

The unspoken plea coming from her eyes would be Luc's downfall if he remained trapped by them.

Her rounded chin lifted. He sensed she'd gone into battle mode. "Because of Papa's decision, my words will ensure that the Ferrier board at least listens to me where Remy is concerned.

"But the greater weight will come from knowing it's Remy I've chosen to run the company because *he's* the rightful head who should have taken over the moment his father died. *He's* the one who can fix the company. Deep down, every staff and family member knows this, even if they won't want to admit it. I'm counting on enough of them doing the honorable thing and supporting me."

She'd left Luc nonplussed.

"If you want to tell me to go to hell right now, I won't blame you because you have every right. I certainly understand if you believe I have no conscience to get you here without your knowing all the facts. The truth is I *do* have a conscience, but this is a matter of righting a wrong, and I'm willing to do whatever it takes. Even not being totally honest with you until now."

True, she hadn't been straight with him up front. On the other hand, he'd never met a more wonderful, principled person. Without meeting Remy Ferrier, she was willing to go to these lengths for her grandfather because of the great injustice done his cousin. She wanted nothing in return for herself.

It was a heart-wrenching story, one that had a stranglehold on Luc. He'd been thinking about Remy and the tragedy that had prevented him from doing the work he'd obviously enjoyed. Even without meeting him, Luc had developed a soft spot for him, all due to Jasmine's powers of persuasion. His emotions were overwhelming him.

While he was deep in thought, she started searching in her bag. Out came her checkbook. "Since I've already committed my sin of omission with you, I'll pay you now for your time, the lunch and the mileage for your two trips to Grasse and bid you *adieu* with my heartfelt thanks."

Adieu had several meanings, one of which was "goodbye forever."

She'd just pressed the wrong button. Since the plane crash, Luc had been living cautiously in all the areas of his life. But this woman had gotten under his skin to the inner core. He didn't like the impotent way it made him feel.

A rare burst of temper welled up inside him. Forcing himself to get it under control, he said, "Why don't you put that away. The only sin you've committed is jumping to a conclusion about me."

"No—" She gave what sounded like a mournful

cry. "Not over you personally, Luc. Any banker with your responsibilities and reputation would be having serious reservations after the history I've laid out for you. To plead my case with your board when I'm not legally the head of the company yet would mean you'd be doing something dishonest.

"I can't ask that of you. It's too big to expect of anyone, but I had to try. The next banker I approach will be presented the whole truth first. Please forgive me."

She tried to hand him the check she'd written, but he refused to take it. "Our clash on Yeronisos caused us to get off on the wrong foot. Before we write off this experience, let's see what kind of success we have with Monsieur Boileau. Obviously your whole plan hinges on obtaining this property to convince Remy that your papa meant business."

Without hesitation, he pressed the number to get the information operator on the line.

CHAPTER FIVE

JASMINE PUT THE check back in her purse, almost in shock that Luc was still willing to work with her after her dishonesty. Not many men would have handled the time-fused grenades she'd thrown at him with such calm; it filled her with wonder. She waited with a pounding heart while he made the vital phone call. His back was turned so she couldn't hear what he was saying.

As he shifted his weight during the conversation, she couldn't help but stare at the way his muscles moved beneath his shirt. When he suddenly turned around, she was caught studying him and there was no getting out of it with grace. Men did it to her all the time. The only thing to do was get past the moment.

"Did you reach Monsieur Boileau? What's the verdict?"

His black eyes gleamed between narrowed lids. She stifled a moan because her legs were trembling. "I was about to ask you the same question."

Hadn't she thought there was something of a bad boy about him the minute she'd seen him on Yeronisos? For the second time since she'd met him, visible heat swept over her. *You fool, Jasmine.*

"I was trying to figure out how I would have saved your unconscious body if you'd been dashed against the cliff of Yeronisos trying to outswim a great white."

One side of his mouth lifted in a devastating smile. "That's an intriguing thought. Any ideas?"

Breathe. "Not yet."

"While your scientific mind comes up with an answer, we have a date in his office at one-thirty. That ought to give us enough time to stop for lunch. I don't know about you, but I'm starving," he said in a husky voice.

She let the comment about his hunger pass. In the last few seconds, she'd realized Luc could be a terrible tease. He swallowed her with those black eyes. "Monsieur Boileau saw you on television the other night. The man couldn't accommodate our request fast enough."

"That was nice of him."

Luc threw his head back and laughed. The rich male kind you felt invade your insides. "Do you want to follow me?"

"Since you're the hungry one, I think that's probably the wisest idea. When Dad gets hungry, he finds the shortest distance between two points. Wherever he is and *food*. I'll try to keep up with you."

More laughter ensued as they got in their cars and headed down the hillside to town. Jasmine felt so alive, she hurt with a strange kind of pain pleasure. On one of the little side streets, they found parking spaces and walked two blocks to the Gros Moine. She learned he'd eaten lunch there many times too.

A waiter seated them outside, where they enjoyed grilled swordfish and salad. "Wine?" Luc asked her.

"No, thank you. Not while I'm working." *Not while I'm with you.*

His lips twitched. "You call this work?"

She stabbed her fork into the fish. "Anything I have to do that forces me to keep my wits rules out alcohol."

He flashed her a devilish smile. "I'll remember that."

While she was attempting to recover from his re- mark that suggested there would be other times, the owner, who was in his fifties, came outside and headed for their table. "*La belle* Jasmine—it's always an honor to serve you."

"*Merci*, Jules. The fish is excellent as usual."

His brown eyes darted to Luc. "Is he the secret you wouldn't reveal the other night?"

"I am," sounded the deep voice she'd heard in the background of her disturbing dreams.

Luc— Her gaze flicked to him in astonishment.

Jules put a hand over his heart. "Ah…*l'amour, l'amour.* Your secret is safe with me." He looked from her to Luc. "The waiter will bring you a complimen- tary dessert. Our signature *gâteau aux framboises.* Enjoy!"

The minute he walked off, she said, "You were even more audacious than Michel Didier during the inter- view."

He scrutinized her over the rim of his wineglass. "I couldn't resist. Jules has a crush on you as bad as the TV anchorman's. So does my assistant, Thomas. Monsieur Boileau is already salivating in anticipation of your arrival."

She smiled as she shook her head. "I have to admit, you're good at talking the talk, Lucien Charriere." With the exception of that time on the island when she'd thought he was trying to pick her up, it was better than any talk she'd ever heard from another Frenchman. It was because when he spoke, it didn't sound like a line.

One black brow lifted dangerously. "Then I've passed your test?"

"Which one is that?"

All the amusement left his eyes. "The only one that counts."

If she spent much more time with him, she would need to visit a cardiologist. "If I were to meet your mother, I suspect she'd tell me you were a handful the moment you could stand up in your crib."

"Much more than that," he quipped. "My parents are away on a trip at the moment. When they return, you can ask her. I'll make a point of it."

The waiter didn't deliver their raspberry tart a moment too soon. She took several bites. In France you didn't bring a woman home to meet your mother unless you'd been brought to your knees. She could hardly breathe.

"What size family do you have?"

"An older sister and brother, both married with children. My extended family is large. We have aunts, uncles and cousins everywhere in the vicinity. I'll answer your next question now. My father heads a multi-national financial services corporation specializing in retail brokerage."

"Why aren't you working with him?"

"The stock market involves too much risk. I prefer not to head into old age with ulcers. My grandfather enjoyed a less frenetic existence in the banking world and lived to a ripe old age."

More guilt attacked her for asking so much of him. She rested her fork on the plate. "I've put you between a rock and a hard place, haven't I?"

He finished off his tart. "I always enjoyed *The Man in the Iron Mask*. For once in my life, it might be challenging to help the side of a nobler cause and put the rightful king on the throne. The idea of it appeals to a part of my deeply buried instinct for adventure."

Jasmine was intrigued by the admission. Something of significance lay behind it. "Why deeply buried?"

"One of these days, I might tell you." That sounded cryptic. "If you've finished, shall we go?" He put some bills on the table. "The Realtor's office is on the other side of Grasse. I'm eager to watch you work the magic that went out over the airwaves on Friday evening to mesmerize your fascinated audience."

He helped her up from the table and they left for their cars. She got in behind the wheel and looked at him through the open window. "Working with my papa *was* magical. But the whole time I was talking, I feared Remy and his family might be watching. Then again, he probably made sure he didn't see any of it to block out the horrendously painful memories."

Luc pressed his forehead against the top of the door, bringing their faces closer together. "I'd like to be the proverbial fly on the wall when you present your case to him. Your concern for him broke my heart, Jasmine. If he's the man you say he is, then your words will transform him."

Her throat almost closed. "I pray they do," she whispered.

She had the impression he wanted to kiss her. Or maybe it was because she wanted him to. While she waited for it with an ache that wouldn't go away, he turned and strode swiftly toward his car, devastating her. Appalled and frightened by these new emotions pouring out of her, she rummaged shakily for her keys and started the engine.

When she'd started out from the house this morning, she'd hoped Luc would give her a chance once he'd seen the property. Now that he was doing his part on blind faith, to want anything more from him embarrassed her. She'd actually sat there waiting to feel his mouth close over hers!

"I'll be right behind you," she called to him. Her heart raced as she tried to keep up with him. He drove fast before finding the building in question, where they each found a parking spot. The prosperous agency listed a dozen agents with Monsieur Boileau's name being at the top.

Luc entered the reception area with Jasmine. The receptionist soon led them down the hall to his office. The sixtyish, balding Realtor was all smiles as he got up from his chair and hurried toward them. Luc introduced her.

"It's a real honor to meet the new chief at Ferriers, Ms. Martin."

"Thank you for meeting with us so quickly."

"Monsieur Charriere indicated your business borders on an emergency."

She owed Luc everything and darted him a quiet smile. "He's right. There's a time element involved."

"Then let's all sit down and you tell me what I can do for you."

Luc sat back in his chair and handed the file to her. It was clear he was leaving this up to her. In that regard, he reminded her of her papa, who had seen her as an equal and never talked over her head. She appreciated that more than he could know.

"I'm aware it hasn't been advertised, but I understand the old abbey property is for sale again. I would like to buy it for the company." Jasmine spent the next few minutes explaining what she wanted it for and how it would be developed. She handed him some papers from the file. "The owner couldn't object to the projected use of the land. With this sale, everyone would be handsomely compensated and preserve the tradition of the fields."

His bushy eyebrows knit together. "I'm sorry to say that someone else has already put in a bid for it."

"I was afraid of that."

"Do you have an earnest money agreement?" Luc questioned.

A ruddy color entered the older man's cheeks. He cleared his throat. "I'm not at liberty to tell you that."

"A verbal bid isn't solid, which means you don't have one yet," Luc came back with startling authority. The Realtor didn't really have a buyer and Luc had known it at the outset. It was all a bluff to see how much money the agency could wangle out of Ferriers, but Luc wouldn't let him get away with it. "What's your asking price?"

Monsieur Boileau named an eight-digit figure that was higher than she'd anticipated, causing her spirits to plummet.

"No wonder you don't have a sale yet. If your other client exists, which I doubt, then I presume they're in the process of finding the backing needed. But knowing the market as I do, you're not going to get that price from anyone," Luc rapped out.

His remarks had unsettled the older man.

"Lower it by two million euros and Ms. Martin might be interested. You have it in writing that Ferriers will treat the land the way it was meant to be used. That will satisfy the seller. Otherwise it will sit there for another twenty years, and you know it."

The other man sat there touching his fingertips together while he considered the offer. Jasmine was afraid to make a move. Luc had taken over with a fearsome mastery that proved why he'd been made director of the bank at such a young age. In action, he was awesome. His shrewd business skills had read the situation accurately.

Another minute and the man sat forward. "You're ready to sign now?" She could see the dollar signs in his eyes. That meant Luc had gotten to him.

"If you'd give me and my client a minute to confer, we'd appreciate it."

"Of course."

He got up from his desk and left the room. After he'd shut the door Jasmine turned to Luc in panic. "You haven't presented anything to your banking board yet. I thought you told me it would be too risky as long as I wasn't the official CEO yet."

"I have more information to work with than I had when you first approached me. Here's what needs to happen, Jasmine. I'll be happy to authorize your signing an earnest money agreement today with the Realtor, provided you approach Remy Ferrier right away. He needs to be in agreement with your plan, and then he needs to meet with me. If all goes well, then I'll grant the loan and you can come back here to buy the property."

"But I don't want you to jeopardize your position at the bank! Naturally I'm overjoyed at what is happening, but not at the cost of you doing something you could regret."

"Don't let that be your concern right now. As far as I'm concerned, it's Remy Ferrier you need to worry about. You can show him the signed earnest money agreement offer. It should be the proof he needs to know you're behind him a thousand percent. I'll take care of the rest."

She shot out of the chair. "But not if it isn't aboveboard. I won't let you do something that harms you!"

"It won't. To be honest, you've convinced me the man's life is at stake, along with a company that should have been his. If there's risk involved, I find myself wanting to take it for the sake of an ideal."

There couldn't be another man in the world like Luc, but she couldn't possibly let him do it. "Don't think I don't appreciate what you're trying to do here, but we're going to leave. On the way out, I'll tell the Realtor I've changed my mind."

Luc barred her path. "What were Carton's last words in *A Tale of Two Cities*? 'It's a far, far better thing that I do, than I have ever done.'" His eyes burned like coals. "You've taught me that, Jasmine. Monsieur Boileau is ready to do business, so do it!"

There were dimensions to this man she couldn't have known were there when they'd first met. Was it only several months ago?

"But, Luc—what if Remy won't be able to accept what his cousin wanted to do for him?"

He eyed her with singular intent. "Then you'll lose the money on the earnest agreement, that's all. However, I believe in you to get the job done."

"But what if I'm wrong and Remy can't save the company? Then everything you've done will have been in vain."

He shook his dark head. "You do have a backup plan, *n'est-ce pas*?"

She took a shuddering breath. "Of course. I'll find a buyer for the property and pay you back with triple interest. If I can't accomplish that in a reasonable period of time, I'll deed La Tourette over to you."

Her papa had already willed the house and property to her. She in turn planned to will everything back to Remy as planned. But if he refused what was rightfully his, and she couldn't find a buyer, then she would make certain it went to Luc.

"You see?" he inserted. "None of this will have been in vain. One step at a time, Jasmine. Shall I tell him to come back in?"

She lifted her eyes to him. "Are you sure about this?"

He moved closer and squeezed her arm. She felt its warmth seep in. "I've never been so sure of anything in my life."

His belief in her ability to carry this off rated even higher than her papa's belief in her, if that was possible. Luc wasn't family. Less than two weeks ago they had been strangers except for the incident on Yeronisos island. She couldn't pretend to understand his true motive for getting involved like this. But she wasn't so naïve that she didn't know he would demand something of her in return.

However one fact was clear. He *did* trust her. What greater gift had anyone ever given her? While she was still trying to comprehend it, the Realtor tapped on the door and poked his head in. "Do you need more time?"

His voice jerked her back to the present. She turned to him. "No. I'm ready to put down earnest money with a time frame of one week." Jasmine had to track down Remy and that might prove difficult.

The older man rubbed his hands together. She'd anticipated that reaction. Within twenty minutes the transaction was complete with funds out of the account her papa had set up for her. More handshakes ensued before Luc walked her out to her car.

"What are you going to do with the rest of this day, as if I didn't know?" he asked after she'd climbed in.

She put the file of papers aside and glanced up at him. "You mean this red-letter day that wouldn't have been possible without you? While I'm still full of endorphins from your selfless gift, I'm going to figure out the best way to meet Remy. I have to approach him at the right time."

"It was anything but selfless."

Jasmine had to take another quick breath. His real reasons for deciding to help her were still unexplained, but she'd find them out later. "Whatever motivated you, I'm in your debt."

"I only ask one favor." *Here it comes.* She braced herself. "Whatever the result of your meeting with Remy, call me when you've had your talk with him."

That favor was far too easy to grant. The blood pounded in her ears. "You'll be the first person to know everything, but I have no idea how soon I'll be getting in touch with you. I don't know how soon Remy will be available."

"True, but a flower farmer isn't long parted from his crop."

He understood a lot. "You're right."

Luc backed away from the door. "You know where to find me."

In the next breath, she glimpsed an unexpected look of triumph in the recesses of his eyes. For an inexplicable reason, her body underwent a curious shiver. Reaction was already settling in over the enormity of what she'd just allowed to happen.

"À bientôt," he called over his shoulder before heading for his Jaguar, leaving her with an ache as she drove home to La Tourette.

On Thursday morning, Jasmine headed for the old, small Fleury farmhouse on the outskirts of Grasse. She owed Luc for helping her get this far, even if she didn't know at what cost yet. Because of him, she was able to put her plan into action much sooner than she'd thought.

Now it was up to her to make it all bear fruit for this seminal moment in two lives. But so much was against her, she trembled with fear.

When Jasmine looked at herself in the mirror, she had a hard time seeing anyone but herself. Those around her who knew her father saw his dark blue eyes and nose in her. Those who knew her grandfather saw his rich dark hair and the shape of his brows in her. Those who knew her mother saw the pure oval of her face.

But the majority of her world saw the overlay of

her grandmother Megan in Jasmine's countenance, from the outline of her smile, to the rare frown on her forehead, to the occasional wistful expression, to the shape of her figure.

That's what frightened Jasmine. Two cousins had loved her grandmother with a wild passion that would go on through eternity. Megan had loved them both. But though Remy had found her first, it was to Jasmine's grandfather she'd given her heart.

When Remy looked at Jasmine, would he be able to get past the reminder of her grandmother long enough to listen to what she had to say? Did the pain still pierce so deeply, he wouldn't be able to bear it?

Her entire body trembled as she drove along the modest piece of ground laid out in rows of violets on her way to reach the house. She slowed down when she saw a man hunkered down tending one of the plants under the morning sun. He wore denims and a white shirt with the sleeves shoved up to the elbows. His back was to her.

Even from the distance she recognized the burnished red hair and was reminded of Luc's comment about a farmer and his crop. Being sixty-six hadn't faded the color or changed the strong physique that could have belonged to a much younger man. Jasmine had thought him very handsome in all the pictures.

He hadn't seen her yet. She pulled the car to a stop.

This was it.

Putting the file in her straw bag, she got out of the front seat and stepped over the ridge of ground to reach the *terroir*. The heavenly scent was close to overpowering. She got to within a couple of yards of him.

"Eh bien." She cleared her throat. "I'm looking for Remy Fleury Ferrier."

He jumped to his feet and turned around. For a timeless moment he looked at her until his green eyes began to burn and he staggered backwards. She knew the woman he was seeing. No doubt he had watched Jasmine's broadcast. Even deeply tanned, she could tell he'd paled.

"Mon Dieu," he whispered as if he'd seen a ghost.

"You and I don't share the same blood, but I share a love of this land you love to the marrow of your bones. You're the son who should have been put in as the head of the Ferrier empire the second your father died."

Emotion darkened the green of his eyes.

"I'm Jasmine, a nose of little consequence. My grandfather used me so I could get you installed to your rightful place as CEO of a company that you built years ago. It needs you desperately."

Taking advantage of his speechless state, Jasmine reached in her bag and handed him the file. "Read this and you'll see that the Banque Internationale du Midi is loaning us the money to buy the old abbey property. The CEO, Lucien Charriere, wants to meet you. Here's the record of the earnest money agreement. If you're willing to take over the company, then this land will be ours and we're going to plant thousands more of your fabulous Parma violets.

"I've already made up the perfume from the ones I bought at the flower market on Saturday.

"Here's a sample." She pressed the little bottle into his other hand. "I think we should call it Parfum Reine Fleury, after your mother.

"With you at the helm, the company will come back

so much greater than it's been. Unfortunately life dealt the family a monstrous blow under the rule of your despotic father. Forgive me for being so brutal, but not all men who can make a baby are fit for husbandom or fatherdom."

She took a step closer. "I've heard about you all my life. Except for the ability to get inside your skin, I know the long, twisted, painful history that drove you away. Papa loved you so much and told me everything."

A strange sound, suspiciously like a sob, escaped his throat.

She pulled out the picture. "This is my favorite photo of you that your mother put up on the stairway. The stairway of *your* house, Remy. Here's the deed made out to you. You're the legal owner of the house and the property. No one else." She handed it to him. He took it. By now, his arms and hands were loaded. He moved as if he were in a dream.

"I feel a bit like King Richard who knighted Robin Hood and said, 'All former residences and manors are restored to you.' What do you say to that, Sir Robin of Loxley?"

His throat was working. She could feel the emotions erupting inside him.

"Will you let me hug you, dear Remy? I've loved you for so long and have been waiting for this moment for what seems like an eternity. Please," she begged in an aching voice.

After a stillness that almost destroyed her, he put the things down, then extended his arms. She ran into them and they hugged while unspoken messages passed between them. His body quietly heaved.

Tears rolled down her cheeks. "Papa cried to me over you more times than you can possibly imagine. His plan was to put me in charge until I could convince you to come back home where you always belonged." She eased away, but still held on to his arms, which she shook.

"You have to believe that. Papa went to the other side early, but I know he'll never rest in peace until you accept his love and forgive him. Don't you know in your soul he loved you? He said your name on his dying breath."

Remy expelled a great, shuddering sigh. "I loved Max too. He didn't do anything wrong. My father was the one responsible for hurting my mother and me. But in my anger I blamed Max for everything. It took me years to come to grips with the truth about my life, about Megan. She and Max had always been honest with me, but I chose to believe they betrayed me.

"When I married Louise and we had a baby, my feelings started to undergo a change. But my wife was too upset about never having enough money and left me and Jean-Louis. The truth is *he* became my salvation.

"After he got older and married, I talked to him frankly about my life. That's when I decided to go to Max and beg *his* forgiveness for the way I treated him." Tears filled his eyes. "But he died unexpectedly."

"It was a shock to all of us."

"I wrote a letter to Megan telling her what was in my heart. She wrote me back, telling me that my letter had released her from pain. I suffered another shock when I heard about her death so soon after."

"Oh, Remy." She hugged him again. "Don't suffer

anymore. I'm sure they both now know how you feel and are content. The only thing left is for you to take over the company."

He smiled. "Except for one thing. I don't believe the family is going to throw their arms around an ancient, formerly bitter, recovered alcoholic as you have done."

"You're not ancient, and they aren't your blood. *You're* the true Ferrier, and they will thrill to the knowledge that you're going to save everyone's skins because there isn't anyone else! Give them a chance. There are years of life ahead! You *are* going to accept!"

A chuckle escaped his throat. "Do I have a choice?"

"None!"

"Come to the house and meet the family."

"I'm dying to." He picked up the things. She linked her arm through his and they started walking. "Any noses born yet?"

He actually laughed through the tears. Except for Luc's, it was the most beautiful sound she'd ever heard.

Friday morning, Luc's cell phone rang. After two hellish nights with no sleep, he sprang out of bed and grabbed the phone off the nightstand. At last! The one name he'd wanted to see on the caller ID had finally appeared.

He clicked on. "Jasmine?"

"Forgive me for calling you this early, Luc, but I wanted to catch you before you left for work. I need your advice. Would you have time for a quick breakfast first? I'll meet you at Chez Arnaud near your bank. It'll be my treat."

Since they'd parted company the day before yesterday, the torturous wait to hear from her had driven him up a wall. Luc's pulse raced. "How soon can you get here?" He would have told her he'd meet her anywhere, but since she already had a plan in mind, so much the better.

"Half an hour."

"I'll be there."

"My debt to you keeps growing." On that note, she clicked off.

Those endorphins she'd talked about filled his system. Today wasn't going to be the day without her in it he'd been dreading. He showered and shaved in record time. Reaching for one of his suits, he dressed for work. Already he had plans for the end of the day that would include Jasmine. She just didn't know it yet.

His breathing altered when he arrived and saw her seated at one of the small round tables outside, dressed in another blouse and skirt like she'd worn yesterday. She was ready for work. If there was any difference in her, it was the full smile she bestowed on him. It illuminated his insides. Jasmine had good news or her eyes wouldn't be shining a bluer blue than the sea beyond them.

"Thanks for meeting me on such short notice, Luc. I took the liberty of ordering breakfast for both of us so you wouldn't be held up."

"I appreciate that." He sat down opposite her. "Right now I want to hear about Remy. You caught up with him obviously."

After the waiter served their breakfast and poured coffee, she said, "Yesterday morning, I found him on his farm tending the violets. It proved, among other things, that you're clairvoyant."

"This is the land of flowers. You can't drive by a field without someone in it. Now tell me what it was like to meet him."

Her eyes filled, but the tears stayed on her dark lashes. "Oh, Luc—he's so wonderful!"

Jasmine's compassion for another human being's pain had stirred Luc's deepest emotions. "How long are you going to keep me in suspense?"

She laughed gently. "For the first five minutes, I did all the talking. I thought he'd never respond. At the height of my agony, he held out his arms." Her shoulders started to shake. She was trying to hold back her emotions in front of him.

"It's strange, but he feels so familiar to me, like he's my long lost great uncle. Our talk was cathartic. I love him, and I know he's more than up to the job of running the company. You'll think so too after talking to him."

That was the moment when Luc recognized something earthshaking had happened to him and there wasn't anything he could do about it.

"We spent the rest of the day and last night discussing everything," she went on talking. "He's willing to take on the company, but he knows it will be an uphill battle to win a majority vote. I told him you want to meet him since you're the person he'll be doing bank business with in the future. How soon do you want him to come to your office?"

Luc had to think fast. Thomas could clear part of today's schedule. "This afternoon? Two o'clock?"

"That's perfect! He'll be there." Her eyes glistened.

"One more thing I'd like to ask of you if you don't mind. I need your advice about something else only you can help me with."

He didn't know how much more of this he could take. "What would that be?"

"When your grandfather put your name up to be considered to take his place, how did he do it when there were other men older than you with experience who wanted the position? Did he meet privately with each member of the board?"

Luc was so blindsided by the realization that he was madly, painfully in love with Jasmine Ferrier, he hardly heard her questions. He'd known love's power in his late teens, but tragedy had struck, turning him into a different man, who'd been closed up ever since.

No longer a teenager, he was a grown man of thirty-four who'd possibly lived half his life already. But a big portion of that life had been half lived to avoid future pain of loss. In scientific terms, it meant he'd lived to a point when life had fallen to half its value and the other half would grow unstable. That was the path he'd been on.

"Luc?" The sound of Jasmine's concerned voice jerked him back to the present. "Are you all right?"

He fought to recover. Her request for his advice had humbled him, but he worried. Once she didn't need him anymore, would she want him as much as he wanted her? He needed to get back to the office and think.

"Forgive me, Jasmine. I want to answer your questions, but not here while we're both still facing a full work day ahead of us. On my way over here, my assistant alerted me to a problem I need to take care of before my first appointment. I'm sorry, but I have to go."

He finished his roll and drank some coffee. "Why don't I call you after my meeting with Remy and we'll talk then." He got up from the table.

"Of course," she said in a quiet voice. "Thank you for agreeing to meet me at all, Luc."

Their eyes met. "I told you to let me know after you'd seen Remy. I'm looking forward to meeting him. Talk to you later." He put some bills on the table and walked off. Though he thought he heard her call to him, he kept on going.

When Remy Ferrier arrived at his office at two that afternoon and sat down with him, Luc couldn't have been more surprised over the man's dynamic aura. He felt as if he were talking to a man in his fifties! Maxim Ferrier's cousin was every bit as charming, sophisticated and intelligent, but in an entirely different way.

They talked at length about the new technology his son had developed. After discussing some of Remy's marketing ideas for the future of flower farming, Luc realized this extraordinary man had vision and depth of character. Ferriers couldn't possibly go wrong with him at the helm.

"If the board can't see their way to voting me in, then so be it. For Jasmine to come to me on behalf of my cousin has meant everything. She has touched my life and I'll always be grateful. Thank you for all you've done."

"It's been my pleasure." Luc could hear Jasmine's defense that Remy was wonderful. She was right. He was a wonderful person. He talked about his love for his cousin, who'd tried everything on earth to get him to come back and head the company after Paul died. But he couldn't do it then.

Before Remy left the office, he said, "I know none of this would be possible if you hadn't listened to Jasmine. She has a lot of her grandmother Megan in her. Yesterday when she came to the farm and begged me to take over the family business, it was like being with Megan again." His voice sounded husky. "There's a sweetness and earnestness in her. I found I couldn't say no. I couldn't love her more if she were my own granddaughter."

Remy had revealed a world of information with that admission. Luc had known there was an underlying problem that had kept Remy away. That problem had been a woman, Maxim Ferrier's wife. In the end, Remy hadn't been able to say no to Jasmine either. Luc didn't know the story. One day, he'd get Jasmine to tell him.

Once Remy left the bank, Luc phoned the woman who was continually in his thoughts. She answered on the second ring. Besides being anxious to hear about Remy, he hoped she'd been just as eager to hear Luc's voice. She had his insides so twisted up, he didn't know himself anymore.

"In a word, Remy is the man for the job in every way. I have no doubt of it. Why don't you and I take a drive to the top of the gorge this evening? There's a quaint inn that serves lamb wrapped in mint leaves and roasted over a wood fire."

"I haven't been there in years, but I remember it was delicious."

"Good. It will give us all the privacy and time we need to talk strategy."

She took her time before she said, "I probably won't be through with work before six."

"Fine. Let's say seven at your house. I'd rather pick you up there than at your lab. That way we suffer less chance of being seen together before you drop another bomb in your family's lap. I'm looking forward to our meeting tonight." That was the understatement of all time.

He clicked off and went in his house to get ready. After a shower and shave, he put on an open-necked sport shirt and trousers. The talk with Nic earlier in the week had helped him get his feelings out in the open. As his friend had said, move past all the business first. That's what Luc intended to do so they could get down to the personal. He needed to be with her tonight.

When he left the house, he decided to keep the top down. The scent of the flowers rising from the farms in the warm evening air affected him like an aphrodisiac.

Luc knew where to go. He'd been to the Ferrier home many years ago with his grandfather on business. He'd sat outside in the sedan while he'd waited for him. With the cypress and orange trees lining the gravel drive, the setting was the envy of everyone who visited the perfume fields of the Midi.

Little had he known that a certain young granddaughter had been a frequent visitor quietly following in Maxim Ferrier's footsteps. Maybe she'd even been there at the same time as Luc. His heart thundered in his chest anticipating being with her tonight. He had no intention of ever letting her get away from him. To make sure of it, he'd pulled out every stop to ensure there could be no escape route.

As he drew up in front of the house, she appeared

wearing a filmy, soft orange-colored dress. He'd come early and there she was. The skirt draped around her long, elegant legs with every step. She'd caught her hair back with a clip. Luc's breath caught at the mold of her enticing figure.

Their eyes met as he got out of the car and walked around to help her in. "You're wearing a different perfume this evening."

"I didn't put on any. It must be the shampoo."

"You smell like fresh peaches."

She darted him a glance after he'd started the engine. "I hope you like them. Papa developed the scent. For a non-nose, you have a keen olfactory sense. Maybe you're in the wrong business."

Luc chuckled. "Before we leave, shall I put the top up?"

"Please don't. I love the breeze. You can smell everything growing."

"That's why I bought a convertible."

She smiled. "I'm surprised everyone doesn't drive one here. For years I've worked in a shadowy lab. It's a treat to be in the open air and breathe all the scents. When I'm home, I live outside."

Her comment threw him. His head jerked around. "You *are* home."

"No. You could say Grasse has been my second home because of my grandparents. But my home is in Driggs, Idaho, where I help on the ranch. There's nothing I love more than riding my horse through the sage. When it has just rained, the scent is so heavy, it's almost as overpowering as the jasmine in flower. I miss it. As soon as Remy takes over, I'll be leaving."

"You mean on a well-earned vacation."

"No. I mean for good. I'm afraid I'm like Papa. I don't want to be the head of anything. That's why I'm so grateful you've helped me get everything into place this fast."

His hands gripped the steering wheel with so much force, he had to slow down before they had an accident. Suddenly his world was blowing up in his face. "I don't understand. Your papa designated you to be the nose for the company. All the years you've put in…"

"Luc, I had to get my degree in something and will never regret any of the time I spent with him. But now that I've secretly created a violet perfume from the violets Remy has been growing, I have other interests and have worked it out with him."

"Worked out *what* exactly?" he demanded. His adrenaline had kicked in.

"When he wants to put another new product on the market, he'll use the other chemists in the lab. If they run into a problem, he'll call me and I'll fly over to help."

His mind was reeling. In his gut, he sensed there was only one reason Jasmine planned to go back to the States.

A man.

But she was keeping it a secret until she'd carried out her agenda here to install Remy. That's why she'd avoided the question the anchorman had asked about someone special in her life.

Was he a rancher like her father? Had she already committed to him? She wore no ring, but that didn't mean anything if she was in love with him.

If that was the case, why hadn't he been with her in Cyprus?

Luc was riddled with questions, particularly since he'd felt the sensual tension growing between them from the moment they'd met. He couldn't have been wrong about that. It was so real he didn't recognize the man he'd become since their meeting on Yeronisos.

Before tonight was over, he intended to find out the truth. Hearing about her plan to fly away forever gave him a feeling that wasn't any different from being in the plane after it lost power. When he'd seen the earth coming up to meet him, his world had flashed before his eyes then too. But he wasn't about to relive that aftermath a second time.

CHAPTER SIX

NIP IT IN the bud. That's what you did when you didn't want the plant to grow bigger.

Judging by the quiet coming from Luc, she'd accomplished her objective. But that didn't help her state of mind. Far from it.

Remy had told Jasmine about his son's new scientific discovery, called a bio-timer mechanism. It helped synchronize growth and control the rate. This would allow the farmer to save on man power and shipping because maturing crops wouldn't all flower at the same time. It could save Ferriers hundreds of thousands of dollars.

"We'll maximize our yield and reduce the cost of harvesting because you can do it all at once and reduce waste."

The phenomenal discovery was another weapon in Remy's arsenal, but she'd just applied it to the situation with Luc Charriere.

Jasmine was already in deeper than she wanted to be with him. Once she'd picked his brains tonight, she didn't plan on seeing him again. Being up-front with him right now about where her life was going was its own control mechanism.

By making it clear that her meetings with him had been for business only, she would stop the growth of something that couldn't be. It was time to make the break. Her future was in Idaho. She'd promised this to herself and her parents, whose hearts she'd broken. Then maybe her guilt would go away.

Jasmine had been living with all kinds of remorse since her parents' last visit. The pain and disappointment in their eyes had tortured her until she couldn't live with it any longer.

When Luc reached the inn, they were shown around the side and seated in a garden. So far they were the only diners in this section, but it wouldn't be long before more arrived. A mist watering the flowers cooled the hot air around them. The delightful setting provided the perfect ambience for her business meeting with him. But with her heart in her throat, she'd never felt less businesslike in her life.

When she eyed him with a covert glance, his newly shaven jaw still retained its shadow and had taken on a chiseled, almost primitive cast. It reminded her once more of his Ligurian ancestry, those warriors who'd fought with ferocity against the Romans. The thought unnerved her no end.

A waiter took their order for the lamb. Jasmine asked for coffee. "Make that two," Luc spoke up. Then he lounged back in the chair and came straight to the point.

"To answer the question you asked me at breakfast, my grandfather knew it would be an uphill battle to get me appointed. He couldn't see that a meeting with each board member would change their prejudice. Their perception, naturally, was that I didn't have the gravitas. In the end, he called them together in one body and let me speak. Either I could make my own case with a vision of where the bank should be going, or not."

"Your grandfather knew you could pull it off," Jasmine said, studying him intently. "That's why it worked. Thank you for giving me the answer I needed. After being with Remy, I know in my bones he'll wield that same power."

Luc sat forward. "He has the necessary gravitas?"

"Yes. As for you, you were born with a unique power to get things done. I saw it in front of Monsieur Boileau. No one could have taught it to you, Luc. Remy has that same kind of power. Though he's a son of the soil, he's also a man of the world with refined sensitivity who understands people. The board is ignorant of his value, but they won't be for long.

"Instead of my trying to convince them, I'm going to take a leaf out of your grandfather's book and let him speak for himself. Once they hear him present his ideas and understand his great grasp of the company he put on the map, he'll hold them in the palm of his hand."

"I agree, Jasmine. He impressed me in surprising ways. I know he'll have that same effect on your board members."

"I'm so glad you feel that way!" she cried. "After he speaks to them, I'll remind them that the only reason there's a company today and the only reason they have a job is because of Remy. Hundreds of families who work for the company in the region still feel a deep loyalty to him and will cheer his election.

"Though Paul had a nose, it wasn't that great and he couldn't have succeeded without Papa. And before you can make up a perfume recipe and sell it, you have to have the knowledge and the infrastructure behind you. That was Remy."

She waited for Luc to say something.

"When is the meeting?" he asked at last, but she saw no warmth in those black eyes. What wasn't he telling her? Something troubling was going on inside of him.

"A week from Monday, but I'm going to move it up to a week from today."

"That's very soon."

"Exactly. The element of surprise will work in Remy's favor."

Once the waiter served them, Luc asked, "Won't it still work if you wait until the Monday already chosen? Why the great rush?"

She ate some tender morsels of lamb. "You don't know the family board members. They're festering now. The less time they have to speculate and make the situation more difficult, the better."

"And the sooner you can go home," he muttered before eating his food.

"Yes. I can't wait to get back to my family."

Jasmine averted her eyes, conflicted by her own decision to leave France and get on with a new life. All sense of family had disappeared here in France once her grandparents were buried. Since then, her guilt over spending so much time away from her parents had caught up to her. She needed to go home and make up for all the lost time.

But the striking male seated across from her could have no idea how his existence was causing her emotional upheaval that she couldn't have imagined before meeting him on the island.

He still didn't say anything and it made her nervous. "The house is Remy's. I've already started packing up my things. I told him to start moving in. Papa never allowed anyone to disturb Remy's or his mother's suite of rooms. All his treasures are still there waiting for him. His son and wife and the grandchildren will be overjoyed. They're cramped in the Fleury farmhouse."

Filled with anxiety at this point, she blurted, "But I haven't forgotten my promise to you—if the family won't vote for Remy, at least he'll have his home and land back. I'll find a buyer for the old abbey property. Fortunately I have a few sources I can contact to make certain you're paid back with interest."

"Let's not worry about that right now."

He remained quiet throughout the rest of their dinner. Feeling more and more uncomfortable, she said no to another cup of coffee. There'd be no sleep for her tonight as it was.

Finally she couldn't stand the tension any longer. "It's growing late and I've taken up enough of your time. I'm ready to leave when you are."

One black brow lifted. "Are you meeting with Remy tonight?"

"No."

"Then why the hurry?"

Heat swarmed into her face. "Because I got you up early this morning and feel guilty about it. You have a half-hour drive ahead of you tonight and a full banking day tomorrow."

"I'm a big boy now in case you didn't notice. I get up and go to bed when I please."

"Of course. I'm just so grateful for everything you've done, I'm embarrassed at how much time of yours I've taken when—when—" Rarely had she ever been at a loss for words.

"When I could be with another woman? Is that what you were going to say?"

"No," she lied.

"In other words you're not interested in my private life."

"It's none of my business." The charged atmosphere had her trembling.

"Go ahead and ask me if there's a woman in my life."

She lifted her head in torment. "Luc—"

"There've been many women over the years, but I never wanted to live with one of them, let alone get married."

Beneath the cynical sounding revelation, Jasmine thought she detected a thread of pain. "Why?"

He shook his dark head. "It's your turn. Who's the man of special interest in your life in Idaho you can't get back to soon enough? A cowboy who's waiting impatiently for your return?" he drawled.

She couldn't believe he'd just said that and grabbed on to his assumption like a lifeline. "And if there is?"

When you didn't want to answer a question, then answer it with another one. That fictional man had to be out there somewhere! Jasmine was counting on it because she'd promised to live with her family from now on. She wanted a husband and family of her own where they could all be together.

Jasmine didn't think Luc's eyes could go any blacker, but they did. "Is he a friend of your family?" he kept it up. "A fellow rancher perhaps?"

"I'd rather we got off the subject if you don't mind."

"Why?" he persisted. "Is it too painful to talk about?"

Taking a deep breath she said, "Maybe I'll answer your question when you answer mine."

The hard line of his mouth relaxed. "So you *are* interested."

He had her there. "Only if you feel like sharing."

She could hear his mind ticking. "I fell for a girl in high school. We were planning to get married in the fall after graduation. *Je l'aimais à la folie.*" To hear him say he'd been madly in love sent a pain to her heart. "When you're young, you feel everything intensely and imagine yourself immortal. One weekend, our group of six, including my best friend, decided to go skydiving."

What Jasmine heard next tore her up inside. It was a miracle he'd survived the crash.

"I'd always been the one to suggest the more dangerous activities. But my sense of adventure overtook common sense one too many times. There was a price to be paid. One of the results was that I discovered you can't count on the permanence of life.

"Marriage was no longer part of my future agenda. But that doesn't mean to say I don't enjoy women thoroughly…as you've already discovered," he added.

She couldn't look at him for a minute. Her pain for him went too deep.

"Now it's your turn, Jasmine."

But all she could think of was the terrible pain he'd lived through. "That explains why you were so vehement about me not going cliff jumping. It makes sense now. I could tell you were more than a little upset. How horrible for you, Luc. I'm so sorry."

"It happened a long time ago. I hadn't thought about it in years until I heard a couple of the teenagers scream and I had a flashback. When I saw you start for the steps of the cliff, I was seized by fear for you. I was afraid there could be another tragedy."

"I understand and I was an idiot not to let you know I didn't plan to participate."

"Not an idiot. You had no idea who I was or what I might have been up to. Unfortunately there are enough awful things that happen to innocent people to force you to protect yourself."

She looked around, seemingly conscious of the other diners. "Why don't we talk in the car on the way home? We're not the only people out here anymore."

"You're right, and everyone is staring at you. Whether they recognize you from television or not, you will always draw attention, just like your grandmother, Megan."

Her gaze flicked to his. "Remy must have talked to you about her."

"Only that you reminded him of her and he couldn't say no to you. Did he love her?"

"Yes," she whispered. "You figured that out?"

"It wasn't something he could hide. I doubt he was even aware of it."

"Papa always feared Remy would never get over loving her too." Jasmine looked away. "Let's go."

On the way to her house, Luc drove past the land she intended to purchase and pulled over to the side for a minute. Night had fallen over the landscape. He reflected that the soil here in Grasse was coveted by the farmers of the world for its exceptional ingredients, producing flowers of the highest quality.

But as he looked out to the sea, Luc realized Grasse possessed many more qualities not found anywhere else. With the gentle breeze blowing off the water to dishevel Jasmine's hair, the land, the twinkling lights of villas seemed locked in a kind of intangible enchantment.

Without eyeing her, he said, "Can you honestly walk away from this and leave Remy to carry the load alone?"

He heard her shallow intake of breath. "He's getting his life back and has his own family to help him. I have loved ones waiting for me at home."

Luc turned to her. "Why wasn't this special man with you on Yeronisos?"

She wouldn't look at him. He sensed her calm was forced.

"Ranching isn't unlike farming. To coin your phrase a different way, Luc, a rancher isn't long separated from his cattle herd."

"Not even for the woman he loves?" She was evading him. "Is he divorced with a child?"

She gasped. "Why on earth would you ask that?"

"It's a legitimate question. A rancher has a foreman to take care of things if he wants to get away, but if he has a child to consider, that makes it more complicated to arrange a trip. Is that why you're turning your back on part of who you are? Has he asked you to marry him and help raise his child? To consider what you're planning to do means you would have to be driven by a compelling reason."

"For heaven's sake, Luc—"

She was sounding more and more flustered. He flicked her a glance. "I can't fathom a man who wants to marry you leaving you alone for a second. How much do you truly love him when you've been separated so much of the time?"

Her inability to come up with a response convinced him she was hiding something. He had enough patience to wait until they were in a less public spot to find out what was going on inside her. After a couple of cars drove by, he pulled back on the road and headed down the gorge.

The moment he pulled up in front of her house, he saw her hand reach for the door handle. "Careful. I haven't turned off the engine yet. Why are you acting so frightened of me?"

She took an unsteady breath. "It's not fear, Luc. I simply don't want to take up any more of your time."

"Would you still say that if there weren't a man waiting for your return?"

A sound of exasperation came out of her before she turned to him. "Yes!"

"So you have no interest in me except for what I've been able to do for you."

Her features hardened. "I came to you with a business proposition. You *know* how grateful I am for what you've done for me—"

"But it's all work and no play, even though you're separated from your beloved by thousands of miles?"

Those blue eyes looked haunted. "What do you want from me?"

"How about honesty."

"I'm being honest," her voice trembled.

"The hell you are—" he whispered fiercely. Having taken all he could, he pulled her close so their mouths were almost touching. "I'm feeling something I've never felt before and I know you're feeling it too, but your guilt is preventing you from admitting it. The fact that guilt is getting in the way means you couldn't possibly love this man the way you should."

A strangled moan escaped her lips.

"I'm going to kiss you, Jasmine, and then we'll know for a certainty."

Luc found her mouth and coaxed her lips apart. In the next instant he felt her begin to kiss him back with such answering hunger, it took his breath.

He'd wanted this kiss to happen for so long, and now that it had, he couldn't stop. Her passionate response took them to a deeper level until they both moaned with pleasure.

He was so far gone and so enamored of her that when she suddenly wrenched her mouth from his, it brought a protest from him.

"No more," she cried. Breathing heavily, she eased herself out of his arms. She sat back and said, "I knew deep down there would be a price to pay for your generosity that went beyond bank boundaries. Am I to presume *this* is the payment you're really after for bending your own rules to help me?"

In that second while the unexpected question caught him off guard, she moved away and got out of the car.

He stared at her through narrowed lids, making no move to stop her. "Now we know the truth, don't we? A moment ago you were right with me, kiss for kiss, and obviously feeling even more guilt about it than I realized. Otherwise a woman like you who is sacrificing everything for the good of one man and the company would never accuse me of buying you to get you in my bed.

"Need I remind you that you came to me first? In case you think your moment of righteous indignation for whatever you believe I'm guilty of has ruined everything, be assured our deal still stands. I'm a man of my word. *À bientôt*, Jasmine."

As he drove off, Luc thought he heard her calling him back, but in his savage state of mind, he knew it safer to keep on going.

Mortified was the only word that even came close to what Jasmine experienced as she watched Luc disappear from sight. The insult she'd flung at him was unconscionable and could never be erased. The second his mouth had descended, she'd started kissing him back with a fervency she hadn't known herself capable of. But it had frightened her so terribly she'd torn her lips from his.

What kind of evil streak did she possess to kiss him as she'd done while pretending there was a man in her life? And then to turn on Luc with such cruelty because he'd guessed the truth.

Luc would never have to buy a woman. He could have any woman he wanted. He'd been honest with her about his painful loss. He'd opened up to her. That couldn't have been easy to do. In fact, he would never tell something that private to a person he didn't care about. In so many words, he'd let her know there was no significant other in his life since that terrible time.

And look what she'd done to him—

Tonight he'd wanted to kiss her. Heaven knew she'd wanted him to kiss her, but after she'd felt his mouth devouring hers, she'd been afraid it wouldn't stop there. *And not because of him.*

Jasmine wanted to crawl in a hole. Without his willing help, who knew how long it would have taken to get a bank loan somewhere else. She had to do something to fix this, but didn't know how.

Maybe he hadn't heard her call out for him to stop. If she tried phoning him right now, would he answer? He'd only been gone a few minutes.

Desperate to stop the bleeding, she pulled out her cell and pressed the digit for his number she'd programmed into her phone. To her chagrin, the call went directly to his voice mail. When she heard the prompt, the words came pouring out of her.

Another phone call had gone to Luc's voice mail. In this black mood, he didn't dare talk to anyone. It was probably his sister calling again about the party for Sunday she was planning for her husband's birthday. She wouldn't relent until he let her know he'd be there with a girlfriend.

After the dark moment with Jasmine, he wasn't fit company for anyone. Tomorrow he'd clear out for the weekend. Luc had no idea where he'd go. He only knew he had to get far away.

Further ahead of him, he saw lights flashing. There'd been an accident. He had to stop behind a line of cars. While he was forced to wait, he glanced at the caller ID on his phone. Seeing Jasmine's name there almost caused his heart to palpitate out of his chest. In the next instant, he listened to her message.

"Luc? You have to forgive me for what I said. I didn't mean it. You know I didn't."

He could hear her voice shaking over the line.

"I'm aware I don't deserve a chance to explain, but I have to. You have to let me. Please turn around and come back. I won't be able to sleep tonight until I've talked to you. You don't need to call me. Just come. I'll wait for you. Please."

That urgent throb in her tone connected in a more powerful way than her words. He came close to causing another accident by turning around and peeling down the road toward Grasse.

The ten minutes it took to reach her house were the longest he'd ever known. He levered himself from the car and strode to the front door. As he started to knock, it opened. Jasmine's nervous expression left little to the imagination.

"I've been waiting, but I can't believe you came back. It proves what a good man you are." That was the second time she'd told him that. She opened the door wider. "Come in and we'll go out on the terrace."

He followed, watching the sway of her womanly hips as she led him through the hallway to the salon. From the French doors, they walked out to a terrace with lawn furniture. It overlooked a flower garden. He walked over to the stone balustrade. The sweetness of the blossoms intoxicated him.

"What is that smell?"

"Rose de Mai. Papa's Aunt Dominique loved this garden."

"Heavenly stuff," he murmured after turning to her. She'd perched on one end of the swing.

"You have to forgive me," she began. "I've never been intentionally rude to anyone in my life. That makes twice now with you, but I don't want you to think I'm the girl you thought I was on Yeronisos."

He lounged against the balustrade, still struggling to deal with his emotions. "In other words, I bring out something in you that makes you cross a line, is that what you're saying?"

She leaned forward with her arms on top of her legs, clasping her hands. "You didn't do anything wrong. I take full responsibility." Her head was down, causing her gleaming dark hair to slide forward. "I'd like to blame my cruelty on a nervous breakdown or temporary insanity or some such thing. But it wouldn't be the truth."

Honesty from her at last…

"I've lived a very selfish life, Luc. Been given every gift without counting the cost."

His brows furrowed. Where was she going with this?

"When you told me how you felt after the plane crash, it pressed on a nerve inside me.

"I'd always had this feeling of immortality too, that I could fit everything into the life I wanted, when I wanted. I had time for all there was to accomplish. There'd be no bell tolling for me.

"Then I woke up on my twenty-sixth birthday and realized the day had come when everything was now on my shoulders. Papa had put me in charge to carry out his wishes and trusted me not to fail. Up until then it had seemed like some dream that wasn't based in reality. But it wasn't a dream!" She lifted her head. "Suddenly I felt my mortality for the first time, and I was terrified. I still am…"

Luc knew that feeling all too well.

"It's not just the fear of failing Papa. It's the realization that I failed the parents I adore. So many missed chances that I can never recapture."

He moved closer. "I've been following you until now. What do you mean, missed chances?"

She got up from the swing. "To show them my love. I've been a selfish daughter, Luc. I—I've been as horrible to them as Paul Ferrier was to his son." Her voice faltered. "I neglected them by putting my interests first. Papa was such a fascinating figure, I loved being with him. In the process, my father took a back seat without my meaning for it to happen. He and Mother made it so easy for me. *Too* easy. I see that now."

"Aren't you being too hard on yourself? I'm sure your parents recognized you had a special destiny. A good parent enables their child to live up to her full potential."

Her face was a study in pain. "Even so, I recognize what I've done and want to make it up to them. My siblings have always been there for them when I was nowhere around."

Luc was beginning to put all the pieces together. "So now you're going home to live and make things right."

"If it isn't too late to repair the damage."

"Jasmine—there's no damage. Your case isn't anything like that of the prodigal son. You had their blessing. When you spent so much time in France, you didn't turn your back on them or fritter away your inheritance."

"But in a sense I did, Luc! I left my father's home and the life he'd planned with Mother for *our* family." She started to sob. "I'm worse than Paul Ferrier."

Without conscious thought, Luc reached out to crush her guilt-ridden body in his arms. "Hush," he murmured into her hair. He'd finally gotten the truth out of her. There was no man waiting for her. But the realization had thrown him into a new quandary.

Luc could have handled that form of competition. But he had a much greater adversary in the form of her father, whom she now wanted to shower with love for the rest of her life. That meant her leaving France for good.

If she were to get involved with Luc, he'd be the one standing in her way. That's why she'd said something hurtful to him when he'd known in his gut it was totally out of character for her. Luc had found out that when Jasmine did something, she went at it with all the energy of her soul.

He got it.

This was a moral dilemma staring him in the face on a whole new scale. Luc didn't know if he had the fortitude to do the right thing and walk away. But if he continued to feel her beautiful body pressed against his, he'd start to make love to her.

Do you want to take the chance that she'll say something hurtful again and mean it this time, Charriere? Do you want your life to be utterly destroyed by loving this woman whose destiny lies on the other side of the world? Get away while you can.

To his dismay, she must have been reading his mind because she eased away from him first and hugged her arms to her waist. "Thank you for giving me the chance to explain."

Luc took a deep breath. "You're under a tremendous amount of stress. I'm going to leave so you can get to bed." *Get out of there before you're tempted beyond endurance.* "If you need me for anything, call me. Good night, Jasmine."

He left her standing on the terrace and hurried out to his car. This time she didn't call him back. How in the name of all that was holy was he going to handle it?

CHAPTER SEVEN

The day of the board meeting had finally arrived. The Ferrier members on the board hadn't been at all happy about her bringing the date forward to Friday, but so far none of them had formed a mutiny. Everyone had assembled in the conference room of the perfumery.

She'd found it hard to sleep since Luc had left La Tourette a week ago. His brilliant mind had figured out what she'd been trying to tell him. So far he hadn't phoned her. She'd known he wouldn't, but it devastated her to the point she felt ill.

Over the last week she'd spent all her time with Remy. They'd planned he would stay out in the reception area with his family until she called for him to come into the room and be introduced to the board. Remy had been amazing through it all.

He knew the board might not vote for him, but Jasmine could see he was handling it because her grandfather's ghost had been laid to rest for good. Getting back the house and the estate where he'd grown up had made a huge difference in him. Jasmine knew he would go on being a flower farmer and helping his family, but with one difference. He'd be happy.

Before she walked in the conference room, she said

a little prayer. "I've done everything I could, Papa. The rest is no longer in my hands."

Squaring her shoulders, she entered the room and walked to the head of the long conference table. Giles LeClos sat on her left, Roger Ferrier, her oldest uncle, on her right. Her eyes traveled around the table, lighting on her relatives and staff members, all fourteen of them.

None of them had been able to accept the fact that their father and grandfather had chosen her. She knew the feelings of resentment, even anger against his choice, had been roiling inside of them and she understood.

"I can't thank you enough for dropping everything to be here this afternoon. Some of you had to fly from Paris. If it weren't of the most vital importance, I wouldn't have called for a meeting even earlier than planned." Several of her family sent each other off-putting silent messages.

"I'll make this short. First of all, I've made the decision not to be associated with the company any longer. Secondly, I won't be working as a nose anymore. I'm moving back to the States for good."

A collective gasp reverberated in the room. They stared at her like they'd seen a ghost.

"However, I'm leaving you in the hands of the only person who has the right to run this company as he sees fit. There would be no company to run if it weren't for the genius of this man, who did everything his father never could. I'm talking about Paul Ferrier's son and heir, Remy Ferrier."

A strange silence enveloped the room.

If Jasmine had announced the end of the world, she

doubted the reaction would have been any different. "Giles? Please give everyone a file that contains all the pertinent information they need to see on Remy. While you do that, I'll ask Remy to come in. He's right outside."

The other man looked shocked, but he did her bidding. She went to the doors and beckoned to Remy. He came in and stood next to her. She squeezed his hand and introduced him to everyone; then she nodded to her grandfather's attorney. "Please read the part of Papa's will none of you have heard yet."

Her heart was pounding furiously as the older man stood up and put on his glasses. "Beloved family and staff members—Remy was the brother I never had. I loved him." Jasmine squeezed his hand again and never let go. "He should have run the company from the start, but it wasn't meant to be while Paul was alive and insisted that I run things.

"After he died, I begged Remy to come back and run the company, but by then he had other interests. It is my wish that he be installed now. I've used my sweet granddaughter Jasmine shamelessly to make this happen.

"You who are my children and grandchildren have all been wonderful stewards of the company. So has my faithful staff. No one could have asked for better. But no one has the right to head Ferriers except the man who worked in the trenches of the company as a boy and knows every jot and tittle of what makes it tick.

"With Remy's vision, he'll do miraculous things that will put the company on top and stay there. Be his friend. Accept his guidance. Remy has a reputation among the work force of our company in the Midi. When they hear he's been installed, you'll see them wearing a smile again because he's one of them. In no time at all you'll find out that Ferriers has a weapon like no other."

Jasmine had been watching their faces during the reading. The whole demeanor of the room had changed. They acted like they were in a trance.

For a sixty-six-year-old man, Remy looked younger and sensational in an olive suit with a light green shirt and tie. He'd worked in the fields most of his life when he wasn't racing or drinking. Besides having an amazing physique with no fat on him, he was still handsome and bronzed by the sun. Naturally, he'd aged, but his dark red hair was still vibrant and thick.

She smiled at him. "We'd all like to hear from you, Remy."

He kissed her cheek. "I can see we're all in shock," he quipped. "Max and I grew up under the same roof and were like brothers, being only two years apart. I remember a time when a rival in the perfume industry caused an explosion at the lab in Hyeres. By now, my father was dead and it was right before Max got married.

"Everyone thought the act of sabotage had killed him. During that horrendous time when we couldn't find his body, I felt like I wanted to die. That's when I realized what his life meant to me. We can thank God he wasn't killed. You've all heard stories and rumors, some true, some not. The fact is, he and I went through hell and back together, but in the end, we're still brothers.

"Like my psychiatrist told me when I went to him

REBECCA WINTERS   139

for my former drinking problem, he told me that unless I was willing to work with him, then there was no reason for me to continue seeing him. That's my speech to you. If you're willing to work with me, I'll do everything I can to earn your trust."

Jasmine grabbed his arm. "His Parma violets will be the envy of every perfume house. For the last year, I've worked on a perfume with essential oil from the violets he's been growing.

"He's the only person in the world to grow this variety, and thousands more are going to be planted. He calls them Reine Fleury. As you know, Remy's mother's name was Rosaline Fleury. I've given each of you a tiny sample bottle of perfume to open now."

In a few minutes the room smelled like a garden of violets. The sounds of *ahs* and pleasure from everyone told the story as nothing else could.

"When this perfume is out on the market, it will turn the company's revenues around. With that said, I propose we now take a vote by secret ballot."

Remy excused himself and left the room.

"I'm going to vote my conscience and know you will do the same. Giles? If you'll start the process."

A few minutes later, Giles read the verdict. "The vote is unanimous in favor of Remy Ferrier."

Your dream came true, Papa.

Jasmine ran to the door and asked Remy and his family to come in. When they entered, everyone stood up and started clapping. She could hardly see the green of his eyes for the tears in her own. She hugged him hard. "It was unanimous. Welcome home, dear Remy."

Everyone gathered round him and his family to shake their hands and congratulate him.

Unable to stand it any longer, she whispered, "Do you mind if I leave you for a little while? You're in good hands. I'll meet you back at the house later."

"Where are you going?"

"I need to see the man who made all this possible."

Jasmine flew out of the perfumery as if her feet had wings.

En route she phoned her parents and told them the joyous news. "Everything I wanted to do for Papa has been accomplished. It won't be long before I'm home for good. I love you both so much, you can't imagine."

Luc couldn't concentrate. He'd stayed away from Jasmine for the last week and had been in hell. He knew the board meeting at the perfumery had been called for today. He checked his watch. Three-thirty. Though he'd promised himself he wouldn't do it, at some point he knew he was going to break down and phone her.

He had one more phone conference with the branch manager in Colle-sur-Loup, but he couldn't bring himself to deal with business right now.

"Thomas? Get Emil Rocher on the phone for me and tell him we'll have to do the conference tomorrow. I'm leaving for home now." He stood up to leave.

"You can't go home yet."

"Why not?"

"You've another appointment waiting for you out here."

"Tell them I'm sorry, but they'll have to schedule for another day."

"I don't think you want me to do that. She's on her way in now."

The main door to his office opened. "Luc?"

Jasmine's excited cry sent adrenaline flooding through his system as she hurried inside and paused a few feet away from his desk. Her eyes glowed like sapphires.

"It worked! Everything worked. Remy's the new CEO by unanimous vote. It's because of you that any of this happened! Can we go somewhere private to talk so I can thank you? Do you have time?"

Luc looked into her face beaming with happiness. "What do you think?" he said fiercely. "We're going for a boat ride and you can tell me everything. We'll drive back for your car later."

There was no argument from her as he hustled her through the rear door and they climbed in his car. Luc's cruiser was moored at the main boat dock for easy access two miles away. The drive only took a few minutes. He left the car in the parking area and they walked along the floating dock to his cabin cruiser.

After handing her a life jacket, he removed his suit jacket and tie. Once he'd rolled up his shirtsleeves, he undid the ropes and idled the boat at wake speed. When they'd cleared the buoys, he opened it up and they flew across the blue water away from shore.

To be with her like this had lit him on fire. The fact that she'd come running to him instead of phoning him with the news proved she was on fire for him too. Right now, he refused to think about her leaving France. She was here on his boat. She was with him. Nothing else mattered. No tomorrows. This time was for them.

The sun made the sea air balmy. Now that they were away from people, he cut the motor. "Come and sit in the back of the boat with me." They made their way to the seats.

Jasmine had worn a pale pink two-piece suit with short sleeves to the meeting. Between her coloring and her outfit, she looked good enough to eat. She tucked one leg under her and turned to face him. He stretched his arm along the top of the seatback near her.

"I want to hear it all from the beginning. Don't leave anything out."

She brushed some strands of hair out of her eyes. "Luc? I meant what I said earlier. None of this would have been possible without you. It got Remy there. Then the attorney read part of Papa's will no one had heard yet. In it, he paid tribute to Remy, the man he'd loved like a brother. The words were so touching, there wasn't a dry eye in the room."

Hers had filled with tears. "It *was* a far, far better thing you did for him than anyone else has ever done for him before. Thank you doesn't begin to express what's in my heart, but I'll say it again anyway." She leaned closer and kissed his cheek. "Thank you, thank you, thank you," she cried until he couldn't hold back his hunger.

Seven days apart had been too long. Luc had needed to feel her mouth moving beneath his again. He covered those lips, smothering the words, and there was no more talk. The taste of her was a revelation. Time had no meaning as each kiss deepened and lasted longer.

She gave freely, thrilling him to the core. He'd been with other women, but he'd never known ecstasy like this. Cradling her face, he brushed his lips relentlessly over every lovely feature, so precious to him. "You're incredibly beautiful, Jasmine. I'm sure you've heard that all your life, but I've seen inside the part of you that hides the secret of your beauty. It comes from your soul. I didn't know anyone like you existed."

They kissed again with a devouring hunger neither could hide. "Because of your faith in me, I could say the same thing about you. As I told you the other night, you're a good man." Her eyes burned like blue flames. "Do you have any idea how rare you are?"

He kissed her back, longer and harder. But he couldn't get close enough to her while she was wearing the life jacket. "I'm going to drive us to that little cove you can see from here where we won't be bothered by the wakes from other boats. Stay right there and don't move. Promise?"

"I promise, but where would I go?" Her breathing sounded shallow.

Somehow, he didn't know how, he left her long enough to drive them the short distance to a stretch of beach. He cut the motor and the hull glided on to the sand. With his heart pumping too fast, Luc walked back to her.

"Let's take off that preserver so I can get my arms around you properly."

She undid it before he could help and threw it on the floor. A little smile lifted one corner of her delectable mouth when she said, "Now I'm going to find out just how difficult it would have been to save your unconscious body after your rental boat crashed into a shark."

He pulled her into his arms. Finally there was no space separating them.

Her eyes melted into his. "You know something? You're a lot more man than I realized, Luc Charriere, and gorgeous besides. So gorgeous I have a hard time taking my eyes off of you. Thank heaven you weren't killed in that plane crash." Her voice shook. "Then we would never have met, and you wouldn't have made me the happiest woman alive today."

His breath caught. "I know what getting Remy that loan has meant to you."

"That's true, but you know very well I'm talking about you and the way you make me feel. I thought my problems would be over once he was installed, but now I discover I've got a bigger problem."

"What's that?"

"You." A tortured sigh escaped her throat. "What am I going to do about you?"

A charge ignited his body. "What do you *want* to do?"

"I have my dreams, but they can't come true, so there's no point in talking about them. I've got to be content with what I have right here, right now, with you."

This time, she searched for his mouth with stunning impatience, telling him without words. Their kiss went on and on until he felt transported.

But a different kind of pain than he'd known before shot through him because this was her goodbye kiss. He pulled her right up against his chest and buried his face in her neck. She really was going away. This wasn't something he could talk her out of.

"Jasmine? Before you leave for the States, I have to spend some time with you. I'll take my vacation now. How soon do you have to go?"

"I promised to be home on August seventh. It's my parents' thirtieth wedding anniversary party."

So soon? Everything in him rebelled. His mind cal-
culated the time. "That gives us a week."

A moan sounded before she moved off his lap and
stood up. "No more make-believe, Luc. I couldn't go
anywhere with you."

He stared up at her. "Why not?"

"You *know* why. Your life is here. Mine is on the
other side of the Atlantic. How could it possibly be
good for either of us to go off for that long, knowing
we're going to say goodbye at the end? The thought
of it is too painful to even contemplate." Her voice
throbbed. "At least it is for me. But you're a man, so
it's different for you."

"Explain that remark."

Jasmine wouldn't look at him. "You can go away
with a woman and enjoy the time thoroughly. When
it's over you can move on. But women are different.
Not all, but some. *I'm* different. To travel and make
love with you, only to get on a plane at the end of that
journey and wave goodbye, sounds like a kind of pur-
gatory I have no desire to live through."

He grasped her hand. "Then we won't sleep together."

She looked down at him and smiled. "You're a
Frenchman, aren't you?"

"I'm a man like all other men, and the thought of
making love to you has been on my mind since I saw
you on Yeronisos. But that isn't why I want to go away
with you. If you think making love to you is all I'm
after, then you have an odd conception about me.

"The other day I told you I have feelings for you
I've never had for another woman. If all I can do is
hold you and kiss you while we're on vacation, it will

be enough. What I'd truly regret is not being able to get to know Jasmine Martin, the fabulous woman inside the girl who makes me want to be a better man."

"Luc."

"It's true. Is life so cut and dried and riddled with deadlines, we can't take time out for ourselves to feed our own needs? The cruiser sleeps two comfortably and can go anywhere on the Mediterranean. We'll explore grottos and ruins. While you're still in France I can indulge in *my* dreams. I have them too, you know."

She looked shocked. "You really could get away now?"

He got to his feet. "My work will still be here when I get back. You *won't* be. We've cleared up all the business there is to do. Now I want to spend every second possible with you not worrying about anything or anyone but each other."

"I want that too," she admitted at last. "But I can't be gone a whole week. I have a few more preparations to make before I leave."

That was all he needed to hear. Now that Luc could breathe again, he had to think fast. He handed her the life preserver to put on. "Let's pick up your car and I'll follow you to Grasse. Once you've packed a bag, we'll come back in my car. I'll gather my things and we'll set off in the cruiser. When we find a spot we like, we'll lay anchor for the night."

Taking advantage of her silence, he walked to the forward part of the cruiser and jumped to the sand to push it into the water.

He should have followed her up that cliff last May. They might still be on Cyprus, too enthralled with each other to care about anything else. But there was no point in looking back. The next few days were what counted. He couldn't think beyond that.

Several hours later Jasmine sat across from Luc as they skimmed the water along the Italian coast in the sleek white, seaworthy cruiser. "See those lights ahead?" She nodded. "Now that we've passed Alassio, we're coming to Baba Beach, where we're going to spend the night. It won't be crowded."

With Luc, she was going to see the charming delights along the Cote d'Azur she hadn't had time to explore while she'd been working. The scene ahead looked like fairyland.

He pulled into a protected bay. She saw a sailboat farther on, but Luc had been right. They were virtually alone. Once he'd dropped anchor near the shore, she removed her life preserver. At the house, she'd changed into jeans and a top. It was still warm out so she didn't need a jacket yet.

Luc had dressed in sweats and a T-shirt. On their way to the pier, he'd driven her to his villa near the Grimaldi castle in Cagnes-sur-Mer, a medieval town with a warren of alleyways and decorated wooden doors. Flowers abounded and cascaded from the balconies. It was a dream home. This had been the hometown of the Charrieres for generations. She'd been enchanted.

He propped a couple of loungers side by side on the deck. "What do you say we relax for a while before going downstairs to bed?"

"Ooh, yes! Who could go to sleep yet on a night like this?"

His eyes smiled at her. "Want a soda?" Luc was attentive to her every need. Jasmine had dated a little in college, but hardly at all in the last two years. She'd almost forgotten what it was like to be waited on and pampered.

"Not right now, thanks. What about you?"

"I'm perfect," he murmured.

They'd stopped for dinner on the way back from Grasse and had bought some food and drinks to stow on board. Right now, they had everything they needed.

She lay down on her stomach with her face turned toward the beach. Luc stretched out on his side facing her with his hand propping his dark head. Jasmine chuckled. "You're turned the wrong way."

"I've been here before and am seeing the sight I want."

Everything he said filled her with warmth. "You're terrible."

"You're breathtaking. My grandfather had a copy of your grandmother's book in his library. I've read it and looked at all the pictures. You're more beautiful than she was and have the coloring of your grandfather. The combination is startling. Remy must have been shocked to see you face to face."

Jasmine turned on her side. "I know he was."

"Tell me the other reason besides pride that kept him from coming back to run the company after his father died. I know it had to do with your grandmother."

Nothing got past Luc. She took a deep breath. "Do you remember when I told you that he went to Paris to run the company while my grandfather was on a trip to South America?"

"I do, but I didn't know he'd gone so far away."

"After his first wife and unborn baby died, the doctor told him to take a long trip."

Luc sat up. "I didn't know about a baby."

"Not many people do. It would have been his first-born. He had a few friends who enjoyed archaeology the way he did, so he joined them. Before leaving, he asked Remy to go to Paris and run the company. While Remy was there, he wanted him to attend the annual perfume awards banquet with the staff. Papa was glad to get out of it."

"That's right. He hated publicity."

She nodded. "Remy went. It was held at the Hotel de Ville. Everyone who was anyone was there, including the president of France and some famous film stars like Yves Montand and Simone Signoret. While they stopped by the Ferrier table to talk to Remy, a woman bumped into him by accident, causing the champagne he'd been drinking to stain his ruffled shirt. That woman was my grandmother, Megan Hunt."

"Why was she there?"

"Henri Brescault, a reporter for the *Paris-Soir*, was covering the event for the paper. He was hoping to get an interview with my grandfather, who kept winning the perfume award year after year. This reporter had a sister who was best friends with my grandmother. The uncle who raised her after her parents were killed was an Egyptologist and had given her a necklace that predated Christ."

"You're joking."

"No. He worked at the Peabody Institute. Anyway, Henri asked her to wear it because he'd heard my grandfather would be in attendance. He hoped the necklace would catch Papa's attention and garner him an interview."

Luc smiled. "But nothing worked as planned because Maxim wasn't there."

"That's right. Remy took one look at her and fell madly in love. She'd just graduated as a translator from the Sorbonne. He didn't want to lose her to a job in England, so he begged his Aunt Dominique to hire her to help at the boarding school she ran in Switzerland. The night he asked her to marry him, she told him she cared for him very much, but she wasn't ready to commit to marriage yet.

"In his pain, he drove off and got into a car accident with his Porsche. He ended up in the hospital. He was supposed to have driven her to Switzerland the next day. Unbeknownst to him, my grandfather returned from his trip a week earlier than planned because his aunt hadn't been well and he was worried about her. When he walked into his apartment in Paris, he received a call from Remy, who was still in the hospital. Remy had thought the apartment retainer would answer, but it was my grandfather.

"Remy told Papa he'd fallen in love and was planning to be married at Christmas. Remy led Papa to believe he and my grandmother were engaged, which of course they weren't. As a favor, he asked Papa to please pick up my grandmother at her apartment and drive her to the train leaving for Switzerland early the next morning."

Luc shook his head.

"It was the perfect storm. Instead of putting her on the train, Papa drove her to Lausanne because he intended to drop in on his aunt, who'd already promised him she would close the school and stay home in Grasse.

"On the drive, he found out my grandmother wasn't engaged and the two of them fell so deeply in love they didn't know what to do. After Remy recovered from his accident, he discovered what had happened and his heart was broken beyond repair. He went after Papa in Grasse. They had a literal physical fight before Remy left for Paris and never came back home."

"So the rest was history?" Luc surmised.

"Yes. My grandmother was in Switzerland when she found out about the fight. Knowing she was the cause of it horrified her because she loved Remy too, but not the way she loved Papa. In despair she left for the States, where neither man could ever find her, hoping that if she disappeared, the two of them could mend their differences. But Papa hunted her down until he found her in Driggs, Idaho, where she'd been born. They got married there and he brought her back to Grasse."

"Mon Dieu."

Jasmine sat up. "Perhaps now you understand why Papa suffered so much grief. Not only was Paul's cruelty unforgiveable, Remy saw my grandparents' love affair as a great betrayal. Neither Papa nor my grandmother meant for any of it to happen.

"If you want to know the truth, before my grandmother died, she confided in me about Remy. The things she loved about him touched my heart. Papa wasn't the only one who suffered. Grandma wanted to love Remy the way a woman loves a man. She tried so hard. In fact, she admitted to me that if she'd never met my grandfather, she would probably have ended up marrying Remy.

"For nights, I listened to her tell me about their love story. He was so good to her while she was studying for her finals. Remy was prepared to give her the world. During those talks, I felt so close to him. Between my grandparents' confidences about him, I felt like I knew him even though I hadn't met him. I truly love him. Do you find that strange?"

"Not at all." She could tell by Luc's expression he'd been moved. "But it would take a strong man to overcome that kind of emotional pain."

"Still, it didn't break him, and Papa knew it. That's why he begged me to help Remy. Grandma begged me too."

He stared at her. "You have a look of your grandmother. It must have been like déjà vu for him when you showed up in his violet field."

"That's exactly what I thought when he turned around and saw me. I never prayed so hard in my life for a miracle to happen."

"I had no idea so much was at stake. You've carried a heavy load."

"Which you lightened by listening to me and helping me. I'm so thankful for you, Luc." She could feel tears smarting her eyelids. "Enough talk about my life. I want to hear about the girl you loved. Tell me about her."

Lines darkened his handsome features. "Sabine's family moved to Cagnes from Paris our senior year. She was different from the other girls I knew."

"In what way?"

"She was funny, and fun. I was intrigued and invited her to hang out with me and my best friend, Philippe. A group of us did all sorts of crazy things when we weren't studying. She fit right in."

Jasmine smiled. "Define crazy."

"My parents labeled me a daredevil at an early age. That's what we did. We dared each other to push the envelope, no matter what it was."

"Like the guys on the island."

He nodded.

"Were you lovers?"

"Yes."

His answer shouldn't have hurt, but it did.

"We were crazy about each other. I got this idea that after we graduated from high school, we'd get married and take my sailboat around the world. You know. Stop for a while here and there to earn a little money, then move on to the next stop.

"Considering that my family had their own specific dreams for me, they would have been horrified if they'd known what I'd planned. But a selfish eighteen-year-old isn't thinking about anyone else."

Remembered pain seeped in. "I was the same way, Luc. Without giving my parents' wishes a thought, I wanted to go to the Sorbonne, where my grandparents had gone." She shook her head. "Forgive me for interrupting you. Go on," she urged.

"There isn't anything else. The day we graduated, we decided to go skydiving. It was my idea. Our big adventure sounded like the perfect way to start the summer. We took off in a single-engine plane near Cannet-des-Maures. One minute, we were all laughing and getting ready to parachute. In the next minute, the plane lost power and we plowed into a hill."

He got up from the lounger and walked over to the side of the cruiser. In agony for him, she jumped up and joined him. "I can't imagine the horror of it. Were you in the hospital a long time?"

"Three months with a bruised spine. My parents and grandparents never left me alone. At first, the doctors didn't think I'd ever walk again. At the time, I didn't care. I'd lost Sabine. It was my fault she and Philippe were dead. I wanted to die."

Luc was no stranger to guilt of the worst kind. "Surely you still don't blame yourself? You couldn't have known that plane would crash."

"You're right, but it took me a long time to throw off the burden."

She studied him for a moment. "I'm so sorry for your suffering."

He wrapped his arms around her and rocked her in place for a long time. "It all happened a long time ago. I haven't talked about it for years."

Jasmine lifted a hand and caressed the side of his hard jaw. "I shouldn't have brought it up."

"I'm glad you did." He kissed her fingertips.

"How did you pull out of your morose state?"

"My physical therapist told me he was being replaced. I asked him why. He said that when there were other patients fighting to get better, he couldn't work with one who had a death wish. Since the doctor had given me the prognosis of a full recovery if I worked hard, he found me utterly selfish and pathetic and refused to waste his time."

"Oh, Luc—"

"'Oh, Luc' is right. When he walked out on me, I got angry. That was the first real emotion to wake me up to my sickening state of mind. In another six months, I could walk with a cane. A year later, I'd thrown it away and started university at Sophia Antipolis in Nice where I took courses in economics and management.

"It was there I made good friends with Nic Valfort. We both went to graduate school in Paris. Life got better from that point on. Speaking of Nic, he has invited me to his house on Saturday evening and wants me to bring someone. When we get back from our trip, I'd like you to go with me. You'll enjoy his wife, Laura, who's your age. She's from San Francisco."

"An American? That's interesting. But I'm not sure if I'll have time. My flight leaves the next day."

"Then we'll make sure you find the time. He saw you on TV and wants to meet the famous head of Ferriers."

"After today, I'm no longer anything. That's the trouble with fame. Here today, gone tomorrow," she quipped.

Luc winced, not able to appreciate the humor when he knew she was going to leave him. He walked her back over to the loungers. "I don't want to talk about tomorrow. We came on this trip to get to know each other better. I want to hear about all the various men in your life."

She sank back down. "You make it sound like there have been legions."

He sat opposite her, tracing the outline of her cheek with his finger. "I have no doubt legions of men have desired you, but I want to know about the one or two who were lucky enough to enjoy your company."

"I dated some in high school, mostly group dates. But there was one guy named Hank Branson."

He grinned. "Sounds like a cowboy."

She nodded. "The year I met him I was seventeen. Dad had taken the family to the rodeo. My father was a famous bull rider at one time and he's always had an active association with the rodeo. Both my brothers got into it for a while. They became friends with Hank, an eighteen-year-old steer wrestler from Rexburg, a town a half hour away. I was introduced to him.

"In the arena he was known as Hank the Tank because he was big and tough. And cute.

"Every girl around was nuts about him. I was smitten. When he took time off, he came by the house during the year while I was home. I was in heaven riding around the ranch with him, going out on the occasional steak fry with him and our family.

"We went to movies and did some hiking in the Tetons. He gave me my first kiss and told me he was going to marry me when I was all grown up. We dated on and off for about three years, but because I spent so much time in France, it was hit and miss.

"The family really liked him, and dad kept telling me I couldn't do any better. Hank has gone into business with his father, who owns a big, successful ranch. They're good people. But at one point I realized my crush on him had worn off. When he brought up marriage again, I had to tell him I wasn't in love with him and that ended it."

Luc closed his eyes. "The poor devil," he muttered, once again stunned by the revelations falling from her lips. "Are you sure he's still not waiting for you when you go home?"

"For his sake, I hope not."

"What about the men you met at the university in Paris?"

"I went out with several guys, but I never had a lover if that's what you're asking."

Never? "Surely there must have been someone who mattered to you."

"There was one named André. We dated some until I realized he was too dictatorial. He tried to order me around."

"You mean the way I did to you on the island?"

She nodded. "For a few moments, you reminded me of him."

"So that's why you were so angry with me."

"Only for a moment, Luc. Now you know about my legions of love affairs. I'm afraid I've put you to sleep."

"If anything, it's your voice that sounds tired. Maybe we ought to head downstairs. I think I've worn you out after all that's happened today."

He pulled her along with him and they went below. To her surprise, he didn't linger in the doorway to her cabin.

"I need to put the boat to bed. So you'll feel safe, I'll turn on the cruiser's warning device. Sleep well." After a brief kiss to her lips, he walked back toward the stairs, leaving her with an ache that would keep her awake all night.

CHAPTER EIGHT

As she got ready, Jasmine realized she wasn't on Luc's mind right now. How could she be after she'd forced him to relive his tragic past? But she was glad she knew. The experience had helped him to become the remarkable man he was today. *The man you're going to leave after this short vacation is over.*

In order not to think about that, she took out a map of the Mediterranean he'd given her to study and got in bed. Tomorrow he'd let her pick their next spot to explore. Jasmine couldn't recall ever having had this kind of joy in her life. There was only one reason why. *Luc.*

But he was probably up on deck recalling his former dream of sailing around the world. Unfortunately, his dream had been dashed. Jasmine shuddered and tried to focus on their destination for tomorrow, but that didn't work.

After studying the map for a while longer, she fell asleep. She came awake the next morning with a pounding heartbeat. Nothing could slow down her heartbeat knowing Luc was on board. After a shower, she dressed in a plum-colored bikini. When she'd put on a matching beach wrap, she went up on deck to find him.

"Luc?"

"There's my Amazon warrior. I'm out here!"

With a chuckle, she turned in time to see his dark, handsome head while he treaded water. "Come on in! It's the perfect temperature."

Jasmine needed to tie back her hair first, but that meant going below. His invitation was so inviting, she forgot about it and made her way to the transom. Then, removing her wrap, she dove into the brilliant blue water. He swam toward her. The sight of him with his black hair slicked back and those jet-black eyes devouring her thrilled her so much it was hard to breathe.

He reached for her hand and drew her into him. "I've been waiting for my breakfast and here you are." His white smile was devilish. "I'm not sure which part of you I want to eat first."

Jasmine laughed nervously until he captured her mouth and twirled them around. Having lived by the water all his life, Luc swam like a fish. He kept them buoyant as he turned on his back with her lying on top of him so they could drink deeply of each other. They played and kissed both in and on top of the water. For a while, she lost all sense of time, never wanting sensual pleasure like this to end.

Though going to bed with a man was one experience she hadn't known yet, Luc was teaching her ways to enjoy the exquisite pleasure of being with a man. Nothing in life had prepared her for happiness like this. He lifted her high above the water while he turned in circles. When he lowered her again, his eyes played over her hair.

"Do you know the individual strands sparkle in the

sunlight like there are little jewels in them? I never saw anything like it."

Her heart quivered. "When I was a little girl, my dad told me the same thing. From that point on, he called me Sparkles."

Luc bunched her hair in his hands. "It's beautiful, just like you." After kissing it, he found her mouth once more and kissed her with an urgency that carried her away. At the height of her excitement, he said, "If I keep you out here much longer, I'm going to eat you alive." The glitter of desire in his eyes melted her insides. "Since I made you a promise, we'd better go back to the cruiser quick and find me something else to eat."

She groaned in disappointment, but knew he was right. Together, they headed for the end of the boat. He paced himself to stay with her. The feeling of oneness couldn't be described in words. It was too overpowering for that.

He climbed on the transom first, then pulled her up. She reached for her wrap and followed him on to the deck. Luc stopped at the top of the stairs to look at her. "While I put the food on the table, why don't you get the map and show me where you'd like to go."

Jasmine hurried to her room and secured her hair with an elastic. After putting on a T-shirt and shorts, she joined him in the galley and made the coffee. In a few minutes, they were poring over the chart of the Mediterranean while they ate.

"I'd like to head for Palmaria island if it's all right with you. My grandmother told me there's the most fantastic beach, but you can only reach it by boat. She also mentioned a cave."

He nodded. "Pozzale. I haven't been there in years. We should be there by early afternoon. It's the perfect place to swim in crystal-clear turquoise water and explore the caves."

"There's more than one?"

Luc flashed her a smile that sent a shockwave through her. "The side of the island in the Gulf of La Spezia faces west toward the open sea. It has high cliffs that overhang the water, in which there are many caves. You're going to love it."

She discovered that she loved doing anything with him. When this vacation was over, she would never be the same again. By coming with him, she'd crossed a line and was playing with fire, but she couldn't help it.

"I can't wait. Let's get going. I'll do the dishes, then join you."

He got up and planted a kiss on the side of her neck. "Don't be too long. I'm already lonely without you."

So was she, at the thought of never being with him again.

Three hours later, Luc weighed anchor and together they swam to the beach. "What do you think?" he asked Jasmine, clasping her hand as they reached the sand.

"Look at all these polished pebbles! They're fantastic! This whole place is unreal!"

"It's very unique with its unspoiled natural landscape and rocky backdrop."

"I want to find some to take home to my nieces and nephews." And one for herself to remember this day.

"I'll help you take them back to the cruiser, then I'm going to show you the Blue Cave while there aren't any tourists around. You'll understand the reason for its name when you see it."

For the next half hour, she studied the pebbles until she found the ones she wanted. Then they swam back to the boat. In another few minutes, he drove them around to the north side of the rocks. As they rounded a curve, they came to the cave opening.

She gasped. "Luc—I've never seen such a heavenly blue color."

"It's almost as heavenly as your eyes. During your television interview, they glowed like hot blue stars."

Jasmine was afraid to look at him. She feared that to spend much more time like this with him was the greatest mistake she would ever make and she would suffer for it for the rest of her life. "Can we swim in?"

"Of course. But not too far because I want to take you past another cave you'll find even more interesting."

The fun of entering the cave via the water was only eclipsed by their journey to the next cave Luc called the Grotta dei Colombi. Translated, it was the *Cave of Pigeons*.

"You have to descend by ropes, but you need a guide. In this cave, they've found fossilized bones of Pleistocene animals. I have a feeling your grandmother explored this cave with your grandfather."

"I'm sure you're right."

"If you're ready, I'll drive us around to the civilized side of the island and we can explore before it gets too dark."

One adventure after another awaited her as Luc dropped anchor and they swam ashore to do a little exploring through the broom.

"Um...I can smell sage."

He put his arm around her waist and hugged her to his side. "With a nose like yours, I'm not surprised. Do you have any idea what those trees are ahead of us?"

They walked closer to see red-orange balls among flowers on the evergreen leaves. Jasmine couldn't believe it. "This side of the island is covered with strawberry trees! I've got to taste one."

"You're sure you want to do that?"

"Absolutely. They're edible. I'm curious about the essential oil." She bit into one then made a face. "It's very bland."

Luc laughed. "Not as tasty as a regular strawberry?"

"Not quite." She pulled another one off for him. "Are you game?"

"Try me."

She put it to his mouth and he took a bite. "It's mealy too. I think it's time to get back to the boat and fix dinner, but I want another kiss first."

Jasmine knew she'd remember this kiss, this moment, for the rest of her life. She clung to him against a setting Mediterranean sun, enjoying the taste and scent of him, including the hint of strawberry on their lips.

By the time they'd finished eating, night had fallen. Luc pulled into a small protected bay and set the anchor. It had been a hot day, but the light breeze off the water cooled them enough to make the air perfection. He placed the extended loungers side by side again and stretched out on one of them.

But when Jasmine came up on deck, she propped hers forward and sat down. He sensed she had something serious on her mind. In the dim light from the boat's navigational system, her features looked more severe. "What's wrong?" he whispered.

She stared at him. "This."

He sighed and sat up. "It's been a perfect day."

"I know," she whispered back. "Too perfect. I can't do this anymore."

"Do what?"

"Be with you."

A grimace marred his features. "In other words, you've had enough of me."

Jasmine rubbed her arms. "I wish I'd phoned you the good news about Remy and left things alone. I was out of my mind to burst into your office, and then think I could take a vacation with you before leaving France without paying a huge price.

"Please don't misunderstand. You haven't once stepped out of bounds with me. Just the opposite in fact. But it's already a painful situation for me and needs to end. I'd like to return to Cagnes-sur-Mer tomorrow."

Lines bracketed his mouth. "Even if it pains me?"

"Luc—it's no use," she blurted. "I wish there were a drink of forgetfulness so I could fly home with no memories of any kind. But that's not reality. You know I'll never forget you, so to spend even one more minute with you will only make things that much worse." She sprang from the lounger. "We haven't known each other that long, but whatever it is I'm feeling, it'll tear me apart if I don't get away from you as soon as possible."

"What about the party at Nic's on Saturday night?"

"I don't think it's a good idea. I need to sever all

ties with you. I don't want to meet your friends or your
family. It's better this way."

His anger flared. He got up from the lounger and
put his hands on her shoulders. "Why would you say
that?"

"You *know* why! You're the CEO of the biggest
bank in the South of France. Your life is here. Your
family is here. My life is there with my family. I'm
afraid if I don't go home now, I could lose their love.
Being with you simply can't work. That dreadful cliché
about ships passing in the night describes our situation. Please let me go. This isn't getting us anywhere."
Her eyes had taken on a haunted cast.

"You want to go back that badly?" He almost hissed
the words.

"Yes, because I don't trust myself with you any
longer."

He slowly exhaled before releasing her. There
was more than one way to fight this battle, but this
wasn't the time. "If that's what you want, then we'll
leave now. Go down to bed. By morning we'll back in
Cagnes-sur-Mer and I'll drive you home."

Her face had gone pale. "Luc—" She was swallow-
ing hard. "I'm sorry. So sorry."

"Don't be. I've enjoyed every second we've spent
together. It's been a thrill, but it will have to be enough.
Bonne nuit, chérie."

The moment she disappeared below deck, he pulled
up anchor and started the engine. He'd spent his life
maneuvering in these waters and welcomed the night
ahead of him since he knew he wouldn't have been able
to sleep. Luc had too much thinking to do and would
need the whole night to figure things out.

If Jasmine slept at all during the night, she didn't remember. All she knew was that when she awakened at seven with her pillow still sopped by tears, the engine had stopped and there was only the motion of the cruiser rocking gently back and forth.

She freshened up and caught her hair back with a clip. Once dressed in a top and shorts, she packed her few things and went up on deck to discover they were back in Nice without incident. Not that there would have been any problem with Luc at the wheel. He'd been sailing these waters all his life.

He'd already tied up the cruiser against the dock. In the distance she could see his tall physique coming back from his car, where he must have taken a load of things from the boat. More guilt consumed her because he was doing all the work. He should have wakened her to help, but he was too much of a gentleman for that.

His jet-black gaze scrutinized her from the crown of her head to the soles of her sandaled feet. He might as well have been touching her for the way it felt. "I knew you wanted to get home as soon as possible, so I packed up any provisions left to take to the villa."

"Thank you. I couldn't possibly eat right now. Is there anything else I can help take to your car? You must be exhausted after having to be awake all night."

"I'm fine and it's all done. Are you ready?"

"Yes."

He took her bag for her and steadied her arm while she stepped on to the dock. Then he let go of her and they walked to the parking area separately. Once they got in the car and were on their way, he turned to her.

"Would you like to stop for coffee on the way back to Grasse?"

"I don't need anything, but thank you."

After a few miles he said, "Are you definitely leaving Sunday?"

"Yes."

"Then this will be our last time together."

"Don't get me started, Luc. I don't want to say goodbye to you, but I *have* to."

"I know. You've done a wonderful thing for Remy and the company. You've honored your grandfather's wishes. Now there's nothing left except to go home and love your family. I understand more than you think.

"After my accident, my parents stood beside me and refused to let me wallow in self-pity forever. They gave me life and were my mainstay of existence through that tumultuous period. I've tried to be a devoted son ever since.

"You're doing the honorable thing, Jasmine. I can only imagine how thrilled they'll be to know you won't be leaving again. You've got years to enjoy the life you were born into. I want you to know how much I admire you for what you've done. I'm sure your papa couldn't be happier with the way things turned out. Working with you has helped me to know him and Remy, two great men. I thank you for that."

If he didn't stop talking, she was going to scream in pain.

"That goes both ways, Luc. I don't know another man who would have done what you did to help me. Your decency and goodness is a revelation. I don't know how you thank someone for that. I only know I'm in awe of you."

"I think we're even. Since we're coming into Grasse, tell me how to reach the Fleury farm. I'd like to see it before I take you home."

Her heart pounded out of rhythm while she gave him directions. Pretty soon they were driving along the side of the violets where she'd seen Remy. Luc unexpectedly pulled over and stopped. "I'll only be a minute."

What on earth?

In fascination she watched him get out and walk over to pick a small bunch of them. When he returned to the car, he inhaled their fragrance. "These will always remind me of you." He handed them to her. "Sweet, like a spring morning." He pressed a warm kiss to her mouth, then started up the car once more.

Jasmine sat there in shock while he drove her the rest of the way to the house. He pulled up next to her Audi. "This is it. What a journey since Yeronisos. I don't know about you, but I wouldn't have missed it."

Instead of lingering, he got out and reached for the small suitcase he'd put in the back seat. After he opened the passenger door for her, she had no choice but to climb out with the flowers and her straw bag. Luc walked her to the entrance of the house.

He put it down next to her. "I detest long goodbyes. Have a safe flight home, Jasmine." With her hands still full, he cupped her face in his hands and kissed her once more, this time hotly on the mouth.

Her legs were close to giving way by the time he got back in his car and disappeared around the bend in the gravel drive. She fell against the door, needing to hold on to the handle for support.

Luc... Luc...

On Saturday afternoon, Luc drove into the Martin ranch on the outskirts of Driggs, Idaho. The stunning view of the Teton mountain range dominated the sage-covered landscape. He found the pine-scented air warm even at the six-thousand-foot elevation. *Glorious.*

The two-story log ranch house had the authentic rustic flavor of the American West. He saw signs of various ranching equipment and several trucks parked around the side. After parking the rental car, he got out and walked up the porch to the main entrance. A dog started barking inside before Luc rang the buzzer.

He heard a woman admonishing the dog to be quiet. Soon, the door opened and he came face-to-face with a woman, fiftyish, wearing a western shirt and jeans. She was a real beauty in her own right, with a great figure, and couldn't be anyone else but Jasmine's mother.

This had to be Blanchette, the youngest daughter of Maxim and Megan Ferrier. Luc knew so much about this family it felt strange to be this close to a first descendant of the famous couple.

Blanchette had inherited her mother Megan's blond hair. But she'd bequeathed the shape of her face and features to her daughter Jasmine.

"*Bonjour*, Madame Martin," he spoke in his native tongue. "Forgive me for arriving at your doorstep without calling first, but I couldn't find your phone listed. I've flown all the way from Nice to meet you and your husband. My name is Lucien Charriere. Your daughter Jasmine and I have been doing business over the last few weeks."

"Ahh—" was the only sound she made while her brown eyes lit up before playing over him. "*You're* Raimond Charriere's grandson who took over at the bank after his death—"

"*Oui.*"

"According to her, you made it possible for Remy to become the new head of Ferriers. My father suffered terrible grief over that situation. Thank you for the part you played in helping Jasmine right a horrible wrong. Please. Come in. *Entrez.*"

"*Merci.*" He followed her inside to a great room that was three stories high to let in the sun. She indicated one of the leather sofas. "*Asseyez-vous, monsieur.*"

"Luc."

"Call me Blanchette. I dislike formality." She sounded so much like Jasmine just then, it stunned him. "My husband, Clark, has gone into Driggs for supplies and groceries. We're going to have a big party on Monday night to welcome Jasmine home. She'll fly into Jackson early Monday morning on the company jet. Clark should be back soon." When she sat down, the black lab lay down at her feet.

"I knew I was taking a chance. I'm sure you're wondering why I'm here, so I'll come straight to the point. I've taken time off from the bank for a vacation. There's only one way to say this. I've fallen in love with your daughter and hope she'll end up marrying me. I'm here to obtain your permission. Because your approval means everything in the world to her, it means everything to me."

She put a hand to her throat in surprise. "Have you already proposed to her?"

"No. I haven't even told her I'm in love with her. She's made it clear that her home is here in Idaho with you. When we were last together she told me we were two ships passing in the night, but I could never accept that. I realized that if I hope to get a yes out of her, then I'll have to move here.

"I love her too much to lose her, Blanchette. If she'll have me, I'm prepared to live in Idaho and earn my living here in order to be with her."

A soft cry escaped her lips. "You'd step down as CEO of the Banque Internationale du Midi and move here for her sake?"

"She told me you gave up a life in France to marry your American husband and live here with him. As you found out, when you're in love, the other things don't matter if you can't be together. I'm not different and have been considering several options of work here.

"In the meantime, for most of the day, I've been with a Realtor in Jackson who has shown me several small ranches for sale around Driggs. I'm thinking of buying one so Jasmine and I could live close to you. That's more important to her than anything else in the world. Since she's the most important thing in my life, I'll do anything because I can't live without her."

Her mother got to her feet, visibly shaken. "Does she know you've flown here?"

"No. And I don't want her to know. Not yet… We said a final goodbye a few mornings ago after coming back from a little trip along the Mediterranean to Palmaria in my cruiser. She's an amazing woman. It was a selfless act, to get Remy installed as CEO of

Ferriers in order to honor your father's wishes, but naturally you already know that about your daughter."

"She's exceptional."

"I agree, and I think you and your husband are exceptional to have given her the life she's been able to live. After she's been home a few days, I'd like to come by and see her with your permission.

"But I'll wait for a call from you before I do anything in case you learn that she wouldn't be happy to see me. If she wants nothing to do with me, then I'll leave and I won't be back. Most important, I never want her to know I was here." He got up to leave.

She studied him for a long time. "Where are you staying?" He had the feeling she understood a lot he hadn't told her because she'd been through a similar experience.

"At the Teton Valley Cabins. Just ask for me at the front desk."

"Clark will be sorry he missed you."

"I'm sorry too. I'd like to meet her hero, the ultimate cowboy."

Blanchette broke into a smile so much like Jasmine's it was uncanny. "I promise to call you."

"I can't ask for more than that."

"*À la prochaine*, Luc."

Next time? Hoping there was going to be one, he left the house and took off in the rental car. There was another property he wanted to check out before dark. Tomorrow there'd be more to look at. He'd stay busy until that phone call came.

At seven on Monday morning, Jasmine's plane touched down on the tarmac in Jackson Hole, Wyoming. She walked down the steps of the Ferrier jet into the arms of her family who'd come out *en masse* to welcome her home.

She had a ton of luggage and boxes of precious mementos that Remy and his family had helped her load onto the jet before she'd left Nice. She in turn had given him her Audi for an extra car he'd need. Other Ferrier family members had gathered, even Giles, who had presented her with a bouquet of jasmine on behalf of her papa. That unexpected gift broke her down. She'd been the recipient of more gifts than one human being deserved. There'd been a lot of tears.

As the jet took off, she'd looked out on Nice, the jewel of the Mediterranean, and her life had flashed before her eyes. Luc was down there. Her beloved Luc. She knew the exact spot and felt such a stab of pain she thought she was going to pass out.

For the rest of the flight home she remained in a numbed state. Nothing seemed real as her brothers and family scrambled to pack everything in three sets of cars for the drive back to Driggs just twenty minutes away. Another beautiful August morning with the sun outlining the backside of the magnificent Tetons.

The view was so different from the flower fields she'd looked out on one last time from her bedroom balcony yesterday. Both views were spectacular.... Both represented matchless slices of life and experiences.

You're a lucky girl, Jasmine Martin. You've been given every blessing except one. Don't dwell on what can't be. Don't be greedy. You're home where you belong. It's enough. Embrace it.

Her dad opened the front door and the dog came

flying. "Buck!" she cried and gave him a hug. "I've missed you too." She played with him for a minute before she insisted on a couple of boxes being opened. Jasmine had brought presents for everyone and wanted her nieces and nephews to enjoy their gifts now.

Several hours later, everyone left, but not for long. She found out her parents had planned a big party for the evening and had invited neighbors as well. Grabbing a suitcase, she walked upstairs to the same bedroom she'd had when she was a little girl. Nothing had changed.

Her dad followed her and stood in the doorway to her room. The smile on his face warmed her heart. "Hey, Sparkles. Do you have any idea how thrilled we are that this day has come?"

"I feel the same way, Dad."

"I know you do, but I see something else too."

She averted her eyes. "What do you mean?"

"Since the last time we saw you, you've changed from a girl to a mysterious woman."

A nervous laugh escaped. "There's nothing mysterious about me."

"Oh, yes, there is. You stood quietly in the doorway of the jet for a minute and I noticed it right away. I haven't had a heart-to-heart talk with you for a long time. How about it? I've got all the time in the world."

Jasmine flicked her gaze to him in consternation. "I don't know what you're getting at."

"Who's the man you left behind?"

Heat swept into her face. She'd never been able to hide anything from her father, let alone lie to him. "He's exactly that. Someone I left behind."

"Tell me about him."

"I'd rather not."

"Why? Because it's too painful to talk about?"

She took a deep breath. "Yes."

"What's he like?"

Jasmine sank down on the side of the queen-sized bed. "Grandma Megan said it best when she talked about Papa. Her words could be mine."

"What did she tell you?"

"'He's in a class by himself, Jasmine. No other man could hope to compete. It would be futile. In comparison, he makes all the other men I've ever known seem bland and unexciting. It isn't fair that one man could be so endowed. It isn't his fault. His charisma is something inherent, so are his looks and personality.'"

"Well, well. Your mom and I have wondered if this day would ever come." He sat down by her and put an arm around her shoulders. "When are we going to meet him?"

She shook her head. "You're not. It's over."

"Why?"

"Because it *has* to be," she cried. "He's the head of the Banque Internationale du Midi! He's a Frenchman whose roots go back hundreds of years. He has a big family and friends and a fabulous life. He's as married to his life as you are to ranch life."

"I see."

"To want a life with him is like this big dream that couldn't possibly come true. That's why I don't want to talk about him, not ever again. Do you mind?"

"No, sweetheart. We'll consider the subject closed." He kissed her forehead and got up from the bed. "I'll be downstairs with your mom getting things ready for the party."

"Dad? Don't misunderstand. I'm so happy to be home with you and Mom."

"You think we don't know that?" He smiled. "Go on and get settled in, then come on down and I'll fix you one of my super-duper roast beef sandwiches with your mom's homemade bread."

She ran across the room and hugged him hard. "I love you."

"Ditto."

Seven hours later, the ranch house filled up fast with family and neighbors, old friends Jasmine hadn't seen in ages, most of them wearing cowboy boots and hats. There was no formality here. Her mom had prepared a barbecue out on the back patio with corn on the cob by the tubful and plates of her homemade rolls that disappeared by the dozens. They'd lit some torches to add to the atmosphere. Country-western music played in the background.

Jasmine dressed in jeans and a western shirt. After pulling on her well-worn cowboy boots, she brushed through her hair, having left it long, and went downstairs to help. Her sisters-in-law had prepared salads and desserts while her dad and brothers fried steaks for everyone on the two grills he'd set up. The little kids ran around having fun.

A few more guests dribbled in. Jasmine was headed for the kitchen to bring out another potato salad when she saw a few more familiar ranchers wander outside to the patio. They were all in cowboy hats and boots. But there was one she didn't recognize who stood out from the others. He had black hair and was wearing a black Stetson. One of the ranchers must have brought him along.

He was a little taller, a little more well-built. She noticed he filled out his tan fringed shirt in such a way that she couldn't possibly look anywhere else. As he started to fill his plate, she saw the play of muscle across his shoulders and back.

She moved closer, feeling the hairs stand on the back of her neck. He reminded her of Luc on the day they'd gone to see the property she'd wanted to buy. Maybe she was missing him so much that she thought she was seeing him. After the talk with her father earlier in the day, she hadn't been able to get him off her mind.

There couldn't be two Lucs in the world, could there?

Jasmine had to find out and walked over to him. "Hi! I'm Jasmine Martin. I don't think we'v—"

But she didn't get the last word out because he'd turned toward her with the plate still in his hand. The second she saw that five o'clock shadow and those black eyes, she was afraid she was hallucinating. His seductive half smile turned her entire body to jelly.

"Luc—" she whispered in a state of absolute shock.

"Oui."

Her eyes grew bigger. "I—I don't believe it," she stammered. Suddenly she understood about the talk with her dad in the bedroom. Luc had already been to see her parents!

"What don't you believe? Your folks invited me to come to your welcome-home party. Naturally I wouldn't have missed it. They thought you'd probably be lonely on your first night home after being away so long." He started eating.

"Luc—" She struggled to find words. "You're really here."

"Where else would I be?"

"But when did you get here?"

"On Saturday."

"You came before *I* did?"

"That's right. I don't like goodbyes."

She began to tremble. "You—you shouldn't have come!"

"Does that mean you want me to leave right now?" He put down his plate.

"You *know* that's not what I meant."

"Then what *did* you mean?"

"Shh. Everyone's watching us." She looked around guiltily. "Come with me."

"I'm glad you said that, but it has to be someplace alone. There are a few things I need to say to you and I don't want an audience."

She bit her lip. "Follow me."

"Where are we going?"

"Upstairs."

"As long as I can get you to myself, I don't care where we go."

A deep blush crept into her face as they left the dining room. She felt him right behind her all the way up the stairs. The second he shut the door, he threw his hat across the room and reached for her.

"*Luc—*" she cried, but didn't make another sound as he lowered his head and smothered her with a kiss that went on and on. They ended up on her bed.

He turned her on her back so he could look down at her. "I swear you're the most bewitching woman I ever met in my life. I love you more than life, Jasmine. You have to marry me, the sooner the better. I'm asking you right here and now."

"But—"

"No buts, *mon tresor*. Just so you know, we'll be living here from now on. I've been looking at ranches. There's one four miles down the road from here that would be perfect for us. My family will fly over for the wedding. We'll do what your parents did and fly back and forth to visit family. It can work."

"How can you say that when your life is in France?"

"Not anymore. You and I are not ships passing in the night. We're madly in love and we'll never be happy if we don't live together forever starting this instant. Say you'll marry me, Jasmine. Without you, life will never mean the same to me again."

"I feel the same way," she exclaimed. "I love you beyond reason. Yes I'll marry you." She threw her arms around his neck and kissed his eyes. "Yes." She kissed his nose. "Yes." She kissed his mouth, heedless of everything except her love for this incredible man. "I love you with all my heart and soul, darling. There's not another man alive like you. I've already found out that to be without you is a living death."

In another instant his total demeanor changed.

"Dieu merci," he whispered against her throat. She felt his body tremble against hers. *"Je t'aime, mon amour."* His voice had grown husky. *"Je t'adore."*

CHAPTER NINE

December 24

"COME TO BED, JASMINE."

"I will. I just have to finish wrapping this Christmas present for your mother." The French wedding reception to celebrate their August marriage had been held earlier in the evening at Luc's parents' villa in Cagnes-sur-Mer. Now they had to get ready for Christmas Day.

"I thought everything was done."

"It is, but this little gift is special and wasn't ready until I dropped by the perfumery yesterday. I had to find the right packaging for it. Since you said periwinkle is her favorite color, I hunted for the right paper. I'll be through here in a minute."

He walked over to the dressing table where she was sitting and put his hands on her shoulders. By now, her body was so sensitive to his touch, she trembled if he even came near her. The mirror reflected the two of them. Her heart thudded heavily as she anticipated going to bed with him tonight.

Every night since the wedding had been like their wedding night. Luc was an insatiable lover who took her to the heights and taught her the meaning of self-less loving.

"You've been very secretive about this gift."

"That's because your mother is a very special person. I want to honor her because she gave birth to the most wonderful man in existence. I love your parents."

He kissed the curve of her neck. "They love you. Won't you give me a hint what it is?"

She put the package down and turned in his arms. "If you really want to know, I developed a perfume ages ago and was waiting for the right person to give it to. After realizing how much your mother loves roses, I knew it would be the perfect present for her."

His black eyes traveled over every feature. "Are you talking Rose de Mai?"

"Yes." She brushed her lips against his. "You remember!"

"They were growing off the terrace at La Tourette. The scent was clear and sweet."

"Just like your mother, darling. But what you loved was the light note of honey."

"Which only you could detect."

"That's why it's so sweet. I called Remy several months ago and asked him to take Fabrice some flowers from the garden with instructions to make up a small fresh batch of my rose recipe and have it ready by the time we flew over."

"Who's Fabrice?"

"One of the chemists."

"Do I want to know about him?"

She smiled. "No, you fool."

"Maman won't believe it when you give her a bottle

of her own perfume made by the greatest nose since the death of your papa. That's an honor she'll never forget."

"I certainly wasn't the greatest that night at La Tourette after you brought me home from dinner."

"That's all behind us, *mignonne*." He turned off the lights before picking her up in his arms. When they reached the bed, he followed her down. "Do you miss the lab?"

"No," she answered honestly. "Do you miss walking into the bank every day?"

"You know I don't. Thanks to the miracle of technology I can consult from our den in Driggs, and have time to grow an alfalfa crop in the backyard. I've got to learn all I can. When our children come along, I want to be able to measure up to your father."

She held his handsome face between her hands. "You don't need to measure up to anyone. You're magnificent just the way you are. I'm so crazy about you. Love me tonight, darling. I want your baby."

With those words Luc made love to her with abandon. At the height of their passion, he kissed her almost savagely, but she welcomed it. She wanted to trap him in her arms and never let him go. He was so strong and so incredibly gorgeous she could look at him and love him all night.

Toward morning, he let out a long deep sigh and tangled his legs with hers. "Jasmine," he murmured against her lips.

"What is it?"

"I have a little Christmas present for you right now. I've memorized something I want you to hear."

She blinked and sat up so she could look at him. "You have me intrigued. What is it?"

He rubbed his hand over her hip possessively. "Your papa was the poet. I've taken license with his words. 'Jasmine is the flower for nostalgia. Like the flower that grows in doorways and winds over arches, she links me to the intimacy of our love nest. Her cheeks bloom as the days become hotter, and she releases her scent at the hour when tables are set in the garden, or in narrow lanes, or in the dark of night in my arms. She reminds me of the melancholy of dusk if she's not with me. Her presence brings out the conviviality of summer evenings when I'm with her. Her fragrance permeates the air, making it a background for the love I feel for her.'"

"Oh, Luc." She started sobbing, so deeply touched she started making love to him.

The sun was well up in the sky before she let him go.

"Do you want to know a secret on this joyous Christmas morning?"

They were both worn out. *"Bien sûr,"* he murmured, close to being too exhausted to talk.

"I love scents…but there's no flower on earth that can compete with my favorite scent."

At that remark his lids flickered open. "What's sweeter than a flower?"

"I've labeled it 'The Scent of Her Man.'"

"Does that mean you developed a cologne for men a long time ago? Something synthetic?"

"No, darling. It can't be created or manufactured." She pressed her mouth to his. "It's the scent of *you.* There's no other scent like it on earth because there will never be another Lucien Charriere. You're my heart's blood, but I think you already know that by now.

"In fact, I think you sensed it before you ever left Yeronisos island. If only you knew how much I'd wished you'd been lying in wait for me *after* I came back down. You can't imagine my disappointment."

"Now she tells me," he cried and proceeded to plunder her mouth over and over again.

* * * * *

MEET THE FORTUNES!

Fortune of the Month: Jensen Fortune Chesterfield

Age: 30

Vital Statistics: Tall, dark-haired, impeccably groomed—with a swoon-worthy British accent.

Claim to Fame: Sir Jensen is a prince of a man…literally.

Romantic Prospects: Stellar, if only he was interested. Sir Jensen keeps his heart locked up as tight as the Crown Jewels.

"That kiss with Amber Rogers? People are making way too much of it. It was all Amber's idea, to distract the paparazzi from my sister. She was just doing a favor for a friend. We are just friends. To think that a down-to-earth cowgirl would get together with a fellow like me is— well, it's pure fiction. A lovely fiction, perhaps. Her long blond hair, those big brown eyes… oh, blimey! We're. Just. Friends."

****

The Fortunes of Texas: Cowboy Country:
Lassoing hearts from across the pond!

A ROYAL FORTUNE

BY
JUDY DUARTE

MILLS
BOON

Published in Great Britain 2015
by Mills & Boon, an imprint of Harlequin (UK) Limited,
Eton House, 18-24 Paradise Road, Richmond, Surrey, TW9 1SR

© 2015 Harlequin Books S.A.

Special thanks and acknowledgement to Judy Duarte for her contribution to the Fortunes of Texas: Cowboy Country continuity.

ISBN: 978-0-263-25101-2

23-0115

Harlequin (UK) Limited's policy is to use papers that are natural, renewable and recyclable products and made from wood grown in sustainable forests. The logging and manufacturing processes conform to the legal environmental regulations of the country of origin.

Printed and bound in Spain
by CPI, Barcelona

To Cindy Kirk, Marie Ferrarella, Michelle Major,
Nancy Robards Thompson and Allison Leigh—
the amazing authors who took part in
The Fortunes of Texas: Cowboy Country.

It was a joy working with each of you. I'd take a trip
back to Horseback Hollow with you anytime!

Chapter One

Jensen Fortune Chesterfield slipped out the back door of the small Texas ranch house in which he was staying, hoping to escape the chattering crowd and to find a little peace and quiet.

Inside, his family had gathered to celebrate Christmas on Boxing Day with their new Texas relatives. But he wasn't in the mood for all the holiday gaiety—and hadn't been since his father died nearly four years ago.

After Sir Simon Chesterfield suffered a fatal heart attack during a polo match, Jensen had been plagued by a bah-humbug mood that began in December and lasted through the better part of January.

In some ways, he wished he'd stayed in England, but his mother wanted him to join her in Horseback Hollow, where his sister Amelia now lived with her husband, Quinn Drummond.

His mother was staying with her sister, while his younger siblings had rooms at a local bed-and-breakfast. Jensen was staying with Amelia and Quinn. The space was a bit tight, but the arrangement suited him. As he stood in the yard, he took in a deep breath and surveyed the grounds. If you removed the vehicles in the drive, the Drummond ranch would've made the perfect Western setting for a cowboy movie. He actually found it quite appealing, but then, he'd always been a fan of classic American Westerns, even the old black-and-white ones he occasionally caught on late-night cable when he couldn't sleep.

Despite his wealthy London upbringing, he liked being in the country. Plus, with him here and Amelia's due date fast approaching, he'd be able to watch over her while Quinn was out working the ranch.

Fortunately, her pregnancy had been uneventful as far as medical concerns. But, emotionally, she'd had a time of it early on, when the paparazzi had pounced on her, making her life miserable. And they'd been especially annoying lately. He wouldn't put it past them to try to infiltrate the family gathering today, which was one reason he was on guard.

He reached inside his pocket and withdrew his gold watch, a habit he'd picked up over the past four years. The treasured heirloom had once belonged to his father, and for some reason, he drew comfort from the weight and the feel of it in his hand.

As the back door squeaked open, Jensen glanced over his shoulder to see his mother stepping out and onto the porch. She was dressed impeccably in a simple forest-green dress and heels, her silver hair coiffed as though her personal stylist had accompanied her on the transatlantic trip to Dallas/Fort Worth and then the quick hop on a charter flight to Lubbock.

"Jensen," she called. "What are you doing outside when the chill is so frightful?"

"I wanted some fresh air." To prove the imaginary excuse, he took a deep breath, relishing the brisk winter breeze.

His mother, Lady Josephine, made her way toward him—no doubt concerned about him distancing himself from the others. But he was in Horseback Hollow, wasn't he? And not out each evening at one of the many parties he'd attend if he was home in London.

Whether she believed it or not, he was actually trying his best to fit in with the numerous Horseback Hollow cousins who were gathered in the house, most of whom he'd only recently met.

His mother frowned—the first sign of distress he'd seen since her arrival in the provincial Western town.

"Is something wrong?" she asked.

"No, not at all." Again he scanned the yard, taking in the barn, the new corral Quinn had built, the old-style windmill that creaked in the breeze. "On the contrary, I was just enjoying the scenery."

"I see," she said, yet her frown failed to lighten. "Are you disappointed about us celebrating together?"

His mother had always known she was adopted, but two years ago, she learned that she'd actually been a triplet. Her brother, James Marshall Fortune, had remained with his birth family. But the two baby girls, Josephine and Jeanne Marie, had been given up and raised in separate households.

"No, Mum. I'm not bothered. I was actually out here counting my blessings."

And if truth be told, that's exactly what he should be doing. He wasn't a loner by nature, but he hated the melancholy that seemed to hover over him during the family get-togethers, especially those associated with the holidays. That's why, at least in December, he preferred to stay in London, where the nightlife, parties and his many social obligations kept him busy and distracted.

She reached out and gave his arm an affectionate squeeze. "We truly have been blessed, haven't we?" Her blue eyes twinkled, and a wistful smile chased away her frown. "I had a lovely childhood, although it was a bit lonely with no siblings. I still can't believe I have a sister and brother—and so many nieces and nephews. Imagine, me—a Yank!"

As if on cue, little Kylie Fortune Jones, Toby and Angie's youngest, popped her head out the door. "It's time to open presents. Are you coming to watch, Aunt Joseph…iiine…I mean, Aunt Lady?"

His mother laughed. "Aunt Josephine will do just fine, love. And we'll be right there."

The title of lady had been honorific, but many of the local Texans were excited to have "royalty" in their midst and tended to make more out of it than Jensen or the rest of the family liked. The press and paparazzi did too, often referring to him and his siblings as sirs, lords or ladies, when neither of their parents' titles had been inherited.

"Isn't Kylie precious?" Josephine said. "I love having young children around again, especially at Christmas."

His mother had always begun her holiday preparations—the shopping, as well as overseeing the decorating and baking—on the first of December. In fact, she'd gone above and beyond to make the holidays happy for all of them.

"I'm glad you can spend this time with your sister," he said.

"So am I."

Still, he found it impossible to explain to an outsider. His mum, who'd grown up on a country estate in England with all the things money could buy, was staying with her newfound sister Jeanne Marie and her husband in a modest ranch house—and clearly delighted with the arrangement. You'd think she was in a five-star hotel with a full staff to cater to her every need.

To be honest, Jensen was a bit surprised by her swift acclimation—culturally speaking. But she was clearly happy. And for that reason, he was happy for her, too.

"Amelia was asking about you," she said.

At that, Jensen's brotherly instincts kicked into full throttle. "Is everything okay?"

"She's fine—other than the usual discomforts to be expected during the ninth month. She asked me to find you because it's nearly time to open the gifts."

Relieved, he nodded. "I'll be right in."

He expected his mum to re-enter the small, two-story house that was busting at the seams with family, leaving him a moment or two longer to relish the quiet.

Instead, she lingered and said, "I wish your father were here."

Jensen's grip on the pocket watch tightened. Sir Simon had been a loving husband and father, and they all missed him terribly.

She sighed, then added, "He would have been a wonderful grandfather."

Jensen slipped his arm around her and pulled her

close to give them both comfort. "You'll be a smash-ing grandmum, too."

Her eyes glistened. For a moment he feared she would cry and dampen his spirits even worse, but when a smile stretched across her face, he realized grief hadn't made her teary.

"I can hardly wait to hold that baby," she said.

"I'll just be happy when it gets here—and happier if we can keep the bloody photo hounds at bay. They've been sniffing around for a story—or rather, hoping to make up one." Fortunately, Jensen had become adept at avoiding them.

"I do wish you'd come into the house, son. This is the best Christmas I've had since… Well, in years. And I want you to share it with me."

She'd been devastated when his father died and she'd lost her soul mate and the love of her life.

Jensen slipped the gold watch back into his pocket and took her by the arm. "Then let's go inside."

They entered the house through the service porch and headed into the kitchen, where they found his sis-ter making another batch of eggnog. With her long, dark brown hair and doe-like brown eyes, Amelia had always seemed a bit lithe and fragile to him—but more so now that she was due to give birth within the next month or so.

She turned and, upon seeing them, smiled. "Oh, good. Now we're all here."

Well, not all of them. Her once slender waist was as big as the globe in the library back home, reminding Jensen that soon there'd be one more Fortune to add to the world—albeit with the Drummond surname.

"Can I help you with that?" he asked.

"Yes, thank you. I'll tell everyone they can begin passing out their presents now."

Jensen took the bowl and made his way to the living room, which was filled to the brim with relatives, every chair taken, others forced to stand or to find room to sit on the faded rag rug. But apparently, he was the only one who'd found himself on edge.

Jeanne Marie Fortune Jones, who resembled his mother in looks, but not in style, was just as bright eyed and happy as his mum to have the family together. Her husband, Deke, stood by her side, somewhat stoic but with the hint of a grin tugging at his lips.

Their children were all here. Stacey Fortune Jones, along with her fiancé, Colton Foster, kept a close eye on her daughter Piper, who was toddling around the Christmas tree and trying to keep up with her older cousins.

Liam and his fiancée Julia Tierney were posed next to Quinn's upright piano. Jensen suspected someone would suggest they sing a round of Christmas carols before the day was over.

Jude, with his fiancée Gabi Mendoza, stood near the children, all of whom appeared to be on sugar highs. Yet the happy couple held hands and looked on at the festivities as if they couldn't imagine being anywhere else but here.

Even Christopher, who'd been absent from several Horseback Hollow social gatherings last year, was here, along with his fiancée Kinsley Aaron. Apparently, he was back in the family saddle after his rejection of ranch life created discord with his father earlier in the year.

Jensen blew out a sigh. So many engaged couples. Would they all be this happy next year, after their vows were spoken? He hoped so, but he tended to be skeptical about things like that.

Of course, Toby and his wife, Angie, who watched their newly adopted children tear into their gifts, certainly appeared to be as happy as ever.

Rounding out the family gathering were Jensen's brother Charles and his sister Lucie, who were staying in nearby Vicker's Corners at the closest B and B they could find. The two were smiling, but they looked a little uncomfortable among the exuberant American relatives. Jensen wasn't uncomfortable, though. He, better than any of the British Fortunes, probably understood the Texas way of life. He was merely awed by it all.

About that time, his mother approached the serving bowl for a refill of eggnog, which was unusual for a woman who watched her calorie intake. But apparently she was celebrating and throwing caution to the wind.

"It's so good to see you happy, son."

What was she talking about? Had he been smiling?

She slipped an affectionate arm around him. "Have I told you how delighted I am to have so many of my family together?"

The smile, which he must have been wearing, deepened. "Several times in the past hour."

She lifted her free hand and fluttered her fingers in a little wave at her sister, Jeanne Marie, who wore a new pair of her signature stretch-denim jeans and an oversize Christmas-themed jumper.

Again, Jensen was reminded of the sisters' differences. They'd grown up worlds apart—one on an English estate and the other on a small working cattle ranch—something that could be seen easily in their style of dress. Still, they shared many similarities, including a love that knew no bounds.

"This is what it's all about," his mum said. "*Family*."

Jensen suspected she was talking about more than just a holiday reunion. She'd made no secret of her wish to see him and his siblings settle down. Hopefully, Amelia's baby would take her mind off matchmaking.

But then again, it seemed that everyone else in the room had marriage on their mind. His four engaged cousins had planned a huge wedding for Valentine's Day.

Jensen looked across the room, where Quinn stood next to Amelia, his arm wrapped around her. When she grimaced, Quinn immediately picked up on her discomfort, his expression growing as serious as a first-year pupil meeting his housemaster at Eton.

Amelia smiled, whispered something to her husband and placed his hand over her baby bump. His eyes grew wide and then he smiled, too.

Hopefully Amelia would breeze through labor with no snags or problems. But what if something went wrong during birth? What if…?

Jensen tried to shake his troublesome thoughts. What he really ought to worry about was the press infiltrating the couple's privacy. They'd resorted to all kinds of trickery to learn whether the baby was a girl or boy. But Amelia and Quinn had chosen to be surprised at birth, which none of the reporters believed.

A rap sounded at the door just as laughter burst out at something Toby's precocious daughter had said to her red-haired brother.

Jensen heard another noise, although no one else seemed to take note of it. Had someone knocked?

* * *

Amber Rogers stood on the Drummonds' front porch and rapped on the door again. She'd driven to the Rocking U Ranch to deliver a gift for Amelia, Quinn's new wife. It was a handmade baby blanket, although the sections Amber had quilted weren't as neatly stitched as Gram's.

But it was the thought that counted, right?

There were a whole slew of cars parked outside and a god-awful commotion going on inside the house, but apparently no one had heard her knock. So she rang the bell.

Moments later, a tall and sophisticated stranger swung open the door. He was wearing a well-tailored suit and tie—something so out of place and unexpected on a small Texas ranch that it caught her off guard and made her think about the back-to-back episodes of *Downton Abbey* she'd been watching with Gram.

Surely Lady Josephine hadn't brought along her butler and the entire Chesterfield Estate staff.

But then she realized exactly where she'd seen the drop-dead gorgeous guy before—on the front page of a tabloid down at the Superette—and she swallowed. Hard.

Before she could think better of it, she blurted out, "Oh, it's you."

"I beg your pardon?" he said in a rich British accent.

Amber cringed inwardly. Obviously they'd never met, and she'd just implied that they had. Why did she always have to stick her foot in her mouth?

She opened her lips to apologize, but she merely stammered instead, her cheeks warming.

Dang. She could be such a goof at times.

"What do you want?" he asked—and not very nicely. This wasn't going at all well.

She lifted the wrapped gift. "I'm sorry. I brought this for Amelia…um…Mrs. Drummond…or should I call her Lady Amelia?"

Amber hadn't meant to sound so uncertain, but Sir Jensen's good looks, royal appearance and hoity-toity attitude had nearly knocked her out of her cowboy boots.

His eyes narrowed. "Do you *know* Mrs. Drummond?"

"Not really. I just—" Before she could explain that she'd only recently moved back home to Horseback Hollow, and that she was Quinn Drummond's neighbor, the stuffy Brit snatched her package right out of her hands.

"I'll see that she gets it," he said. Then he shut the door right in her face.

Of all the nerve. He'd just dismissed her! She had half a notion to lean on the bell until someone else came to the door, someone who knew her. But she merely stood there, gaping, dumbfounded by the man's rudeness.

Three seconds later—and yes, *seconds* because she'd counted them off as an attempt to hold her temper—the door swung open again. This time, Jeanne Marie peered out and broke into a smile. "Hi, sweetie. Come on in."

Amber hesitated. "I'm not so sure I should." Nor did she want to. Her mother had been longtime friends with Jeanne Marie, but even the woman's warm welcome couldn't lessen the insult of the snobby man's bad manners. What a jerk.

"Don't pay any mind to Jensen. He's just an overprotective big brother."

This was Horseback Hollow—not a Revolutionary War battlefield. What possible threat could Amber be? She was just trying to be neighborly. But she held her tongue before she popped off with something rude herself. Instead, she would graciously drop off the gift and make a proper excuse to leave. Once she'd shut the door, she could turn on her booted heel and stomp off. She'd never have to step foot on the Drummond place until the entire British side of the family—all except Amelia, of course—went back to their side of the pond.

Jeanne Marie took her hand and pulled her into the midst of the bustling holiday revelers. "Look who's here, everybody!"

Amber never had been what you'd call shy. In fact, as a former rodeo queen and barrel racer, she was used to riding into an arena full speed with her flag flying. But she hadn't expected to walk into a big ol' family Christmas celebration.

Heck fire. Yesterday was the twenty-fifth. She'd known better than to show up then.

"I'm sorry," she said. "I hadn't meant to horn in on your family celebration. I thought by waiting until the twenty-sixth, I'd miss it."

"With everyone having so many family gatherings to attend, this seemed to be the easiest way to get together."

Amber glanced at Jensen, who'd answered the door like a jerk and now appeared rather sheepish. Well, *bully* for that. It served him right for being such a snob.

Amber knew how some of the wealthy British behaved, thanks to Gram's recent addiction to the *Downton Abbey* series. And Jensen reminded her of the snooty upper crust.

Jensen approached Amber and reached out his hand in greeting, his sheepish expression morphing into one that was almost…dashing. "I'm sorry for being rude when I answered the door. We've been bombarded by some rather innovative members of the press, as well as the paparazzi lately, and I was merely trying to ward them off at the pass. Allow me to properly introduce myself. I'm Jensen, Amelia's older brother."

If Amelia's handsome big brother thought that she'd acted like a fool at the royal sight of him, at least he was gentlemanly enough not to mention it.

And while Amber had always had a stubborn streak, she'd never been one to hold a grudge. Besides, it was the Christmas season—God rest ye merry gentlemen and all of that.

So she took his hand and gave it a hearty shake. "Apology accepted. We own a spread down the road a piece."

"Do you raise cattle—like Quinn?" he asked.

"No. We breed and train cutting horses."

"Really?" He seemed to perk up and ease closer. And he held her hand a moment longer. "I'd be interested in seeing your operation sometime."

No kidding? Where did that come from? Not that she'd object. It's just that…well, he'd gone from stuffy to friendly in zero to sixty, and she wasn't quite sure what to make of it. Nor was she sure what to make of the warmth of his touch.

"Sure," she said, withdrawing her hand from his. "You can come out for a visit. I'd be happy to give you a tour."

"Would tomorrow be convenient?"

So soon?

She shook off her momentary surprise. "That's fine. The Broken R is about four miles down the road. There's a big green John Deere mailbox in front of a white wrought-iron gate. You can't miss it."

"Would there be a more suitable time for my visit?"

My, the man was certainly formal. And persistent. But then again, he was probably used to getting his way. With the ladies, too, no doubt. She smiled. "This is Texas. Our ranches are always open and ready to receive company. How about nine? Or is that too early for you?"

"I'm up bright and early. So that's not a problem."

A smile stole across her face. She wondered what time the royals considered early. She and every rancher she knew usually woke before dawn.

"So," she said, "the press has been pestering y'all?"

"Like hounds on a fox. We've grown up with it, so we usually take it in stride. But they've taken great pleasure in the fact that Amelia has fallen in love with a cowboy. And now that she's settled in Horseback Hollow and is expecting a baby, they've been making it extremely difficult on her."

No wonder he'd thought Amber was up to something when she'd rang the bell.

"In fact," Jensen said, "now that the birth is so close at hand, they've been especially wily and persistent."

"Just so they can take photographs?" she asked.

"Yes, and to be the first to report whether the new little one is a boy or a girl."

Amber, who'd always been as curious as she'd been stubborn couldn't help but turn to the handsome British royal and ask, "Which is it going to be?"

"Even if I knew, I wouldn't breathe a word of the secret. But Amelia and Quinn have decided to be surprised." Jensen crossed his arms and tossed her a cocky smile, reminding her of a Cheshire cat and making her heart scamper.

Fortunately, before she had to decide what to do about it, Jeanne Marie approached. "Can I get either of you a cup of coffee? Or maybe you'd rather have Jensen pour you some of Amelia's eggnog? You can have it with rum or without."

"You might fancy a cup with rum," Jensen said. "It's quite good. And a holiday tradition in our family. I'll pour you a spot."

Amber thanked him.

"It's been fun blending our holiday traditions," Jeanne Marie added.

"I guess change isn't always a bad thing." Amber wished she would eventually come to believe that herself.

Jeanne Marie sighed. "I don't know about that. When it comes to family, it's been fun. But not when it comes to our town and community."

"Are you talking about Cowboy Country USA?" Amber knew where Jeanne Marie was going with that. The town had seemed to split in its support of the new Western theme park that was being built near Vicker's Corners. Some thought it would draw tourists and business to Horseback Hollow and others were staunchly against its construction because they feared it would make a mockery of the Western life they held dear.

"Now, I'm not one to get political," Jeanne Marie said. "And I'm not about to make a fuss down at city hall or give speeches in Town Square on Founder's Day. But I like Horseback Hollow just the way it is."

Amber understood her concern—and that of the others, too. But she was excited to have an amusement park so close to home. She loved roller coasters and thought it would be cool to show the tourists from the rest of America how their country counterparts lived.

She'd also been approached by the casting department of Moore Entertainment about starring in their Wild West Show. And she was going to accept the offer because it would provide her with an opportunity to rope and ride again in an arena, while not having to leave Gram to run the ranch alone. She hadn't told anyone, though. No need to risk getting run out of town on a rail.

Besides, she wouldn't hurt Jeanne Marie for the world. The woman had become a second mother to her after her own mama had passed.

When Jensen returned, Jeanne Marie and Lady Josephine excused themselves and went to find seats closer to all the holiday activity.

"Here you go, Miss…" Jensen paused as he handed Amber a glass of eggnog, along with a holiday napkin. "I'm afraid I didn't catch your last name."

"It's Rogers," she said, as she took the drink and thanked him.

Jensen—Lordy, the man was handsome—tossed her an earth-tilting grin. "Are you any relation to Roy?"

"You mean Rod, who owns the R and J Auto Body in Vicker's Corners? No, I'm afraid not."

"Actually," he said, "I was referring to Roy Rogers, the old-time movie star."

Amber stole a glance at the Brit. Who in America, especially the state of Texas, wouldn't know who Roy Rogers was? She just hadn't expected Jensen to. But rather than point out their obvious cultural differences, she said, "I'm afraid that was a bit before my time."

"It's before mine, as well. But since I'm an American Western film buff, I'm familiar with all the old movie stars, such as Tom Mix, Randolph Scott, John Wayne..."

She crossed her arms and shot him a playful grin. "So you assumed that, just because I'm a cowgirl, that I should be familiar with all things Western, even from sixty and seventy years ago?" He probably also thought she sang on her horse as she cantered along in her fringed pink vest à la Dale Evans.

"I'm sorry. It appears that I'm making all kinds of false assumptions today."

"Apparently so. But you don't have to be so formal. You can call me Amber."

"Well, Miss Amber Rogers, if you'll excuse me, it looks like that eggnog needs to be replenished again."

That seemed an odd job for a man—especially a fancy-pants one like him, who was just a guest in the house anyway. Was he trying to get away from her?

As much as she'd wanted to avoid him in the past, she was a bit sorry to see him go. He was actually charming—when he wanted to be.

As he made his way to the punch bowl, which was indeed nearly empty, he was stopped several times along the way—first by one of his cousins, then by one of the children. He would smile and comment, yet he appeared to hold back, to remain somewhat aloof.

He'd seemed to lower his guard with her, though, but just for a moment. And only when they'd talked about old movies and horses.

She couldn't help watching as he moved through the

house, chatting with his family, yet milling about looking as neat and formal as his professionally pressed suit.

Jensen was a looker—if you liked the fancy and stylish kind of man who could grace the cover of a men's fashion magazine.

Of course, she'd always favored the rugged outdoorsman, like cowboys and ranchers. Real men, not city boys.

Still, Jensen Fortune Chesterfield was a sight to behold—and to study, to admire, as long as he wasn't aware of her interest.

Funny thing, though. For a man who seemed to have it all together—amazing good looks, a boatload of money, a royal family and position—he seemed to distance himself from the others.

But then again, she could see why someone as stuffy as him would be a loner. And she couldn't help feeling a bit sorry for him.

There was something about Jensen that gave her a feeling of…well, she couldn't quite put her finger on it. But it was a feeling she just couldn't quite name or shake.

It was as if she knew him—or was destined to know him.

Hmm. Now *that* was weird. Because it made zero sense. He was British royalty and wool suits. And she was one hundred percent Texas cowgirl and worn jeans. They were as ill-suited as a cutting horse at the Grand National.

You'd think that would be the end of it. But oh, no. He'd gone and invited himself out to the Broken R tomorrow. And like the goof that she was, she'd agreed to a tour. So she was stuck seeing him again.

But after that, she'd cut herself out of the herd and make a quick getaway. Because what possible good could come of a friendship between a down-home country girl and the lord of the manor?

Chapter Two

Amber had expected to see Jensen show up at the Broken R the next morning since he'd asked if he could see her breeding operation. But she'd thought he'd probably take his jolly good time, as the aristocracy was prone to do, and arrive late, driving a borrowed ranch truck, kicking up dust and trying to get used to having the steering wheel on the correct side of the vehicle.

What she hadn't expected to see was him all decked out in English riding clothes and mounted on Trail Blazer, the gelding Quinn Drummond had recently purchased from her.

Still, here he was. And she'd promised to give him a tour. So she walked down the porch steps, carrying a mug of fresh-brewed coffee, and waved as he rode up.

When he dismounted in a swift, fluid motion, she sucked in her breath at the way his jodhpurs hugged his muscular legs.

Yet she stifled a grin, too. Who the heck wore fancy English riding britches in Horseback Hollow?

"Hi," she said, which was about all she could muster, as she watched him stride toward her in a pair of swanky brown equestrian boots.

Did he think she'd invited him over to play polo? If so, he was as out of place on the Broken R as she would have been sipping tea in Buckingham Palace.

And speaking of being out of place, so was that little flutter that was racing up and down her spine.

He held the horse's reins in one hand and reached out the other to her in greeting. "Good morning."

Well, dang. The gent was certainly formal. She shifted the steaming mug to her left hand and accepted his handshake. But the moment his fingers wrapped around hers, her pulse rate spiked.

Then, upon his release, which was slow and drawn out, that little flutter took off like a flock of turtledoves, and she nearly dropped her coffee on the ground.

"I hope I'm not too early," he said.

He was too everything. Too early, too formal, too good-looking. But her grandmother had raised her to be a gracious hostess, and she didn't give voice to her racing thoughts. "Of course not. Can I get you a cup of coffee? Or tea? You guys probably prefer tea, right?"

"We guys?"

"You Brits."

He smiled and gave her a slight nod of his head. "Actually, I was hoping for a nice pot of chicory cooked over a campfire. That's what you country-and-western 'guys' drink, correct?"

The glint of amusement in his eyes sent her already soaring pulse rate into a loop de loop, but she reined it back down to earth the best she could and tossed him a smile of her own. "Fair enough. I guess we probably shouldn't make assumptions about each other. So...? Coffee or tea?"

"Neither, thank you. Amelia cooked a huge breakfast this morning. I believe she's going through what the maternity experts call 'the nesting period.' She can't stop cleaning and organizing and freezing big pans of food Quinn refers to as casseroles."

Amber laughed at the animated confusion in Jensen's eyes. "I've heard about nesting. I would imagine the responsibility of bringing another life into the world would be a little overwhelming. She probably just wants to get everything in order."

"I take it you don't have children?" Jensen glanced down at her left hand.

She moved the mug handle around, not wanting to draw attention to the fact that her ring finger was very much unadorned.

"Nope," she said. "No kids. But maybe someday."

"My aunt Jeanne Marie said you live here with your grandmother?"

"Yes, it's just me and Gram." She dumped the rest of her coffee into a shrub near the barn, then set the mug on the fence post. "Actually, I only moved back to Horseback Hollow a few months ago."

"Where were you living before that?"

My, he was certainly full of questions for a man who'd closed the door in her face when he'd thought she'd been a nosy reporter. She wondered how he'd like a taste of his own medicine. But she didn't have anything to hide. Well, other than her possible job with Cowboy Country USA. But if that came to be, and it certainly looked promising, it would soon be out in the open as front-page news for the *Cross Town Crier*, the county weekly paper. And boy, was she dreading that day...

"I traveled around," she admitted. "I was on the professional rodeo circuit for a couple of years and spent most of the time living out of a trailer."

She waited for him to lift his snooty British nose at that revelation, but he just nodded his head as if he'd expected her response.

"Like a caravan?" he asked.

"A what?"

"A *caravan*. Isn't that what you Americans call a recreational vehicle?"

"I guess—if it's a whole bunch of them. Sometimes we stayed in motels or would bunk at a friend's ranch. It's a far cry from the glamorous world you're probably used to living in. But I loved the rodeo life—the traveling and the camaraderie." In fact, after only a few months away, she was already missing it.

"It sounds quite exciting, actually. Like Dale Evans, Queen of the West."

Was he comparing her to a movie star from the fifties? Seriously?

"Dale Evans?" she asked.

He nodded, and his dark brows lifted as if he was... well, if not intrigued, then definitely interested.

She shrugged. "I guess it was kind of like that, but with faster riding and less singing."

He smiled. "I actually have a film library and collect all the classic American Westerns and some documentaries. I've even watched some of the rodeos on television. But besides an appreciation for thoroughbred racing—especially the Kentucky Derby—I'm afraid my knowledge of other American horsing sports is somewhat limited."

The tension in Amber's shoulders eased. So that's why he was here. He really *was* a greenhorn, interested in the Wild West. And if he was still going to be in town this summer, when Cowboy Country USA opened for business, he'd probably be the first in line to buy a front-row seat.

Well, she could deal with that kind of fan. And while his style of dress was better suited to a polite game of polo than to bronc busting, she'd give him a tour, just as she'd promised.

She rubbed the bay gelding's nose. "So what do you think of Trail Blazer? Though I realize you're more into the English style of riding."

"He's a fine horse. Quinn said your grandfather trained him."

"That's right. Trail Blazer is one of the last colts out of Moonshine, my pop's pride and joy. The other is Lady Sybil. She's one of our more spirited fillies."

"Lady Sybil? As in the character from *Downton Abbey*?" He arched his brow.

Amber's cheeks warmed at the connection. The last thing she wanted was for Jensen to think she was some sort of British noble wannabe like a few of the other Horseback Hollow residents. But since he was such a Western movie buff, maybe he wouldn't judge her too harshly. "Gram is a big fan of the show. Anyway, come on into the stable and you can meet her."

"Lady Sybil or your grandmother?"

Amber laughed as Jensen followed, the bay gelding trailing behind him. "No, Gram went to Vicker's Corners this morning to meet with her quilting club. And the rest of the hands are still off for the holidays. It's just me, you and the horses."

As soon as the words were out of her mouth, she wanted to snatch them back. "What I meant was that nobody else is here to bother…I mean, we're alone… Oh, heck. What I'm trying to say is that there's no reason to keep me from showing you around. Why don't we start in the barn?"

She kept walking, not wanting to turn and face him since the blush in her cheeks had probably deepened to the exact shade of red in her plaid shirt. Fortunately, the cool confines of the stable and its familiar smell of straw and horses brought her back to her senses and provided a better state of mind.

For the next thirty minutes, Amber showed him the broodmares and several new foals. "Almost all of the mares were bred and trained on our ranch. We ride and work with them, so we know their strengths and weaknesses. We're also honest and fair. If we don't have what a buyer is looking for, we can usually refer them to another breeder or trainer."

"I know horses and can see that you have some good quality stock here."

She thanked him, then led him out of the barn. While he waited near the outside corral, Amber saddled Lady Sybil, the spunky bay filly she was still training—and not planning to sell, although there'd been several substantial offers already.

"I appreciate you taking the time to give me a tour," Jensen said. "You must be especially busy with your staff on holiday."

"It's not too bad. We planned ahead and took care of all the major chores before they left."

"If there's something I can do to help," he said, "just let me know. Quinn is staying close to the house this weekend, so I have some free time."

Jensen might be an accomplished rider, but she couldn't see him helping out on the Broken R.

"Thanks for the offer," she said. "I'll keep that in mind."

He remounted Trail Blazer and together they set off to see the rest of the ranch.

Throughout their morning ride, he asked polite but inquisitive questions about their operation. It was easy to see that he had an avid interest in the ranch, although several times, she'd caught him watching her in a way that had her zinging and pinging all over.

She'd stolen a few glances his way, too. But that was to be expected. After all, the Brit was so foreign to her, it was no wonder she couldn't keep her eyes off him.

Right? That's all it was. Jensen could have been from another planet—or even another century, like the one in which Jane Austen had lived. The early 1800s, if Amber remembered what she'd learned in her English Lit class.

"You have a lovely piece of land," he said. "And an impressive operation."

"Thank you. It's been in the family for generations."

As they made their way back to the stables after their tour, it was just about noon. She wondered if she ought to ask him if he'd like a sandwich—or if she ought to send him on his way.

Seemingly he was in no hurry to leave because he dismounted first and tied up his horse while she rode Lady Sybil into the paddock.

So, now what?

She bit down on her bottom lip as she slowed her mount, giving a lunch invitation some thought, when a rumble grew in the distance.

Lady Sybil whinnied.

"Easy, girl." Amber tightened her grip on the reins and stroked the filly's neck, but with the approaching engine's roar, the horse grew more apprehensive.

A loud green car churned up a cloud of dust as it tore down the long driveway toward the ranch house, fish-tailing its way toward them.

Lady Sybil whinnied again, tossing her head back and forth. Amber leaned low over the agitated animal's neck to avoid getting thrown.

Jensen jumped over the railing and ran to her side. Obviously, he didn't realize that Amber was perfectly capable of handling the horse—or used to picking herself up after a fall—because he grabbed the horse's bridle and murmured to Sybil in his soft English accent.

The horse stilled, and Amber began to dismount. But the darned vehicle backfired and the mare bolted to the right, which threw Amber off balance.

She stumbled toward Jensen, and he slipped an arm around her, steadying her just as effectively as he'd steadied the filly.

Yet as his fingertips dug into her waist, sending a bolt of heat to her core, he unraveled just about everything else holding her together, and she darn near dropped the reins.

Thank goodness he had a hold of them, too. And her.

When he looked at her, assessing her with eyes the color of fine Texas bourbon, their faces just inches apart, her breath caught and her lips parted. But before

Amber could either think or blink, Lady Sybil tossed her head once more, and she came to her senses, pulled away and took control of the horse, just as the roaring muscle car parked in front of the house.

A dust cloud swirled around the windows, making it difficult to see who was inside, but there were two of them—a man and a woman. When the engine shut off, the driver's door opened, releasing the big band sounds of the Glenn Miller Orchestra.

Uh-oh. That explained it all. Gram had come home with that man again.

But this time, there was an upside. At least, Amber had an excuse to put some distance between her wacky hormones and the fancy British nobleman who'd aroused them.

For the briefest of moments, while Jensen had rushed to Amber's assistance, something had passed between them—an intimacy that had shocked the living daylights out of him.

The minute his hand slid around her waist, he couldn't help pulling her closer—and not just in an attempt to save life and limb. Then, when her lips parted, there'd been a moment—a single heartbeat, actually—when he'd been sorely tempted to kiss her.

Amber must have felt it, too, because she'd had such a lovely expression of bewilderment—that is, until Lady Sybil and the big green machine had put a stop to it all and reality had set in.

The driver of the green Dodge Charger, a squat older gent in his early eighties, climbed out of the car and yelled over the sound of swing music, "I can't figure out how to turn this dadgummed i-radio off."

Then he reached back into the car, took the hand of the lady who'd accompanied him and helped her to slide across the bench seat and exit through the driver's door.

But rather than calling it a day, the older gent spun the woman in his arms and lowered her into a graceful dip that should have only been attempted by the most agile of professional dancers.

Jensen found it all rather amusing.

Apparently Amber didn't because she handed him Lady Sybil's reins, then strode across the yard, reached inside the vehicle and disconnected a cord, ending the song, as well as the impromptu dance. "What are you doing?"

"Practicing our moves for the upcoming dance contest at the Moose Lodge," the elderly gent said. "I'm trying to talk Helen into competing with me, instead of with Harold Witherspoon, who don't stand a chance of winning, even with a woman as pretty as Helen in his arms."

Amber shifted her weight to one booted foot. "Gram, I thought you and Mary Trimble went to have breakfast with your quilting group."

The older lady, who wore a green floral dress and a cream-colored sweater, turned to her granddaughter with flushed cheeks and a pleasant smile. "We did have breakfast, honey. But on the way, we learned that Martha Bradshaw's relatives are all still staying at her house, which is where we usually go. So the group had a change of plans, and we decided to move over to the VFW instead. I ran into Elmer Murdock there, and he offered to give me a ride home so Mary wouldn't have to."

Amber's grandmother, whose steel-gray hair had

been woven into a French twist, fingered the side of her head and tucked a loose strand behind her ear before addressing Jensen. "I'm Helen Rogers. I recognize the horse you're riding, but I don't believe you and I have met."

"It's a pleasure to meet you, ma'am. I'm Jensen Fortune Chesterfield." Then he turned to her companion.

The short, elderly man with a gray buzz cut reached out a weathered hand and gave Jensen a firm handshake. "Elmer Murdock, United States Marine Corps, retired."

Jensen glanced at Amber, who didn't look too pleased with the newcomer's arrival.

"You Jeanne Marie and Deke's nephew?" Mr. Murdock asked him.

"Yes. I'm in town staying with my sister, Amelia."

The man's clear blue eyes traveled up and down, studying Jensen hard, but not in a threatening manner. "Those are some pretty fancy riding breeches."

"Thank you."

"Where'd you find them? Might get me a pair like that."

"Actually, I purchased them at a shop in Windsor."

"Humph. That figures. You being one of them Fortunes from England and all." Mr. Murdock crossed his arms, gave a little nod, then rocked back and forth. "You got any relatives that fought in the RAF?"

"Yes, sir. My father was a pilot in the RAF."

"You don't say." Mr. Murdock stroked his chin. "He see any action in the war?"

"Which war?"

"Any of 'em. Personally, I was too young to fight the Germans. I had to earn my stripes over in Korea. But my older brother Chester went over early and helped get you boys out of that pickle in dubya dubya two."

Clearly, Elmer Murdock was quite the spitfire, but Jensen was used to the bravado of elderly soldiers when it came to World War II and their role in it. "Then I thank both you and your brother for your service."

"You're welcome. The US of A has no match on the battlefield, which some of your kin found out for themselves back during the Revolutionary War."

"Jensen," Mrs. Rogers said, before the men lapsed into a patriotic rivalry, "I was just about to fix lunch. I hope you'll join us."

Jensen glanced at Amber, who still held Mr. Murdock's music device in her hand. A frown marred her pretty face, but he didn't think it was because he'd been invited to stay. Instead, he had a feeling it was because her grandmother had included Mr. Murdock.

And while Jensen probably ought to gracefully decline, he remembered hearing the ingredients of the franks and tots casserole Amelia planned to make for lunch, doubling the recipe so she could freeze the leftovers. Suspecting his odds for a tasty meal would be much better here on the Broken R, he said, "Thank you, Mrs. Rogers. I'd like that."

Besides, he'd enjoyed his tour of the ranch and had found Amber even more intriguing. The cowgirl had been so animated when she'd explained their operation, and when she'd talked about animal husbandry, it had sounded as if she had an advanced degree. He couldn't help wanting to spend more time with her.

"I'm so happy you'll be joining us." Mrs. Rogers flashed a smile at her friend, then hurried into the house.

Amber walked around the front of the early model Dodge Charger, assessing the vehicle that had delivered her grandmother home from Vicker's Corners. "Is this your car, Mr. Murdock?"

"Sure is. I'm getting this beauty ready for the classic car show me and some of the boys down at the VFW are planning to put on next fall. We're calling it Cruisin' Vicker's. All the cars have to be built in 1975 or earlier."

While Jensen didn't think this old heap would win any competitions, he kept his opinion to himself.

"The cars don't have to be American made," Murdock added with a sly nod at Jensen. "So if you want to ship one of your fancy MGs or Jaguars this way, you can."

"That's kind of you to invite me," Jensen said, "but I'll be in town only for a short duration."

"Well, hopefully you'll stick around for a few more weeks." The old man patted the hood of the car. "I should have the new paint job done by then, and Rod down at R and J Auto Body promised he'd order a passenger-side door, too, since I can't get the fool thing to open."

"Rod Rogers?" Jensen asked, letting the old man know that he was picking up on a few names and business owners in the area.

"Yup. That's him."

"I don't suppose he's any relation to Roy Rogers," Jensen said, more to tease Amber than anything.

"Shoot, no," Murdock said. "But he might be related to Amber and Helen."

Jensen turned back to the cowgirl he'd likened to Dale Evans, the one who'd told him she wasn't related to either man, and winked.

"No," she said. "I'm not related to Rod Rogers, the car mechanic, or to the singing cowboy."

"Well, I'd rather be related to Rod any day over that mansy pansy Roy Rogers," Mr. Murdock said.

"Really?" Jensen asked, "What's wrong with Roy? I like the Western films he made."

"Westerns?" Murdock humphed. "If you wanna watch an authentic Western, you go see something by John Wayne. Now there's a real actor. 'Course, I like him in *The Green Berets* on account of that's a good war movie, and I'm a military man myself."

Amber rolled her eyes just as her grandmother stepped onto the porch. "Elmer, can you come help me with the sweet tea?"

"'Scuse me, you two. I gotta go help sweeten Helen up." He raised his weathered hands in a sign of surrender. "What can I say? The woman sure does love my sweet tea."

Mr. Murdock lumbered toward the house and Amber shook her head.

When he was out of earshot, Jensen said, "I take it you're not a fan of Mr. Murdock."

"I like him just fine. I've known him all my life. He's a funny old codger, and I usually get a kick out of being around him. But now that he's been spending more time with Gram, it just doesn't feel right."

"What do you mean?"

"It's not that I don't want my grandmother to be happy. I do. But it's going to take a special man to take my pop's place. And I just don't think there's one out there who won't disappoint her."

Or perhaps disappoint Amber?

In all honesty, Jensen knew just how she felt. His

mother had lost her true love and soul mate when his father passed away, and he doubted she'd ever find another man to take his place.

"Besides," Amber said, "those two are so different from each other. They have nothing in common and are complete opposites. It would never work out."

"Are you sure about that?" Jensen asked. "I know Mr. Murdock seems a little…"

"Rough around the edges?" Amber said.

"Perhaps a bit. He's certainly colorful."

"Yes, and Gram is a quiet sort. She likes to stay home and bake and sew. Her idea of excitement is going to church or to an occasional movie in Vicker's Corners. But then in walks Elmer Murdock—or should I say, 'in charges Elmer.' And now she's doing all kinds of wild and crazy things."

"Like what?"

"Going on hikes with backpacks—and just because he'd made a bet with some buddy that he could get Helen Rogers to agree to go with them."

"And Mr. Murdock was able to talk her into it?" If that was so, then maybe the old girl had more feelings for him than Amber realized.

"Elmer told her that it was a charity event with all the proceeds going to the Wounded Warrior Project."

"He lied to her?"

"Elmer Murdock may be a lot of things," Amber said. "Eccentric and even annoying at times. But you'll never meet a man more patriotic and more supportive of our troops and military. He'd never make light of something like that. The event was sponsored by the Moose Lodge. He won the bet and even turned over the five dollars to the charity, as well."

"I'm not sure I—"

Amber slapped her hands on her hips. "My gram is seventy-five years old, Jensen. She shouldn't be carrying backpacks and going on hikes with a bunch of military veterans as if they were picnics in the park."

It sounded as though Mrs. Rogers might have enjoyed the outing, but Jensen didn't mention it. Not when Amber was so clearly miffed.

And miffed indeed. A fire—sparked by fierce loyalty and compassion, no doubt—lit her eyes and revealed her true spirit.

A smile tugged at his lips. He'd never much liked to see a woman annoyed, but this one was actually quite lovely—perhaps because her annoyance wasn't directed at him.

"And now this." Amber swept her hand across the length of the muscle car. "What in the world was Gram doing, blowing around town in that green death machine?"

Poor Mr. Murdock. Amber wasn't going to make this courtship easy for him.

"Perhaps she's just having a bit of fun and it will all blow over soon."

Amber let out a sigh. "I hope you're right."

When she looked up at him with soulful brown eyes, Jensen was taken aback—transported, actually—to that moment when Murdock arrived and Lady Sybil had acted up. When Jensen had stepped in to help Amber dismount and briefly thought of kissing her.

But that wouldn't do.

It wouldn't do at *all*.

"Well, we'd better put the horses away," Amber said. "Then I'll help Gram get lunch on the table."

It would seem that Mrs. Rogers already had help with that task, but Jensen kept his thoughts to himself. Instead, he watched the sexy cowgirl walk toward the barn, enjoying the way her denim jeans curved on her derriere.

He had to admit that Mrs. Rogers and Mr. Murdock didn't seem any more suited for each other than he and Amber were.

Maybe Amber had realized his interest in her and this was her way of letting him know that she didn't believe in the old adage that opposites attract.

If so, that was too bad.

Physically, Jensen was captivated by the cowgirl, but he was a rational man who understood that duty came first. And right now, his duty was to his family.

Besides, in a few weeks, six at the most, he'd be back in London, which was in an entirely different universe than Horseback Hollow. And he wouldn't think of the beautiful Amber Rogers again.

Unfortunately, for the time being, he feared that he wouldn't be able to think of anything else.

Chapter Three

Lunch went much better than Amber had expected—thanks in large part to Jensen's presence. The Brit had a dry wit and a way of making everyone feel comfortable, a skill he must have perfected as an aristocrat attending various charity events and rubbing elbows with the lower classes. Not that she knew anything about the life he actually led, but she did glance at the headlines of the tabloids whenever she stood in the checkout line of the Superette, and so his social activities were no big secret, even if he didn't have an official royal title.

Amber had expected the meal to be awkward, but unlike yesterday, Jensen hadn't seemed the least bit snobbish today.

"Thank you for a lovely meal," he said, as he rose from the table. "You're a wonderful cook, Mrs. Rogers. I enjoyed that chicken salad. And your chocolate cake was one of the best I've ever had."

"Why, thank you," Gram said. "I'm glad you liked it. But please, call me Helen."

"All right, I will." He then reached across the table and shook Elmer's hand. "It was a pleasure, Mr. Murdock. Good luck refurbishing that car. I hope you win the competition."

Elmer stood as tall as his five-foot-four-inch frame would allow. "And just so you know, there's been some talk about you English taking over Horseback Hollow. Some are downright pleased and giddy about it, while others are fretting about a British invasion. But I'll have you know, you're A-OK in my book."

Jensen chuckled. "I'm pleased to hear that."

"Come on," Amber said. "I'll walk you outside."

Once they left the house and were out of earshot, she blew out a sigh. "I hope that wasn't too trying for you."

"Actually, I enjoyed myself. And I wasn't just being polite. Your grandmother is a good cook."

"I think so, too. But a man like you has eaten meals from the best chefs all over the world. So I have a feeling you've just gotten your fill of casseroles lately."

He laughed—a hearty, resonant sound that lifted her spirits, making her forget all about the green Charger parked near the house or the man inside who'd insisted upon helping Gram with the dishes.

"You have a point," Jensen said. "But that chicken salad was excellent. And so was the chocolate cake, which could rival any I've ever had the pleasure to eat."

As they made their way to the barn, where they'd stabled Trail Blazer, he added, "I hope you didn't take offense when I laughed at some of the things Mr. Murdock said. I know how you feel about him and your grandmother, so I hope you don't think I was having fun at your expense. And I'm sorry if having me here made you uncomfortable."

"Actually, having you here made it easier. And to be honest, Elmer can be a real hoot at times." Amber shook her head, then blew out a sigh. "It's just that… well, besides the fact that I think they're so unsuited— and that Gram deserves someone better than him…"

"Someone more like your grandfather?"

Amber glanced up at Jensen, caught the look of compassion in his eyes, the understanding. "Yes, there's that, too. My grandfather was an amazing man, and I'm not ready for her to find a replacement. In fact, I doubt that I'll ever be ready for that."

Jensen slipped his hands into his pockets. "I know what you mean. I lost my father four years ago. He and my mother were soul mates, and I can't imagine her ever finding another man to take his place."

They stood like that for a moment, caught up in a shared moment—probably the only thing they really had in common. Then Jensen withdrew his pocket watch—a beautiful gold-embossed piece. She expected him to open it and check the time, yet he merely turned it over a time or two, then slipped it back into his pocket.

"Perhaps your grandmother is just enjoying a little camaraderie with Mr. Murdock and they've merely struck up a friendship of sorts."

"You may be right. And if that's all it is, I guess I shouldn't worry. But Elmer always has some fool wager going on. And I'm afraid she'll get hurt—emotionally, physically or even financially. Like I said, no good can possibly come from it."

Jensen stiffened. "If the man has a gambling problem, I can certainly see your concern."

"Well, it's not as though he's mortgaged his house or ran his credit into the ground. I think it's all penny-ante stuff. But he'd wager a nickel or a postage stamp or the button off his shirt, just to make things competitive. And Gram is so honest and straitlaced, she wouldn't take a shortcut home."

Jensen placed his index finger under Amber's chin in a move so sweet, so tender, that it should have been comforting—and it was—yet it stirred something in her blood, too. Something warm and sparkly.

"You're a good-hearted woman, Amber Rogers." And…

She waited for what seemed to be the longest time for him to complete the thought—or maybe the connection he'd just made. But he did neither.

Doggone it.

But why would he? She and Jensen Fortune Chesterfield weren't any better suited than Helen Rogers and Elmer Murdock. And she was a fool to even let her thoughts drift in that direction. Because, like Gram and her silly crush, no good could come of it.

On the last day in December, while Quinn spent the afternoon at home with Amelia, Jensen took the opportunity to go for another ride on Trail Blazer.

He was still getting used to the stockier quarter horse breed and the Western tack. And while he was an exceptional horseman, he was adapting slowly.

As he cantered along on the spirited gelding, he pondered the possibility of purchasing a saddle of his own to keep in his brother-in-law's stable. In spite of his affinity for cowboy movies, he still preferred the English equestrian style for his own use.

He hadn't anticipated doing much riding at all when he'd flown to Texas for his sister's due date. But given the frequency of weddings and births taking place in America, he'd come to the realization that he would be most likely spending more time here in Horseback Hollow than he'd ever expected, so he didn't see it as a foolish investment.

After he rounded a large oak tree, he spotted a lone rider galloping toward him. He recognized the long blond hair flowing beneath the rim of the cowboy hat and watched as the cowgirl urged her mount forward.

Amber Rogers was quite the horsewoman, and Jensen pulled back on his reins, slowing so that he could fully enjoy the sight of her.

"Good morning," she said, as she pulled her horse alongside his.

"Hello, there. I thought I was still on Drummond land, but I must have crossed over onto your property line."

"Actually, this is neither. The county owns this area. It's full of riding trails, and if you follow this path far enough, you'll end up at the Hollow Springs Swimming Hole."

"A real swimming hole? Like that old movie with Marcia Mae Jones?"

At her confused look, he wondered whether Americans ever watched their own classic Western films.

But his excitement at seeing a true testament to the Wild West frontier couldn't be diminished.

"I would love to see it," he said. "How much farther do I need to ride?"

"About two miles. Come on." She turned her horse toward the narrow trail. "I'll take you up there."

He followed her slow pace and tried to keep his eyes on the trail and not her shapely bum. Thank goodness she wasn't riding at a quicker speed, otherwise he'd be completely useless ogling her graceful movements in the saddle.

When the trail widened and he pulled up alongside her, she said, "I didn't realize you were such an avid rider."

"Did you already have set expectations of me?"

"I really didn't know what to expect. The gossip magazines show you walking the red carpet and attending fabulous parties all over Europe. Of course, you're rarely smiling in those pictures, so I didn't know whether you disliked the photographers or if you're just one of those stoic Brits who doesn't know how to cut loose."

Did he really come across as that stuffy? Sure, he didn't always fancy the parties and the social commitments that came along with being a Fortune Chesterfield. But he smiled. Occasionally.

At least, he used to. Before his father's death. Yet, he didn't think mentioning this served any purpose. At the very least, it would put a damper on the present mood.

"Well, even the Brits know how to have fun," he said.

"And what, Mr. Jensen Fortune Chesterfield, do you do for fun?"

"I play polo. I attend the symphony. And I'm thinking about taking flying lessons." There he went with another reminder of his father. But instead of maintaining that painful topic, he changed the subject. "What do you do in your leisure time, Miss Amber Rogers—no relation to either Roy or to Rod?"

"I suppose you could say that I train and ride horses."

"From what I read online, you were one of the best barrel racers last year on the pro circuit."

"Oh, come now, you of all people know you shouldn't believe every news story you read." A flush of pink stole up her cheeks.

Was she embarrassed by her achievements? Or humbled by them? The tabloids had certainly exaggerated or downright lied about the things they often reported. But he assumed what he'd read about her was true.

"So then you haven't won several national titles?" he asked, wanting to hear more about her rodeo life.

"Not national titles. Just a few state ones. I was on track to go to the nationals in Las Vegas, but midseason, Pop passed away, and I left rodeoing to come back to the ranch and help Gram run things." Her eyes dimmed somewhat and took on a wistful gaze into the distance.

So he'd been right. She was being modest. From all accounts he'd read, she'd done very well in a short period of time and showed enough promise that the papers had expected her winning streak to continue. But she gave it all up rather quickly, and Jensen was learning the reason.

"Your grandparents raised you?" he asked.

"I was actually born in Lubbock, but my father died when I was five, and my mother and I moved in with his parents, Gram and Pop, after the funeral. Pop was a retired rodeo cowboy who bred and trained cutting horses. He was the one who trained me and encouraged me to follow my dream."

It sounded similar to Jensen's own father, who had encouraged him to play polo rather than follow family tradition and join the Royal Air Force. In fact, he and his father had been in the process of purchasing a polo

farm and investing in a couple of prize mares from
Argentina when Sir Simon died four years ago, taking
some of Jensen's dreams along with him.

"So you've put your future on hold to help run the
family business," he said.

"Pretty much. Besides the rodeo, I've never had
much of a plan for my life. I mean, it's not like Horseback Hollow is jumping with opportunities for barrel-
racing rodeo queens. I always figured I'd end up back
on the Broken R someday anyway, working with horses.
I suppose you can say that I just started doing that a bit
earlier than I expected."

Jensen nodded. "When my father passed away, it
forced me to step back and look at my life and what
I ought to be doing with it. Someone had to take over
the reins of the family investments and enterprises, as
well as Chesterfield Ltd., and since I'd been educated
and groomed to do so, I took the helm. Fortunately, I
can handle a lot of it remotely—although, with the time
difference, I'm working online and on Skype at some
strange hours."

"When do you sleep?" she asked.

"I find the time. I also take a nap now and then. The
most important thing to me has always been my family, and now that my father's gone, the responsibility
of looking after them has passed along to me. Hence
the reason I was so rude to you when you came to see
Amelia the other day. I fear I'm terribly overprotective."

Amber smiled. "I can understand that. I never had
any siblings. You're very lucky to have such a big family."

"I try to remind myself of that, although it does take
quite a bit of getting used to. As you may know, we only

recently met all of our Fortune cousins, so I'm still coming to terms with such a large addition to the family."

"But your British side of the family wasn't all that small."

No, it wasn't. His mother had been married before—to Rhys Henry Hayes. It hadn't been a happy union and had ended in divorce. The one good thing, though, was that it had produced Oliver and Brodie, Jensen's older brothers.

Fortunately, his mum had met Sir Simon, the love of her life, soon after. Together they'd had Jensen, followed by Charles, Lucie and Amelia.

"I suppose a family of six siblings sounds pretty large to an only child," he said.

"Large? I'd call it enormous. Do you get along?"

"Other than a few little tiffs now and again, yes. But I'd have to say we owe that to the parenting skills and the love of our mum and my father."

They rode through a tree-lined summit that opened up to a pristine and scenic waterfall. The red rock cliffs surrounding the swimming hole provided a stunning backdrop to the calm blue water below.

"Here it is. Horseback Hollow's hidden gem."

"I can see why the residents would want to keep it private. It's beautiful. Do you swim in it?" The thought of Amber Rogers in a two-piece swim costume stirred his blood in a way he hadn't expected.

"Not this time of year." She swung off her horse and tied the reins to a low-hanging branch of a nearby weeping willow tree. "But come summer, the place is hopping with kids and teenagers trying to beat the Texas heat. Personally, I like it best during the winter, when it's quiet and empty and a person can just ride up here and be all alone with their horse and their thoughts."

"Really? I wouldn't have pegged you for the quiet and introspective type." He regretted his word choice when she lifted a delicate brow at him.

"Do you picture me singing 'Happy Trails' around a campfire wearing fringes and a sequined hat like Dale Evans?"

"Maybe not singing, but I definitely can see you wearing fringes and sequins, riding faster than lightning through a cheering arena." He'd actually seen photographs of her when he'd looked her up on the internet.

Her shoulders slumped, and she gazed at the waterfall in the distance.

"I'm sorry," he said. "I didn't mean to hurt your feelings."

"No, it's not that. I guess I really do miss the rodeo life more than I expected. The glitz and the crowds are just a small part of my job. The practices and the injuries and hauling my horses and my gear all across the country was the hardest and biggest part, but all that work was worth it when the horn would sound, and I'd take off racing for that first barrel. I guess I should be lucky that I still get to work with horses and ride whenever I feel like it."

"But you still miss the excitement?"

"I really do. But I'm glad to be helping Gram, which, trust me, comes with its own share of excitement—as well as its confusion. I can't believe she'd even consider entering a dance contest. She never did anything like that with Pop. I didn't even know she *liked* to dance."

"Maybe she didn't know that until she met Mr. Murdock. My mother didn't know she'd come to love Texas barbecue until she came to Horseback Hollow for her first visit. Now, every time she flies back to England, she stuffs her luggage with jars of homemade rubs and sauces. A few months ago, she brought home a cooler filled with brisket and had our cook commission a company to install a smoker on the back lawn at our Chesterfield Estate."

Amber laughed, causing him to feel ten feet tall for bringing her out of her funk. "You're right. I'm sure you didn't realize how much you would love riding in that Western saddle."

"Oh no. You're wrong. As much as I like cowboy movies, and as hard as I've tried to adjust, I just can't seem to get used to this ghastly thing. I'm going into Lubbock later this week to custom order a proper English saddle. The pommel, the stirrups, everything just sits wrong on these American rigs."

"Really?" A mischievous glint flickered in her eyes. "Is that why you ride so slowly? Are you afraid you might lose your seating, fall out of that sturdy saddle and dirty those fancy white breeches?"

The corner of her mouth tilted. She was a cocky little thing—and in need of a lesson.

As Jensen strode to his horse, he wished he had one of his thoroughbreds back home for the challenge he was about to issue. "I'll wager I can ride faster than you, despite this inferior equestrian equipment my brother-in-law provided me."

"What do I get if I win?" she asked, already mounting up.

He thought for a moment, then grinned. "If I win, you fix me a proper English tea, complete with crumpets and clotted cream. If you win, I'll take you to a real-life authentic Texas barbecue joint." He adjusted the reins in his hands, knowing that the outcome of the bet was a win-win situation for him. Either way, he would get to spend more time with the lively and fun Amber Rogers.

"Well, Sir Jensen, I hope you like ribs, because next Monday night they have an all-you-can-eat special at my favorite spot in Vicker's Corners." With that parting comment, she took off.

He nudged Trail Blazer with his heels and leaned down over the gelding's neck, pretending he was racing for the polo ball with his mallet. Not only had he been team captain the last two years at university, but after graduation, he'd gone on to play competitively for England at the international level, so he had no doubt he could give her a good run. But after all the casseroles he'd been politely tolerating the past couple of weeks, he had a strong craving for some lighter fare—like some English cucumber sandwiches.

Still, in all honesty, some good ol' Texas barbecue wouldn't be bad, either. Especially in the company of a beautiful blonde cowgirl...

"How far are we going?" Amber called behind her, her hair whipping about her graceful neck.

"To that fork in the road where we met," he yelled back, trying to watch the trail and not her hips moving fluidly in the saddle.

When they finally reached the finish line, Amber was at least two lengths ahead of him. She pulled up first and slowed her horse to a walk as he did the same.

He hadn't enjoyed losing a race so much in his life.

They were both out of breath, but her shirt was the only one that had come unbuttoned at the top. He couldn't take his eyes off the way her breasts were heaving under the fitted plaid material.

He lifted his gaze long enough to see her smile. Maybe making the wager was a bad idea. Now he owed her dinner, yet he didn't know how he could sit across from her at a restaurant table and keep his thoughts strictly on the food.

"So when is dinner?" she asked.

"How about next Friday night? That way, we can avoid the New Year's holiday, as well as the all-you-can-eat crowd."

"That works for me."

"I'll pick you up at six."

"Sounds like a date," she said. "But under the circumstances, maybe it would be best if I met you there."

He pondered her suggestion for a moment longer than he probably should have because she added, "Don't you agree?"

And in truth? Probably so. No need to set the paparazzi to thinking there was another British royal enamored with a Horseback Hollow local. "You're right. Knowing the tabloids the way I do, they'd love to make something out of nothing."

"Well, they can't blame you for eating dinner with a neighbor."

"That's right."

"Oh, and please let Quinn know I'll be bringing Amelia's cutting horse over Friday." Then she turned in the direction of her ranch.

Jensen felt a bit like a heel when he and Trail Blazer headed in the opposite direction. He'd become adept at dealing with the tabloids. They printed blaring exaggerations about him all the time.

But the truth of the matter was, he didn't want Amber to get the wrong idea about them. He might be attracted to her, but that's as far as it would go.

So as they each headed home, the symbolism of them going their own ways at the fork in the road was both sad and true.

Bright and early Friday morning, on the second of January, Amber handpicked a filly she thought Amelia would like and brushed her until her coat shone. Then she loaded her in the trailer and drove her to the Drummond ranch.

Along the way, she spotted two cars parked on the side of the road, neither of which she recognized. She slowed up, mostly because she was going to turn, but also because curiosity niggled at her.

There seemed to be some whispering going on—a camera snatched out of one car and taken to another?

Uh-oh. Jensen had mentioned the media had tried all kinds of tricks, wanting to snap photos of a pregnant Amelia. She turned into the drive, yet continued to check her rearview mirror.

No cars…

Wait. A light blue sedan was parked in the shade of an oak tree. A man climbed out of the rear passenger seat. He was wearing black slacks and a white shirt. And he carried a camera with a huge telephoto lens.

The driver remained behind the wheel, but a second man got out, as well. And they proceeded to walk down the drive toward Quinn's house.

Nosy reporters.

Amber pulled up close to the barn and parked, but she left her purse in the truck. Then she marched up to the front door and knocked, prepared to tell Quinn or Amelia or whoever answered that there was possibly a cameraman and a reporter nearby.

Dang. Where was everyone? She knocked again.

Maybe they weren't home. Something told her they wouldn't like those reporters trespassing. Jensen had implied as much last Friday. But what should she do? Run the paparazzi off? Did she have a legal right to do that?

About the time she was going to walk away, the door swung open, and she looked up to see Jensen standing in the entryway.

"You came just in time for all the excitement," he said. "Just before dawn, my sister went into lab—"

"Jensen!" Amber had to shut him up. And there was only one way she could think of that would do so quickly. So she wrapped her arms around his neck and drew him into a close embrace, whispering, "There are a couple of reporters skulking around right behind me. Play along." Then she rose up on tiptoe and kissed him.

Chapter Four

*P*lay along?

The moment Amber wrapped her arms around Jensen's neck and pressed her lips to his, it was easy to fall into the little scheme she'd concocted. His mouth was much too busy to speak, so he couldn't possibly blurt out that his sister had gone into labor. Nor could he tip off the reporter that Quinn had taken her to the hospital just a couple of hours ago, leaving Jensen the only one home on the ranch.

In fact, as Amber's peaches-and-cream scent enveloped him, as her lips parted and he tasted—brown sugar and…spice?—she leaned into him. He couldn't help but draw her close and caress the curve of her waist, the slope of her hips.

Who would have guessed such a feminine creature hid beneath all that denim and flannel?

And who would have known that the pretty cowgirl could kiss like this?

When the camera flashed behind them—not once, but a second time—Jensen came to his senses, ending the little sideshow they'd put on for the paparazzi. Amber may have saved his sister from being headline news, but she'd inadvertently given the tabloids another gossip-worthy story to publish. But he'd have to deal with that fallout later.

In the meantime, he took her by the hand and pulled her into the house—and out of the camera's view. Then he quickly shut the door behind them and turned to face her.

"I'm sorry," she said, "but I spotted a couple of men outside who had to be reporters. And I was afraid you were going to say something about Amelia being in labor, and I figured you wouldn't want them to hear that. So I did the only thing I could think of to shut you up."

She was quite flushed—not just her cheeks, which would explain a bit of embarrassment, but her throat and neck, too.

Had that kiss aroused more than gallantry on her part? It would seem so, and he couldn't help but smile.

"What's so funny?" she asked. "You were saying that Amelia was in something or other. And I jumped to the conclusion that she might be in labor."

"You're right. That's what I was going to say. And no, I didn't want the reporters to hear."

Amber brightened. "So Amelia really *is* in labor?"

"Yes, since early this morning. Quinn took her to the hospital in Lubbock right before dawn."

"So what are you doing? Waiting for a phone call?"

"That's exactly what I was doing. She wasn't due

until the first of next month, although her obstetrician didn't seem overly concerned. Still, I can't help worrying about it, though."

"I can understand that."

"She was under a great deal of stress early on, and those reporters made her life miserable. I can't help thinking that might have brought on early labor.

"But now they're outside again, ready to steal her joy and happiness again. They probably plan to camp out at the ranch until the baby's birth. Fortunately, she and Quinn managed to slip away while it was still dark, but now I'm undoubtedly stuck. I'm not sure how I'll go about leaving without them following me."

"Do you have the keys to that ranch pickup that's parked behind the barn?"

"Yes, the key should be hanging on the hook near the back door."

"Then maybe I can help. The reason I came was to bring that filly Quinn asked me to deliver. Why don't I go outside and make a big show of getting her out of the trailer? I can saddle her and do a little trick riding in the corral that's on the other side of the house. If the reporters are watching me, maybe you can slip out the back without them noticing you."

"How very Annie Oakley of you."

"Are you making fun of me?"

"On the contrary. I actually think it's quite a clever plan that just might work. And I do hope it does. Otherwise, I'll have to wait here and try to sneak out under the cloak of darkness."

"How very Sherlock Holmes of you."

He laughed. "What a team we make."

Now it was her turn to chuckle. "That's true. But just wait and see. We'll *git 'er done*, ol' chap."

"Apparently, we will. And those reporters won't know we've been having a go at their expense. Thanks for being my partner in crime."

"Anytime. That's the cowboy way." She glanced down at her scuffed boots, then back at him. "Hey. About that kiss…"

"Don't give it another thought, Amber."

She smiled, and the concern that had once troubled her brow eased. "Okay, then I won't."

He was glad that she seemed to shake it off as though it had never happened—the kiss and the reporters who'd recorded it all.

Unfortunately, he'd be thinking about it for the both of them—and not just the camera flash and the rippling effects of what that might mean. Because the memory of her taste, the feel of her in his arms, the flush on her cheeks and throat, would linger in his mind for a long, long time.

She'd jumped in to save the day, and it had worked in a surprising, blood-stirring way.

What an odd, mismatched team they made. The polo enthusiast and the cowgirl. The Brit and the Texan.

The tabloids were going to have a field day with that one.

Amber hadn't heard a word from Jensen or anyone remotely related to the Drummonds or the Fortunes since she'd run interference for them two days ago. And while she'd hoped someone would call to give her news about Amelia, she really hadn't expected them to.

She just hoped that everything went okay—and that the baby was healthy.

Other than her scattered thoughts, it had been business as usual on the Broken R. After breakfast, she'd lined up the foreman and ranch hands on the chores that needed to be done. Then she'd checked on the broodmares and worked with Lucky Charm, a gelding who was showing a lot of promise.

It had been a productive morning. That afternoon, Gram drove into town to run some errands and to pick up groceries at the Superette, while Amber went into the office and spent the next two hours paying bills, reconciling the checkbook and catching up on some year-end bookkeeping.

She'd no more than printed off a report for the accountant when the sound of an approaching vehicle caught her attention. She glanced out the window just in time to see Gram's Ford Taurus speed into the yard and skid to stop, a swirl of dust settling around the black sedan.

The mild-mannered woman never drove over the speed limit, and to come racing home…? Why, that bordered on recklessness.

See? Elmer Murdock *was* a bad influence on her.

Determined to ignore the behavior and not make any more fuss about Gram's dating habits, hoping that the excitement would run its course and fizzle out, Amber glanced down at the printout. That was, until Gram's shrill voice called out from the kitchen.

"Amber Sue Rogers! Get on out here as fast as your little legs will carry you. What in blue blazes is this all about?"

It had been ten or more years since Gram had lit

into Amber, although even then, she'd been fairly soft-spoken and mellow about it. So she was clearly worked up about something, and the angry shriek kicked Amber's pulse rate up a notch.

So after pushing back the desk chair, Amber hurried to the kitchen to see what all the commotion was about.

She found Gram standing beside the scarred oak table, holding a newspaper—or rather a tabloid—clucking her tongue and shaking her gray head.

"What's wrong?" Amber asked.

Gram turned the paper around and flashed a front page photo of a couple kissing. Well, not just any couple. It was Amber and Jensen standing smack-dab on Quinn Drummond's front porch.

Her heart thudded and rumbled like flat tire on a wheel that was falling off its axle.

How the heck did a national tabloid get a photo printed so quickly? Those dang reporters must have emailed it to the home office as soon as they took it, along with some cock-and-bull story to explain what they imagined they saw. Because other than the pictures they took of her riding the mare, there was nothing to report because she hadn't said a single word to them.

"Girl," Gram said, "you're front-page news. It doesn't list your name, but I know it's you. And so will everyone else in town."

Sure as shootin', it was Amber, all right. And there was no mistaking the headline, either. Sir Jensen and Texas Cowgirl Caught in Royal Liplock!

"What's this all about?" Gram asked.

"It wasn't a real kiss, if that's what you mean. And there's no romance going on between us. It was just an act, a ploy to distract a tabloid reporter who was hanging around the Drummond ranch."

"Distract him from what?"

"From learning that Amelia was in labor and that she'd been taken to the hospital."

Amber snatched the paper and scanned the article, which didn't appear to mention the Drummonds at all, other than to say that the Fortune Chesterfields seemed to be fixated on the "bucolic commoners in quaint Horseback Hollow."

What a crock of bull. They made normal, down-home country folk sound like a novelty that the rich and famous would soon grow tired of.

"Did the ploy work?" Gram asked.

Amber glanced up from her reading. "In terms of taking the heat off Amelia? Yes, it appears that way."

But now, it seemed that heat had been transferred on to Amber, who'd gotten her fifteen minutes of unwarranted and unwanted fame.

As she continued reading about how a brazen cowgirl had launched herself into Sir Jensen's arms in an attempt to rope a British royal…well, heck. She wanted to crawl into a hole and die.

Better yet, maybe she ought to rope herself a couple of reporters and hog-tie them until *they* wanted to crawl into a hole and die. It'd serve the nosy snoops right. She did have to admit, though, the shots of her in the saddle were pretty good. She smiled, remembering the clicking of shutters and photographers' gasps as she nailed several of her trademark riding tricks. When it came to showmanship, she definitely had the knack.

"Speaking of Amelia," Gram said. "How is she? Did she have her baby?"

"I don't know." Amber set the tabloid on the table and tapped her finger at the photo that took up most of the front page. "After that silly kiss, I went outside and took the filly out of the trailer. Then I saddled her and proceeded to ride around the yard, doing a few tricks. If you turn the page, you'll see a couple of shots where I'm showing off for the cameraman and the reporter, which is how Jensen was able to slip away and head to the hospital."

Gram reached into the grocery bag, withdrew a tub of spreadable butter and placed it in the refrigerator. "I hope he appreciated your help because I'm afraid that article is going to make you look like a hussy."

Amber lifted her hand and fingered her lips, recalling the kiss that had shocked the wits out of Jensen— and had nearly stolen the breath out of her.

He seemed to have appreciated the diversion, although now she wasn't so sure. She might have just helped him exchange one sticky wicket for another.

The telephone rang, and Gram answered. "Hello? Yes, it is."

Amber didn't give the call much mind, thinking it was some kind of telemarketer or one of Gram's quilting friends wanting to be the first to know whether it was truly little tomboy Amber Rogers plastered all over the racks above the grocery store checkout aisles.

"Goodness, it's no bother at all. And yes, she's right here."

Her? As in *Amber*? Who could it possibly be? She didn't give people of any importance, like friends or someone from the casting department of Cowboy Country USA, the telephone number to the house. They called her cell. And speaking of that casting director—Perry or Terry What's-His-Name…

The guy had gotten it in his head that she could not only rope and ride, but that she'd look great dressed up as a saloon girl. So he'd been trying to talk her into auditioning for a part as a dance-hall girl in some indoor stage show they planned to have called Madame LaRue's Lone Star Review.

Never mind that Amber had never been to France and couldn't do the cancan. Apparently, they had dance instructors who could teach her all she needed to know.

"May I tell her who's calling?" Gram asked.

Boy, that guy was sure persistent.

"Why, hello, Jensen. I'll get her." Gram covered the telephone receiver and whispered, "I knew it was him, but I didn't want him to think I was all gaga over him like some folks in town—especially after that stupid tabloid hit the newsstand."

She was right. Some of the locals saw dollar signs whenever they spotted one of the Fortunes because they considered them as rich as ol' fury. And with the Fortune Chesterfields now in town, some people acted as though they were related to the queen of England.

Amber took the receiver, cleared her throat and willed her voice to sound as though kissing royalty and being on the front page of a tabloid were just as normal as…well as wearing a saloon-girl costume and dancing the cancan.

"Hey," she said. "I'm glad you called, Jensen. How's your sister? Did she have the baby?"

"She's doing splendidly. She had a beautiful baby girl early this morning—about six o'clock."

She was in labor for two days? "It sounds as though she had a rough time of it."

"Actually, her labor would start, then stop. And because she wasn't due until the first of February, her doctor was reluctant to induce her labor—or to send her home. She wasn't overly uncomfortable until last night, when her water broke—and then they gave her an epidural."

"How much did the baby weigh?"

"2.7 kilograms."

Amber's breath caught. "That sounds awfully small. Is everything okay?"

He paused. "Oh, I'm sorry. I forgot that you Americans aren't on the metric system. She weighs about six pounds—maybe a bit less."

"Then she wasn't too small. You Brits do things so differently."

"I'm afraid it's the other way around, my dear. But I'm much too happy to argue with you. Mother and daughter are doing very well."

"I'm glad to hear it." Amber blew out a sigh of relief. "I'd been wondering how things were going—and I'd planned to call Jeanne Marie and ask."

"You would have had to call her on the mobile. She's here at the hospital with us."

"That's not surprising. I'm sure she's been nearly as excited about the new baby as your mother is."

"That's true. They're both beside themselves and planning shopping trips already—now that they know the baby is a girl." Jensen laughed.

"Well, thanks for calling," Amber said.

"I also wanted to let you know that Amelia would like to speak with you."

Amber glanced at the tabloid on the kitchen table. No doubt Jensen's sister had gotten wind of the latest gossip. The realization poked at her like a pinprick to a helium balloon, and all the levity she'd experienced a heartbeat ago whooshed out, leaving her empty, deflated.

Was the new mother upset about her providing more Chesterfield fodder for the news rags? Had it caused her more grief and uneasiness on a day that should have been one of the happiest of her life?

Maybe Amelia wanted to ask Amber to stay away from her, Quinn and the baby from now on.

If that was the case, this would be her first—and maybe her only chance—to see the baby. At least, until Jensen left town and news of the poor and desperate cowgirl's attempts to land a royal husband died down.

"Can you slip away for a while?" Jensen asked. "The nursing staff have strict orders not to allow any visitors, other than the ones who are already here and are now leaving, but I can get you in."

"Amelia wants to see me in person? *Today?*"

Couldn't it wait until she was released from the hospital? Until she was feeling better?

"Yes," Jensen said. "So I thought it might be best if you met me someplace discreet."

No doubt because the reporters hadn't shown up at the hospital yet. And since they probably assumed Amelia and Quinn were still at the ranch. Maybe they were staked out there, so Jensen was afraid to go home. Or maybe they were now following Amber.

"Sure," she said. "Of course. Where do you think we should meet?"

"I know this sounds pretty clandestine, but if your

grandmother wouldn't mind driving you into town later this evening, she could drop you off at one of the local eateries. Then maybe you could slip out the back door, and I could pick you up."

"Perhaps I should wear a costume of some kind."

"I don't know if that would be completely necessary."

Amber had meant the comment to be tongue-in-cheek, but Jensen clearly hadn't picked up on it. So she took it a step further. "A black trench coat might be better than cutting eyeholes out of a brown paper bag and wearing it over my head."

"Are you annoyed?" he asked.

"Mostly with myself and this darned predicament I seem to have gotten us into. I should have known better than to have kissed you."

Silence stretched across the telephone line for a moment, and she was suddenly more embarrassed about bringing up the kiss rather than the entire incident itself. And why was that?

"For the record," he said, "I thought that kiss was rather nice."

"Nice? Well, that's a relief. At least you didn't find it dull or nasty."

"In spite of what you said to the contrary, it appears that I've managed to offend you yet again and that was never my intention."

Amber blew out a sigh. "I'm sorry, Jensen. It's just that I'm looking at a blasted tabloid and reading about how I've set my sights on marrying a British prince so I can move to London and drink tea with the queen. And all I was trying to do was help you and your family. Now people are going to think I'm some kind of highfalutin gold digger."

"I know better than that. And I would wager that most people who know you would agree."

A slow smile stretched across her face. "Thank you for that. I just hope your sister and the rest of your family does, too."

"We're aware of how the paparazzi creates stories out of nothing. This is old hat for us. So don't worry about anyone from my family believing that rot."

She supposed that was true. But his sister was trying to live a normal life in Horseback Hollow, and she probably didn't care for any extra notoriety these days.

Still, Amber couldn't imagine why Amelia would want to speak to her, especially now—and in person. It couldn't possibly be about anything other than the media headlines. And to be honest, Amber dreaded the meeting.

But she wasn't a coward. So she'd have to face the music—or in this case, the new mama.

In spite of Jensen's assurance that they act normally, it still seemed pretty cloak-and-dagger to Amber.

At exactly seven o'clock, she and Gram pulled into the parking lot of the VFW, where they left the Ford Taurus next to Elmer Murdock's army-green Dodge Charger. Amber wore her customary Wrangler jeans, although she'd chosen a white feminine blouse and a new black sweater to ward off the winter chill. She'd also applied more makeup than usual and had left her hair long and loose, the tendrils glossy and curled on the ends.

Then she and Gram went inside to meet her grandmother's unlikely gentleman friend. Amber stayed long enough to drink a diet soda, to make small talk and to ask Elmer to drive Gram back to the ranch. Needless to say, the Korean War vet was more than happy to oblige—and Gram was pleased with the game plan, too.

Twenty minutes later, as dusk was settling over Horseback Hollow, Amber excused herself and walked to the feed store, which was closed. But that didn't matter. She had no intention of going inside. Instead, she slipped around to the back, where Jensen was waiting for her in Quinn's pickup, the engine idling. Then she opened the passenger door, climbed inside and off they went.

They traveled a circuitous route to the hospital in Lubbock, arriving well after dark—and right before visiting hours ended for the night.

As they entered the lobby, which still bore Christmas decorations although New Year's had just passed, Amber said, "It looks like we managed to avoid those pesky reporters."

"This time, and when you outwitted them two days ago and helped me escaped. You're a clever actress. Your ploy worked."

Jensen probably had no idea how his compliment pleased her, how it pumped her confidence and encouraged her to go ahead and audition for Madame LaRue's Lone Star Review. Why not? It might be fun, whether she landed the spot or not.

When they stopped at the elevator, he pushed the up button, then turned to her and smiled. "Perhaps you should be living in Hollywood instead of Horseback Hollow."

Fortunately for her, with Cowboy Country USA opening just outside town, she wouldn't have to move from the ranch at all. "Thanks. Play-acting is a tal-

ent I'm just learning to perfect." And just in case he'd
read too much into that little kiss she'd given him, she
added, "So don't get too caught up in the local gossip
about me being swept off my boots by you. That little
smooch was all part of the show."

"Is that right?" His lips quirked into a sly grin.

He might be having fun at her expense, but she ignored the tease and merely nodded.

"Then you really are a jolly good actress." He
reached out and fingered her throat, where her pulse
fluttered. Dang. Did he feel it trembling?

She swallowed, no doubt giving him something else
to feel in there.

Where the heck was that darn elevator?

But she shook off the pesky little flutters and trem-
bles. "What are you getting at?"

"That kiss on Quinn's porch. The one you said was
no big deal."

"What about it?"

"Afterward, when we went inside, your cheeks were
rosy. But so was your neck and throat. How did you
manage to get that flush to spread like that? I'm amazed
that you were able to just close your eyes and conjure it
there with no help from me or any good, old-fashioned
chemistry. Like I said, you're a very good actress. Either that, or a very bad liar."

She had to admit she'd been shaken by the kiss, although she hadn't wanted to admit it to him—or even
to herself.

But the trouble was, she had been thinking about it a
lot more than she should. It may have started out as an
act—all fun and games. But she'd never experienced a

kiss quite like that before and she doubted she'd ever experience the like again.

Fortunately, the elevator door finally opened, interrupting the intense questioning of his eyes and allowing her to pretend as though they'd been talking about something else.

"All aboard," she said. "Which floor is Amelia on?"

"The fourth."

Before she could push the button, two other people joined them. *Thank goodness! Saved by strangers.*

A couple of elevator dings later, Jensen walked Amber through the double doors that led to the maternity ward and on to room 411, where they found Amelia comfortably nestled in her hospital bed, holding her daughter in her arms.

The tired but glowing new mother looked up from the precious swaddled bundle. "Oh, good. You're here. Thank you for coming, Amber."

"Where is everyone?" Jensen asked.

"Mum and Aunt Jeanne Marie just left with Quinn. They're having dinner at a restaurant down the street. I believe they'll be heading back to Horseback Hollow, but Quinn will be staying the night with the baby and me. And he promised to bring me back some shepherd's pie. I don't know when these pregnancy cravings will go away, but this hospital food isn't really to my liking."

Amanda eased closer to the bed and peered at the sweet newborn who dozed in her mother's arms. "She's beautiful. And so small. But I'm sure she'll be playing dress up with her cousin Piper and pushing dollies in their strollers in no time at all."

"I'm sure you're right. Plus, Quinn's sister Jess just

gave birth to a baby girl two nights ago. So she has another new cousin to play with."

"Three little girls all close in age," Amber said. "Won't that be fun?"

"What's especially nice is that Jess and Mac have five sons so, needless to say, they're delighted to finally have a daughter to love and spoil."

"I'll bet they are!"

As Amber and Amelia marveled over the sweet newborn, Jensen asked his sister, "Is there anything you need? I'd be happy to pick it up for you."

"I talked to Stacey," Amelia said, "and I think I'm going to need more nappies."

"I'm sure you will," Amber said. "From what I hear, newborns don't sleep through the night for several months. So you won't be getting much sleep."

Jensen furrowed his brow. "What does sleep have to do with it?"

"Taking naps?" Amber asked. "I would think that your sister will need to take plenty of them."

Amelia laughed. "I was talking about diapers. We call them nappies in England."

"You've sure done some strange things with our language," Amber said.

Jensen gave her a little nudge. "I beg to differ. If I remember my history lessons, the English language was well established before your little American colony began butchering it."

Amber elbowed him right back. "And we dumped your tea into the harbor and taught you a lesson or two, if I remember correctly."

"Listen, you two, if your revolution reenactment wakes the baby, I'll have to ask you to take it outside my hospital room," Amelia said, as she smirked and nuzzled her newborn closer.

"We'll save it for later," Jensen said. "Besides, visiting hours are nearly over."

"Then, if you don't mind, I'd like to talk to Amber alone."

"Of course," Jensen said. "I'll step outside into the hallway."

Here it comes. Amelia was going to lay into her for practically mauling her brother in public. But Amber was a big girl. She could take her licking.

"Thank you for distracting that reporter at the ranch," Amelia said. "It allowed Quinn and I to have our privacy during this special time in our lives."

"You're welcome. Although, I apologize for opening up a whole new can of worms for those crazy tabloids. Now they think Jensen and I are a hot topic."

"Would that be so bad?"

Amber drew back. Was she kidding? While a lot of mothers opted for natural childbirth, the British woman must've chosen to use drugs. Was Amelia flying high on some kind of medicine that bypassed her baby's bloodstream but had her dreaming romantic fantasies?

Amelia studied Amber carefully, smiled and nodded. "You're just what Jensen needs."

Seriously? Amber slowly shook her head. "I'm afraid you've got it all wrong. It was just a little kiss between friends."

"The camera caught a spark. And I've seen the banter between you. My brother hasn't lit up like that since before my father passed away. And even then…well, I think there's something going on."

Oh, boy. Maybe the euphoria of being a new mother

was making her see things that clearly weren't there. "I'm afraid it was all an act."

Amelia shook her head. "You can deny your feelings the way I denied mine for Quinn. But it will be futile. Once my brother sets his sights on a prime piece of horseflesh, he can be as stubborn as Churchill's bulldog."

Had Amelia just called her a horse?

The Brits had such an odd way with words. Maybe it was best that Amber not take offense, especially when the new mother had been so sweet and so understanding.

Amelia glanced down at her little one, then checked the baby's diaper. "Well, what do you know? I'm going to have to change her nappy, then put her down for a nappy."

They both laughed.

"I'll let you get to it, then," Amber said. "And it's probably a good idea if you both get some rest. Thanks so much for understanding about that darn photo." Even if Amelia didn't understand that nothing was going on between Amber and her brother.

"Thank you. We might need you to pull another stunt to help us sneak home undetected."

"I don't know about that. I'm afraid this cowgirl isn't used to being front-page news. But I'll run the idea past Jensen." She tossed her new friend a smile. "You have a beautiful baby, Amelia. Take care."

Then she slipped out of the room and went in search of Jensen. She found him near the water fountain in the corridor.

"That was quick," he said. "What did she have to say?"

"Not much. She thanked me for helping lead the paparazzi astray. That kind of thing."

As they continued out of the hospital, he glanced her way a couple of times. She figured he wasn't buying her explanation. But there was no way she'd tell him what Amelia had really said, especially about there being some kind of spark in that kiss—as nice and moving as it was. Or that he needed someone like Amber. Imagine that.

He opened the lobby door, and they stepped out into the winter night.

"I forgot to ask if they'd chosen a name for the baby." In truth, she'd been so worried about the conversation Amelia intended to have with her that she'd been thrown off step.

"Clementine Rose."

"How cool is that? Your sister gave her daughter a Western name."

"What do you mean?"

Amber broke into song, singing the familiar old diddy that Pop used to hum all the time, "Oh, my darlin', oh, my darlin', oh my darlin', Clementine…"

"Actually," Jensen said, "the baby was named after my father's mother—Clementine."

"Oh. And the Rose…?"

"Amelia just likes the name."

Jensen opened the passenger door of Quinn's pickup, and Amber slid inside. Then he climbed behind the wheel and they were off.

The ride back to Horseback Hollow was pretty quiet, the silence stretching between them like a taut rubber band that was ready to snap.

When they finally reached the feed store, where

they'd met earlier, he parked in front, under an old streetlight that wasn't working. It was only a couple of doors down from the VFW, where Gram had left the Taurus for Amber to drive home.

When Amber reached for the door handle, Jensen asked, "What's really bothering you?"

She turned back, deciding to finally level with him. But instead of taking her time to think up a careful explanation, her words came out in a near rush after being pent up for so dang long. "It's just that Amelia thinks we're really a couple, and I know that's not true. Heck, we're barely even friends. Anyone can see that. A man like you would never want a girl like me, and you're probably laughing on the inside and—"

Jensen leaned across the seat, placed a hand behind her neck, drew her lips to his and stopped her deluge of words with a kiss that soon deepened to the point that her hands didn't want to stay put.

Amber wasn't sure how long it would have lasted or what it might have led to if Jensen hadn't inadvertently leaned against the horn, setting off a loud, ear-splitting honk that made them jerk apart and left them both breathless.

"What...was...that...kiss?" She stopped, her words coming out in raspy little gasps.

"...all about?" he finished for her.

She merely nodded.

"I don't know. It just seemed like an easier thing to do than to discuss."

Maybe so, but being with Jensen was still pretty clandestine, what with meeting in the shadows, under the cloak of darkness.

The British royal and the cowgirl. They might be attracted to each other—and she might be good enough for him to entertain the idea of a few kisses in private or even a brief, heated affair. And maybe she ought to consider the same thing for herself, too.

But it would never last. Especially if the press—or the town gossips—got wind of it.

So she shook it all off—the secretive nature of it all, as well as the sparks and the chemistry, and opened the passenger door. "Good night, Jensen."

"What about dinner?" he asked. "I still owe you, remember?"

Yep, she remembered. Trouble was, she was afraid if she got in any deeper with him, there'd be a lot she'd have a hard time forgetting.

"We'll talk about it later," she said.

"Tomorrow?"

"Sure. Why not?"

"I may have to take my brother and sister to the airport, although I'm not sure when. I'll have to find out. Maybe we can set something up after I get home."

"Maybe so." She wasn't going to count on it, though. Especially when she had the feeling he wouldn't want to be seen out in public with her—where the newshounds or local gossips might spot them.

But as she headed for her car, she wondered if, when he set his mind on something, he might be as persistent as those pesky reporters he tried to avoid.

Well, Amber Rogers was no pushover. And if Jensen Fortune Chesterfield thought he'd met someone different from his usual fare—he didn't know the half of it. Because he'd more than met his match.

Chapter Five

Jensen wasn't surprised that his younger sister and brother wanted to return to London as soon as Amelia came home from the hospital with baby Clementine Rose. He'd briefly contemplated flying back with them, then returning for the weddings next month. But his mother wanted him to stay awhile longer, and he'd agreed for more reasons than one.

He'd broken things off with Monica Wainwright just before the holidays, so the trip to America had allowed him to put some distance between them.

The early days of their short-lived romance had been somewhat pleasant, but then she'd let down her guard and had shown him a selfish and haughty side he couldn't tolerate.

Besides, he owed Amber dinner for that horse race he'd lost, something he was actually looking forward to. But as soon as the weddings were over in February, he'd be making this trip to the airfield himself, rather than driving his two younger siblings and dropping them off.

So, with the flight plan set, Jensen waited for Quinn to retrieve the car keys.

"Here you go," the proud new father said.

"Thank you. It won't take long."

"It doesn't matter. Keep the car as long as you want."

Lady Josephine, who'd just entered the living room from the kitchen, said, "Wait for me, Jensen. I'd like to ride with you."

"You don't need to do that, Mum. I'm sure Charles and Lucie will understand if you'd rather stay here with baby Clementine."

"Yes, I know, but Quinn and Amelia would probably like some time to themselves, and I'd enjoy an outing. It also gives me a chance to see Sawyer and Laurel. I haven't talked to my brother's son or his wife since Christmas. Just let me freshen my makeup. I'll meet you in the car."

A few minutes later, Lady Josephine had not only applied a fresh coat of lipstick and face powder, but a subtle touch of Chanel No. 5. After she slid into the passenger seat, Jensen drove them to the B and B in Vicker's Corners, where Charles and Lucie had been staying.

Just as he'd suspected, his younger brother and sister were waiting in front of the quaint, three-story building with its green-and-white striped awnings. After they loaded the luggage in the car, they headed to the small airfield.

As Jensen turned onto the country road that led to the small terminal, his mother glanced over her shoulder and into the backseat, where Lucie and Charles sat. "Be sure to check on Oliver and ask about Ollie. I miss

that little boy so. And let me know if there is anything
I should be concerned about."

Oliver, their oldest half brother, had divorced last
year. His toddler son lived with his ex-wife.

"We'll do that," Charles said. "But I'm sure Oliver
would let you know if there was anything to worry
about."

Jensen wasn't so sure about that. He wasn't the only
one who didn't like to see their mother overly concerned
about things she had no control over.

"But, Mum," Charles asked, "can Lucie and I trust
you to take care of baby Clemmie for us?"

At that ridiculous notion, laughter erupted. Even
Lady Josephine smiled at her youngest son's attempt
to lighten the mood.

She was still grinning from ear to ear when Jensen parked in front of Redmond-Fortune Air, the flight
school and charter service owned by Sawyer Fortune
and his wife, Laurel.

The new building they'd built last year, with its gray
block walls, smoky glass windows and chrome trim,
had modernized the small airport, which up until that
point had only amounted to a small control tower, a
couple of modular buildings, several hangars and the
airstrip.

Jensen had no more than shut off the engine when Josephine exited the car and was heading for the entrance.

How strange. But then again, Mum had mentioned
that she was eager to see Sawyer and Laurel.

Lucie trailed their mother while Jensen and Charles
brought up the rear, carrying the luggage.

The small reception area was empty, although Orlando Mendoza, one of the pilots, sat in a chair, holding his smartphone and sending a text.

Upon seeing Lady Josephine, the handsome man with graying hair and sun-bronzed skin broke into a smile then stood and took her hand. "Good afternoon. What a pleasure to see you."

She flushed. "Will you be flying Charles and Lucie to Dallas?"

"No, I'm afraid not," Orlando said. "I had an early day. I just completed a charter flight to Houston, so I'm heading home. At least, I will be as soon as Sawyer returns." Orlando glanced out the window toward the parking lot, then back to Jensen. "I don't suppose you happen to be heading back through town?"

"No, but it's not too far out of the way. Why?"

"I had car trouble this morning, and my nephew, Marcos, gave me a ride to work."

Marcos Mendoza and his wife Wendy owned the Hollows Cantina.

"I'd be happy to drop you off," Jensen told Orlando.

"Are you sure it won't be any trouble?"

"Not at all."

While Orlando made small talk with his mother and siblings, Jensen wandered off to look at a table that held a plastic-enclosed display of miniature-sized scale-model aircraft. As he did so, he reached into his pocket and felt the gold watch that rested there.

He and his father used to stop by the small airfield near the Chesterfield estate, where they would watch the planes take off and land. It had been a special time, when they talked about life and hopes and dreams. Not a plane flew overhead without Jensen remembering those days.

A door swung open, and he turned to see Laurel Redmond Fortune enter the reception area of the terminal. The lovely blonde pilot had once flown jets for the United States Air Force.

After greeting Josephine and then Lucie with a warm embrace, Laurel shook hands with Charles, who could be rather stuffy at times.

"I'll be flying you to Dallas today," Laurel said. "Are you ready to go?"

Charles reached for his bags. "We certainly are. We've had a lovely time, but Lucie and I are eager to get home."

"Hey." Laurel glanced at Jensen, who stood off to the side—no doubt appearing to be as stuffy as Charles and, perhaps, more distant. "I don't suppose you're heading back into town after this?"

Jensen left the miniature airplanes, as well as his musing behind. "Orlando mentioned he needed a ride, so I'll take him wherever he wants to go."

Laurel gave him a thumbs-up, then walked out the door to the airfield, with Lucie and Charles on her heels, each carrying their own bags.

"Marcos promised to have someone fix my car while I was gone," Orlando said. "So, if you don't mind dropping me off at the Hollows Cantina, that would be perfect."

"Splendid," Josephine said. "Jensen and I haven't eaten yet, and I've had a craving for a crock of their crab dip and those tasty rice crackers."

What? No hurry to get back home to the new grandbaby? Apparently, his mum really did want the new parents to bond.

"Great," Orlando said. "I'll buy you a margarita for your trouble."

Jensen was just about to tell him that wouldn't be necessary when his mum blushed and patted the pilot's arm. "That would be lovely, Orlando."

Since when had she switched from wine to margaritas? Interestingly, Texas was beginning to have an odd effect on her.

Yet wasn't it having an odd effect on Jensen, too?

Horseback Hollow certainly didn't have a drop of culture, nor did it offer any of the nightlife he enjoyed in London. Yet he found the quaint Western town appealing—from a tourist's standpoint, of course.

He was far more comfortable on his country estate and playing polo at the nicest clubs in the UK, but he'd make the best of it for the month or so that he'd be here. Which meant spending more time with Amber Rogers.

Should he call her and ask her to meet him at the Hollows Cantina? Maybe not. But to be perfectly honest, at least with himself, he wouldn't mind sharing another kiss with her—or possibly even more than that.

Amber's stomach had been growling all throughout her Wild West Show tryout and, as she'd pulled up to the Hollows Cantina, she thought her belly would soon be ordering for her. Less than an hour ago, she'd delivered a performance that would've really knocked the socks off those so-called journalists who'd been camped out around the Drummond property.

She put the old truck in Park and checked the trailer she'd been towing to ensure that Danny Boy was resting comfortably after the barrel racing display he'd helped her put on earlier today. When she'd sat down with the bigwigs at Cowboy Country USA afterward, she let them know that if they signed her as one of their lead acts, she'd only use her own horses.

The executives had made her a surprisingly good offer, and she'd promised to have her attorney look over the contract and get back to them within a week.

She gave Danny Boy a pat and promised him a treat after dinner. Then she hitched her purse higher on her shoulder and headed into the restaurant, which was sure hopping tonight.

It was a cool place to gather, but it had gotten some flack from the locals who considered it a "rich folks' establishment" and feared that it would ruin the small town's ambiance.

The same people were against Cowboy Country USA, although their number appeared to have doubled as more of the locals jumped on the bandwagon to complain about the theme park. Even Deke and Jeanne Marie hadn't kept their objections secret. And from what Amber had gathered, most of their kids agreed.

Still, Marcos and Wendy Mendoza were seeing an increase in business these days, thanks to the Cowboy Country bigwigs frequenting the Hollows Cantina and holding some of their meetings here. So she suspected they weren't opposed to the theme park, although they were smart enough to keep their opinions to themselves.

Once inside the busy restaurant, she was met by the hostess, Rachel Robinson, who was new in town and resembled a less-glamorous Angelina Jolie.

Rachel flashed a bright-eyed smile. "Good evening, Amber. We're pretty full tonight. You're looking at a fifteen-to-twenty-minute wait unless you want to sit upstairs."

"I'm meeting my grandmother for dinner, and since things get a little chilly and loud up there, I think we'd better wait for a table down here—hopefully in a quiet, out-of-the-way spot."

"Mrs. Rogers is already here with Mr. Murdock," Rachel said. "They mentioned that someone would be joining them. I didn't realize it would be you. And they're seated upstairs."

How do you like that? Elmer Murdock was a party crasher.

"I can show you where they are," Rachel said.

"That's okay. I'll find them." Amber made her way to the middle of the room and climbed the staircase with wide iron railings and rustic wooden steps to the second floor.

She'd no more than reached the landing when she spotted Gram's trademark French twist at a table near the dance floor. Normally her grandmother kept to the quiet corners of any location, but the place was so packed, they must have seated her in the only available spot.

Amber made her way to the table and greeted her grandmother with a kiss on the cheek, just as a huge margarita glass was thrust in front of her.

No, make that *two* huge margarita glasses, each with a shot glass filled with tequila attached to the side.

And the server was none other than Elmer Murdock. "Two of the cantina's finest drinks for two of the finest women in the joint."

Gram smiled up at the man. "Why, thank you, Elmer."

Apparently, the retired marine was too busy to notice Gram's appreciation since he was asking the server, who was carrying his beer, to bring over a salt shaker and some limes.

What was he doing here? And why was he under the impression that Gram would be throwing back margaritas and shots of Jose Cuervo like a coed on spring break?

The uninvited bearer of alcoholic beverages pulled out a seat and sat a little closer to Gram than was entirely necessary, given they were at a table for four.

If he noticed Amber's lack of enthusiasm, it didn't seem to bother him. "Drink up, gals. It's a twofer one special, and we got another thirty minutes before happy hour is over."

Amber had barely registered the cheapskate comment before Elmer threw her for the next loop of the evening. "So, girlie, how did the big audition go?"

"Shhh!" Amber hoped he'd lower his voice, but she was afraid she'd have better luck trying to get a stampede of wild broncs to jump through a Hula-Hoop.

"Why?" he asked. "You ought to be pleased as punch that they'd come after you like they're doing. They know a class act when they see one."

What in blue blazes did someone like Gram, who was so refined and quiet, see in such a loudmouthed character like Elmer Murdock?

Amber took a gulp of the margarita and decided the quick hit of liquid calm would be worth the brain freeze she'd get from downing the cold drink so quickly.

Fortunately, Gram came to her rescue. "Elmer, dear, Amber wasn't quite ready to tell anyone about—"

Amber gave a discreet cough.

"Whoops." Elmer took a sip of his beer and reached into the communal basket of chips. "I won't say another word about it, then. Old Elmer Murdock is like a vault. You wouldn't believe all the secrets I know."

That was a relief. And if she took the job at Cowboy Country USA, which she planned to do, everyone would find out anyway. The lines were already being drawn in the town sand since many of the locals weren't exactly giving a warm Texas welcome to the Wild West theme park, and she'd soon be grist for the gossip mill.

She took another sip of the sweet-and-sour drink, this time a little slower than the first. She scanned the restaurant, trying to see who might have overheard the comment made by Gram's third wheel.

Of course, from the way Elmer was showing her grandmother how to lick the salt and then squeeze the lime after drinking down her tequila, Amber would have to assume that *she* was the third wheel.

"Miss Rogers! I'm so glad you're here."

Amber glanced up to see Perry—or was it Terry?— from the Cowboy Country casting department.

He must have noticed her befuddled look because he reached out his hand and said, "Larry Byerly. Cowboy Country USA."

She knew who he was. They'd met before and talked on the phone several times. It was merely his first name she was having trouble with. But she let it go at that and shook his hand.

"After that little performance you put on today down at the county fairgrounds, news traveled like wildfire. And I was told to sign that girl come hell or high water."

She'd already agreed to sign with the Wild West Show if her attorney didn't see a problem with the contract, so news didn't travel nearly as fast as Larry thought it did.

"What can I do for you?" she asked.

"It's what *I* can do for *you*. If I could just have a minute or two to speak with you in private—that's really all I need. The PR department is chomping at the bit to get a pretty local girl to feature in our ads and quite possibly the Lone Star Review. And Miss Rogers, we're all convinced that gal is you."

Again, Amber scanned the room. Luckily, there wasn't anyone around who seemed to be paying attention—other than Gram and Elmer, who were leaning into the conversation as though the fate of the entire world rested on Amber's answer. Or at least, life as they knew it in Horseback Hollow, which was crazy.

The only one she was really concerned about seeing her talk to the enemy, so to speak, was Jensen. But why stress about that?

The Hollows Cantina might be the nicest restaurant in town, but it wouldn't be Jensen's cup of tea. Besides, what did he care what she did with her life or her future anyway?

The Hollows Cantina was busy tonight. Each of the outdoor tables that lined the sidewalk was taken, the heaters blasting to keep the bundled-up diners protected from the brisk, January evening.

The second story, an open-air terrace adorned with little white lights, appeared to be just as full.

Jensen opened the door for his mother, and she stepped inside, followed by Orlando.

The distinguished pilot greeted the hostess, a lovely brunette with long straight hair and striking blue eyes. "Looks like you have a full house tonight, Rachel."

"We do, but I have a table upstairs. It's not quite

ready. If you don't mind waiting a couple of minutes, I'll take you to it."

"That's fine," Jensen said. "Thank you."

"You were telling me about your sons," Josephine said to Orlando.

"Yes, Cisco and Matteo have just settled in Horseback Hollow. I'm glad to have them nearby."

"I'm sure you are. I'll be spending more time here, now that..." She scanned the area, then lowered her voice. "Well, you know."

Orlando nodded. "I completely understand. Maybe you should consider getting a small home here, unless you want to stay with your daughter and son-in-law."

"That's a good idea, Orlando. I'll give that some thought. Maybe I can encourage my other children to buy vacation homes in Horseback Hollow. I think it would be especially good for Oliver and Brodie to have a closer relationship with their new family—at least for part of the year."

Jensen couldn't imagine either of his older brothers leaving the UK. Goodness, even Charles and Lucie couldn't get home fast enough as it was.

"Your table is ready," the hostess—Rachel—said. Then the attractive woman led them upstairs.

Jensen had no more than reached the landing when he spotted Amber seated at a table near the bar with a man he didn't recognize.

The gent was older than she—in his forties perhaps. Not bad looking—if you liked men who wore golf clothing when they socialized.

"Is this table all right?" the hostess asked, drawing Jensen's attention, but just barely.

"It's fine. Thank you."

Orlando held a chair for Josephine, yet Jensen couldn't seem to take a seat. His interest was drawn to that table for two, especially because the older man leaned forward as though pressing Amber, urging her to…?

What?

"Is there something wrong, sir?" the hostess asked.

Jensen snapped his attention back to the people he was with. "No, I'm sorry. I thought I spotted someone I knew."

His mum chuckled softly. "You did, son. Isn't that Amber Rogers, the young woman who owns the ranch near Quinn's?"

"Um. Yes," he said. "So it is."

"If I'm not mistaken, that also appears to be the young woman the tabloids spotted with you…perhaps… Photoshopped a perfectly simple picture to look like the two of you were kissing."

Jensen reached for a glass of water and took a sip. He knew exactly where this conversation was heading, and he wished she'd let it drop—especially in front of Orlando.

"I wonder who that man is?" his mother asked. "He seems quite enamored of Amber. But then, what man wouldn't be. She's actually quite lovely."

Jensen ought to be annoyed with his mum for taunting him, but he was too caught up in what was going on at Amber's table. He couldn't help his interest—nor the sharp poke of jealousy that needled him.

Somewhere along the way, they'd placed drink orders, and he'd ended up with a longneck bottle of beer. But he couldn't seem to focus on anything but Amber and that older man who was doing all the talking.

What in the hell was he saying?

She actually looked as though she'd rather be somewhere else.

Did she want to escape? Jensen was feeling rather chivalrous.

His mother was saying something, although he'd be damned if he knew what it was. He'd completely lost track of the conversation at his table and decided to put an end to his curiosity.

So he picked up his bottle of beer, stood and said the only two words he'd wanted to say since laying eyes on Amber just minutes ago. "Excuse me."

Amber wasn't sure how long Jensen had been in the restaurant before she spotted him, but he hadn't kept his eyes off her for a moment.

About the time she was trying to snatch her hand out of Byerly's and tell him she was no cancan dancer and that she didn't care if the company was prepared to hire a dance instructor to help her prepare for the stupid audition, a cool British voice said, "Miss Rogers. What a surprise."

A flood of warmth rushed through her. She wished she could say it was the effects of Jose Cuervo making its way through her system, but she was afraid it was none other than Jensen Fortune Chesterfield who'd done the trick.

Either way, she welcomed the distraction and used it as her excuse to break away.

"I'm so glad you're here," she said, tearing her hand from the casting director's grip. "Mr. Byerly was just proposing a project he wanted me to consider, but I really need to get back to my table."

Just a few minutes ago, she'd called the ranch foreman and had asked someone to come and give Danny
Boy a ride home. She hadn't planned on having a drink
tonight—but then again, she hadn't expected to feel the
need for one.

"You have my card," Byerly said. "Please call me."

"I told you I'd think about it. And I can't do that if
you won't give me the time I need. So do us both a favor
and let me be the one to make contact, okay?"

Once she'd left Byerly's table, she thanked Jensen
for the interruption. "That guy doesn't take 'we'll see'
for an answer."

"Then I'm glad I could help."

"I'm…uh, here with Gram—and Elmer Murdock,
apparently. It seems my grandmother is full of surprises."

"Actually, I'm here with Orlando Mendoza and my
mother. We just came in from the airfield, where we
dropped off my sister and brother, who are heading
back to London. When I saw you, I thought I'd come
over and say hello."

Amber glanced at Gram, who'd lifted her hand and
was waving her fingers at Jensen.

He'd no more than walked over to their table and
greeted them when Elmer pointed toward the stairs,
a gleam in his eyes. "Oh, Helen, look. Here come the
Baumgartners. Let's go schmooze it up with them and
find out what song they're planning for the dance contest. Keep your friends close and your enemies closer,
I always say."

With that, Elmer pulled back Gram's chair and
helped her to feet that had never danced even a two-
step, at least as far as Amber knew.

But before he could sweep Helen away, Amber placed her hand on her grandmother's arm and asked, "Since when are you and Estelle Baumgartner enemies?"

"Elmer is just teasing, honey. He says they're our stiffest competition. Besides, I think he's just trying to give you and your young man some time alone."

"Try the twofer happy hour special, son. They make a mean margarita here, and you can't beat the price." Elmer winked at Jensen as he ushered Helen away, his gnarled hand a little too low on Gram's back.

Jensen was most certainly not her young man. And while she appreciated Elmer giving them some privacy, she didn't like him putting fanciful notions in her grandmother's head. It was bad enough the tabloids were spreading that rumor all over the county—and the world, for that matter.

"I hear they're having quite the bang-up price on them until seven o'clock." Jensen, still standing, nodded toward her margarita glass. "Can I get you another one of those frozen drinks?"

"Oh, goodness no. Thank you. I didn't even want this one."

He raised his eyebrow at her almost empty cup, as if questioning why she would've drunk the thing down in three gulps if she hadn't wanted it in the first place. And with the way he was looking down at her, she was reminded of the first time they met. Although this time, it was her neck hurting, not her pride.

"Are you sure you wouldn't like to sit down?" she asked.

"Maybe for a moment." He took the seat next to hers. "So how did the airport run go?"

"Without a snag. My brother and sister are on their way back across the pond as we speak."

"So you're staying on here a little longer?" She wanted him to think she was just making casual small talk and that his decision to stay in town wouldn't make the slightest bit of difference to her. It wouldn't, of course. But thoughts of that second kiss he'd given her after dropping her off near the VFW the other night made her insides turn to gelatin and her mouth go dry.

How did one explain the chemistry in a reaction like that?

Her hand shook as she reached for her empty glass. Well, duh. Now what? The only thing in front of her was the shot of tequila Elmer had ordered—the drink she hadn't planned on drinking.

Trying to play it cool, she downed that, then winced.

"Here." Jensen handed her his cold longneck bottle of beer.

She took a swig, then winced even more. "What is this?" She turned the label around and saw the harp logo on the front.

"It's Guinness. My cousin Wendy stocks up on it for us, since we're not used to the American ales. They're too watered-down."

Too watered-down? Was he crazy? Give her a cold light American beer any day over this thick drudge. But she bit her tongue as she handed his bottle back to him.

He signaled a waitress and asked her to bring another margarita and some water.

"Have my mother and Mr. Mendoza ordered yet?"

"No, sir. My lord. Um, I mean…" The young waitress stammered, most likely at a complete loss.

"Please, just call me Jensen. Will you let them know that I'll join them in a few moments?"

"Of course, Sir Jensen." The blushing woman hurried back to the bar.

As Amber watched her go, she wondered when the town would finally get used to this British invasion. The Beatles probably had it easier than the poor Fortune Chesterfields did.

"Speaking of your mom," Amber said, "Lady Josephine and Orlando seem to be hitting it off well."

"That's bloody unlikely." Jensen chuckled at the possibility. "Mum is just being social. She's quite the mingler. Besides, Mr. Mendoza and she are true opposites." He took a sip of his Guinness. "If she were to ever…well, become romantically involved with anyone, it would be with someone like my father. He was her soul mate—and one in a million." He paused and looked off in the distance.

In fact, he looked beyond Mr. Mendoza and Lady Josephine, who appeared so deep in conversation that they probably didn't even notice that Jensen was no longer sitting with them—much like Gram and Elmer did whenever Amber was around. Talk about a couple of third wheels. Amber had to laugh. Now that's something she and Jensen did have in common—the fact that they found themselves as odd men out.

"Anyway," the handsome blue blood continued, "why would my mum ever remarry when the only man she'd ever find would be someone who would fall short in her eyes?"

Amber looked over at the silver-haired British woman and the suave Orlando Mendoza. The two didn't seem to be all that mismatched to her.

But what did she know about romance or soul mates?

Then again, maybe Jensen was actually talking about his feelings for Amber—warning her that even though they shared a passionate kiss, he would never marry someone who clearly fell short in his eyes.

That had to be it. Okay, that was a no-brainer.

The waitress returned with the margarita that Amber didn't want, but she took a sip of it anyway to still her emotions and to cool whatever flush might have risen to the surface. But this time, she could blame it on the alcohol.

Fortunately, Gram and Elmer returned to save Amber from any further speculation of how unsuitable she and Jensen were.

As Elmer helped Gram into her seat, he said, "I'd have to say that me and Helen have the dance contest in the bag. They're going with Tony Bennett. Again. Talk about Snoozeville. I'll slip Clem Hodgkins a fiver to make sure we go after them. The Baumgartners will put the crowd to sleep, and then me and Helen will come along and bam! We'll wake 'em right back up."

Gram's laughter tinkled out, and Amber had to wonder if she was merely being polite, or if she actually enjoyed the old man's antics.

"So what music did you two select?" Jensen asked.

"Cotton-Eye Joe," Elmer said smugly.

Amber slapped her hand to her forehead.

"What?" Elmer asked. "Do you think it's too slow paced? Should we choose something livelier?"

Gram looked at her dancing partner, a furrow in her sweet brow, and Amber dumped the tequila shot into her margarita and took another drink. Heaven help her.

"Would you excuse me?" Jensen asked. "I need to tell

my mother and Orlando that I've temporarily jumped ship."

When he walked away, Elmer leaned forward and lowered his voice. "Did you do any fancy trick shooting for your audition?" Then he looked at Gram. "Maybe we should incorporate some pistols or something in our dance routine to really give it some pizzazz."

"No!" Amber nearly shot out of her seat. When the other diners turned to look at their table, she lowered her voice. "No, you two may not do any trick shooting. It's bad enough I have to worry about Gram breaking a hip, I don't want to worry about her accidentally shooting somebody's eye out."

"What's this about trick shooting?" Jensen asked, as he returned to the table.

"Amber is the best," Elmer said.

"Like Annie Oakley?" Jensen's smile was eager and almost hopeful.

The guy really needed to get a grip on this whole over-the-top Wild West fascination. Of course, it was people like him who would be paying customers, eager to see her show.

"Yes," Amber admitted, "but when I do trick shooting, it's in a controlled environment."

"Oh." The corners of his lips dropped and a look of dejection crossed his face. "So you don't really know how to shoot then."

Heck, the man acted as if she'd just told him Santa Claus wasn't real. "Of course I know how to shoot."

"A real gun?" His eyes sparkled with that same gleam Elmer's had right before he'd confronted the Baumgartners.

"Yes, a real gun. I'm an excellent shot."

"Care to make a wager on it?" Jensen smiled and cast a glance at Elmer, who'd scooted to the edge of his seat.

"I believe you still owe me from the last wager we made," she pointed out. Their barbecue date had understandably been waylaid by Amelia's recent delivery. And Amber had been looking forward to it.

"So then double or nothing," Elmer shouted out, having no idea what the bet was in the first place. The man just loved a competition.

Amber lifted her brow at Jensen, waiting to see how he would react to the old marine's suggestion.

But he didn't give it a second thought. "Yes. Double or nothing."

Chapter Six

Jensen wasn't sure what the old man had planned for today's shooting competition, but he knew one thing for certain—he had no plans of winning.

If he lost, he'd get to take Amber out on *two* dates, since he'd yet to collect on their original wager. And he'd been looking forward to their barbecue dinner.

Losing didn't come easy to a man who'd grown up competitive. And he'd never thrown a bet in his life.

But for Amber, the temptation had been far too great to resist.

He shook his head at the silly trail of thoughts. The bloody competition had yet to even begin and he'd already planned his surrender. The little Texas cowgirl was making his mind spin in funny directions. Something about her had him doing things he'd never think of doing back in England.

He rolled the window down. Maybe it wasn't Amber. Maybe it was something in the western breeze that blew tumbleweeds across the fields in summer and English bachelors willy-nilly in January.

Even his penchant for old cowboy movies couldn't explain the relaxing effects of being in Texas. And for once, overseeing the family investments and holdings, as well as Chesterfield Ltd., and keeping his siblings out of the tabloid limelight no longer seemed like the only things that mattered.

For some damned reason, he now found himself watching airplanes take off, riding horses on bulky Western saddles out to watering holes and kissing a rodeo queen behind a darkened feed store. He also found himself smiling for no reason at all, which he hadn't done since…well, in longer than he cared to ponder.

Now, as he eased Quinn's pickup along the dirt driveway and headed toward a parking area near the Broken R barn, he spotted Elmer Murdock and did a double take.

The stocky, elderly was man toting liter-sized bottles of soda out of the back of the spiffed-up muscle car. But why was he dressed like a leprechaun playing in a polo match at the VFW hall?

Jensen parked and exited the truck.

The old man, wearing tight white jodhpurs on his short, bowed legs, waved him over. "Top o' the morning to ya."

As Jensen made his way to Mr. Murdock's open trunk, the elderly man handed him a crate holding eight plastic bottles filled with bright neon-pink soda.

Jensen looked at the array of containers. What in the

world was he doing with so much…? He glanced at the label. Caliente Pepper Fiz?

"Were they having a special at the grocery?" Jensen asked.

"They sure was, but not at the Superette here in town. I picked these up over at the discount drug place on the way to Lubbock. Seems they didn't sell as well as store-owners hoped, so they were just sitting on a pallet out back, expiring in the sun."

"Did they go bad in the heat?" That would explain the unnatural neon-pink color.

"I don't reckon so. This here is their strawberry-cream-flavored line. The regular hot sauce flavored soda is pretty tasty, but no one seemed to like it much when they added the strawberries to the original mix."

Jensen looked again at the label. These Texans and their food products could sure be inventive. "Hmm. You'd think they wouldn't be able to keep hot sauce-flavored cola on the shelf."

"I know," Mr. Murdock said, not recognizing Jensen's sarcasm. "Oh well, it's the Caliente Company's loss and our gain, right ol' chap?"

Jensen was raised to be polite, but there was no bet in the world that would make him drink strawberry-cream-and-hot-sauce-flavored cola—let alone nearly fifty bottles of the wretched stuff. "Tell me why it's our gain?"

"They make perfect targets, son. When your bullet hits one of these suckers, boom! Hot-pink juice explodes everywhere. Not only is it fun to look at, it saves the range master some footwork. He doesn't have to run back and forth to measure the targets. And since that'll be my job for this here competition, I figured I'll save my legs for that upcoming dance contest."

Just then, Amber stepped out of the ranch house cradling a rifle and a box of ammunition.

She looked just as serious as Wyatt Earp himself making his way to the OK Corral. Of course, Wyatt Earp didn't look as sexy. Her snug jeans hugged her curvy hips, tempting a man to want to go out and buy her a dress… Or maybe some silky lingerie.

Jensen came to a complete stop, not even noticing the weight of the bottles in his arms as he watched Amber walk toward him. She wore a shiny silver belt buckle along a tiny waist a man could span his hands—

"Are you ready to get beat by a girl, Sir Jensen?" she asked.

He forced himself to pull his gaze away from her dangerous torso to her seductive brown eyes. And to be honest, if he was ever ready get bested by a girl, it was today. And it was this girl. Or rather, this woman. No doubt about that.

His throat worked to swallow, but his mouth was so dry he almost opened one of the discolored sodas and took a huge sip.

What a mistake that would be.

Back in London, he'd never been tongue-tied around the beautiful socialites and jet-setters who made up his social circle. Then again, they didn't have anyone quite like Amber Rogers in the British Isles—or all of Europe, for that matter.

A hand smacked against his back, pitching him forward. "Keep it moving, son. I got an appointment with my podiatrist at one o'clock to see about my bunions. And if I win our bet, Helen said she'd go with me afterward to that remodeled movie theater over in Vicker's Corners."

Jensen picked up his pace, hoping Mr. Murdock wouldn't miss out on his opportunity to squire Helen to the cinema.

Because there was no way Jensen was going to miss out on his own date with Amber. Instead he said, "I appreciate your vote of confidence."

"Hell, son," Murdock said. "I didn't bet on *you*. I bet on our Amber over there."

Amber's hand held steady as she chambered the first, which was surprising since she'd caught the ways Jensen had studied the jeans she normally saved for when she wasn't working on the ranch. At first, she'd thought he might be assessing her choice of clothing, since the uptight Brit was so stoic and difficult for her to read.

But riding the pro rodeo circuit provided her with plenty of opportunity to study the male species and their mating rituals. And there appeared to be one thing that applied to all men around the world. They couldn't hide their sexual interest in their eyes.

Whether Jensen was wearing a top hat or a Stetson or no head covering at all—like today, with just the Texas breeze to ruffle his dark locks—the intensity in his gaze couldn't mask his obvious physical attraction.

Nor did Amber want it to. It caught her off guard and made her tremble as she walked toward the makeshift range Elmer had set up alongside the barn. It even filled her head with intoxicating ideas of what that gaze could lead to. It also made her feel like a desirable worldly woman, one who hadn't given up her career to breed horses at the family ranch in the middle of Texas.

She didn't know what it all meant, but she certainly liked the way it made her feel, the way it made her walk a little taller and with a little more sway to her hips. And she'd be darned if she wouldn't win this shooting competition and have a night on the town with him because in no time at all, he'd return to London, leaving her in Horseback Hollow, where she'd be forced to read about his dates—rumored or real—in all the tabloids.

She'd once dreamed of riding the rodeo, traveling the world and tasting all it had to offer. And she did accomplish her goal—sort of, given that she'd never made it outside the borders of North America. Jensen provided a glimpse into that lifestyle that she would never have. But Horseback Hollow and the Broken R had always been home to her. And when push came to shove, she'd always known she'd end up back here one day anyway.

And if that meant she had to shoot her best today to get a small taste of glamour for two nights at best, then that's exactly what she would do.

So she lifted the stock to her shoulder, took careful aim at the Caliente soda bottle and squeezed the trigger.

"Hot damn!" Elmer shrieked as the neon pink liquid sprayed into the air.

Gram clapped politely from her seat off to the side. "Three more shots to go."

Amber made all of them, blasting strawberry-cream-and-hot-sauce-flavored soda with each direct hit.

"That's our girl!" The retired marine patted her back, then hurried out to place new targets for Jensen's turn.

Amber passed the rifle over to her competitor and smiled.

"Well-done, Miss Rogers." Jensen loaded the shotgun, took aim and shot through the bottle, blasting a spray of pink liquid. Then he turned to her and winked. "I prefer the British Boss over the American Remington, but I believe this rifle will get the job done."

Amber crossed her arms. "We'll see who's 'boss' when it comes to shooting then, won't we?"

"So we shall. And to be perfectly honest, I'd enjoy competing with you just to have what you Americans call bragging rights."

"We'll see who's bragging when it's all said and done, Sir Jensen."

He flashed her a handsome grin, then proceeded to fire again, nailing the next two targets.

Amber's pulse rate soared. She'd always enjoyed the adrenaline rush of competition—friendly or otherwise. But this was different. Each time Jensen cast a glance her way, his brow lifted, his lips quirked in a boyish grin, a glimmer in his eyes, her heart did all kinds of loop-de-loops.

Talk about a rush…

As Jensen took aim at the last target and drew back on the trigger, he pulled his right shoulder back a bit too much, and his round veered into the fence post.

"Whoop-dee-doo!" Elmer shouted. "We won!" He lifted Amber into the air and twirled her around in his stocky arms.

While she appreciated Elmer's support and enthusiasm, she didn't want to rub Jensen's loss in his face. She might be a born competitor, but she was also a good sport.

So was Jensen, it seemed, because losing didn't seem to bother him at all. In fact, a smile tugged at his lips, and a glimmer lit his eyes. Surely he hadn't missed his last shot on purpose…?

When Jensen set down the rifle, and Elmer set her down to hurry over to Gram, Amber held out her right hand.

"Good game," she said.

Jensen accepted her offer of sportsmanship with grace and class, although he held her hand a bit longer than necessary, and his smile deepened. "Make sure you wear those jeans when we go to dinner."

With that, he released her, but his gaze held her steady and tight—so much so that she had to will herself to take a breath. Finally she glanced down at her Wrangler jeans. "Why do you want me to wear these?"

"They're a nice fit."

She'd been thinking about wearing a dress, but maybe he hadn't meant their dinner date to be a…date.

"All right. It's a da…deal."

Jensen glanced toward the back porch, where Gram was sitting, smiling with Elmer, and winked.

Amber was more surprised to see that it was Gram who actually returned Jensen's wink.

Amber walked into Smokey Joe's, her favorite barbecue joint and honky-tonk in Lubbock. Normally the place was bright and loud during the dinner rush, then the staff moved the tables and dimmed the lights. That's when the drinkers and line dancers showed up.

She wore new boots—and the jeans Jensen hadn't been able to keep his eyes off that morning. She also found a black, ruffled halter top in the back of her closet and threw a short suede jacket over it. She doubted Jensen would be up for any dancing afterward, but she dressed in layers, just in case.

It may be cool outside, but when the crowds settled

in and the music got going, small places like Smokey Joe's could heat up quickly.

She was met by the hostess, a peppy college-age girl with a vivacious smile, a low-cut blouse and a pair of Daisy Duke–style shorts.

"I'm meeting someone," Amber said.

The young woman, whose name tag read *Maddie* and whose legs looked as if they could use a lot more covering than what the skimpy denim provided, smiled. "A tall, formal, good-looking dude?"

At Smokey Joe's? That description couldn't possibly describe anyone else. Amber nodded, then followed the hostess.

For the eighth time that night, she wondered if she'd put on too much makeup or if she'd overdressed. She ran a hand through her long and loose hair, wishing she'd clipped it back or pinned it up.

This wasn't a date. And she didn't want Jensen getting the idea that she was trying to dress to impress him. But it was too late to change course now, so she continued on, past the makeshift seating on the dance floor and then the bar itself. They even passed the kitchen with its open window letting out scents of smoked meat and tangy sauce.

She'd eaten here plenty of times, but she had no idea there was more seating this far back. Where the heck was Maddie the hostess taking her?

Maybe she'd misunderstood. Maybe there were two tall, handsome, formal dudes in this neck of the woods.

Dang, maybe there was some private party going on, and Amber was about to crash it. But just as they rounded a corner, Jensen, who'd been seated at a small table in a hidden alcove, stood to greet her. "Hello, Amber."

She looked around, still curious about this secluded corner. "Well, what do you know? I had no idea they had a room back here."

"I thought it would be quieter than out front."

And a lot more private. Did he do this sort of thing with all his dates?

Not a date! she reminded herself—and with a mental scolding.

He pulled out a chair for her and she took a seat. "I took the liberty of ordering a margarita with the tequila shot in it for you. You seemed to enjoy them when Mr. Murdock ordered them for you at the cantina."

Great. Just what she needed—the possibility of losing all her inhibitions with the man. She should advise him not to take dating cues from Elmer Murdock.

Instead, she smiled and thanked him for his thoughtfulness.

Maddie handed them the menus. "Your waiter will be with you shortly. I'll let him know where you are."

You'd better. Something told her they could be left to die back here until closing time.

She scanned the area, where they were the only diners. "I wonder why they put us way out to pasture."

"Oh, that was at my request. I asked them for something more private, where there would be less risk of being bothered by others."

"You know, part of the barbecue experience is the communal tables and environment. I mean, I know this place isn't swanky, but it has good food."

"I can ask the hostess to reseat us, if you'd rather be in the dining hall area. I just assumed you would want to be away from the prying eyes of the public, and I didn't want any more cameras catching us doing something as innocuous as sharing a meal."

She hated to sound ungrateful. Besides, she didn't want him to be uncomfortable if he preferred their out-of-the-way table. "No, this is fine."

Although, it was much warmer back here. They must be sitting on the other side of the kitchen with its hot smoking pits. She took off her jacket and hung it on the back of her chair before turning and catching the surprised look on his face.

He was staring at her blouse, and suddenly, she was glad she'd done so much riding and roping recently because she knew her shoulders and tight arms were her best features.

A waiter in a black Stetson came to take their order. "Wow. I heard we had a celebrity back here, but they didn't say who it was."

"I trust you'll keep it to yourself until after we leave," Jensen said.

"I sure will." The young man cast a smile at Amber. "But I don't suppose I could get your autograph before you go, Miss Rogers. It isn't every day that we get a rodeo queen in here."

She smiled. "Of course, you can."

The waiter's cheeks flushed. "My sister was a huge fan and followed your career. She even tried to barrel-race like you. 'Course she isn't nearly as pretty as you are."

"Thank you." Amber glanced at Jensen, whose expression had grown serious.

After the waiter took their orders and returned to the kitchen, Jensen said, "Maybe we should move. It was cooler on the other side of the restaurant, and then you'd be able to keep your jacket on."

"No, truly, this table is fine." Didn't Jensen like her top? He definitely didn't seem to like their waiter, who'd continued to study her while they'd ordered.

After the waiter finally served their drinks, Jensen took a long draw from his bottle of Heineken, since there weren't any stout British ales served here.

He chugged another long gulp.

Was something still bothering him?

Maybe she was reading too much into his expression.

"How's Amelia feeling?" she asked, wanting to get back on neutral territory.

He looked up, his serious demeanor fading into a slow smile. "Quite well. She's glad to finally have baby Clementine home."

"I can imagine. I once had to go to the hospital to get my appendix out, and I couldn't wait to leave. I missed everything about home, from Gram's cooking to my horse. I promised to stay in bed for a week if the doctor would just let me leave, which was a pretty big promise for a twelve-year-old girl with a new horse and an up-coming junior state barrel-racing competition to make."

"And when they finally did release you, did you stay in bed?"

"For one whole day. Pop caught me sneaking out to the stables a couple days later and let me ride for a few minutes before Gram found out and lit into us some-thing fierce."

"Your sweet grandmother? I can't imagine her yell-ing."

"She didn't need to. She told one of the ranch hands to take Miss Muffin, my new horse, over to the Drummonds' place so I couldn't ride her. Then she went on strike in the kitchen, making Pop eat frozen dinners and cereal for the next two weeks to remind him that being an accomplice to a twelve-year-old's whims, especially when she was recovering from surgery, wasn't his smartest move. Needless to say, both Pop and I learned our lesson."

"So you didn't get to go to the junior state rodeo?"

"No, I still got to go, but I'd barely had any practice beforehand, so neither Miss Muffin nor I were up to speed. Literally. I came in second place to Starlight from Vicker's Corners."

"Well, then it all worked out well in the end."

"No, it was the worst moment of my life. I hate coming in second place. And I hated it even more that snotty Molly Watkins won the buckle that should have been mine if it hadn't been for my stupid appendix getting in the way of my training schedule. She was so smug with her perfectly curled red hair and expensive outfit that was better suited to a homecoming queen than a barrel racer."

A glimmer lit Jensen's eyes. "A bad sport, then, this Molly girl?"

"The worst. She told everyone that the reason I didn't do well was because I'd tried to kiss Billy Carmichael behind the warm-up fences, and he'd pushed me away, making me too upset to do my ride."

Jensen, who'd clearly been engaged in their conversation before, leaned forward. "Who was Billy Carmichael?"

Surely he wasn't the least bit jealous of a thirteen-year-old boy—but she liked the idea that he might be interested in her romantic history—as short and unremarkable as it had been. "Billy's dad was one of the rodeo clowns, and Billy was the top calf roper at the National Little Britches Rodeo Finals two years running. Let's just say that for a junior high school girl, he was a big deal."

"So Billy Carmichael didn't defend your honor?"

"Nope. He liked everyone thinking that I had a crush on him."

"What a cad."

"Exactly."

Jensen smiled, and her heart picked up speed. She took a drink of her margarita. With the way he was looking at her, she would've downed the whole thing. Luckily, the waiter, whose name tag read *Danny*, brought their food just then—as well as a sheet of paper he'd printed out with a photo of her in her barrel racing days.

She signed it to Bonnie Sue, wishing her all the best in her career.

"Would you mind posing for a photo?" Danny asked.

"Yes, we'd mind," Jensen said.

Danny's shoulders slumped. "I'm sorry. I didn't mean to interrupt your dinner. I could come back afterward."

"I asked for this table because I like my privacy," Jensen said. "I don't want my picture taken."

"Sorry, sir." Danny said again. "I didn't want you in it. I was hoping you'd take a shot of Amber and me with the camera in my cell phone."

Amber laughed. It served Jensen right to realize there were some people more popular in Texas than a British noble. "Be a sport. It'll only take a minute to make a girl's day."

And it did.

Moments later, after the happy waiter went back to

the kitchen, Amber and Jensen dug into their meals. "So, did you ever get back at Molly what's-her-name?" Jensen asked after spearing a bite of cooked rib tips.

"I got back at her every year after that. In the arena, that is. I never came in second to Molly Watkins again."

Jensen laughed, and Amber tried the Campfire Beans.

"Oh, didn't you order any of these?" she asked, looking at his plate.

"No, I chose the homemade coleslaw and the Belt-Bustin' Baked Potato. And they're very good. You were right. This is the best barbecue restaurant I've been to yet, although I'm afraid I'm still what you'd call a novice."

"Here, try this." She spooned a taste of seasoned beans into his mouth.

He reciprocated by giving her one of his rib tips.

They talked and shared food with each other as if they'd had countless dinners together. She fed him macaroni salad. He buttered cornbread and held it up to her mouth.

It wasn't until the meal was over that Amber realized they could've easily just used their own utensils and eaten off each other's plates. They didn't have to feed one another.

She rubbed her bare arms, suddenly embarrassed at the shared intimacy.

Jensen's eyes focused again on her skimpy top just as a fiddle player started warming up in the main dining room.

"Looks like the band is getting ready." She felt a little silly for pointing out the obvious.

"Do you dance much?" he asked.

"I can hold my own. What about you?" She hoped he'd invite her to two-step.

"Yes, but not to this. Frankly, this may come as a surprise to you, but they don't teach us country-and-western line dancing in cotillion class."

"Really? And yet the waltz is so terribly popular in my neck of the woods." She smiled, just as the band launched into full swing.

"Shall we have a dance-off then, Miss Rogers?" he asked as he scraped his chair back and offered his hand.

"I'd love to." She pushed aside the Jose Cuervo she hadn't touched and rose to join him. "But I should warn you." She leaned toward him, her mouth aimed toward his ear as he guided her to the dance floor. "One day soon I aim to do a mean cancan."

She caught herself the moment the words rolled out of her mouth, especially since she was merely entertaining the idea, especially after drinking a margarita.

"The cancan? My goodness, Miss Rogers. You're full of surprises. I'd love to see that sometime—especially if you're in costume."

Gram planned to work on her fancy outfit, and if Amber gave her the go-ahead, that was something Jensen would never see. So she laughed off her slip of the tongue.

As she stood, Jensen said, "Don't forget your coat."

"Are you crazy? It's too hot to think about wearing something like that on the dance floor." She did, however, take her purse, which was a tiny little bag barely able to hold her keys, her ID, a credit card and some cash.

Jensen seemed to study her momentarily, and she patted the purse that hung at her side by a narrow shoulder strap. "I travel light when I plan to spend some time on a dance floor."

He seemed to ponder that a moment, then spun her into his arms. A beat later, they joined the others two-stepping across the parquet floor.

Jensen did much better than she'd expected, and they were soon laughing and twirling their way around to various renditions of classic George Strait and Alan Jackson songs.

After the first set, the band paused for a break. She'd worked up a thirst. Jensen asked if she wanted to order another margarita, but since she was driving, she told him she'd prefer a glass of ice water to cool her down.

"This has been the most enjoyable night I've had since my arrival in Texas," Jensen said, then he leaned in closer. "You're an excellent dancer, Amber. And an enjoyable companion."

She told herself that the loud music had forced them to talk into each other's ears the past hour, and that they leaned into each other as a matter of habit.

"Companion, huh?" she said, maintaining the intimate proximity.

He glanced at the top she wore, which helped to keep her cool in the heated quarters. But there was another kind of closeness, another heat that had her steamed up. Him, too, it seemed.

When a cowboy walked by, carrying a longneck bottle of beer, he gave her a flirtatious grin and tipped his hat. But he hadn't really meant anything by it. She was used to being recognized.

Jensen's smile faded. "There are too many people ogling us in here. Maybe we should go outside. Why don't you get your jacket?"

Just who was he to be concerned about them ogling? He certainly hadn't staked his claim, and even if he had, she wasn't about to let anyone tell her what she could and couldn't wear out in public. The blouse wasn't all that skimpy!

And while she wouldn't mind going outside anyway, she fought the urge to go for her jacket. Her rebellious streak wouldn't allow it, especially since Jensen was doing that judgmental upper-crust thing again, like he'd done that first day she'd met him on his sister's porch.

That being the case, he'd need to learn that she wasn't going to be intimated by him or his snobby attitude. "Apparently you don't like my top."

"It's fine."

The female singer stepped onto stage just as the chords for a Patsy Cline song sounded over the speakers. Couples made their way back onto the dance floor, but Jensen stood facing her—and looking down his aristocratic nose.

"If you were Pinocchio, your nose would stretch out a foot right now. And birds would be swooping down to build a nest on it."

"There's not a bloody thing wrong with your blouse," he said. "Which is why every man in this place has been staring at you."

She looked around. The cowboy was long gone by now, and she didn't see anyone else staring at her, other than a man in a John Deere hat near the bar. But that guy was probably watching the scene they were causing rather than the way her shirt rose above her waistline.

She uncrossed her arms, tucked her thumbs in her front pockets and shifted her weight to one hip. "Nobody is staring at me, Jensen. And so what if they were?"

"You know what? You're right. So what if they are? They can stare all they like because you're here with *me*. And the sooner all the other single guys find that out, the better."

He wrapped his arm around her waist and pulled her onto the dance floor, holding her close as the singer belted out lines about being crazy for loving you.

She tried not to think of what he was so all-fired worked up about. Was it really *her*?

Truth be told, she fancied being locked in his embrace all night long. And if, down the road, things blew up in their faces, it would serve the both of them right for playing with fire. They were a mismatched pair— and nothing could ever come of it.

So why did she even harbor the slightest little dream that things could be different? But clearly, they weren't.

Before she could wonder about Jensen's intentions, the man in the John Deere hat held up his smartphone, the flash of the camera going off.

Chapter Seven

Jensen took Amber's hand and led her off the dance floor, through the throng of people who'd gathered around to watch the cowboys and their dates slow dancing to the sounds of "Crazy," and out of Smokey Joe's.

As they moved, Amber scanned their surroundings. "The guy who took the photo isn't following us. And he wasn't one of the reporters who was at Quinn's ranch the other day."

"If he was one of the paparazzi, he'd be out here now, snapping more photos."

"Then why did we have to leave?"

"Because I wasn't up for a photo shoot—no matter who was behind the lens—or what kind of camera it was."

Besides, amateurs sold photographs to the tabloids all the time—something the Fortune Chesterfields knew too well.

Jensen slowed their pace as they were outside and in the clear, then he walked Amber to her pickup.

"If you don't mind," she said, "I'd like my jacket now."

"I'll go back inside for it."

She crossed her arms, ignoring the gooseflesh which had risen to the surface of her skin. "Not so fast. What's the deal, Jensen?"

"You're going to freeze out here. Are you just plain contrary?"

"It's the principle. I make my own choices when it comes to my wardrobe—and to my inner thermostat. When I was hotter than blazes inside, you wanted me covered up. And I'd like to know why."

"Sorry. I just didn't like seeing all the men in there ogling you."

She lifted a brow. "But it's okay for *you* to do it?"

When she stated it that way, he supposed it wasn't. Although he liked the black lacy blouse—and the way it revealed her tiny waist and sexy midriff.

But he wasn't being the least bit fair, was he? Not when there wasn't a chance in hell that the two of them would make any kind of match—lasting or otherwise.

Well, perhaps otherwise might be an option, but he'd be damned if he knew how to broach a subject like that. He might have his share of ladies offering to be his lovers, but he wasn't what you'd call a Casanova.

He'd never had to be.

Yet, again, that wasn't fair to Amber. So if their friendship or relationship went in that direction, the decision would have to be hers to make.

"I had a lovely evening," he said.

She stopped, turned, slapped her hands on her

denim-clad hips and completely disarmed him with a look of astonishment. "Did you just completely ignore my question?"

"The one about your top and how sexy I found it this evening? Why, yes. I was moving on to a safer topic."

"And my sexy blouse is dangerous because...?"

She was provoking him, setting him up. Prompting him to continue.

All right. He'd take the bait. Perhaps it would lead to the direction he'd like things to take—her choice, of course.

"Because a conversation like that would surely lead to me kissing you senseless in the parking lot, especially since we seem to be the only two out here, without any witnesses to sully your reputation."

For a couple of heartbeats, silence played cat and mouse in the moonlight.

"And kissing me would be a bad thing?" she asked.

"You tell me."

With that, the lovely, irrepressible and delightful Miss Amber Rogers—no relation to either Roy or Rod—did better than that.

She showed him by rising up on tiptoe, wrapping her arms around his neck and kissing him...utterly senseless.

Her scent—something that reminded him of ripe peaches in full harvest—enveloped him. His hands sought to draw her close, to hold her, to capture the essence of the woman who tempted him beyond reason, while his tongue dipped and twisted and mated with hers.

Then, just as quickly as it all started, she pulled her sweet lips from his, dropped her arms and spun around.

Before he could blink or think, she reached into her tiny purse, pulled out a key fob and said, "I'll see you later." Then she climbed into her pickup and turned the ignition as if nothing between them had happened.

And perhaps it hadn't. Because a couple of heartbeats later, she drove off, leaving him standing in the moonlight, bewitched, bothered and more than a little befuddled.

It had taken every ounce of Amber's strength and willpower to control her weak knees, trembling arms and pounding heart to leave as if she was completely unaffected by that good-night kiss. But what she might lack in sexual experience and worldliness, she made up for in gumption.

Jensen may have thought he'd made her feel better about things, but he hadn't. And that's mostly because there was a whole lot he didn't know, a whole lot she hadn't told him.

How would he react when everyone in town, including the *Cross Town Crier*, learned that she'd accepted the job of riding in the Cowboy Country USA Wild West Show? Or that she'd been asked to audition for a part in Madame LaRue's Lone Star Review—which meant donning a saloon-girl costume that Gram was stitching up for her because Elmer Murdock suggested it would give her a "leg up"—the pun very much intended?

Not that she'd decided to try out for sure. But doggone it. She was certainly tempted to do just that because she could almost hear Patrick Swayze's voice booming out in the cab of her truck: *No one puts Amber in a corner.*

Okay, so *Dirty Dancing* had always been one of her mom's favorite movies, and Amber had watched the DVD a hundred times.

But bottom line? Amber was both a competitor and maybe even an entertainer at heart. And she wasn't meant to spend her entire life marooned on a ranch. Of course, that didn't mean she didn't love the Broken R or Horseback Hollow or Texas, for that matter. They would always be home to her.

It's just that, deep down in her heart, she'd wanted to shine and to be someone. And now Cowboy Country USA was providing her an opportunity to have it all. Well, if Jensen ever got wind of her involvement, that would surely put the end to anything that might come of any romantic opportunities there.

But who was she kidding?

A few heated kisses didn't mean anything without an invitation to go along with them. And at this rate, this *thing* or *friendship* or whatever you wanted to call it, wasn't apt to go anywhere—nor was it going to last more than a week or two at the most.

And even if they did sneak off and do more than just kiss, the whole thing would fizzle out soon enough. They were a mismatched pair—and nothing could ever come of it.

So why did she dare even harbor the slightest little hope that things could be different?

Actually, the way he wanted to keep things secret made her mad as heck and fired her up.

Who whisked their dates out under the cover of darkness to a quaint little out-of-the-way place, treated them to a romantic dinner and shared a soul-stirring, knee-wobbling good-bye kiss only to let them go their own way?

Okay, so she'd been the one to leave. And just like Cinderella at the ball, she'd left her suede jacket behind when she ran off in a rush to escape the inevitable reality of the situation.

He'd called her an hour later to make sure she'd gotten home all right and to tell her he had her suede jacket. She'd thanked him, and they'd made small talk for a while, although they didn't broach anything remotely serious, like jealousy or heated kisses.

But she clearly wasn't Jensen's type. Nor did she belong in his world. She was a fool to even entertain a fleeting dream that they could ever share more than a few sneaky dates and a couple of stolen kisses.

And Gram and Pop didn't raise her to be no fool.

Amber pulled the rig into the side yard just after dark. It had been a long day and she'd just delivered a couple of cutting horses to one of their clients on a ranch near Lubbock.

Normally, she wouldn't be so exhausted so early in the evening, but she hadn't been able to sleep last night after dancing with Jensen and remembering how good it felt to be held in his arms.

Or how his kiss had rocked her to the core.

As she shut off the ignition, she noticed the green Dodge Charger parked near the back door. The light was still on in the kitchen.

Obviously, Gram had company for dinner. Again.

It's not that Amber minded Elmer being at their house so much lately. It was just that she didn't want to have to make conversation tonight or have the perceptive old man quiz her about Jensen and about what he suspected might be going on between them.

Because the truth of the matter was, even if Amber wanted to be perfectly open and up-front, she didn't have an answer for him—or for anyone.

While she'd worked the horses this morning and then during the drive both to and from the ranch near Lubbock, she'd run the whole situation backward and forward in her mind. Yet, she still had trouble knowing what to make of it all—the fun she had when they were together, the attraction she felt for him, the sexual feeling he aroused in her. And he seemed to be experiencing those same things—although she could certainly be reading into that all wrong.

Sometimes, when she found herself losing focus or direction, she'd put on headphones and pump Garth Brooks as loud as she could stand it, just to help her mind clear. And if her mind ever needed some clearing, it was tonight.

Yet, cruising down the highway, with the horse trailer hitched behind, the last thing she wanted to be reminded about was how things between her and Jensen could never work out. So when Garth had come on the radio, singing about Papa lovin' Mama into an early grave, she'd switched the dial to a loud rock station. There'd be no songs about fatal attractions or star-crossed lovers for her tonight.

Now, as she walked toward the front porch, her ears were still ringing from the electric guitars that had blasted the entire ride home.

She didn't want to deal with Gram or Elmer Murdock or even the empty horse trailer she'd left hitched to the truck. All she wanted was a piece of Gram's leftover cornbread and maybe a cold glass of milk before taking a nice hot shower and hitting the sheets.

When she entered the house, she spotted Elmer resting comfortably in Pop's old leather recliner. So comfortably, in fact, that his age-spotted hands were crossed over his extended belly and his mouth hung wide open. His snores were loud enough to trigger the lowering of the guardrail on a railroad track.

Amber didn't appreciate another man taking Pop's place in the ranch house, but at least Elmer was sound asleep. Thank goodness for small favors.

She heard the sink water shut off, so she made her way into the kitchen, where Gram was drying dishes with an old flour sackcloth.

Helen Rogers always claimed a woman did her best thinking standing in front of a kitchen sink. And Amber had found that to be true, as well. In fact, the kitchen was a special place. Some of their best conversations happened right there on that worn spot of pine boards in front of the faucet. So she picked up another cloth and took a wet plate from the dish rack, as Gram turned and greeted her with a warm smile.

"I see you've got company." Amber nodded her head toward the living room, where the television hummed with the nightly newscast.

"Poor Elmer plum tuckered himself out today, so I figured I'd let him rest up before he had to drive home."

"How'd he wear himself out?" Amber asked, before she could stop herself. She didn't mean to imply that the man was lazy. A tornado couldn't keep up with him. But he was clearly basking in Snoozeville while Gram was cleaning up.

Of course, Pop never had lifted a finger around the

house, since it had always been Gram's domain, but still, he'd worked hard on the ranch.

"Elmer cooked dinner," Gram said. "He made an amazing beef Wellington and the most delicious fingerling potatoes. He even baked a chocolate soufflé for dessert. You wouldn't guess it by the way he won that chicken wing–eating contest over at the Moose Lodge last week, but he's quite the gourmet."

No, Amber wouldn't believe it. And she was tempted to check the fridge to see if there were any leftovers in there to prove it. But she'd take Gram's word for it.

"So how did the delivery go?" Gram asked, thankfully changing the subject.

"Pretty well. Stumpy Thomas was pleased with the gelding, and his granddaughter went nuts over the young mare. He cut me a check while I was there, so if you're going into town tomorrow, could you swing by the bank?"

"Well, I do have that tea planned with the garden committee. It's not even spring and already they're planning for the Blue Ribbon Floral Spectacular. Elmer thinks my roses are going to bloom early this year. And he was online all yesterday afternoon researching alternative fertilizing techniques."

Amber couldn't see the old man maneuvering his way around the World Wide Web, but he certainly knew his way around winning competitions he had no business entering. So if Elmer was backing Gram's rose bushes, that blue ribbon was as good as hers.

"So what's going on with you and Elmer, anyway?" Amber asked as she put away a bowl and reached for the wet silverware. *Please say you're just friends.*

"I guess the same thing that's going on with you

and that Sir Jensen you've been spending so much time with."

Sure, Amber told everyone she and Jensen were just friends, and while things had definitely been getting a lot more than friendly between them, she didn't want to think that something similar between Gram and the retired marine might be heating up, as well. Gross.

But since Amber didn't want to have *that* conversation with her grandmother, she kept her mouth closed.

After a couple of minutes, Gram dried her hands and took off her apron. Then she turned to Amber. "Why don't you like Elmer?"

"It's not that. I've always enjoyed his humor. Who doesn't? He's very entertaining. But as far as the two of you go, I guess I just don't get what *you* find so appealing about him."

"He has a romantic streak."

Amber glanced over her shoulder and into the living room at the snoring old coot. "You gotta be kidding."

"This afternoon, he took me to the Golden Horseshoe, the old theater that was refurbished last fall, the one offering old classics at a low price."

"You found that romantic? The place charges three bucks to see super old movies that you can watch on TV for free."

"But it's not the same as sitting side by side, sharing Milk Duds in the dark and watching them on the big screen."

Amber took another look at the man and wondered if sticky caramels were good for his dentures, which were, at this very moment, at risk of sliding out of his slack mouth.

"Plus," Gram added, "on Sundays they do a senior

special. And Elmer said he saved five dollars on our tickets and popcorn combo."

Not that Pop had been rolling in the dough, but Gram deserved a nicer date than some discount movie theater. Of course, Mr. Murdock was probably on a limited income with his military retirement, but did he have to be so obvious in his money-saving techniques?

"Okay," Amber said, deciding to focus on the positive. "I'll give you that the theater definitely has ambiance. So what did you see?"

"Urban Cowboy."

"And you thought *that* was romantic?"

"Actually, yes. Have you ever seen it?"

Amber nodded. "Once. About a year ago, when I couldn't sleep. It was on television. The music was pretty cool—for an old classic—but I can think of a lot better romantic movies."

"Do you remember how Bud, John Travolta's character, used to drive Sissy around town in his truck?"

"Debra Winger played Sissy, right? I remember that. He had that big black Ford with those little personalized souvenir license plates in the back window. What about it?"

"Come with me." Gram motioned for Amber to follow her out to the mudroom, where the porch light illuminated the back steps. Still, she reached into the cupboard and withdrew a flashlight before taking Amber outside.

When they reached the Dodge Charger, Gram walked around to the back and flashed the light on the rear window, where someone had painted *Elmer* on the driver's side and *Helen* on the passenger side with a cursive flair.

"He had it done while we were at the movie theater," Gram said. "Rod Rogers, from the paint and body shop, came over as a favor to him, and did it while we were inside. Isn't that the sweetest thing you ever did see?"

Oh, for Pete's sake.

Okay, maybe it was a little romantic, but did Amber really want her sweet and prim grandmother hot-rodding around town in that green death machine with her name emblazoned across the back?

"So what does this mean? Are you and—" Amber pointed to his painted name "—are an official item?"

"Oh, I don't know what to call it. We're too old to worry about labels and nonsense like that. All I know is that Elmer makes me feel special, and I like spending time with him."

"But now everyone in town will know that you guys are together. These new graphics make quite the statement, Gram."

The older woman reached over and patted her hand. "Dear, I know it's not as subtle as, oh, say, a front-page picture spread on an international tabloid."

"Point taken," Amber said, shoulders slumping. "But he's just so different from Pop."

"What's wrong with different?"

Everything, right?

Before Amber could begin to list the reasons people searched for soul mates, her cell phone rang. She was half tempted to ignore it, but decided to check the display first.

Jensen?

"Just a minute, Gram. I need to take this." She swept her finger across the screen, accepting the call. "Hey. What's up?"

"Not much. I just wondered if you'd like to go out on a date."

She smiled, and her heart lightened. "A *real* one?"

"Yes, and then we can go to dinner afterward. But it might be wiser if you met me."

"Of course. I understand. Where?"

"At the Golden Horseshoe Theater."

Was this a joke?

"Seriously?" she asked.

"I heard it was unique and a lot of fun."

And Amber had given Gram a hard time about Elmer Murdock taking her to that ol' place with the two-bit movies.

"What's the matter?" Jensen asked.

"Nothing. I was just wondering why you'd suggest we meet there."

"Elmer told me it's quite the rage. And while I was in town earlier today, I noticed a flyer advertising a movie I'd like to see."

Amber didn't know what to say. The Golden Horseshoe had to be "quite the rage" at the VFW or the Moose Lodge or the senior center because none of her friends had mentioned it.

"Are you busy tomorrow night?" Jensen asked.

"No."

"Then would you like to join me?"

It wasn't that. She was trying to figure out if he was stringing her along. Or just what the heck was behind all of this sneaky, I'll-meet-you business.

Was his real reason for meeting her at obscure places to avoid the paparazzi?

Or was he just hoping no one would see them out and about and realize they were together?

She had half a notion to decline the invitation. And if she hadn't had such a strong urge to see him again, she would have done just that. Instead, she said, "Okay, I'll meet you there." But her heart really wasn't in it.

Like Gram, didn't Amber deserve to be romanced, too?

Chapter Eight

While Jensen and Amber waited in the concession line at the refurbished Golden Horseshoe Theater, he stood like a young boy in a candy shop, studying the reprints of old movie posters that lined the walls.

Could there be anything more perfect for a clandestine date, which wasn't supposed to be a date, than a darkened cinema on a Wednesday evening?

And to top it off, *The Big Country* was playing tonight.

Sadly, at least for the proprietor, there weren't too many people taking advantage of the low price and 1950s ambiance, but there was still a bit of a wait at the concession stand.

Now, with his hand resting on the small of Amber's back, his arm itching to circle around her, he didn't care how long the lady in front of them took to place her order.

When it was finally their turn, a young man in his late teens wearing a pair of black slacks, a white shirt and a red bow tie asked, "What can I get you?"

Jensen asked Amber, "What's your preference?"

"Something to drink—and maybe some munchies, like popcorn, I suppose."

"Very well then. We'll have a large buttered popcorn, a Kit Kat, a package of red licorice, those funny American sour candies shaped like naughty children and two large colas."

"Seriously?" she asked. "How long is this movie?"

"If I remember correctly, it's two hours and forty-five minutes, but it's one of the few long classics without a proper intermission, so I thought we should stock up."

The clerk tallied the order, and as Jensen paid the bill, it took only a moment to realize Mr. Murdock had received one hell of a senior discount. No wonder the proprietorship was able to get by charging such an inexpensive admission fee. They more than made up their loss on ticket sales here at the concession stand. Not that Jensen was complaining by any means. It was merely his habit as a financier to crunch the numbers and decide whether an establishment would succeed or not. Clearly, this place would do well on popcorn alone!

He reached for their refreshments and tried to balance one of the packs of candy and the popcorn container in his left hand, while grabbing his drink with the other.

Amber, proving herself to be quite practical, as usual, took the candy out of his hand and tossed it, along with the other packages, into her handbag before picking up her own cola and following him into the theater.

"Look, they have balcony seating," he said, not the least bit embarrassed about his excitement over the novelty.

"It seems kind of far away from the screen." Amber raised an eyebrow. "I don't think many people choose to sit in the nosebleed section these days."

"Come now. It's not that high. Besides, it'll be much more private up there."

When they settled into the velveteen upholstered seats, he took in all the details of the old-time cinema setting, feeling as though he'd traveled back in time to 1958, when the movie was first released.

The Gregory Peck and Jean Simmons film had been quite popular in Britain back in its day, and Jensen had seen it before on DVD and cable. But with the cinematography so up close and personal, the way the producers had originally intended, the experience couldn't be beat.

He glanced at Amber, who'd placed a red licorice stick in her mouth, her lips wrapped around it, taking it in…

Talk about new experiences. Being seated next to the beautiful and sexy Amber Rogers made it a bit difficult to keep his mind on the screen, especially when he was tempted to reach over and slip his hand in hers. But he forced himself to focus on the movie.

When Peck's character, sea captain James McKay, left New England, moved out west and fell in love with a wealthy cattleman's daughter, Jensen could relate to the man feeling like a fish out of water in a way he hadn't been able to before.

And when McKay dumped the spoiled Patricia in favor of the beautiful Julie, played by Jean Simmons, a funny burble welled up in his stomach—and it had nothing to do with the extra butter on the popcorn or the sugar high coursing through his bloodstream.

Hadn't he recently dumped the spoiled Monica, only to come to Texas and meet Amber...?

No, the similarity ended there. Everything was so much simpler in the movies, which was probably why he always found them to be such a pleasant escape from reality. But in the real world, men like him and James McKay had no business playing cowboys out west.

Yet, sometime during the course of the picture show, he'd succumbed to temptation and reached for Amber's hand. And while they sat in the intimate confines of the darkened balcony, he fought the growing urge to take her in his arms and promise her the world—or at least the water rights to a sprawling ranch. But he restrained himself, knowing they'd each have to return to their own lives soon. Their very different, very separate lives.

As the lights turned on and the curtain closed, he continued to sit in his seat, holding her hand, not breathing a word and trying to make the fantasy last for just a few more heartbeats.

Actually, he wasn't quite sure what fantasy he was trying to envision. Was he seriously entertaining the possibility that he and Amber might share something more than popcorn and candy at a movie?

"This was actually very nice," Amber said, interrupting what could surely be a dangerous line of thinking. But she didn't pull her hand away. And when she cast him a pretty smile, he felt as if he'd just won the UK National Lottery.

"I'm glad you enjoyed it." He glanced down at the empty popcorn bucket in her hands. "Hopefully, I didn't fill you up on too much junk food because I had my cousin Wendy set up something for us at her restaurant."

Amber glanced at her wristwatch. "But isn't the Hollows Cantina closed now?"

"Yes, it is. And that makes my surprise all the more special."

Her brow lifted again. Why was she so skeptical of anything he said?

"Are you going to cook for me?" she asked.

"No, not exactly. I've never been much of a chef. Why? Should I have prepared something for you myself?"

"No, of course not. I only...well, it's just that Elmer took Gram on a date yesterday. And they came here to the movie theater. Then he cooked her a fancy gourmet dinner. I was beginning to think that you were getting dating tips from Elmer Murdock."

Jensen laughed. "I can see why you might. And while Mr. Murdock is full of advice, some of which actually has merit, I came up with this one on my own. He merely mentioned the Golden Horseshoe, and I thought about bringing you here. But the dinner afterward was completely my idea."

She sighed with relief. "That does make me feel better."

"I must admit that some of my previous dates might wish that I sought out some dating tips from a real master, though."

The hint of a smile blessed her lips—pretty lips, full and kissable. "I don't buy that, Sir Jensen. The way the tabloids link you with a new starlet or supermodel every other month, it's obvious that the women clamor to be your next conquest."

He laughed as he escorted her out of the nearly empty theater. "Yes, one would get that impression. But don't believe everything you read and see. In reality, my work and family obligations keep me far too busy for much of a romantic life."

"Speaking of work," she said, as he opened the door to his truck for her, "tell me more about what you do."

Was she trying to change the subject on purpose because she wanted to discourage him from thinking about any possibility of a romance building between them? Maybe she was trying to remind him to stick to friendly and neutral topics.

He got in on the driver's side, started the truck and headed toward his cousin's restaurant, telling her about his job as a financier at Chesterfield Ltd. and what it entailed.

He knew his work probably sounded dull, especially when compared to the exciting life of a traveling rodeo star.

She listened, though, which one would expect from a polite woman, but she had to think that he was the biggest wanker with all his self-talk.

Was his life truly as mundane as it sounded?

They pulled up to the darkened restaurant. He parked, and they climbed out. When they reached the front door, he held it open for her, as the sounds of Linda Ronstadt filled the air.

"Well, it's not locked yet, so I guess that's a good sign." She gazed around the empty room.

There was a single table set, but everything else had been cleared away.

"I'm just on my way out," Wendy said by way of greeting. "There's a pan of beef enchiladas in the kitchen and the plates are in the warming drawer. Help yourself to anything behind the bar, and don't worry about cleaning up. The staff comes in early in the morning." Then she handed Jensen a key and kissed him on the cheek before rushing out the door.

As Amber looked around, Jensen cursed himself for allowing his cousin to go a little too over the top in staging a romantic dinner for them.

He hadn't been lying when he told Amber he wasn't the Casanova type and that he never took the time away from his work or his family to pursue serious relationships—other than a week or two with Monica, although their relationship hadn't lasted more than a few months, nor had it been serious enough to gain any special attention from the tabloids.

"Do you mean to tell me that you arranged for us to have the place to ourselves?" Amber asked.

"Well, I called Wendy and told her I owed you dinner and that we would be in the cinema until late. All of this wasn't completely my idea. Unless you think it's terribly impressive, in which case, it was one hundred percent my doing."

At that, she blessed him with a pretty smile, and his nervousness—Jensen was never ruffled around the ladies, so where had that come from?—soon dissipated.

"Can I get you a cocktail?" he asked. "Or maybe some wine?"

"A glass of merlot sounds good."

He went behind the bar, found a nice bottle of California wine and uncorked it. Then he carried it to the table and poured them each a glass.

Hopefully he hadn't laid it on too thick. He didn't want her thinking he was trying to seduce her, but at the same time, he had to wonder if deep down, maybe he was.

"I'll get our dinner."

As he turned toward the kitchen, she followed him. He should have known Amber wouldn't be the type of woman to merely sit still at the table like a regal queen, waiting for someone to serve her.

It was one of the things he liked most about her. She always seemed willing to jump in and lend a hand—to his sister, to her grandmother or to anyone who needed it.

After he filled their plates full of hot and cheesy enchiladas, they carried them back to the intimate table, where a small candle flickered in the votive.

Since he didn't want to give her the impression that he was trying to wine and dine her, he talked about the movie, horses and about anything else that would be considered neutral territory.

"I'm certainly going to miss the delicious southwestern food when I go back to London," he said as he finished his last bite.

She paused, fork in midair. "When are you leaving?"

She seemed surprised—as if he'd announced he was going tomorrow.

Would she miss him if he was to go so soon? Or would she be relieved? He knew she didn't like having her name linked with his in the tabloids.

"Not until after the weddings in February. I'm sure the whole town will be glad to see the lot of us go and take the sleazy paparazzi with us."

"Oh, I don't know about that. I think a few of the townspeople are enjoying the notoriety."

"Maybe. But some of them are just fame and fortune

seekers, looking for the opportunity to get a piece of the limelight. I can't stand people like that. If they had any idea how terribly difficult it is to go about their lives and protect their families from bloodthirsty newshounds stalking them every second, maybe they'd rethink that."

She shifted in her seat, and he wondered if his tirade had made her uncomfortable. He'd never been able to stomach the poor little rich boy image, either.

It wasn't as though he was trying to sell her on becoming a permanent fixture in his life, thank goodness. Because, if he was, he was sure making a jolly muck of it.

And as pleasant as the thought of having her become his temporary lover was, he knew better than that. The two of them were as different as night and day, as oil and water, as…

He glanced across the table at her, wondering if her thoughts had strayed in that direction, too. After all, they'd been tiptoeing around a temporary relationship of sorts—laughing and sharing, holding hands and kissing each other senseless.

The glimmer in her eyes, which had been glowing in the candlelight just moments ago, seemed to have dimmed—or perhaps that was merely his imagination.

If he had made a muddle of things, then perhaps that was just as well. Nothing could come of this—whatever this was. And the sooner he put that fool notion out of his head, the better.

So why couldn't he keep his gaze or his thoughts to himself?

Four days later, Amber entered the side door of the Horseback Hollow Grange Hall, carrying her saloon-girl costume on a coat hanger. Of course, no one knew exactly what it was, since she'd carefully draped a green plastic trash bag over it, hiding it from public view.

To be perfectly honest, she was beginning to have second thoughts about agreeing to show up for the stupid dance rehearsal/audition that Larry Byerly from casting had lined up for today. But after Gram had gone to so much trouble to make the ruffled dress, which was actually pretty darn good, she hadn't had the heart to consider changing her mind.

Besides, she'd been avoiding Jensen ever since their date at the Golden Horseshoe the other night, and moving toward a future without him seemed to be a good game plan—and one that would keep her heart from getting any more involved than it might otherwise be. The problem was, she was falling for the guy—like it or not—and could see heartache coming at her like a raging bull.

And though she had no business dancing the cancan, even in the privacy of her own bedroom, she'd agreed to come out today and accept some "private instruction" to see if she was "teachable." Even if she wasn't, they still wanted her to be the face on their ad campaign and planned to do a trial photo shoot today.

She thought the whole thing was just plain nuts, but she got a kick out of it, too. So she would listen to whatever they had to say.

Nothing like a little down-home notoriety, huh? But if there was something she knew deep in her soul about her fellow townspeople, it was that they were usually a forgiving lot—at least, with each other and when given time.

She knew she wouldn't be a complete dud today.

She'd done a little acting in high school and had twirled around in front of the mirror a lot as a kid. She really couldn't compete with a professional dancer, though.

Besides, riding in the Wild West Show was going to keep her busy enough. So she probably ought to tell Larry to forget it, to go find his local gal somewhere else since most of the townsfolk would be opposed to one of their own having anything to do with Cowboy Country USA.

It was just that she'd never liked people telling her what she should or shouldn't try out for. It only made her more determined to give it her best shot.

"Miss Rogers!" Larry called out. "It's good to see you. I was afraid you might not make it. Come and meet GiGi LaSalle, the choreographer. She'll work with you for twenty minutes, then we'll see how quickly you catch on. It's all very simple."

Yeah, right. She smiled and greeted GiGi, a tall, slender woman in her early thirties. "I…uh…brought a costume. Should I put it on?"

"By all means." Larry pointed toward the rear exit. "The ladies' room is down there."

Amber knew exactly where it was. She'd been coming to the Grange Hall for wedding receptions, family reunions and pancake breakfasts sponsored by the volunteer fire department since she was a kid.

"I'll be right back," she told him.

Moments later, she stood before the mirror, all decked out in the red-satin-and-black-lace ensemble Gram had created, her shoulders bare, her breasts more prominently displayed than she was used to. She tugged at the fabric, hoping to cover up a bit of the swell, to no avail.

She supposed the costume wasn't all that revealing, at least, by some people's standards. But while a lot of women liked showing off their wares, she usually kept her blouses buttoned nearly to the neck—other than that top she'd worn to Smokey Joe's. The one that Jensen seemed to think had caused every cowboy in the place to gawk at her.

Just the thought of his jealousy drew a smile to her lips, and she cocked her head to the side, assessing herself in a way she never had before.

Dressed in denim and cotton, she'd always thought of herself as just one of the cowboys—only a bit on the feminine side. But in red satin and lace, with every curve blatantly exposed one way or another, there was no doubt she was a female through and through—and pretty darn sexy, if she did say so herself.

"Miss Rogers?" Larry called out. "We don't have all day. I have other dancers coming in to audition—and we need to be out of here by six o'clock. The mayor's daughter is having her wedding rehearsal here tonight."

Amber quit her preening and exited the restroom, carrying her folded street clothes and boots with her.

"Oh, wow," Larry said. "I knew it. You were a natural."

She tugged at her neckline. "No, I'm not. I've never had a dance lesson in my life—other than this one."

"You're a natural in that costume. Who'll care if you flub up? Everyone will be watching you in that dress." He glanced at GiGi. "Don't you agree?"

"She definitely has potential, in a Podunk rodeo queen sort of style."

Who was GiGi calling Podunk?

She nearly objected when GiGi reached out and grasped a lock of her hair. "Do you mind?"

"Mind what?"

"If I just improve on what you're working with here. Larry, give me five minutes and be prepared to be wowed."

Amber sighed and gave a little shrug. Gram used to try to dress her up for Sunday school, especially at Easter and Christmas. But Amber usually threw such a fit, the poor woman gave up.

Doggone it, Gram had once said, *if the Good Lord knew how hard it was to get you ready to go to church, young lady, He'd tell me to stay home.*

GiGi walked to the corner of the room, where she had a multidrawer case of some kind. She brought it back and opened it up, revealing a wide display of makeup and things a Hollywood hairstylist might need.

A few minutes later, she'd whipped out some blush, lipstick, eye shadow and mascara and made quick work of applying it to Amber's face. Next, she teased Amber's hair to new heights, then whipped it into a twist or topknot of some kind. "Now go take a look at yourself and tell me what you think."

She thought GiGi and Larry were a couple of over-the-top wannabe stage parents, but she kept her thoughts to herself and returned to the ladies' room. When she glanced into the floor-length mirror, her breath caught.

Wowzer. She looked va-va-voom sexy now. Mae West could eat her heart out. But more to the point, what would Jensen say if he saw her in it?

It was sure to turn his blue blood raging red-hot.

Of course, she didn't look as if she was in the twenty-first century anymore—or in Horseback Hollow, for that matter. But the look Larry and GiGi had been going for was definitely accomplished.

She almost hurried to the corner where she'd left her belongings so she could grab her cell phone out of her purse and take a selfie to show Gram, but she didn't want to come across as a complete country bumpkin.

Oh, well.

For the next twenty minutes, GiGi showed her some moves. She wasn't a complete klutz, and while it took her some time to get it right, she finally caught on and had a few laughs in the process.

After the audition, Larry explained the idea behind Madame LaRue's Lone Star Review. "We'll have someone play the piano, there'll be a comedian, some actors will do a shoot 'em up at the bar. It'll be a nightly dinner show—and a real addition to Cowboy Country USA."

"I'm already committed to ride in the Wild West Show," Amber said. "My attorney looked over the contract, and I signed on. As fun as it could be, I still run a working ranch. And while I followed through on the audition because I told you I would, I won't have time to be involved in two productions. So you're going to have to find another cancan dancer."

"All right, I understand. But speaking of attorneys..." Larry looked at the young assistant sitting on the folding metal chair and taking notes. "Remind me to talk to the suits about making an addendum to Miss Rogers's contract..."

"Why would you do that?" Amber asked.

"After what we've seen today, we're gonna need to add a clause about you being our local PR gal. As far as the dinner show goes, we'll have plenty of saloon girls to perform, but since we plan on having you as the face on the posters, we'll need you to make some appearances."

"I'm not sure I even want to do one appearance." She glanced at her wristwatch. "Listen, I need to take off."

"No problem. We have the next auditioner in the ladies' room. Thanks so much for coming. We'll have our photographer get in touch with you for the upcoming publicity shoot."

"Like I said, we'll need to talk about that later." Amber still only planned to commit to the Wild West Show, although she actually liked the idea of having her photo in the ad, especially dressed in costume.

She snatched up her clothes from the spot on the floor where she'd left them. But rather than stick around long enough to change back into her jeans and shirt, she decided to head home dressed as she was. Besides, she hadn't taken that selfie, and she wanted Gram to see her all dolled up, with her hair and makeup done.

She could hardly wait to see the look on her grandmother's face.

But it wasn't just Gram who'd get a gander at Amber after GiGi and her magic makeup box had their way with her. When she arrived at the ranch, she found a couple of unexpected vehicles parked in the yard. The first was Elmer's green machine, which she supposed shouldn't have been all that surprising. She couldn't say the same for the other one, though, which was Quinn Drummond's pickup, the one Jensen had been using.

Evidently the handsome Brit had decided to stop by unannounced, which was fine with Amber. But from the look on Jensen's face, the surprise was really on him.

While looking in the mirror of the Grange Hall restroom, she'd wondered what he would think if he was to see her in the saloon-girl getup. But in all her imagining, she hadn't been able to envision his actual expression when she climbed out of her truck dressed in red satin, her hair pulled up in that fancy twist GiGi had coiffed, her face painted, her shoulders bare and her breasts ready to burst out of the neckline.

And poor Jensen looked a bit stunned, to say the least. You'd think he didn't know whether he was afoot or on horseback.

Chapter Nine

When Amber climbed out of the ranch pickup dressed like she'd just stepped off the back lot of a Wild West movie set, she could have knocked Jensen over with a feather boa—if she'd been wearing one. And that seemed to be the only thing missing.

She smiled as she closed the driver's door. "Cat got your tongue?"

Apparently, more than his tongue was missing. His brain had been nabbed along with it.

"What's the matter?" A grin tickled her lips. "You're looking at me as though you think I've been out on the town, throwing down whiskey shots and dancing on the bar of every beer joint in the county. Haven't you ever seen a saloon-girl costume before?"

Yes, but she'd caught him completely off guard, and he'd be darned if he knew what to say.

"Have you been driving around town dressed like that?" he asked, hating the jealousy that found its way into his voice.

At that, her grin faded. "No, I just came back from the Grange Hall."

"What, pray tell, were you doing out in public dressed like that?"

She crossed her arms, which thrust her breasts upward—and nearly out of the outfit completely. "Is this some kind of inquisition?"

"No, I'm sorry. It wasn't meant to be. It's just that…" He scanned the length of her, from the upswept hair and—blimey. Had her eyes always been so large, her lashes so thick? And those cherry-red lips…

His imagination, along with his hormones, was running amok. And while he'd never considered himself a jealous man, he didn't like the idea of her running around town so…so exposed.

"Did you stop by for a reason?"

Actually, he had. He'd noticed a breach in paparazzi security at the ranch and thought he'd slip away to see her in person, to ask if she'd like to ride into Vicker's Corners to spend some time together. He hadn't given the details much thought yet, but he wouldn't be opposed to taking her for an ice cream cone and some window-shopping or some other perfectly simple and innocent venture.

He'd been going stir-crazy inside his sister's house, and if he had to look at Quinn and Amelia gushing all over each other anymore, he'd take a polo mallet to the first camera lens he might encounter upon his escape. Luckily, though, he hadn't had to take extreme measures to slip away.

But seeing Amber dressed like one of the vixens of the Wild West, he was no longer thinking of ice cream or considering a date that would end up being either simple or innocent.

"I came by to see you," he admitted. "Just to talk, or to maybe whisk you away for a bit. But seeing you dressed like that—stunning and beautiful… Well, you've just shot my original plan all to hell. And now I'd like to whisk you away all right. But to live out a cowboy's romantic fantasy."

She glanced down at the dress, and his gaze followed, continuing down her shapely legs. *Damn.* It had to be the most grievous of sins to keep limbs like that covered in denim.

"The folks down at Cowboy Country USA were looking for a local girl to be in their ad campaign. They also…" She paused, glanced at her bare feet, which made him wonder what shoes she'd been sporting earlier. "Well, they had some other coals in the fire, which is what Larry Byerly had been talking to me about the other night at the Hollows Cantina. So Gram stitched up this costume for me, and I met him and another fellow at the Grange Hall earlier. It was all fun and games on my part. Sort of. I probably should have changed before I came home, but—"

"I'm glad you didn't."

They stood like that for a moment, in the waning light of dusk—the beautiful saloon girl and the…

What? Who was he, really? A British royal—or a polished, stuffed toff?

Right this minute, though, it seemed that the only answer that really mattered was the one Amber could give him. And as the silence enveloped them, the layers of his facade—some gold, perhaps most gilded, but all of them carefully erected over the years or maybe even the centuries—seemed to slowly peel away.

The sounds and scents of the Texas ranch in the evening set an interesting stage for an intriguing fantasy that was building by the minute. And in spite of his social standing, his upbringing and his better judgment—which he couldn't seem to fall back upon—a question rolled out of his mouth. "Is there someplace where we can be alone?"

Amber gazed at him with soulful eyes, and as she did, something passed between them—although he'd be damned if he knew what it was, since he'd never experienced the like.

"Gram and Elmer are in the house," she said, "but there is somewhere close by where we can talk in private, although it's not suitable for royalty."

"I'm not royalty. I'm just…Jensen."

And tonight, that's exactly who he was.

Amber took his hand and led him to the barn. Once inside, she turned on the light. "There's no one around to see us in here—other than the horses. And I can assure you that they won't gossip or take photo ops."

"That's a relief." He led her over to a hay bale, and they took a seat. But once they did, things turned awkward.

When he'd mentioned getting her alone, he hadn't meant to sit and talk. And doing any more than that in a barn…well, it just didn't need contemplating.

He had no idea what to say, other than how utterly beautiful she was—and how just looking at her gave him an out-of-body experience. Bloody hell, it was an out-of-this-century experience, as well.

To get things back on an even keel, he said, "I'm not sure how much longer I'll be in Horseback Hollow. My mother wants me to stay until after the weddings in February, but I have business obligations back home."

"Yes, you said that the other night. Is that what you came to tell me?" she asked.

"No, it's not." Perhaps he should be honest. "I came because I thoroughly enjoy being with you. I lo—I like your wit, your sense of humor, your spunk. And you've made my time in Horseback Hollow most pleasant."

"Pleasant? I hope that's more complimentary in London than I'm taking it about now."

"I'm sorry for the language barrier we seem to have, but yes, I find myself thinking of you at all times of the day and night. And when I do, those thoughts make me smile."

"I'm glad to hear that, Jensen, because I feel the same way. When I first met you at Quinn's house the day after Christmas, I didn't like you. And I thought we'd have issues if we ever met again. But I actually like tangling with you."

He laughed. "Tangling, huh?"

"Yep."

They sat there for a moment, side by side on the hay. Then he reached out, took her hand and felt the work-roughened palm he'd come to admire.

"Is that why you wanted to be alone? So you could tell me that?"

He pondered the wisdom of pure honesty, but only for a moment. The lack of pretense was what he liked best about his relationship with Amber. And yes, it had become more than a friendship lately, although he wasn't entirely sure how much more.

"Actually," he admitted, "I wanted us to be alone so I could tell you that I wouldn't mind…"

He'd never been at a loss for words with women before, but this was different. Amber was different. And not in the most obvious of ways.

"You wouldn't mind what?" she asked.

Now it was his turn to grin. "Tangling with you tonight."

At that, she turned to him, her lips parting. "You want to argue and banter?"

"No, not at all. I didn't mean sparring verbally." He brushed a kiss across her lips—lightly, tentatively. "There are other ways to tangle. Like this."

"When put that way, I'd be agreeable to tangling with you." She broke into a pretty grin, transforming the saloon girl into a… Hell, he wasn't sure what, exactly, but princess certainly came to mind.

"This barn wouldn't be conducive to what I'd actually had in mind," he said, "but if you give me a little time, I'll plan a romantic evening. That is, if you don't mind a temporary fling with a man who finds you an amazing, intriguing and delightful woman."

With that, she gave his hand a squeeze. "I'm up for a temporary tangle, even though I'm not into one-night stands or casual affairs. But I've come to care for you, Jensen. And because we live in different worlds, there doesn't seem to be any other way for us to see where our kisses might lead."

"So you'd be okay with a no-strings attached affair?"

"To be honest, if you leave town and I never see you again, I'd always regret not knowing what we might have shared—even if it's just a one-time thing."

"Then I'll find us a perfect romantic getaway."

"No need to do that. I have one available—right here, right now."

In a dirty, dusty barn? Surely she wasn't serious.

But when she placed her hand on his cheek, he realized that she was indeed serious. And with that gentle touch, the slight roughness of her palm uncovered a raw desire that sent his hormones soaring and his blood racing, and he realized he'd agree to anything she suggested.

"Come with me." She stood and took his hand, walking toward a ladder that led to the hayloft.

As Amber led Jensen up the steps, as he watched the sway of her hips, he was glad that he'd thought to bring a condom with him. Not that he planned to have need of one tonight, but he didn't take chances. And he'd... well, he'd hoped something like this would happen, although he'd never expected to have a saloon girl suggest that they make love in a hayloft.

Still, he found the whole idea rather exciting.

When they reached the top rung, he couldn't believe what he saw. Several quilts had been spread over the hay-littered flooring near a rickety nightstand that held a battery-operated lantern and a portable radio.

For a moment, he had to wonder if she'd been expecting him and had planned to invite him to join her here all along.

"I haven't been up here in a year or longer," Amber said, "so it might be a little dusty. But it's comfy."

Rodeo posters of cowgirls lined the walls, and a small bookshelf held several paperbacks and a stack of magazines.

"This was my hideout when I was a teenager. I used to come up here to read and think. And often just to dream." She shrugged, then strode over to the night-stand and turned on the lantern, as well as the radio, which played the sounds of soft rock. "It might not seem like much to you, but it was a castle in a faraway land to me back then."

"It looks pretty special to me now."

And so did she.

As they stood in the hayloft, in the yellowed glow of the old lamp, he felt rather heroic, like a Western sheriff who'd fought the bad guys and returned to town after earning the right to woo his lady's heart.

Her heart? All daydreaming aside, their reality didn't allow him the luxury of assessing the emotions involved, although admittedly they were brewing under the surface.

But right now, all he could think about was how lovely and alluring Amber was, dressed in that sexy red satin and looking at him as though she was feeling every bit as aroused and tempted as he was.

He reached out and unpinned her hair, allowing it to fall along her bare shoulders and down her back. She smiled, then scooped her soft curls aside and turned so he could unzip her costume. He took a moment to linger, to inhale her peach blossom scent and to graze his fingers along her skin.

Finally, he reached for the zipper. As the garment opened and slipped to the ground, she turned to face him wearing a black strapless bra and matching pant-ies. His breath caught. The cowgirl had morphed into a goddess, a sight to behold.

Her body, curvaceous yet lithe, was everything he'd imagined it to be and more.

Talk about fantasies coming to fruition. But for the life of him, this was one fantasy he never wanted to end.

As Jensen drew Amber back into his arms and claimed her with a heated kiss, she leaned into him, ready to give him all she had to offer—and to take whatever he was willing to give.

If the kisses they'd shared had been a sample of what was to come, making love with Jensen was going to be magical—memorable. Yet it wasn't just a sexual act. Not as far as she was concerned.

He ran his hand along the curve of her back and down the slope of her hips, then pulled her hips forward, against his erection, letting her know how badly he wanted her. A surge of desire shot clear to her core, and she pressed back against him, revealing her own need.

When she thought she was going to die from the ache of her arousal, she ended the kiss long enough to un-snap her bra and let it drop to the straw-covered floor.

"I knew you were beautiful under that denim and flannel, but I had no idea you were so…stunning, so perfect." He reached for her breasts, his thumbs skimming her nipples and sending her senses reeling.

She knew better than to think about concepts like forever when they only had tonight—or perhaps a few more like this. But everything about Jensen and what they were doing seemed so right.

When she feared her knees would no longer hold her up, he scooped her in his arms and carried her to the quilt. Then he dropped to one knee and gently lay her down. A true knight—with or without the official royal title.

He studied her for a moment, passion glazing his

eyes, then he proceeded to remove his shirt, baring himself to her. When he was undressed, and she caught the full sight of him, the sheer beauty of his chiseled chest and abs, she scolded herself for ever thinking polo wasn't a serious sport. The man was well-muscled perfection, and she wanted to pull him down to her so they could start kissing right where they'd left off.

"I hope you don't think I came here planning to do this tonight, but I did bring some protection along with me."

"If I'd known this was going to happen, I would have had fresh linen, rose petals and candles."

"I'm glad you didn't think of candles. I can't imagine how we would have explained a barn fire, especially if the news reached the *Cross Town Crier.*"

She laughed. "And then the paparazzi would have had a real heyday with that."

"They might have said our scorching hot affair had set the quilt on fire."

"Think we should risk it?" she asked.

"I might spontaneously combust if we don't."

She laughed, then opened her arms. He joined her, and they continued to kiss, to taste, to stroke each other, skin to skin. As her thumb brushed across his nipple, he sucked in a breath.

For a moment, her feminine confidence, which had been soaring through the roof only moments ago, waffled. "I'm sorry my hands aren't as soft as the other women you've—"

He grabbed her by the wrists and gave them a firm squeeze, his gaze locking on hers with an intensity that stilled her voice, her thoughts and even her fears. "Your skin and hands are perfect, Amber. And your work ethic is one of the things I find most attractive about you. Don't ever apologize for that. Your touch stimulates me in a way I've never experienced."

"You aren't just pulling my leg?"

His expression softened, and a smile tugged at his lips. "I meant what I said about tangling with you earlier, so I might tug your legs a bit before the evening is over. But all translations aside, your hands are exquisite."

Then he kissed all her insecurities away until she was drowning in need. After he slipped on the condom, he entered her. And as her body responded to his, as their tempo increased until there was no one else in the world but the two of them, it seemed that they were in that magical castle she'd always imagined this old barn to be.

This wasn't Amber's first time making love, but it certainly felt like it. Jensen was an amazing lover—no doubt experienced with all the "dalliances" she'd read about, the women he'd dated all over the world.

But she wouldn't think about that now. Not while he was doing such amazing things, making her body move and arch, releasing far more than an uninhibited sexuality she hadn't realized she had. He was triggering emotions she'd only dreamed of feeling.

As his tempo increased, she raised her hips to meet him, feeling as though she was on a sexual roller coaster, her heart racing, her pulse spiking. She went up and up, then raced down and around.

She was in and out of control, yet breathlessly anticipating each and every unexpected jolt and turn. And as she reached a peak, she cried out and let go. Jensen shuddered with his release, and they came together in an earth-rumbling, soul-soaring climax she would never forget.

As she held him close, enjoying the ebb and flow of the most amazing afterglow, she was reluctant to release her hold because making love with Jensen had been a ride to beat all rides.

And since she'd just come to realize that she didn't want to settle for a temporary affair, this was one carnival ride that was bound to break her heart in the end.

Jensen didn't dare breathe, let alone move.

He wasn't anywhere near as sexually experienced as the tabloids reported him to be, but he'd certainly been with worldly women before—and in some rather glamorous locations, including five-star hotel suites, Scottish castles and more than one Italian villa. So needless to say, a Texas barn was a first.

But if he was to compare making love with Amber in a hayloft to the rest, the other ladies and bedrooms would pale.

Whether in denim and flannel or red satin and black lace, Amber Rogers had a way of rocking his world. And in this case, she'd certainly pulled the proverbial rug out from under his feet.

Not to take Texas colloquialisms too far, but how in blue blazes had she done that?

The mutual desire had been a large part of it, sure. When she'd cried out with her climax, he'd released with her in a sexual explosion that had him seeing stars, in spite of the fact that they weren't out in the open and that there was an old wooden roof overhead.

He rolled to the side, yet he continued to hold her

close, reluctant to let her go. He didn't have to ask how it was for her. He'd felt it in her touch, heard it in her sighs.

They lay like that for the longest time, sated and… well, amazed was a pretty good description.

He feared the questions that might follow, things like, Where shall we go from here?

Because, in reality, whatever they'd shared this evening couldn't really go anywhere other than here in Horseback Hollow. As fond as he'd grown of Amber, as much as he'd like to spend every waking hour he had with her while he was in town, he couldn't see them having much more than that.

Their lives were so completely different that it would be impossible to mesh them. Besides, he had family obligations in London and a patriarchal image to maintain.

He could, of course, come visit her from time to time, whenever he was in town to see his family. But he couldn't expect her to put her life on hold, staying single for those few and far between visits.

Still, as he drew her close, as he inhaled her faint peach scent and pulled a piece of straw from her silky hair, he felt as though he held an unexpected treasure.

Amber Rogers was an attractive and intriguing woman, one he found entertaining and a world apart from the upper-class socialites he normally dated. She also made him smile as often as she challenged him, which kept him on his toes.

Not a day went by, and hardly a moment, that he didn't think about her and wonder what she was doing. They'd become close friends, dear friends. And now they were even more than that—they were lovers.

Of course, as soon as the weddings were over in February, he'd be making a trip to the airfield, where he would board a chartered flight on Redmond-Fortune Air to Dallas, connecting to British Airways and flying first class to Heathrow.

But for the first time since in arriving in Texas, Jensen wasn't the least bit homesick for London—or eager to return.

Chapter Ten

Jensen refused to risk Amber's reputation with the threat of the paparazzi still lurking. And even if he wasn't concerned about them making a tabloid-newsworthy spectacle of themselves, he couldn't trust himself to see her and keep his hands off her. Instead, they talked on the mobile several times each day. But it was never enough.

He'd give anything to whisk her away to a deserted island, where he could be alone with her, but they were stuck in Horseback Hollow, where he was finding it more and more difficult to keep their relationship quiet. All his efforts at secrecy made him fidgety—or maybe his wish to spend every spare moment he had with Amber was doing that.

Either way, Quinn had picked up on it and brought it to the forefront during the third week in January, while they had their morning coffee.

"Looks to me like you have a little cabin fever," Quinn said.

Jensen slipped his hands into his trouser pockets, and his fingers wrapped around the gold watch. "A bit, I suppose. I can't seem to slip out of here without the paparazzi sitting up and taking note."

"You sure that's all it is?"

No, but Jensen didn't feel like talking about it. "They'll eventually get tired of hanging out here and go look for a story elsewhere."

"Seems like you'd be used to all that. There's nothing else bothering you?"

"Being away from home for so long has me concerned about the office, the Chesterfield estate and that sort of thing."

"That's it, huh?"

"What makes you think there's anything more than that?"

"Because you're wearing out the floorboards pacing back and forth. And you keep picking up your cell phone—or mobile, as you call it—as if you're dying to place a call. Yet I know what time you typically talk to your assistant back home, thanks to the time change, and that you told me that your office seems to have things well under control across the pond." Quinn took a sip of coffee, stretched out his legs and smiled. "So I thought it might have more to do with a pretty former rodeo queen."

Jensen stiffened, but he didn't give his brother-in-law's theory any credence. At least, not verbally. Ostensibly, his body language might not be so subtle.

"I'm the last one in the world to believe anything

those tabloids print," Quinn added. "But I have to admit, you look a little lovesick to me."

"That's ridiculous."

"You'd know best," Quinn said.

"That's right." But did he really?

Jensen blew out a sigh. "All right, I'll admit it. Amber Rogers has caught my eye—and she's taken up a good deal of my thoughts. But nothing can come of it. And while I'd like to spend more of my time with her while I'm here, I don't want her to have to deal with the paparazzi."

"I hear you. Those jerks made Amelia's life hell for a while—mine, too. And we've been keeping a low profile so they won't do it again." Quinn carried his empty mug to the sink and rinsed it out. "But if you and Amber enjoy each other's company, it seems a shame to let those guys ruin what little time you have left."

He certainly had a point.

After Quinn left the kitchen through the mudroom, grabbed his hat and headed outside, Jensen sat alone, pondering his dilemma. He'd let his worries about his privacy and the paparazzi steal precious time he could have spent with Amber face-to-face. And the clock was ticking. He only had about three weeks left in town.

Who knew when he'd be back? So he reached for his mobile and called Amber.

She answered on the second ring. "Good morning. You're up early."

No need to tell her he hadn't had a full night's sleep since he'd left her ranch the night they'd made love in her barn. "I thought I'd have a cup of coffee with Quinn."

"What? Trading in your teapot for a coffee grinder?"

She tsked her tongue. "Sounds as though the Texas ruffians are having a bad influence on you."

"You may be right." Jensen found himself leaning back in his chair and grinning, as carefree as a child with no responsibilities in the world. "I was wondering if you'd like to go out to dinner with me tonight."

"You already paid off your wager."

"I was talking about a date—a real one."

"Seriously?"

"Yes. And if you have something other than blue jeans, you might want to dress up a bit."

"Like a saloon girl?"

Jensen laughed. "As much as I'd love to see you in that sexy red dress again—in a barn setting or in the privacy of my bedroom—you'd better leave the costume at home."

"All right. Just tell me what time and where to meet, and I'll be there."

They agreed upon seven o'clock at The Garden in Vicker's Corners, and then Jensen set about making plans for the evening.

He was leery of being caught with Amber for more reasons than one. The paparazzi would have a field day with it—The Prince and the Cowgirl... Or, heavens! What if they'd gotten wind of her in that sexy saloon-girl outfit?

Still, Amber was worth the risk of a little notoriety, especially if that meant spending some quality time with her.

That evening, as Jensen prepared to leave for his date with Amber, his mother was seated on the divan at the Drummonds' ranch, her mobile in hand, her head bowed.

"What are you doing, Mum?"

Lady Josephine glanced up, her cheeks flushed. "Sending a text."

Where in the world had she ever learned how to send texts? One of Toby's kids must have taught her. The oldest boy loved anything electronic.

His mother was one of the most technologically challenged people he knew, although it was high time she joined the rest of the world.

She slipped her mobile into the pocket of her tailored slacks, assessed him with a mother's eye and smiled. "My, don't you look handsome. Where are you going?"

"Out for the evening."

"Where? And with whom?"

"I thought I'd take Amber to dinner in Vicker's Corners."

"That sounds lovely." His mum stood and walked over to fix the collar of his Western shirt.

And yes, Jensen was cautiously dipping into Horseback Hollow fashion in an effort to blend in with the locals and draw less attention.

Mum cocked her head to the side. "Are the two of you…?"

"No, not at all." The last thing he needed was for his mother to worry that she'd lost another one of her children, especially the one who'd taken the helm of the family finances and assumed a patriarchal role, to the Texas countryside. "We're really just friends."

"Oh."

"No need to give the tabloids any more fodder for their silly stories," Jensen added, as he took in the quiet cleanliness of the living room. Little Clemmie was sleeping in the bassinet, and his mum had prepared a quiet, romantic dinner for Quinn and Amelia in the kitchen.

Then he noted that she'd combed her hair and freshened her makeup. "So what are you up to this evening? Are you going back to Aunt Jeanne Marie's house?"

"Yes, but Gabriella is hosting a small dinner party for her brothers, Cisco and Matteo, at Jude's ranch this evening, and I've been invited. So I'll be going there first."

Gabriella, Orlando Mendoza's daughter, was engaged to marry Jude Fortune Jones, Jeanne Marie and Deke's son. They were just one of the couples who would be married in the big wedding ceremony that would take place on Valentine's Day.

"Gabriella wanted me to bring you along, and I thought that you could take me. But if you have plans…" His mum trailed off, as though she hadn't expected Jensen to have anything else to do in such a small town.

"I'd be more than happy to drop you off," he said. "It's on the way. And since you've been staying with Jeanne Marie and Deke, you can ride home with them."

"Splendid." She brightened. "Let me just grab my pocketbook."

Fifteen minutes later, Jensen was helping his mother up into Quinn's pickup. Was it his imagination or had she sprayed on some extra perfume?

Not that he noticed those things usually, but she had seemed to take an inordinate amount of time to grab her purse. She must really be missing the London social scene if she was primping this much for a simple dinner party in Horseback Hollow.

"You look lovely," he told her as he started the engine.

She smiled. "Well, I want to make a good impression on the Mendoza family." Her mobile buzzed and she pulled it out, checked the screen, then giggled.

Had his reserved mother actually erupted in childish pleasure? What were Toby's kids up to?

He could ask, he supposed, but he wasn't the type to pry into other people's text conversations. So he continued to drive, thinking about his date with Amber. While he was looking forward to wining and dining her—in a way she deserved—he needed to keep in mind that the two of them were little more than friends, no matter how entertaining he found her.

Or how amazing he'd found their lovemaking.

The sooner he steered his mind in a different direction, the better. He had family obligations, responsibilities, and his life was a world away from Texas.

"Are you getting eager to return to England soon?" he asked his mum.

He knew she liked being close to her daughter, her new grandbaby and her newfound sister's family. But Lady Josephine Fortune Chesterfield was more British than the parliament building.

"I miss being home on the Chesterfield estate, but this funny little town is starting to feel like a second home. In fact, I was thinking of possibly speaking with a real estate agent about purchasing property here."

"Truly?" he asked, completely gobsmacked.

"Not to live full-time, of course. But I plan to visit Amelia and that sweet little Clemmie often. I don't want to be a thorn in their side, always staying at their house. Besides, if I do purchase a home here, it will give you, Lucie and your brothers a place to stay when you come to visit."

"I can't imagine either Oliver or Brodie spending much time in this tiny Texas town."

"Perhaps not. But I would have said the same thing about you a few weeks ago, and you seem to be getting along splendidly here."

Jensen had to admit that he'd enjoyed his time here. But he also had a business and clients to get back to. He couldn't stay out here playing cowboy indefinitely.

But when he thought about saying good-bye to Amber and not seeing her until his next visit to the States, something tightened in his chest.

They had certainly developed some type of connection, but not one that could withstand half a continent and an entire ocean.

Their worlds were too far apart—and not just physically.

He was a noble, a gentleman, not a ranch hand. And she was a rodeo queen, not a lady of the realm. There was no way they could forge a lasting relationship. They were simply too different.

It was better for them to just enjoy each other's company for the time being and not think about what the future most certainly did not hold for them.

"You know, Orlando's sons are single," his mom said as they pulled into the driveway at Jude's ranch.

"Hmm," Jensen murmured, not quite processing his mother's line of conversation.

"It must be so nice for him to have his family now living nearby. Perhaps his sons will find wives soon and settle down in Horseback Hollow permanently."

"It seems to be the common thing to do lately."

"You know, Amber Rogers is single and lives locally.

Perhaps you should mention the Mendoza boys to her. Perhaps, we can introduce them."

"Amber? *My* Amber?"

"Oh, I didn't understand her to be *your* Amber." Lady Josephine smiled, that knowing smirk she often displayed when she'd caught her husband sneaking biscuits or scones to one of the children before dinner time.

"I didn't mean she belonged to me," Jensen said. "Quite the contrary, in fact. But she has quite a bit going on in her life right now. Running her family ranch keeps her busy. So I'm sure she isn't in the market for a new beau."

Or was she? She'd seemed eager enough to consider romance when Jensen had taken her in his arms.

He'd like to think that was because he had instilled that passion in her. But what if it wasn't him? What if she was lonely, and he just happened to come along at the right time?

Still, she wasn't some young woman making her first appearance at a debutante ball in order to snag a husband. And he should know. He'd been to plenty of them—and he knew the look of a woman on the prowl for a husband. Amber Rogers definitely did not fit the bill.

Yet, long after he dropped his mother off at Jude's ranch, her suggestion lodged itself into his mind and he couldn't dislodge it. He'd even been tempted to go inside and meet these Mendoza boys just to confirm that they weren't possibly Amber's type.

But he was already running late. So he'd only walked Lady Josephine to the door. And before he could be invited inside, he'd dashed off.

It wasn't jealousy that had made him leave so suddenly. He was in a hurry to get to the restaurant and reassure himself that his date couldn't possibly be interested in dating anyone else.

He'd never been the possessive type, but he was determined that as long as he remained in town, he would be the only man with whom Amber would spend her time. After that, he wouldn't allow himself to think of her marriage options.

Maybe it was selfish, but he wanted her all to himself. Which was why, when he arrived at the restaurant before her, he again asked the hostess to seat them in a quiet, out-of-the-way corner.

The Garden in Vicker's Corner was a trendy bistro with stained-glass windows, copper ceiling tiles and a vintage art-nouveau crystal French chandelier in the entryway. Despite Amber's travels to some of the bigger cities throughout the great state of Texas during her short-lived rodeo days, she'd never been inside a restaurant this fancy.

"I've heard how great this place is," she said. "People need reservations weeks in advance to get in. How long have you been planning for us to have dinner here?"

Jensen chuckled, then lowered his mouth to her ear. "Not long at all. Despite the need to be on the lookout for constant media hounds and social climbers, wealth and notoriety also comes with some advantages."

Amber stopped soaking in the decor long enough to lift a brow at him. The way "social climbers" had rolled out of his mouth had put a sudden bad taste in hers.

She suspected that gold diggers and people wanting to move up in class and status often tried to take advantage of him, so he'd had to put up an emotional barrier to keep them from getting too close. But now that he was becoming firmly entrenched in their sweet little Texas town, who would he suspect was attempting to climb his social ladder?

Certainly not her. But ever since that night in the hayloft, she felt a little uncertain about where things stood between them. So she found herself reading into everything he said. She'd have to stop doing that.

"I can see where having financial and social advantages would come in handy for you in London Town, but how does that work for you here in Vicker's Corners?"

"You'd be surprised what you can do with some of those green advantages you Americans have—the kind with pictures of your old presidents and patriots on them. I've found them to be quite helpful in making my stay here in Texas a bit more pleasant."

The maître d' himself, a middle-aged man who'd introduced himself as Roland, led them back to a white linen–draped table for two, which was once again in a secluded corner. A single red rose in a bud vase, as well as a flickering candle in a votive, provided a romantic ambiance.

After Roland handed them menus and made sure they had ice water with lemon slices and a basket of fresh bread, he left them alone.

Still, Amber lowered her voice. "So you bribed someone to get us reservations?"

"I wouldn't call it a bribe. It was more like a sizable contribution to ensure our privacy and to enhance our dining experience."

She liked having him to herself. It also gave her an opportunity to get to know him better. So she reached for a slice of pumpernickel and asked, "What was it like to grow up in England? Did you have a happy child-hood?"

"Brodie and Oliver, my older half brothers, may have had it a bit differently before my mum married my father. But I've never heard them complain. So I think they'd agree that we all had the very best of childhoods. We grew up on the Chesterfield estate in England."

"I can't imagine what that might have been like. I suppose you had tons of servants."

"It wasn't like that." Jensen took a sip of water. "Mum wasn't a traditional mother by aristocratic standards."

"What do you mean?"

"She didn't hire nannies to raise her children. She did have help, but she was in complete charge of the nursery, as well as the household. Our family may have been titled and privileged, but she was determined that we wouldn't take our money or royal station for granted."

Amber leaned her arms on the table, eager to hear more, yet not wanting to break the spell Jensen cast upon her when he finally began to open up about himself. So she sat quietly, but attentively, waiting for him to continue.

That is, until the sommelier interrupted him. "May I interest you in one of our wines, sir?"

Once Jensen placed their order for a bottle of zinfandel from California's Napa Valley, Amber steered him back toward the conversation she meant to have.

"So you didn't grow up with a house full of servants?"

"Quite the contrary. We had plenty of them, but they were under strict orders to ensure we weren't spoiled rotten."

The sommelier returned with the red wine, removed the cork and let Jensen have a sample. "It's fine. Thank you."

After filling their glasses half-full, he left them alone again.

"I was an only child," she said. "So I find this fascinating."

Actually, she found Jensen fascinating—and not just the way the candlelight glistened in his hair, the way he held his wine goblet, turning it just so and studying the deep, burgundy-red color. And she was thrilled that he'd finally begun to open up to her.

"After Brodie and Oliver went off to school," he said, "my mother was busy with Charles and the girls, so my father would take me to the stables with him. We spent a great deal of time together, he and I. And as soon as I learned basic arithmetic, he had me adding up his ledger books. He told me never to trust anyone else with the family business or finances. I guess I took it all a little too much to heart."

"How so?" she asked, taking the first sip of her California wine.

"I was always a stickler for the rules. Charles used to tease me and try to get me to lighten up, but the sense of family responsibility had been engrained early on."

He sounded as though he'd been the perfect son, the perfect child.

"I'll bet your teachers loved you," she said.

"They did. I was the one they would send on special errands. In fact, I was a prefect my second year at Eton."

"A *prefect*?"

"It's a student who's put in charge of the others."

"Like an associated student body president?"

Jensen furrowed his brow. "I'm not sure."

Maybe she shouldn't make too many comparisons to their school systems. She didn't want him losing focus.

"So you went to Eton? Even I've heard of that. Where did you go for college?"

"For university you mean? I went to St. Andrews in Scotland, naturally."

Naturally. "Did you always do what your family expected of you?"

He picked up his goblet and swirled the wine in the candlelight, his expression growing wistful. "Father used to say that he could count on me for anything. I mean, he was close to all of his children and loved us all equally. But even Mum will tell you that Father and I shared a special bond. We enjoyed the same things like polo, managing finances, being with our families—even watching old cowboy movies."

"I would have liked to have met him."

Jensen reached into his pocket for a moment, then withdrew his hand. "My father and I even shared a love of airplanes, although he was a pilot and I wasn't."

"Did you ever think of taking flying lessons?"

"Occasionally. But now that he's gone, I think about it even more. What I'd really like to do is purchase a jet. That way, I could visit my family in Texas whenever the fancy struck."

"Seriously?"

Again, he reached into his pocket. "Well, I'll probably take those flying lessons. And I might even buy a jet. But I'd hire the pilots."

She lifted her linen napkin, trying to hide the smile that touched her lips. If he flew here regularly, she'd get to see him more often. But she didn't want to corner him into making promises out of an offhand comment, so instead she said, "You keep reaching into your pocket. Why is that?"

"Oh." He pulled out an antique gold watch. "This was my father's, and his father's before him. It's silly really, but whenever I think about him, I have a habit of toying with it."

"That's sweet. How did he pass?"

His expression dimmed, and for a moment, she thought he might change the subject, but he looked up from the treasured heirloom and continued. "He died of a massive coronary while playing polo four years ago—almost to the day. The family was devastated."

Amber thought of Pop's death, what his loss had meant to her and how she'd given up her rodeo career in order to return to the ranch to be with Gram and to help her through it.

"I'm sorry," she said.

"So am I. It wasn't easy to step in and take over the helm of the family holdings and investments—but not because I couldn't handle it. My father had trained me well, and I was already doing much of that when he died. The difficult part was that I suffered more than just the loss of my father and the family patriarch. I lost my best friend and confidant."

The grief he still carried after four years was etched deeply in his face, and her heart went out to him.

"I suspect that you handled it all with grace—and that you did your best to take care of everyone else."

"My father would have expected it. And my mother needed me to be strong."

"Did you have anyone to lean on at the time?"

What she was really asking was if he had a girlfriend

or a significant other in his life. But even though it had come out innocently and seemed like a natural question to ask, she knew better and winced at her inappropriate curiosity, especially at a time when he was sharing his heart.

It was just that she'd like to have a small part of his heart—if he'd only give it to her.

"I started to talk to my mum about it one day," he admitted, "but she was so heartbroken herself, I couldn't burden her with my grief."

"What about friends or…someone else?" There she went again, probably sounding like an insecure teenager, prying about the other women in his life when she ought to wait for a more opportune time.

But Amber would have given anything to be the one who'd comforted him back then, the one he could have opened up to.

"I realize the tabloids all seem to say that I'm one of England's most eligible bachelors. And while I do attend plenty of social events and usually have a lady on my arm, that's merely an image I project."

"I can't believe women aren't clamoring to date you," she said, a green twinge of jealousy rising up inside.

"Perhaps they are. But my life isn't as glamorous as it seems."

The life he lived didn't seem the least bit glamorous to her—not if he didn't love her back and she couldn't be a part of it.

"Every time I appear in public with a woman, the gossip columns predict a wedding. And if I go on my own, without a date, they wax poetic about why I won't commit."

"That must be aggravating."

"It is. I'm very careful about what I do and the image I project—just as my father was. I wouldn't do anything to soil the family name. But I've learned to take those tabloid headlines in stride. I'm stronger than my sister Amelia in that respect. She went through terrible turmoil last spring when they falsely announced her engagement to Lord James Banning. So don't believe everything you read."

She leaned back in her chair, somewhat comforted. "So no ladies back home are spitting nails because you showed up in the tabloids kissing a Texas cowgirl?"

"Absolutely not. I wouldn't have done what we did the other night if I was involved with anyone that way."

Of course he wouldn't. Amber would expect nothing less of the prim and proper Jensen, but it still felt good to hear him say it out loud.

"So what about you?" he asked, changing the subject. "Did it hurt to give up the rodeo?"

"I told my grandmother that I'd grown tired of the traveling and being away from home. But Gram is my only family. And I didn't want her to think I'd sacrificed my dreams to be with her while she grieved."

The maître d' came by to take their orders—the prime rib for him and the herb chicken and red potatoes for her.

She assumed the topic of their conversation would change, but after he left, Jensen asked, "Why the rodeo?"

"Because I'm good at it, for one thing. But I also did it for Pop. My dad used to compete, which tickled him to no end. But when he married my mom, she thought bronc riding was too dangerous. So he gave it up, moved to Houston and got an office job. After my dad died, she couldn't support me on her own. So she moved home to the Broken R."

"Then you took up barrel racing?"

She smiled. "I couldn't ride broncs, but it was a way to compete in the rodeo—and to make my pop proud."

"From what I heard, you were a natural."

"That's what Pop said."

"So you just gave it up? Just like that?"

She bit down on her bottom lip. She could probably let it slip now—at least some of it. "Yes, I gave it up, but I have an opportunity to ride again. Not in the rodeo, but as part of the Cowboy Country USA Wild West Show."

He stiffened, and she wished she had kept it to herself. Heck, she'd implied that the whole thing was still under consideration. What would he say or do if he knew she was already committed?

The maître d' came by with their salads, and the conversation stalled for a while.

She'd been prepared for a gradual change of subject, but not for the silence that followed. But maybe Jensen was just being introspective.

"Does that bother you that I might ride in the Wild West Show?" she asked.

"Of course not. It sounds like a reasonable compromise."

Did it?

Maybe she should give him some time to chew on it before she told him that she was not only committed, but legally bound.

When their dinner was served, they made small talk while they ate. But the sooner it came time for the bill to be paid and for them to go their own ways, the more

Amber's stomach rebelled at the roasted red potatoes and the herb chicken.

She'd give anything to take Jensen home with her or to drive off to a place where they could be alone, but it looked as though they'd be getting into separate vehicles again tonight.

Even after what they'd shared in the loft.

Her stomach knotted, and she pushed her plate aside even though it was still laden with enough leftover to take home for lunch tomorrow.

Finally, she lifted her goblet and took a sip of wine, preparing to bolster her courage.

"It's a shame nothing can come of a relationship between the two of us," she said, hoping and praying he'd tell her she was wrong.

Jensen reached out and placed his hand over hers, enveloping her with warmth. "As much as I'd like to argue, I can't see how it could."

In spite of the fact that she'd known all along that they'd never have a life together, Jensen's words drove a spike in Amber's heart dead center, creating a crack that threatened to break it in two.

Still, as long as he remained in town, she was determined to spend as much quality time with him as she could.

Because when he left Texas, he'd made it clear that the only part of his life she could claim wouldn't be his future.

It would be his past.

Chapter Eleven

Under normal circumstances, if Amber had heard her grandmother say that she was going on an overnight trip with a single man, she would have been shocked speechless. But when Gram casually mentioned over breakfast that she planned to accompany Elmer on a two-day trip to Lubbock for a reunion with his military buddies, Amber didn't raise a protest or voice a judgment.

Well, she did nearly choke on her coffee. But when she'd finally coughed it into the correct passageway, she decided not to look a gift horse in the mouth.

Having the ranch house to herself meant that she and Jensen could finally have a private place to meet and have the talk she'd been wanting to have since their dinner at The Garden, and she was going to use the opportunity to its fullest advantage.

Once the older couple took off in Elmer's car, their

names branded on the back window, Amber reached for the telephone and, while butterflies swarmed in her tummy, placed the call she'd been dying to make all morning.

Jensen answered his cell on the second ring.

She'd barely greeted him when she blurted out, "What would you say if I told you I had the house to myself for the next two days?"

"Are you suggesting you'd like company tonight?"

"Yes. And not in the hayloft this time."

"That sounds wonderful. I'd offer to cook you a romantic meal, but as we discussed before, my culinary expertise is somewhat limited."

So was Amber's, but she didn't need to advertise that fact. Besides, she had plenty of other skills to make up for it.

"Should we meet at the Hollows Cantina?" he asked. "I've had a craving for carne asada."

"Another private dinner?" she asked. Because if that's what he wanted, they could order takeout and bring it back to the ranch.

"No, I think it's time we dined in the main part of the restaurant with everyone else."

What? No more clandestine meetings? As much as she looked forward to having the house to themselves later tonight, she was glad to know that he didn't want to keep her—or their relationship, if that's what it was—under wraps anymore. And she counted that as a good sign. A very good one.

Evidently they'd reached a turning point. Maybe it was time to level with him about Cowboy Country USA. She could tell him that she'd decided to fully commit to the Wild West Show, although she wouldn't mention anything else. First she'd gauge his reaction to the trick riding.

When the call ended, Amber set about getting ready for the weekend by changing her bedding, setting out scented candles in her room and choosing some romantic CDs to have ready for Jensen's arrival later that night.

Then she took the last two hours to fuss with her appearance—taking a bubble bath, doing her hair and choosing just the right outfit to wear. There'd be no jeans or flannel this evening.

Now, as she looked at herself in the full-length mirror, she studied the low neck of her silky top, one she'd gotten as a gift but had never worn. She wondered if she'd gone a little overboard. After all, it wasn't as if she and Jensen were meeting at a fancy restaurant out of town or in a dark movie theater.

They were going to the most popular restaurant in town—and on a Friday night. Everyone would see them together and, with her decked out in such obvious dating attire…well, it would pretty much be a coming-out party.

She glanced at the swell of flesh peeking out between the low swoop of her blouse. She hoped she'd chosen something that was enticing enough to remind Jensen of what she had planned for the rest of the evening, but not risqué enough to make her look like a truck-stop floozy.

When she had spent as much time as she dared, she reached for the perfume she favored but rarely used and applied a dab, wondering if Jensen would appreciate her efforts.

Or would he want her to cover up? The straitlaced

Brit sure seemed to have a bit of a jealous side. Or had she read him wrong?

He hadn't seemed to mind flaunting other women on his arm. So why her? Was it jealousy or embarrassment?

She shook off the insecurity. Either way, when she told him about Cowboy Country USA, she wouldn't mention the part about the ad campaign. It didn't take a crystal ball to know how the proper gentleman would feel about that, especially if the press got wind of it.

But even though Jensen would be long gone by the time Amber had to start posing for photographs in that saloon-girl costume, she'd keep that little secret to herself.

She took one last glance at herself in her mirror.

The clock was ticking. And she wasn't just talking about this evening and the need to stop primping so she could get on the road.

In a few short weeks Jensen would be leaving for London. And who knew how many more times they'd have to spend together?

For that reason, she would pull out all the stops tonight.

Jensen arrived at the Hollows Cantina before Amber and cursed the bloody paparazzi for his reluctance to pick her up and take her on a proper date.

Rachel Robinson, the hostess, greeted him and asked if he would prefer his usual table in the back corner. But Jensen had decided not to keep Amber or their relationship hidden anymore.

Besides, after the knowing smile Quinn had flashed at him when he'd handed him the car keys, their secret was bound to get out eventually. And maybe, somewhere deep inside, Jensen actually wanted it to. So he'd told Rachel to reserve the table in the middle of restaurant and headed to the bar to wait for Amber.

He'd just placed a drink order when a cowboy turned toward the entrance, broke into a broad grin and gave a slow wolf whistle. Several other men at the bar, along with Jensen, followed his gaze and spotted Amber sashaying into the cantina.

The slinky black blouse she wore wasn't any less revealing than that damn saloon-girl costume. And her jeans fit her like a pair of denim gloves, leaving very little to the imagination when it came to those shapely, not-so-hidden legs underneath.

He stood, fighting the red-hot pulse at the side of his neck. He told himself that the mooning cowpokes in this place were used to seeing Amber dressed in working clothes and that they were merely surprised by the change in her appearance. But the woman was as sexy as she was unpredictable, and he was tempted to whisk her away to someplace private—and not just so he could keep her hidden, but so he could have her all to himself.

She spotted him straightaway because she headed for the bar.

"Hello," she said as she slid onto the stool he pulled out for her.

As if just now realizing that everyone—even the women who'd gathered in the bar—were studying the two of them, she asked, "What're they staring at?"

"You, my dear." From where he stood, he had a clear vantage point of the swell of her breasts, which he'd caressed a few nights before. And he forced himself to look away for fear his words would stall in his throat.

She ran a hand through her glossy hair, as though

taming her long and loose locks could downplay how magnificent she looked. "Am I overdressed?"

"Not at all. You're stunning." He took his seat and handed her the margarita he'd ordered for her—the exact one she'd been drinking the night she'd come with Mr. Murdock and her grandmother.

She looked at the delicate silver-and-turquoise watch on her wrist. "Are they still having the two-for-one happy hour special?"

Did she think he was a tightwad? He'd only been humoring Mr. Murdock before.

"I have no idea what time it is—or if there are any specials. I just thought this was your drink of preference. Did I get it wrong?"

"No, this is fine." She took a sip. "In fact, it's just what I need to calm my nerves."

"Amber Rogers? Nerves? I can't believe the fastest rider and best shot in Horseback Hollow, if not all of Texas, would be nervous about anything."

Did it have anything to do with being seen with him? Did the paparazzi unnerve her, like they'd done to Amelia?

Of course. She probably didn't want her friends and neighbors to know that they were sexually involved. After all, she'd told him she didn't have brief affairs.

And he couldn't blame her for feeling uneasy about it. Even if he was free of familial obligations and they didn't have a geographical barrier, he wasn't sure if he was ready to pursue her in the way his heart and hormones were urging him to.

Amazing. That was the closest he'd come to admitting that he actually cared for her, that he felt more than friendship and that his heart had become invested. And

while he wasn't quite ready to broach the subject in public, he might do that later tonight, while they were alone.

Just as he lifted his drink to take another sip, a slick-
looking gentleman, who looked more out of place in
Horseback Hollow than Jensen felt, approached.

"Why, there's our pretty Amber. It's sure nice to see
a friendly face in these parts." The man, who was in his
late forties, ran a pinky-ringed hand between his fleshy
neck and his collar.

If he'd had a camera, Jensen might have thought he
was a paparazzo.

Amber, who seemed a bit surprised by the intrusion,
turned to Jensen. "This is Max Dunstan, Jensen. He's
with Cowboy Country USA."

Dunstan held out his thick, well-manicured hand
while running a head-to-toe assessment of Jensen.

The men had barely made the customary greeting
when Dunstan pulled out a seat and plopped down on
the stool next to Amber.

Her eyes grew wide, and she glanced around the bar
as though trying to determine whether any of the locals
had noticed that she was hobnobbing with the enemy.

Jensen was an outsider, so his opinion about the
whole Cowboy Country USA controversy didn't count
for much. Nevertheless, while he liked the quaint appeal of Horseback Hollow, he also found the Wild Bill
Hickok and Annie Oakley thing a bit intriguing.

In fact, as Dunstan delivered his fancy Hollywood
talk, Jensen tuned out so he could take in the not-so-
subtle looks being cast their way.

Amber shuffled in her seat a couple of times, as if
she wanted to be anywhere but next to Dunstan. Jensen

found the whole thing quite amusing—until he heard the words *photo shoot*.

He spun back around just in time to hear Dunstan ask Amber if she would bring the saloon-girl costume with her for the ad campaign.

"What ad campaign?" Jensen asked. "And what photo shoot?"

"Our Amber here," Dunstan said, "is going to be the face of Cowboy Country USA. Forget about princesses and Kate Middleton. When we're done with our publicity launch, little girls all around the world are going to want to be cowgirls just like Amber Rogers."

"What do you mean 'saloon-girl costume'?" Jensen asked Amber. "I thought you were only talking about doing some trick riding. And that you hadn't made any decisions yet."

"I planned to talk to you about that later tonight," she said, rather sheepishly.

"Whoops." Dunstan guffawed. "Did I spill the beans?"

Amber shot him a scowl.

"Sorry about that." Dunstan raised his hands in mock surrender. "When I saw the expensive suit and Armani shoes, I figured he was your lawyer and already knew about your contract."

What contract? Why did Jensen feel as though he'd just walked into a movie theater, only to find that he'd missed the integral opening scene?

Using his best "lord of the manor" voice, Jensen said, "No, I'm not her solicitor. I can assure you I'm more to her than that."

"No kidding?" Dunstan raised his brows and looked first at Amber, then at Jensen. "My bad. I didn't expect a saucy cowgirl like Amber to have a stiff suit as a boy-friend. No offense, buddy."

Buddy? Didn't this guy know who Jensen was? And who in the bloody hell was he calling a stiff suit?

"Thanks for stopping by," Amber said. "You have yourself a great night, Mr. Dunstan." Then she waved him off, dismissing him as graciously as Queen Elizabeth would have expelled a naughty dog from the throne room.

As Dunstan walked away, she tipped her shot glass of tequila to her lips as if it were a porcelain cup of Earl Grey.

Yet something told Jensen that she was unsettled by the whole encounter.

Well, he was more than unsettled. He was downright perturbed—especially at being kept in the dark.

"It sounds as though your gig with Cowboy Country USA is all but a done deal." He'd tried to tamp down the accusatory tone of his voice, but without much success.

"I was going to tell you about the contract tonight."

"Tell me what? That they offered you one? Or tell me that you signed one?"

"That I signed one."

"But I thought you were just going to ride in their pretend cowboy show. I didn't know about the dancing-girl business or the photos and publicity."

He hadn't meant to sound so petulant, like a child who didn't get a sticky bun for supper. She didn't owe him an explanation. But for some damn reason, he still hurt like hell—way down deep. And the thought of her parading around in some skimpy costume, modeling for photographers and seeking the limelight was the exact thing that he'd spent his life avoiding.

"This wasn't the way I'd wanted to tell you, but I don't need your permission or approval anyway." She straightened her spine, and he realized she was no longer embarrassed or worried about what the locals were thinking. Or him, for that matter. "When you go back to London, I'm going to stay here in Horseback Hollow and go on with my life the way I see fit."

"I didn't know that performing in a trashy, two-bit saloon-girl costume was on the top of your list for life achievements."

"First of all, it's not trashy. Gram sewed that for me. And second of all, I *like* performing. Not necessarily in a skimpy dress, but on a horse and in an arena. I miss the rodeo and I miss the thrill of riding. I'm not going to apologize for that."

"Nobody is asking you to apologize." He wished she would lower her voice. They were making a scene, and he hated the way the patrons were now looking at him as if he'd insulted one of their own. "I guess I was just taken by surprise. I didn't realize you were into all that celebrity rubbish like the others. I thought I knew... Oh, never mind."

"What did you think you knew? *Me?*" She gave a little snort. "Because if you really knew me, you'd know that I'm not doing this for any other reasons than the ones I already mentioned. The last thing I want is to be a celebrity living out my life publicly on the front page of every gossip magazine. But I guess you have that British nose stuck too far up in the air to see that life is more than hiding out in your sister's house and dating all the wrong people, just so the world will see you the way you want it to—and not the way you really are."

She reached into her purse and pulled out a few bills,

leaving them on the bar, before she got to her feet. "That should cover the cost of my drink. I wouldn't want you to add gold digger or moocher to the list of unflattering qualities you think I possess."

With that, Amber turned around and stormed out of the cantina.

Jensen reached into his pocket, removed the watch and glanced at it. He wasn't sure what had happened, but he'd certainly made a damn mess of everything.

Well, what had Amber expected—a profession of undying love and unconditional acceptance? It took all she had not to burst into tears before she reached the dark and safe confines of her pickup.

Of course she looked like some sort of fame-hungry celebrity wannabe. She could see why someone like Jensen, who'd spent his entire life avoiding the cameras, wouldn't want his precious family name linked with the new face of Cowboy Country USA. But that didn't make her a bad person or somehow beneath him.

But then again, she had no one to blame but herself. She knew where this relationship was going—nowhere. And she'd known that all along.

The two of them were like night and day. Their worlds and their paths never should have crossed.

Still, she'd let herself fall in love with Jensen in spite of all that. And her heart ached at the loss of something and someone she'd never stood a chance of having. She needed to have a good cry, but she'd be darned if she'd do it in the parking lot of the town's most popular eatery.

So she started the truck and drove home, her anger soon replaced with tears and self-recriminations.

When she arrived at the darkened ranch house, she

tried not to look at the romantic staging she'd carefully set up before leaving for dinner—the scented candles that would remain unlit and the Keith Urban CD that would remain unplayed.

Instead, she undressed and climbed into bed, where the soft and clean sheets had been scented with lilac.

She punched her pillow about ten times before succumbing to heart-wrenching tears and crying herself to sleep. But even then, she spent a fretful night, tossing and turning until dawn.

The next day, a cold sense of loss nearly swept her away when she woke at daybreak, alone in a double bed and in an empty house.

She showered and dressed in her work clothes, hoping that would help put a sense of normalcy back into her life. Then she went to the kitchen and put on a pot of coffee.

When her cell phone rang, her heart leaped in her chest. Hope rose, chasing away her sadness. Let it be Jensen, calling to apologize or at least to make amends.

Without taking time to check the number on the lit display, she slid her finger across the screen and answered.

"Hello, dear. This is Josephine Fortune Chesterfield." Amber nearly dropped her coffee mug.

What could Jensen's mother possibly want? Was she calling to gently reprimand Amber for engaging her son in a horrible public display of a lover's quarrel last night?

"I'm sorry to trouble you this morning, but I was hoping you might know where I could find Jensen."

"Not here," Amber blurted out, embarrassed that the royal English aristocrat would think her son had spent the night with her. Of course, if Mr. Dunstan would have just kept his big mouth shut, that's exactly what would've happened.

"What I meant," she explained to Lady Josephine, "was that he didn't sleep with me. I mean, he didn't stay here last night. In fact, I haven't seen him since I left him at the Hollows Cantina."

"Of course not, dear. I'm sorry for assuming otherwise. It's just that he left in Quinn's truck yesterday. But it's back this morning, and one of the horses is gone. Several of the men have ridden out on the trails and haven't seen him. I thought that, maybe, he'd ridden out to your ranch to visit you."

Was Jensen missing? Had he pulled a disappearing act?

"No, he's not here. Does he normally just up and vanish like this?"

"Jensen? Hardly. He's a very reliable person and conscientious. But I'm afraid today's the anniversary of his father's death. And with all the recent developments and changes in the family, Jensen is taking it rather hard this year."

Had his grief been complicating matters?

Of course it had, and Amber had neglected to realize how quiet he'd become after talking about his father's death, how keen he'd felt the loss of the man who'd also been his friend.

She poured out her coffee and placed the mug in the sink. "Don't worry, Lady Josephine. I'll find him."

She just hoped she would be able to keep that promise.

After ending the call, she headed to the barn. If Jensen was on horseback, her best bet to find him would be with Lady Sybil.

But before she could saddle her horse, the brass buckle in the bridle caught her eye, making her think of Jensen's treasured gold pocket watch.

Where would he go if he wanted to be close to his father?

The answer came to her instantly and she ran back toward the house and grabbed the truck keys off the hook in the mudroom.

She drove down the highway much faster than was reasonable. Just before she could pull into the small parking lot at the airfield, she caught a glimpse of a horse and rider at the southern edge of the fence.

She slowed to a stop nearly a hundred yards away, not wanting to startle Trail Blazer, the gelding she'd sold Quinn, or Jensen, who was sitting in the saddle, staring at the small planes parked near the runway. She shut off the ignition and climbed from the truck.

"Hey," she said softly, as she approached.

Jensen glanced over his shoulder. "Hello."

"There's a posse out looking for you, cowboy."

He shrugged a single shoulder. If the dark circles under his eyes were any indication, she'd guess that he'd slept just as badly as she had.

"I'm sorry," he finally said.

"It's okay. We all need to get away and clear our heads once in a while, especially on days like today, when we're missing a loved one. Let me just call your mom and let her know she can call off the search party."

"While I'm sorry for worrying everyone this morning, I was actually apologizing to you for what I said to you at dinner."

She paused, her cell phone in her hand. She probably ought to backpedal about now, quit while she was ahead. But she couldn't help it. She'd fallen for the handsome Brit, and she couldn't roll over and consider their relationship dead in the water before it even got off the ground.

"I said some mean things, too," she admitted. "Cowgirls are tough and they're stubborn. And to make matters worse, I don't like it when someone says I can't or shouldn't do something. I was going to apologize for not telling you about that Cowboy Country USA contract sooner, but then, when I saw your reaction, I got my dander up and, well...I didn't mean to cause such a big scene."

"What you said made sense. I need to stop hiding and start living my life. I'm going to head back to England for a while."

He was leaving? Already? "What about the weddings?"

"I might come back for them. I haven't worked everything out yet."

"Will I see you again?" she asked, not really wanting to hear the answer.

"I don't honestly know. I thought I knew who I was and what I wanted, but then I met you and my whole world was turned upside down. I thought we could have a simple and uncomplicated affair, but that didn't work out so well."

It had worked out nicely the one night they'd spent in the barn. And if they'd had a chance to be together more...

"I'm not like the rest of my family," he said. "I'm not made for a long-term relationship."

Amber bit her lip to keep from protesting. And she blinked to keep from crying. "Did your parents set the bar too high? Are you afraid you won't find what they found?"

"Actually, it's quite the opposite. I don't want to find what they found. Watching my mum grieve for her best friend and soul mate has made me leery of loving someone that deeply. I started to feel much more than I should for you, and then things got tricky. You weren't the only one making a scene last night. I can't believe that I turned into such a jealous and possessive arse, especially when I thought of all those men seeing you in your showgirl costume."

"Well, the costume is a bit much. When Mr. Dunstan said that every little girl would want to dress up as a cowgirl just like me, it made me realize that no parent would want to see their daughter wear a saloon-girl costume. So I plan to make some stipulations in my PR contract. I won't agree to their PR photo shoot unless they agree to let me wear something much more practical for horseback riding."

"Even if you wanted to wear that costume—which is quite beautiful, by the way, so my apologies to your gram for what I said last night—I had no right to imply you shouldn't wear it. My parents never tried to keep me from doing anything I wanted to do. And I shouldn't try to limit you, either."

"But you cared enough to try. Isn't that a good sign?"

"My misplaced jealousy is beside the point. It's better if we end things now. There's a reason I don't let women get too close. If I were to allow myself to fall in love with you and then I lost you, the pain would be devastating. And it might never go away. I can't risk it. I *won't* risk it."

She wanted to object, to argue. But she wasn't about to grovel. Not when he'd already convinced himself that things were over between them.

No, there was nothing Amber could do or say that would change his mind. And while she should be thankful that she could evoke that kind of emotion in him, it only made her pain and her sadness worse.

"Have a safe trip," she murmured before heading back to her truck.

He'd made it sound so simple—and, in a way, so had she. But letting him go without a fight was the hardest thing she'd ever had to do.

She would forever grieve for him and for what they could have had—if they hadn't been so different.

Chapter Twelve

Two days later, Amber couldn't stand it any longer. She needed some answers—and she needed them now.

Had Jensen gone home to London?

Had he stayed?

Her curiosity was eating her from the inside out, and she was dying to talk to him. But she didn't want him to think she was stalking him—or that she'd resorted to begging like a lovesick puppy.

So who should she quiz? Jeanne Marie? That seemed like a more logical choice than Lady Josephine because Amber couldn't very well discuss that sort of thing with his mother.

There was also Amelia. Hadn't his sister said that she thought Amber was good for Jensen and implied they'd make a perfect couple? Well, maybe not perfect. But she'd spotted something between them, just by looking

at the photo of them kissing that had been plastered on
the front page of the tabloid.

You're just what Jensen needs, Amelia had said at the
hospital. *The camera caught a spark. And I've seen the
banter between you. My brother hasn't lit up like that
since before my father passed away. And even then...
well, I think there's something going on.*

Right now, it seemed Amber's only ally was Amelia,
so she whipped her cell phone out from her pocket and
called the Drummond ranch. She told herself that if by
chance Jensen answered, she'd hang up.

But she was in luck—Amelia said hello after several rings.

"Do you have a minute to chat?" Amber asked.

"Clemmie just went down for a nap, so, yes. This is
a perfect time."

Amber filled her in—not about everything, of course.
But she admitted that her attraction for Jensen had led
to...well, there'd been no need to deny or hide her feelings at this point. She'd clearly fallen for the stuffy Brit
who'd set her world on end, then jerked the rug right out
from under her. And she told his sister as much.

"No wonder," Amelia said. "My brother is clearly
confused. He hasn't been himself at all. I'm sure that's
why he left."

"So he *did* go, then." He'd said he would, but she'd
somehow hoped that he wouldn't, that he'd reconsider.
He had, after all, admitted to having feelings for her.

"He'll return soon. I'm sure of it. And not just because of the weddings in February."

Amber wasn't so sure about that. Even Jensen had
said he didn't know if he'd come back to see his cousins
married. That would mean turning around and flying

back across the pond again when the weddings were only a couple of weeks away.

"Thanks for taking time to talk to me."

"Call me anytime. And try not to be discouraged. Jensen will come around. We can always count on him doing the right thing, even if he doesn't know how right that thing is."

Amber didn't feel the least bit hopeful, but she tried not to let his sister sense her discouragement.

In truth, she was better off cutting her losses—no matter how badly her heart ached.

She and Jensen were too ill suited to make a match anyway. He was an uptight aristocrat. And she was going to star in the Wild West Show. She'd have to give up her dreams to live a life with him—although, she suspected that her competitive, cowgirl nature is what drew him to her in the first place. And while she might like to travel and see more of the world, she also loved Texas—and Horseback Hollow especially.

Yet, even if they could work out the geographical issues, there were still so many more differences. He hid from the paparazzi—at least, whenever he was with her. And she would make him front-page news.

No, it would never work out.

She'd be miserable. And so would he.

She deserved to fall in love with an American prince of a man, a real live Texan, a cowboy with roots in Horseback Hollow and not some faraway land where they butchered the English language and didn't appreciate sweet tea drunk from an ice-filled mason jar.

The next couple of days passed slowly. And in spite of Amber's resolve to put on her big-girl panties and get on with life, her cherished Horseback Hollow became a difficult place to be.

She'd avoided going into town whenever she could, but because Gram was often away from the house, spending more and more time with her new beau, running the household fell on Amber's shoulders. And today, they needed some groceries.

So she snatched her purse and the keys to the ranch pickup, then headed out the back door. She'd no more than crossed the yard when Gram and Elmer drove up, big band music blaring from the open window of his Dodge Charger and both of them grinning like teenagers.

"I'll see you later tonight," the retired marine said, as he dropped off her grandmother.

Gram blew him a kiss. "I'll have dinner ready when you get here."

Amber let out a sigh. She supposed she'd have to get used to having Elmer around. He was becoming a fixture, it seemed.

The green muscle car had no more than turned around and sped off, when Gram approached Amber with a big ol' smile plastered across her sweet, prim face.

"What's got you in such a happy mood?" Amber asked.

Gram lifted her left hand, which sported a sparkling diamond ring.

Seriously?

"You're engaged?" Amber asked. "To be *married*?"

"Yes, isn't it exciting? Elmer proposed this morning in front of everyone at The Grill, and I accepted."

Amber's shoulders slumped—and not just because

she thought Gram had tarnished Pop's memory by hooking up with Elmer Murdock. In truth, the sweet old coot had begun to grow on her. But that meant Gram would become a bride before Amber would—not that she'd ever been the kind to get all girly and dreamy over white lace, bouquets and promises.

Still, there was always a first time, she supposed.

"What's the matter?" Gram asked. "Aren't you the least bit happy for me?"

"I'm just a little surprised, that's all. I never expected you to get married again. And, if you did, I thought it would be to someone more like Pop."

"I loved your grandfather dearly," Gram said. "So don't get me wrong when I say this, but I gave up a lot when I married him."

Amber furrowed her brow. "What do you mean?"

"Come inside. I'll put on a pot of coffee, and we can talk."

Ten minutes later, as Amber and Gram sat at the antique oak table in the kitchen, their chat continued over two cups of fresh-brewed decaf.

"Your grandfather was a wonderful man and a good provider, but he was a quiet sort. And marriage to him meant that I had to give up my friends and the life I had in town when I moved to the ranch."

"I thought you liked the Broken R."

"I did—I do. And I never had any real complaints. But I used to have an active social life—something your grandfather didn't appreciate. He was never one for dancing or parties or even attending church socials."

"And so in waltzed Elmer Murdock."

Gram chuckled. "Jitterbugged was more like it. Elmer is always game to try something new or exciting. I know you probably think he's a little...wacky at times. But he's so funny, and he makes me laugh."

"I'm sorry, Gram. I hadn't realized how much he's added to your life. Or that you'd downplayed your own personality when you married Pop."

"It's not just that. On top of everything else, Elmer loves me, honey. And he tells me, which is something your grandfather had a difficult time voicing. What's more, I love him, too. I never expected to feel that zing again. And it's nice." Gram smiled, a spark lighting her eyes in a way Amber hadn't noticed before.

And it made her appreciate the man in a way she hadn't anticipated.

"Will you please give Elmer a chance?" Gram asked. "He'd do anything in the world for me. And for you, too."

Something told Amber that Gram was right about that. So how could she deny them her blessing? "Of course I will."

Gram wrapped her arms around Amber in a warm, loving embrace, which might have triggered an instant healing process if her heart wasn't so badly broken from her own lost chance at love. But Gram's happiness served as temporary balm.

Amber was beginning to realize soul mates came in all shapes and sizes. And one size didn't have to fit all.

At that moment, the telephone rang, interrupting their embrace.

"I'll get it," Amber said, before answering. "Hello?"

"It's Jeanne Marie, sweetie." By the chipper tone in her voice, she obviously didn't know that Amber had been left heartbroken by her British nephew. "How are you?"

"I'm fine." Amber used her brave voice—the one she took on right after she'd had a bad qualifying round. "How about you?"

"Busy with the big Valentine's Day weddings, of course. I was wondering if you'd be available to help us assemble the favors tomorrow."

Was there anyone in town *not* getting married? Amber didn't feel like celebrating the romances of four happy couples, but she couldn't very well say no. Besides, she'd be attending those weddings anyway. And maybe it would give her the opportunity to find out more about what was going on with Jensen. "Sure, I can help. Where are you doing it? And what time?"

"At my house tomorrow—about two o'clock."

"I'll be there." She just hoped she could keep a cheerful front while she worked.

"Wonderful. We haven't seen much of you, Amber. What are you up to?"

"Right this second? I'm heading to the Superette."

"And then what? Are you going back home?"

"That's the plan? Why?"

"Just wondered."

The woman certainly sounded upbeat. And inquisitive. Amber supposed organizing and maintaining strict schedules for four upcoming weddings would do that to a person.

Or maybe Amber was just being overly sensitive. A failed romance certainly sent a woman spiraling into the dumps.

They made small talk for a moment, then ended the call.

Amber continued on with her one errand of the day, but even a quick stop at the local market, where folks often got the scoop on what all the other locals were doing, nearly tore the broken heart right out of her.

Everyone she knew seemed to be having babies or getting married, and she couldn't wait to escape the local gathering place fast enough.

Then, to make matters worse, while she was standing in the checkout line, Mrs. Tierney, the owner of the market, put out the latest issue of the *Global Trotter*, the tabloid that had plastered the photo of her kissing Jensen on the front page several weeks ago.

"Congratulations," Mrs. Tierney said. "You must be over the moon. And I'll bet your grandmother is beside herself."

Amber glanced up from the cart she'd been emptying. "Excuse me?"

"On your engagement." Mrs. Tierney handed her the newspaper, with a bold headline that announced Sir Jensen to Wed His Cowgirl!

Amber would laugh if it wasn't so sad. She finally realized what Jensen had been talking about and how hard it was for people to live their lives—and their heartaches—in front of the paparazzi lenses.

She always thought rodeo girls had tough skin, but hers was newspaper-thin right now. Jensen had to be a robot to not let tabloid lies and rumors get to him.

Mrs. Tierney pointed to a photograph of a sparkling diamond ring—a huge rock, actually—that Jensen supposedly purchased for her and presented while on bended knee.

"I'm afraid there's no truth to that at all," Amber said, lifting her left hand, which was as bare as it could be. "See? No ring, no fiancé. No royal wedding for this cowgirl."

"That's a shame. I wonder who he bought the ring for?"

Amber didn't bother to even answer. Instead, she choked back the emotion and blinked backed her tears until her groceries had been tallied. Was that the business he'd rushed home to London to handle?

Had he been pulling one over on her with that whole never-want-to-risk-falling-in-love-and-losing-someone line? Because as much as the news rags embellished their articles, the picture didn't lie. The man on the front was definitely Jensen, and he was walking out of the Jewelry Shoppe carrying a small white bag.

Of course, he might have gotten his watch repaired.

The store telephone rang, and Mrs. Tierney put the caller on hold while Amber paid the bill. Then as Amber picked up her grocery bags and headed for the door, she refused to give into her sorrow or her suspicion about Jensen leading her on.

The new year had gotten off to one heck of a bad start, but she wasn't going to let it get the best of her. It didn't matter what Sir Jensen was doing back in England or who he was doing it with. Amber had so many new opportunities lined up and so much to look forward to. She lifted her head as she walked to the truck, determined to get right back up on the horse that had thrown her and to embrace a new attitude.

So instead of heading home, she drove to the Hollows Cantina, where she would have her very own belated "Auld Lang Syne"—and a mock toast to the new life she was determined to create for herself.

When Amber entered the Hollows Cantina, she was greeted by the hostess, Rachel. "Are you meeting someone for a late lunch?"

"Not this time. I'll just have a seat in the lounge. Thanks."

As Amber made her way toward the nearly empty bar, she thought she saw Rachel pick up the telephone and make a call, but she couldn't be sure. And what did it matter anyway? So she continued on, pulled out a stool and took a seat.

"What'll it be?" the bartender asked.

"I'd like a split of champagne, please."

"You got it."

She really wasn't a drinker—and the bubbly stuff tickled her nose—but she was determined to find something to celebrate, something positive to look forward to, something that would ease the ache in her heart or at least lighten her mood. And she didn't want another one of those dang Jose Cuervo–shot margaritas that Elmer and Jensen had always ordered for her.

She tapped the tips of her fingers against the top of the bar. First of all, there was her agreement to star in the Wild West Show. And since she no longer had to worry about what attention that might draw to the Fortune Chesterfield family, she could announce it from the rooftops.

Secondly, she'd played hardball with their corporate attorney, Max Dunstan, yesterday and had insisted that they drop the saloon-girl getup if they wanted to use her photograph in the Cowboy Country USA ad campaign, and he'd finally agreed.

"Well, I'll be," a male voice slurred from behind her. "Amber Sue Rogers. I haven't seen you since high school."

She glanced over her shoulder to see Brady Wilkins, the former Horseback Hollow running back who'd gone

on to play a season at Oklahoma State University until
a knee injury sidelined him for good.

"Hey," she said. "How's it going, Brady?"

"Not bad." He held a glass of amber liquid in his
hand—no ice.

Whiskey, she guessed. Maybe bourbon. And from
the smell on his too-close breath, it wasn't his first.

"Can I buy you a drink?" he asked.

"No, thanks. I just ordered."

"Want some company?"

Not really. She'd rather be alone.

And then do what? Mope and feel sorry for herself?

Before she could answer either way, he drew up the
barstool next to hers and took a seat.

About that time, Marcos Mendoza walked in. He'd
no more than glanced at Brady before speaking quietly
to the bartender, who nodded. Then Marcos picked up
his cell phone and sent out a text.

Brady slipped his arm around the back of Amber's
barstool. "So how's it goin'? I heard you gave up the
rodeo to come home after your grandpa passed. That's
gotta be tough. I know what it's like to give up a dream,
especially when you're good—like you and me were."

The bartender brought Amber's champagne, along
with a chilled flute, and opened the split. "You okay,
ma'am? Is this guy botherin' you?"

"Hell, no, I ain't botherin' her, Lester. Me an' her
go way back."

The bartender eyed Amber carefully, letting her
know all she had to do was say the word and he'd make
sure Brady gave her some space. But she could take care
of herself. "I'm okay."

"See?" Brady's hand slipped to her shoulder, and he

drew her closer, as though she'd agreed to be on more friendly terms when, in truth, they'd hardly said a word when passing each other in the hall during high school because they'd run in different crowds.

Funny how a drink and shared heartbreak made bar-room buddies out of near strangers.

Footsteps sounded, and a camera flashed. Amber turned to the doorway, wondering who'd entered the bar. Her breath caught, and she nearly fell off her seat when she spotted Jensen stroll in wearing a black suit, a trail of paparazzi following behind him. And he was heading straight for her.

What the heck?

The cameras—at least four of them—continued to flash, but Jensen didn't blink. He bellied right up to the bar as if he was John Wayne himself, and snatched the only other empty seat next to hers.

Before the reporters could jot down *Sir Jensen in a Love Triangle* on their notepads, Jensen took her hand in his. "Unless you're caught up in a conversation with this cowboy, I'd like to have a word with you."

She'd been dying to talk to him since he'd flown home to London, but his surprise arrival had thrown her so off step, that she wasn't sure if she could wrap her mind around the words she'd been wanting to say. Yet she might not have another opportunity, so she'd better take him up on it. "Let's go into the back room where it's private."

"That won't be necessary." He glanced around the room. "Besides, I'm expecting an audience this time."

She followed his gaze, her jaw dropping when she spotted the people who'd begun to gather around— Gram and Elmer, their arms linked around each other and grinning from ear to ear. Jeanne Marie and Deke, along with Lady Josephine, her hands clasped together, as though waiting on bated breath for something…

Even Mrs. Tierney was here, but who was minding the Superette?

Rachel had wandered into the bar, too, along with Marcos and Wendy.

"What's this about?" Amber asked.

"I needed to talk to you, and I wanted it to be a surprise. So I asked Jeanne Marie to call your house and find out if you were home. She said you were heading to the Superette. I went looking for you there, but arrived too late. Mrs. Tierney said you went home, so I started back to the ranch, then Rachel called Amelia, and she told me you were here."

"How did Rachel know you were looking for me?" Amber asked.

"I suspect Wendy told her since news travels fast in the Fortune family. So I sent Marcos a text and asked him to hold you here, even if he had to hog-tie you."

Amber turned to the drunken former football player, then looked back at Jensen. "I don't suppose you asked Brady to waylay me."

"Not on a bet. Your cowboy friend might be harmless when inebriated, but I wouldn't trust my lady with a man who's not related to me."

"Your *lady*?"

"It's taken me a while to admit it—and a while longer to decide what to do about it. But you've become very special to me, Amber. And I want—no, I need you in my life."

"I didn't think you were coming back."

"The first thing I did when I arrived home was to

spend a little time at the cemetery so I could talk to my father. Just sitting there in the family plot, it became clear to me that I wasn't sparing myself any pain by walking away from you. I missed you so much in those few days I was gone that I couldn't stand it. Like I told you before I left, I was confused. And I had some things to think about."

"Did you?" she asked. "Get things worked out in your mind?"

"Almost. There's just one little bothersome question, but you can settle it for me." He reached into his lapel pocket, withdrew a small, black velvet box and dropped to one knee.

Then he flipped open the lid, revealing a stunning, sparkling diamond ring that looking amazingly similar to the one she'd seen in the most recent issue of the *Globe Trotter*. "I love you, Amber Rogers. Will you marry me?"

Cameras flashed from both sides of them, as people began to crowd around.

"Cat got your tongue?" he asked, a smile sliding across his face, as he used the same phrase on her that she'd once used on him.

"Are you sure about this?"

"Absolutely, positively certain."

She merely gaped at him, unable to believe what he was saying—what he was doing. And in front of an audience, no less.

His words and his sweet romantic gesture were being recorded for all the world to see—or read about in the tabloids.

"My old polo injury is starting to flare up. Are you

going to keep me down on my knees?" he asked. "Or do I have to grovel?"

"Oh, my gosh. I'm sorry, Jensen. I was just so taken aback. And speechless, I...Oh, for Pete's sake." Amber dropped to her own knees. Then she wrapped her arms around his neck. "I love you, too. And yes! I'll marry you. I have no idea what our life will be like together, but it will be a thousand times better than living apart."

Then she kissed him for all she was worth.

When they came up for air, the entire bar hooted and howled and whistled and clapped. Lady Josephine was the first to congratulate them, tears welling in her eyes. "I'm so happy for you two. I knew Jensen would eventually find true love—when the right woman came around."

Jensen stood and drew Amber to her feet. "It seems that I've found my soul mate, too, Mum. She isn't at all like you, but she's every bit as sweet and loving. She's not soft-spoken—and she can raise quite a ruckus when she wants to. But that's fine with me. I've come to enjoy, as my good friend Elmer Murdock would say, a little spit and vinegar."

Amber gave him a gentle punch in the arm. "Did you know that Gram and Elmer are going to be married?"

"Yes, he told me."

"Goodness, Jensen. Did everyone know you were coming back to town but me?"

"I wanted to surprise you."

"Even the tabloids knew. But I didn't believe them!"

"I saw that. The jeweler must have leaked a photograph of the ring. Apparently, that's one story they actually got right!"

"By the way," Lady Josephine said, "I have so much

to celebrate. Oliver is going to visit soon. He'd told me he was too busy to come, but apparently he's had second thoughts and wants to meet little Clemmie. So if you'll excuse me, I'm going to order some champagne for everyone here!"

"That's nice that Oliver is coming," Amber said. "I'll look forward to meeting him."

"I'd like to introduce you," Jensen said. "But something doesn't quite add up."

"What do you mean?"

"There might be more to the story than what he's told Mum. But I suppose we'll find out when he gets here."

Gram and Elmer were the next to congratulate them.

"I'm so happy for you, dear." Her grandmother leaned down and kissed her cheek. "I know that your young man will make you just as happy as Elmer has made me."

"Your grandmother has her heart set on a simple wedding at the courthouse," Elmer said as he, too, kissed Amber's cheek, then shook Jensen's hand. "But if you two have a mind to do one of those double ceremony thingies, I'm sure we can get us a twofer one special at the Grange Hall."

Amber's gaping stare must have conveyed her distress at the suggestion of a double wedding in a multipurpose venue because Jensen rushed in to save her from hurting the old man's feelings.

"Actually," Jensen said, "that's terribly kind of you to offer, Mr. Murdock, but since the town would have already experienced attending a quadruple wedding, I wouldn't want our special events to pale in comparison."

"I got you, son." Elmer winked at them. "Originality is important, especially to the little ladies. Forget about the dual wedding then. We'll just rent one of those jumbo RVs with the extra pop-out sides and do our honeymoons together."

"Lord help us," Amber murmured as Lady Josephine tried to distract Gram and Elmer from further suggestions. "So what about after the wedding and honeymoon," Amber asked Jensen. "Where will we go from there?" They still lived worlds apart.

"I wouldn't mind settling in Horseback Hollow," he said, "although I'd have to travel to London regularly."

"Seriously? That's so sweet. But you don't need to make that big of a concession. I can certainly relocate to England—after I fulfill my one-year commitment with Cowboy Country USA." She supposed she could talk to her attorney about breaking the contract, although she really didn't want to. "Wait, they still don't try to make the ladies ride sidesaddle in the UK, do they?"

"Of course not, although the English tack is certainly a lot more popular. But don't worry about that. Since I'll be purchasing our own jet soon, I'll be more than happy to cart all your eccentric Western riding equipment back and forth for you."

"Back and forth?"

"Well, I assume that with both of us having commitments in different countries, we'll just make the most of both worlds and spend time in each other's hometowns as needed."

Would she truly be getting the man of her dreams and the travel that she'd always craved? It was more than she could've ever hoped for.

"And don't you worry none about the Broken R," Elmer chimed in before Lady Josephine could rein him back. "Your gram and I will take good care of it while you're sipping tea over yonder with those scone lovers. I've got some big ideas about turning that northern pasture into a drag-racing strip for my hot-rodding club."

"Maybe we should stay in Texas for the time being," Jensen suggested quietly.

"Are you sure?" Amber asked.

"No. But I've discovered that I am quite capable of living with uncertainty—as long as you stay by my side."

"Always."

"I know my mother has ordered champagne to celebrate, but I've taken the liberty to create a private celebration for you later this evening—if you're so inclined."

"I'm definitely up for a private party. What did you have in mind?"

"There's a limousine parked out front, and a hotel suite reserved in Lubbock. I was going to be quite lonely if you would have turned down my proposal."

"I could have never done that, Jensen. You're not just my best friend and lover. You're my soul mate. We were meant to be together."

Then she gave him a kiss that promised him all of her love, for all of her life.

* * * * *

MILLS & BOON®

Want to get more from Mills & Boon?

Here's what's available to you if you join the
exclusive **Mills & Boon eBook Club** today:

✦ *Convenience – choose your books each month*
✦ *Exclusive – receive your books a month before
anywhere else*
✦ *Flexibility – change your subscription at any time*
✦ *Variety – gain access to eBook-only series*
✦ *Value – subscriptions from just £1.99 a month*

So visit **www.millsandboon.co.uk/esubs** today
to be a part of this exclusive eBook Club!

MILLS & BOON®

Cherish™

EXPERIENCE THE ULTIMATE RUSH OF FALLING IN LOVE

A sneak peek at next month's titles…

In stores from 16th January 2015:

- **Best Friend to Wife and Mother?** – Caroline Anderson
  and **Marry Me, Mackenzie!** – Joanna Sims

- **Her Brooding Italian Boss** – Susan Meier
  and **Fortune's Little Heartbreaker** – Cindy Kirk

In stores from 6th February 2015:

- **The Daddy Wish** – Brenda Harlen
  and **The Heiress's Secret Baby** – Jessica Gilmore

- **A Pregnancy, a Party & a Proposal** – Teresa Carpenter
  and **The Fireman's Ready-Made Family** – Jules Bennett

Available at WHSmith, Tesco, Asda, Eason, Amazon and Apple

Just can't wait?
Buy our books online a month before they hit the shops!
visit www.millsandboon.co.uk

These books are also available in eBook format!